N-SPACE

N-SPACE

THE HYDRA CHRONICLES – VOL. 1

BRUCE BUTLER

First Edition, September 2023 (rev 12)
Cover design by Bruce Butler

ISBN 978-0-9949538-8-9 (paperback)
ISBN 978-0-9949538-7-2 (e-book)

Published by Bigfoot Press
Penticton, BC, Canada

BIGFOOT
PRESS

If you enjoyed this book, please visit the author's website and check out his
other literary works:

www.brucebutler.ca

DEDICATION

To all who dream of a different past, present, or future.

TABLE OF CONTENTS

ACKNOWLEDGEMENTS

I've been an avid science fiction fan since the first time my parents let me stay up late to watch Lost in Space on TV back in 1965 ("Danger, Will Robinson!"). Then came Time Tunnel, Batman, and Star Trek. Since then, I've consumed hundreds of sci-fi novels, so I'd like to thank the following authors for inspiring me to create my own sci-fi world: Carl Sagan, Douglas Adams, Andy Weir, Larry Niven, Frank Herbert, James S. A. Corey, Arthur C. Clarke, Michael Crichton, Kim Stanley Robinson, Orson Scott Card.

A very special shout out to my beta readers: Terry Harbicht, Kerry Anderson, Ken Ho, Kevin Binnie, Chad Allen, Ray Sewlochan, Scott Hagarty, Audrina McDonald, and Cody Young. This motley mix of geeks, nerds, gears, adventurers, and family (and one nine-year-old!) provided criticism and praise when needed.

Additional thanks go out to those who provided specific content: Ryan Dueckman for the inclined plane solution; Ray Sewlochan for the "nightly riddle" ritual; and Ken Ho for details on UBC's Engineering Physics program circa early 1980s. Thanks to Jerry Jenkins (jerryjenkins.com) for his many video tutorials and newsletters. A nod to Julie Ferguson and her Port Moody Writers' Group (circa 2012-13) for encouragement and feedback.

The "PogoBot" (Chapter 5) was inspired by a real-life event from my youth. The Underwater Research Probe (URP) was invented by Penticton high-school student Donald Lekei, who deployed it in Okanagan Lake in the summer of 1974. He referred to it as "Project SCUID" (Self-Contained Underwater Instruments and Detectors).

Thanks to my partner Dr. Lorna Fadden for being a sounding board and for providing insight into the academic world. Having someone in the house with many letters after her name was extremely helpful.

PROLOGUE

December 9th, 1988

Ann Barnes wiped away the single tear rolling down her cheek as the chairman of the awards committee stepped up to the lectern and began extolling the accomplishments of her son, Matt. Ann was seated in the middle of the second row in the ornately decorated hall and had an unobstructed view of Matt up on the stage; he was fidgeting in his seat, uncomfortable in the suit and dress shoes the ceremony's protocols demanded.

The last time he wore something close to that formal, Ann realized, *was at his high school reunion. He's accomplished so much in only ten years!*

The chairman praised Matt's work for several more minutes, then invited him to come forward and receive his award. The audience was silent as Matt rose from his plush, high-backed chair and walked stiffly towards centre stage. Ann glanced to the right; her husband Nathan was grinning from ear to ear, the proudest father in the world. To her left were Matt's three best friends, barely able to control their excitement.

Award in hand, Matt turned towards the audience. His best friend Renny, seated beside Ann, broke the silence.

"Way to go, Matt! Woo-hoo!"

Ann flinched, then chuckled as the dignitaries on stage appeared to have a collective stroke from this breach of decorum. The surrounding audience members murmured their disapproval. Matt made brief eye contact with Ann, then glanced at Renny, his lips pressed together and mouth stretched in the barest of smiles as he tried hard not to laugh.

These boys don't take anything seriously!

The audience was uncomfortably silent; Ann and Nathan started applauding, forcing the over five hundred guests to join in. Matt's friends clapped louder than the rest of the audience combined; they were on top of the world, oblivious to the protocols of this formal ceremony and didn't care what anyone thought. When Matt published his radical theory three years ago, the scientific community's response had been lukewarm. But after Matt's friends helped him turn his ground-breaking ideas into a practical application, everything changed.

If the world only knew what else these boys have been up to...

ONE

December 3, 1985

NASA astronaut Scott 'Red' Hansen floated four hundred yards from the American space station Liberty, watching it slowly recede. He did the math in his head a third time, and got the same answer.

Yup, I'm a dead man.

His solo spacewalk should have been routine; a short but well-planned excursion to replace a faulty camera mounted to the station's hull. In the five months he'd been aboard, he'd performed ten spacewalks, including three solo ones. All had been, to use NASA-speak, "nominal."

Until today.

He'd completed the camera replacement on schedule, two hours after leaving the station's airlock, and was methodically working his way back along the hull using the "two-tether" safety procedure used by astronauts and rock climbers alike: *always clip one tether to the next anchor point before unclipping from the current anchor*. He'd arrived at one of the few places on the station's tarnished metal hull where there weren't two anchors within arm's reach (a design flaw); that's when things went pear-shaped.

Just as he unclipped his single tether, the sun's reflection off one of the solar panels momentarily blinded him. His reach for the anchor missed by a fraction of an inch; his second and automatic attempt also failed, the

3

effort causing him to spin away from the safety of the station's hull.

A rookie mistake.

He didn't panic. His training kicked in. He radioed his status to the station personnel monitoring his every move, then took several deep breaths.

"Activating SAFER," he said, referring to the Simplified Aid For EVA Rescue, the emergency jetpack worn by all US spacewalkers.

First things first. Null my rotation, then push back to the station. Easy peazy.

He reached for the SAFER's hand controller, mounted to the front of his spacesuit, and thumbed its mode switch from "Standby" to "Auto Attitude."

Instead of the expected gentle pulses from the SAFER's nitrogen thrusters, he felt more than heard several loud bangs. His tumble increased; he bounced once off the station's hull then windmilled away.

Oh, shit!

It took him nearly a minute to wrestle the malfunctioning SAFER under control and stabilize his spin. By then, its precious supply of nitrogen gas was gone and he was drifting away from the station.

Red cursed himself. He cursed the jetpack's manufacturer. He cursed the faceless NASA bean counters who always selected the lowest bid when purchasing equipment. He cursed the engineers who'd forgotten to put enough anchors on the station hull. He cursed the US government for cutting NASA's budget, forcing a reduction in space station crew to where solo spacewalks had become far too common. Then he pushed past the anger, realizing there was no point in spending his remaining hours angry. He clung to hope—hope that the two astronauts inside Liberty could somehow pull off an emergency spacewalk.

Unfortunately, one does not simply throw on a spacesuit and climb out the nearest airlock. Astronauts have to undergo thirteen hours of carefully monitored oxygen pre-breathing and decompression to prepare for the low-pressure, pure oxygen environment inside a spacesuit or risk decompression sickness, a.k.a. "the bends." Medical personnel at NASA's Mission Control in Houston, Texas were scrambling to come up with an abbreviated process so the station commander, Richard Miller, could get to him in time. But the math was unarguable: although Red had four hours of oxygen left, the laws of orbital mechanics decreed that within an hour he'd drift past PNR, the point of no return, far enough he'd be dead by the time any SAFER-equipped astronaut could reach him. It was a minor, yet morbid, consolation that his drift was retrograde—the opposite direction to the station's orbit—so in a few days, the station would catch up with him.

Catch up with my body, actually.

As Red drifted away from the space station with practically no rotation, he consoled himself.

At least I have the best seat in the house: an unobstructed view of the Earth revolving below, and a sunrise and sunset every ninety minutes.

Every few minutes he glanced at the oxygen readout on his chest, the numbers creeping inexorably lower. During his last radio call with Mission Control, they advised him they were bringing his wife and three children to NASA's headquarters.

He sighed. *The next time I talk to Jenny and the kids will be the last.*

He tried to stay calm, slowing his breathing to make his oxygen supply last as long as possible. Praying for a miracle.

Three hours later...

Red was daydreaming, reliving the Hawaiian vacation he'd taken with his family a month before starting his latest rotation on Liberty. The station was now a silver dot just above the horizon, and radio communications had dropped out. He'd just finished a radio call with his wife and kids and was emotionally exhausted. His chest readout showed he had less than an hour of oxygen left; soon he'd start feeling the effects as the O_2 level dropped towards a lethal level.

At least it'll be a peaceful exit.

Then his radio crackled.

"Red, it's Dick. I'm in the airlock and almost through the modified pre-breathing procedure Houston came up with. I should be able to cycle through in thirty minutes." He and Dick had been best friends since high school, played football together, and had gone through the Air Force

Academy at Colorado Springs together.

"Dick, you know I'm past PNR. You don't have enough delta-V to reach me. You can't risk coming out this far—you'll never make it back. Face it, old friend, I'm done."

The silence on the radio spoke volumes—Dick had come to the same conclusion, but wasn't willing to say it out loud.

He let out a long sigh. "I'll make sure you're brought home."

"Understood, my friend. Catch you on the next orbit."

Red returned to the glorious view, somewhat comforted knowing his body would be returned home to the great state of Texas.

Suddenly, there was a bright flash of light off to his right. Where seconds ago there had been nothing but the cold vacuum of space and a tapestry of stars, a milky-coloured sphere the size of a large beach ball now hovered twenty yards away. The milkiness cleared, leaving what looked like a blob of water viewed through an out-of-focus camera.

My O_2 must be getting low—I'm hallucinating.

Debris spewed from the blob in all directions, as if a dirty room was being vacuumed and the blob was the vacuum's outlet.

A minute later, a rectangular metallic box—the size of a loaf of bread and with a black cylinder on one end—emerged from the blob, on the end of what looked like a wooden broomstick. An electrical cable came out of the box, taped along the length of the pole.

What the hell? Is that a... a video camera?

The camera turned slowly, the pole shaking as if someone was trying to hold it steady in a buffeting windstorm.

Yep, I'm definitely in the early stages of oxygen deprivation.

The camera panned past him, stopped, then turned back until it was pointing at him. He weakly waved his arms, an almost impossible task in a bulky spacesuit.

As if responding to his wave, the mysterious blob suddenly jumped ten yards further away, the camera moving with it. He debated mentioning his observations on the radio, but didn't want to panic those in the station or at Mission Control. Resigned to his fate, he opted to enjoy this hallucination in his remaining time. Then the blob vanished, confirming Red's suspicion it had been a hypoxia-induced hallucination.

He felt an odd sensation, something he'd never experienced during his many months in space. He was familiar with that "always falling" feeling astronauts have when in orbit. Now, his inner ears were sending his brain a different signal—he was being gently pushed from behind. The push was weak, the kind one feels when standing on a beach with a light breeze.

Maybe I can sail back to the station, he wondered, giddily.

Small particles of dust and debris streamed past him. Then something bumped into his backpack, causing him to slowly rotate end-over-end. Once he'd rotated one hundred and eighty degrees, the mysterious blob was now hovering only three feet away. The video camera withdrew into the blob, and Red windmilled his arms to cancel his rotation. Faint light emanated from the blob, and inside he saw a distorted shape moving around.

Something emerged: the flat bottom of a red metal cylinder, eight inches in diameter. After two feet of cylinder appeared, it tapered sharply, ending in a stainless-steel handle. What looked remarkably like a climbing rope was clipped to the handle with a large carabiner, the rope disappearing back into the blob. Red grabbed hold of the cylinder with his thick, gloved hands as it bounced around in the invisible breeze. He turned the cylinder; on its side were large block letters, handwritten with a black felt pen: "RESCUE."

You've got to be fucking kidding me!

Red immediately deduced the purpose of this miracle gift from who-knows-where. Never one to dither, he unclipped the carabiner.

I sure hope this works...

◎

Commander Dick Miller opened the outer airlock door and maneuvered through the narrow hatch opening, out onto the station hull.

I'm probably ruining my career, but tough shit.

Miller had refused a direct order from NASA's flight director to abort his spacewalk; senior bureaucrats had decided it was prudent to wait until the space station caught up with Red—correction, Red's body—on the next orbit.

I'm not waiting four goddamn days to get my best friend back. He'd done the math—he had enough oxygen and just enough thruster fuel to do a low-speed transit out and back.

Miller activated his jetpack, just a brief burst to get clear of the station hull, then spun around to go after his friend. Correction—his friend's body. Neither the station nor Mission Control had made radio contact with Red in the past half hour; either he was out of range or... Miller scanned the area of space in the direction Red had drifted. Nothing.

"Dammit, Red. Where are you?" he muttered, forgetting about his voice-activated microphone.

His headphones crackled. "Hey, Dick, over here!"

"Red? Where are you?"

"By the starboard truss."

Miller fired another brief burst, rotating on two axes. A spacesuited figure was drifting towards one of the station's main solar panels, three hundred feet away.

"How did you get over there? Did you get your SAFER working?"

"Uh, not exactly. I could use help getting back, though. I'm a bit off course."

Miller's jaw dropped. Red was moving in a jerking manner, a white cloud appearing near him every few seconds. "Hold your course, old friend. I'm coming."

Miller estimated an intercept course and fired his jetpack. Sixty long seconds later, he'd clipped a tether to Red's suit harness.

"Got you!"

"Glad to hear it!"

"Hey, whatcha got there?" Red's spacesuited arms were folded across his chest, clutching something.

Red chuckled. "You're not going to believe it." Miller carefully spun him around until they were face to face.

"You're going to have to give me a ride back to the airlock. I'm empty," Red said, referring to the cylinder in his arms.

"Where the hell did you get that?" Miller said.

"That, my friend, is the question of the week. Now let's get me inside. I'm pretty low on air."

Once they were back in the airlock, helmets off and starting the recompression cycle, Miller noticed something sticking out of a utility pocket on the right arm of Red's suit.

"Hey, what's that?"

Red pulled out an orange baseball cap sporting a futuristic double-A symbol stitched on the front.

"That symbol looks vaguely familiar," Miller said, but there was nothing else on the hat indicating what the symbol meant. Or where it came from.

"Not sure how I'm going to write up this up," Red said. "But at least I'm alive to do it."

Apparently, I have a guardian angel somewhere...

TWO

August 1962

Ann Barnes emptied the contents of the box onto the dining room table; her son Matthew squirmed in her lap and giggled as the hundreds of cardboard puzzle pieces formed a haphazard pile. She leaned the box's lid against a flower vase in the middle of the table so they could see the image they were trying to recreate: Freedom 7, the NASA rocket that had carried America's first astronaut, Alan Shepard, into space just a year ago. The picture showed the rocket seconds after lift-off, its white fuselage and orange exhaust contrasted against a turquoise-blue Florida sky.

"Wocket, mommy," Matthew said, his blue eyes sparkling. He pointed at the lid and sounded out the large black letters on the rocket's side: "N-A-S-A."

"Yes, dear. Rocket. Very good!"

He just turned two, and he's starting to read! Ann realized. *What a relief!*

Matthew's early development started off "textbook normal"—his first words, "Momma" and "Dada" came just days apart when he was ten months old. But, six months later, he stopped talking altogether and no amount of encouragement helped. Ann and her husband Nathan made several panicked visits to health care specialists; hearing problems were ruled out, as were any attention deficits. Matthew's behaviour even stumped the town's only child psychologist.

"He's fine in all other respects; he just chooses not to talk," the doctor said, shrugging. "Hopefully he'll grow out of it."

To their relief, Matthew resumed talking only a month before his second birthday; in the weeks that followed, he began forming coherent sentences and constantly pointing at things, demanding, "What dat?"

And he never asked about the same thing twice.

Just last week, Ann found Matthew sitting on the floor in the living room with one of his favourite books—Dr. Seuss was a staple of their bedtime reading. At first she thought he was reciting the text from memory, then noticed he was sounding out each word. Ann, an elementary school teacher taking a leave of absence to raise their only son, realized that after a bumpy start, he was developing much faster than normal.

Returning to the puzzle, she started turning the pieces face up and grouping them by colour.

"We should start with the rocket, don't you think?" Matthew nodded.

The phone in the kitchen rang. "I'll be right back, honey," she said, setting him on the floor.

She returned less than a minute later to find Matthew perched on the edge of the chair, teetering towards the table and moving puzzle pieces.

"Matthew Barnes! You're not supposed to climb on chairs!" She scooped him up and sat down, placing him safely on her lap. "Now, where were we? Oh, yes, the rocket."

But the rocket was complete.

That's odd—I didn't do that, did I? Ann looked at her son.

"Honey, did you work on our puzzle without me?"

Matthew's facial expression answered her question—his little face forming a frown, his lower lip coming out in a classic pout.

"That's amazing!" she said. "Show me how you did that."

The frown transformed into a smile as he picked up the nearest puzzle piece, looked at the hundreds of other pieces lying on the table and, within seconds, found its match. Then he did it again. Twenty minutes later, he'd completed the puzzle, Ann only helping when his clumsy little fingers and short arms limited him.

Matthew giggled and clapped his hands. "More!"

11

Unbelievable, Ann thought. *Let's try a harder one.*

After lunch, Ann brought out another jigsaw puzzle, a field of sunflowers in bloom, rated "Difficult: age 12+." Following a hunch, she showed Matthew the picture on the box's lid only for a few seconds before turning it face down. He completed that puzzle much faster than even she could have, then squealed in utter delight.

When Ann's husband Nathan came home from work that afternoon, Ann was waiting at the door.

"You've got to see this. You won't believe what Matthew can do!" She pulled him towards the dining room table where a pile of rocket-puzzle pieces awaited.

"Honey, show Daddy how fast you can solve the puzzle."

Nathan picked Matthew up and sat him in his lap. Nathan's jaw dropped as his son made quick work of the puzzle, finishing it in just under ten minutes.

"Wow, you're my puzzle boy!" Nathan tousled his unkempt brown hair, then lifted him overhead. "Maybe you'll grow up to be an engineer just like your dad!"

Matthew squealed.

After putting their puzzle boy to bed that night, Ann pulled out one of her university textbooks on childhood development. She turned to the chapter titled "Early Development"; every paragraph could have been written about Matthew.

In the following weeks, Ann visited all the school libraries in their small town, researching the subject and talking to primary school counsellors. Once she'd exhausted local resources, she summarized her findings for her husband.

"Research in 'early development' is still in its infancy—no pun intended—so there's very little data. Matthew seems to fit the classic model of a gifted child: accelerated speech and reading, and abnormal pattern recognition skills. I think solving puzzles falls into the latter category."

"Any down-sides?" Nathan said.

"I found one article that mentioned an increase in behavioural problems."

"Such as?"

"Lack of attention. Social interaction—trouble fitting in with other children."

Nathan pondered this. "If Matthew *is* gifted, we should nurture his special abilities." He stared at the wall. "Who knows what he might accomplish?"

Ann nodded. "But he needs to grow up like a *normal* kid."

"Agreed. He has to spend time outside with other kids, playing in the dirt, climbing trees, and skinning his knees. The way *we* grew up."

Like most parents, Ann and Nathan took their roles seriously. Ann maintained a nurturing yet educationally challenging home environment, while Nathan sought out books and toys to further encourage Matthew's abilities. Every week or two, he'd come home from work with a wire-and-string puzzle or a Japanese puzzle block he'd found at the local toy store. Matthew's eyes would light up, then he'd make quick work of them, even the ones rated for kids much older.

By his third birthday, Matthew was reading to his parents at bedtime. Ann broke up his daily play time with flash cards to help him expand his vocabulary and learn basic arithmetic. When Santa left a pail of Lego blocks under the Christmas tree that year, he spent hours building complex shapes and structures. Then he'd knock them over, because, well, he *was* a boy.

The Barnes family lived in a small town in south-central British Columbia, Canada. Nestled between two large lakes in the Okanagan Valley, Penticton was blessed with four full seasons, including a bitterly cold winter and a blazing hot summer. Nathan Barnes and his brother Ed had been orphaned at an early age and raised by their paternal aunt and uncle. The family-owned property on the town's eastern slope and made a decent living managing a fruit orchard that produced apples, cherries, peaches, and apricots. When Ed, the older, stocky brother, graduated from high school, he stayed in town, dividing his time between working as a lineman for the BC Telephone Company and helping run the family orchard. Nathan, the tall, thin bookworm, was more interested in building things; upon graduation, he enrolled in civil engineering at the University of British Columbia in Vancouver, four hundred kilometres to the west.

In his second year at UBC, Nathan met Ann Thompson, a first-year education student, and it was love at first sight. They were soon the most popular couple on campus. He was tall, handsome, and witty with a shock of unruly dark brown hair, and courted by the university's most elite fraternities. She was a medium-height, attractive, willowy blonde at the top of her class, and pursued by several sororities. Nathan's five-year engineering program aligned perfectly with Ann's four-year education degree; they married a week after graduation, then moved to Penticton so Nathan could take a position as a junior engineer with the city. The town also needed teachers, so Ann had no trouble getting hired at one of the town's elementary schools. The newlyweds built a home on the edge of the family property and started a family.

New Year's Eve, 1963

The Barnes household hosted the end-of-year festivities for the staff of the city's small engineering department. Once dinner and dessert were over, it was time for after-dinner drinks, and decks of cards appeared. They'd started with "Crazy Eights" then moved onto Concentration, where players had to find matching pairs of cards from a deck all placed face down. It wasn't an easy game at the best of times, and harder when the participants were only somewhat sober.

"Oh hi, honey, we didn't see you there," Ann said; Matthew had been quietly watching from the sidelines. He'd changed into his pyjamas and come for his good night hug from his parents, but was captivated by the card game.

Nathan's boss, Pete, was taking his turn. He turned over a card: the jack of spades. As he reached for what he was sure was a match, he noticed Matthew out of the corner of his eye, shaking his head.

"Your son thinks he knows this game better than I do!"

Ann read the expression on her husband's face: *He probably does!*

Pete turned over the second card: three of diamonds. "Drat!"

Matthew smiled.

"You think you can do better, son?" Pete said.

Matthew looked to his father for permission, who gave him a nod.

He stepped up to the table, reached out and turned over a card: jack of clubs.

"He got you there, Pete," Nathan said.

"Beginner's luck. Try again," Pete said, turning over the five of hearts.

Matthew immediately turned over the five of diamonds.

At the urging of several of Nathan's slightly drunk co-workers, Matthew finished the game in under a minute.

In the months that followed, Matthew was beating any willing adult at card games, checkers, and other board games where memory and pattern recognition ruled over luck.

◎

By age four, Matthew was working his way through the family's brand-new set of World Book encyclopedias. Ann listened while he read out loud, only helping when he encountered unfamiliar words. She had to stay on her toes; when Matthew wanted to know something, he didn't just ask "why?" like most children his age; he posed penetrating questions.

"Mom, why can't *I* fly?" he said one spring day as a flock of starlings took flight from the large birch tree in their front yard; flapping his arms hadn't produced the desired outcome.

"Dad, why is the sky red *now*?" he said one summer evening during a spectacular Okanagan sunset, referring to the blue sky earlier in the day.

Matthew's thirst for knowledge was insatiable, and the world around him was a wondrous place full of interesting things to discover. His parents often found toys lying around the house in various states of disassembly; once he learned how something worked, he lost interest. As more and more increasingly complex items became magically disassembled, Nathan intervened.

"Son, taking something apart is easy. Putting it back together and making it work is *much* harder." Father and son spent many happy hours together, reversing Matthew's deconstruction efforts and, Nathan hoped, building a foundation of engineering skills.

The world can be a dangerous place for an overly curious child. When Matthew started taking an interest in things plugged into electrical wall outlets, his parents laid down a rule: *never touch anything with wires*.

One spring day, Ann had been outside working in the garden, leaving Matthew inside to play. She came in to get a drink of water and found him sitting on the kitchen floor, surrounded by the parts of the telephone he'd taken apart using tools he'd liberated from his dad's workbench.

"Matthew Barnes! You know you're not allowed to touch things with wires!"

"But Mom—I unplugged it first!" he cried, clearly not sharing her concern. But rules were rules, and Ann sent Matthew to his room. There were no phone calls at the Barnes household the rest of the day until Nathan got home from work and the father-and-son team reassembled the phone. Nathan, wearing his "parent hat," supported the minor punishment his wife had dealt out. With his "engineer hat" on, he was immensely proud.

Nathan was continually thinking of ways to challenge their precocious child, so he added a twist to Matthew's bedtime routine.

"Son, do you know what a riddle is?"

Matthew scrunched his face in intense concentration for a few seconds, then nodded. "A puzzle, but with words."

Nathan smiled. "That's right, son! Okay, tonight I'm going to give you a riddle. I want you to sleep on it, then answer me at bedtime tomorrow night. If you get it right, I'll give you another one."

Matthew's eyes lit up.

"Okay, here's your first riddle: *What colour can you eat?*"

Matthews's brow furrowed for a moment, then his eyes widened. He started to blurt out his answer, but his dad interrupted him.

"Nuh uh, Matthew. You have to sleep on it. Give me your answer tomorrow night."

The next evening, Matthew had the correct answer: *orange*.

"Give me another one!"

"Okay. *What has eighteen legs and catches flies?*"

The riddles and other word games became a nightly tradition. Nathan bought several "brain teasers for kids" books and kept them on the top shelf in their bedroom closet; he'd look up a new riddle every night to keep Matthew challenged.

◎

The Barnes family orchard was on the east side of town, up on a flat geological area known as "Upper Bench." Owing to the remote location, there were few neighbours and no children near Matthew's age. As an only child not yet in school, he only had his cousin Stuart, seven years older, to play with. He didn't mind the lack of peers—he preferred to spend his time alone, reading and solving puzzles. His parents knew that social development was just as important as cognitive development, and were eager to get him around other children. After weighing the pros and cons, they petitioned the school district's superintendent to enroll him in kindergarten at age four, a year earlier than most children.

Kindergarten was Matthew's first exposure to a large group of children. He was the most inquisitive of the twenty children in Mrs. Brown's morning kindergarten class, always asking "Why?" when instructed to do something. His curiosity, combined with his smaller stature from being a year younger, resulted in him being picked on by the other children. Matthew made only one friend, a chubby boy named Joshua Allen who'd also started kindergarten a year early. The other children picked on him for his girth and overly conservative clothing (his parents were practicing Baptists). It was natural that the two outcasts became friends.

The day Matthew brought home his first piece of artwork from kindergarten was another milestone for Ann.

"What a masterpiece!" she said. "Your Dad will be thrilled to see this when he gets home!" She opened a drawer and brought out a new package of fridge magnets, large plastic letters.

"Honey, I've been looking forward to this since the day you were born," she said, tacking the art to the fridge door with a magnet at each corner.

Matthew stared at the fridge, frowning. He reached up tentatively and pulled the letter "M" off the metal door, his eyes widening when it snapped back. He did the same with the other letters.

"Mom, why do they stick to the fridge?"

"It's the magnets, honey," she said, pulling a letter off the fridge and turning it around, showing him the small black objects embedded in the plastic. Matthew peered intently at these magical new things.

"What's a magnet?"

"It's a special piece of material that sticks to metal."

"*How* does it stick to the fridge? Is it like glue?"

"No, it's different from glue. Magnets stick to metal. That's what they do."

"But *why* do they stick to metal?"

I'm out of my element! Ann realized, opting for the default answer. "Let's ask your father when he comes home."

When Nathan got home from work, Matthew pestered him about magnets. Nathan had a solid grounding in physics courtesy of his engineering degree, but was hard pressed to come up with a way to explain magnetism to a precocious four-year-old. The next day, Ann noticed the magnets had disappeared from the fridge door; she found them in random places around the house, some stuck to objects and appliances with metal surfaces, others lying on the floor below non-metal surfaces.

Near the end of his ten months in kindergarten, Matthew developed an odd quirk: occasionally he'd withdraw to the point where he'd ignore instructions from his parents or teacher. It was enough of a concern that Ann booked him in with the town's only audiologist to have his hearing tested. Twice. The results were the same—his hearing was normal. Eventually, his father, after hours of close observation, voiced his opinion.

"Don't you see?" Nathan said. "There's nothing wrong with his hearing—it's his attention. He gets so engrossed in what he's doing, he 'turns off' his hearing."

"You think that's okay?" Ann said.

Nathan shrugged. "It's not normal, but then Matthew isn't exactly the textbook definition of normal. If I had to use an engineering analogy, I'd say that the part of his brain he uses for hearing is busy doing other things. We should keep an eye on it, but I don't think it's worth worrying about."

Ann shrugged. "Well, I hope it doesn't cause problems when he starts school in the fall."

THREE

"**But I don't** want to go to school," Matthew whined. "I want to stay home. With you."

Ann wouldn't be swayed. "Your friend Joshua will be there. And you'll make new friends."

"But I don't want new friends."

Matthew's introduction to Grade 1 was challenging—for everyone involved. Chubby Joshua Allen was in his class, so they had each other for company. But Matthew, exceptionally bright for his age, quickly became frustrated with the slow pace of learning.

When the teacher presented a new topic Matthew found interesting, he learned it then was ready to move on, even if his classmates weren't. If he wasn't interested, it was hard to get him to pay attention. It was as if, at that early age, he was already deciding what information was worth keeping. And what wasn't. He grasped new concepts instantly, often interrupting the teacher with questions while she was still trying to teach the other students. His impatience led to frustration, causing him to speak before thinking, which led to him spending an inordinate amount of time standing in the classroom corner. Those punishments only increased his frustration; by Grade 2, there were more frequent outbursts, resulting in an obligatory parent-teacher meeting.

"We've tried our best to temper Matthew's interruptions," Ann said, "but we're not having a lot of success."

Mrs. Webster sighed. "Neither have I. At first, I thought it was just his being a year younger than his classmates. But last week, after one of his outbursts, I followed a hunch. Instead of putting him in the corner, I sent him to the library and asked the librarian to give him the Stanford-Binet IQ test. We normally give it out in grade six, but I was hoping it might provide an insight into his behavioural issues. Not to mention it would keep him occupied for a while. As you know, a standard IQ test covers knowledge, memory, and visual-spatial and quantitative reasoning. I expected he'd need help with some questions, but our librarian said he never once asked for help."

Mrs. Webster smiled as she slid a thin stack of paper across her desk. "He got *all* the questions right. That places him in the ninety-ninth percentile; in other words, he scored higher than ninety-nine percent of everyone who's written this test. And *this* test is for children four years older."

"So, what's his IQ?" Nathan said.

"Keep in mind that IQ tests designed for children aren't accurate at the high or low end. But according to the charts I have, Matthew's IQ is *at least* 145. I'd guess it's a lot higher."

"Well, we often refer to him as 'our little genius,'" Ann said.

"At his age," Mrs. Webster said, "the proper term is 'gifted.' Many of the world's geniuses were identified as gifted at an early age. Matthew has an innate ability with shapes, geometry, and arithmetic. And, as I'm sure you're aware, his memory is downright phenomenal. If you don't mind, I want to give him more tests—tests aimed at even older children—to see where he stands so we can better challenge him. But we should focus on his social development, or, should I say, lack thereof. He seems to be unaware of many aspects of social interaction. He doesn't read body language well, and isn't able to gauge the emotional state of those around him. And, believe it or not, gifted children often have trouble in school. Do you find that when you're talking to him, he—"

"—interrupts you?" Ann said.

Webster nodded. "It can—"

"—be quite frustrating," Ann said. They both chuckled.

"Well, that's a common trait of exceptionally bright children. When someone is speaking, children like Matthew are continually trying to predict the rest of the sentence. Once they're relatively sure how the sentence will end, they try to move the conversation along. That explains the interruptions—he's figured out what someone is going to say before they finish saying it."

"Any suggestions?"

"Well, gifted children can be a challenge for parents *and* educators. In fact, they can be more work than developmentally challenged children. I'll do what I can, but I do have nineteen other children in my class. I suggest you spend extra time with Matthew on home schooling—let him explore subjects we don't cover in class."

"He's already worked his way through the World Book series," Nathan said proudly.

"Well, that's definitely a good start," Mrs. Webster said. "But don't forget his social development. Other than his friend, Joshua, Matthew is a loner, and the other children have picked up on that. He needs to foster more relationships."

"Could we move him ahead, you know, skip grades?" Nathan said. "I skipped grades three and six."

Mrs. Webster nodded. "Well, that's a possibility. Matthew would benefit academically by advancing. Based on what I've seen, he could be the youngest person in town to graduate from high school. But he's already a year younger than his current classmates, so a big downside is he'd advance more or less alone—making friends would become harder each time he moves ahead and the age gap increases."

Ann and Nathan pondered Mrs. Webster's words for several weeks, debating the pros and cons of moving Matthew ahead. They eventually decided that, for now at least, they'd keep him with his friends, challenge him more at home, and encourage him to be more social.

By the end of Grade 3, Matthew and Joshua added a third member to their group of outcasts. Gary Stocks was a small freckled boy with coke-bottle glasses whose father owned the town's camera store. The three boys shared an interest in science fiction, and with America in a space race with the evil Soviet Union, they always had something to talk about. They spent their recesses and lunches chatting about the new Star Trek television series and drawing pictures of the USS Enterprise and NASA's Gemini and Apollo spacecraft. Like most Canadian boys, they loved watching NHL hockey on TV; Joshua rooted for the Montreal Canadiens while Gary and Matthew cheered for the Toronto Maple Leafs.

And the father-son ritual of the bedtime riddle—word puzzles—continued. Matthew usually knew the answer right away, but Nathan insisted he "sleep on it," not only to improve his cognitive skills but to learn patience. The riddles increased in complexity, from elementary ones such as *What has 13 hearts and no organs?* to longer, Tolkien-style rhymes:

What has roots that nobody sees,
Is taller than trees,
Up, up it goes,
And yet never grows?

◎

"Class, can I have your attention, please?" Miss Morrison announced to her Grade 4 pupils. She scanned the room, making sure everyone was listening.

Matthew was focussed on his assigned task and hadn't heard the teacher speak. They'd been studying geography; Africa in particular. Miss Morrison had given each student a blank map of the continent and asked them to label and colour each country. He found the instructions frustratingly vague, so he turned the assignment into a puzzle: *how do I use each colour an equal number of times, and make sure that no adjacent countries have the same colour?*

Joshua reached forward and poked him in the back with a ruler. "Psst, Earth to Matthew!"

"Matthew Barnes!" Miss Morrison barked. "Pay attention!"

Matthew's head jerked up, his face turning red. Beside him, Gary snickered. The principal walked in, causing everyone to sit up straight. In the hallway behind him, a student lurked. Miss Morrison addressed her students.

"Class, we have a new student today. His name is Renny Harris. Please welcome him to our school."

The principal ushered the new student into the room to polite applause. He was a large boy with a dark complexion and a shock of black hair. His t-shirt was tattered, his jeans faded, and one of his runners had a hole in the toe. Miss Morrison led him to the only empty desk in the room. Beside Matthew.

"Renny, this is Matthew. Matthew, this is Renny. Matthew, I'd like you to be Renny's buddy for the next few days and help him get familiar with our school."

"Uh, yes, Miss Morrison," Matthew gulped.

"And Renny, please let Matthew help you out."

"Eh," Renny said, his voice deep for a Grade 4 boy.

Matthew was terrified of his new "buddy," six inches taller and thirty pounds heavier. Judging by Renny's size, Matthew figured he was at least two years older, having been "held back" once or twice—a common practice when a child didn't perform well enough to move on to the next grade. Renny's face was a mix of fear and hostility—when he lowered his large frame into his seat, the desk creaked in protest.

In the following weeks, Matthew, Gary, and Joshua did their best to include Renny in their daily activities, inviting him to join them outside for recess and sit with them in the gymnasium at lunch. Renny wasn't big on conversation—he mostly sat in silence, glaring at everyone else. He had a couple of mannerisms the boys found odd: he said "eh" instead of "yes," and pointed with his lips instead of a finger. He took part in the boys' lunchtime tradition of trading sandwiches—his were always a single slice of processed cheese between two pieces of white bread. When Matthew and his friends chatted about the space race and drew pictures of spaceships and aliens in their notebooks, Renny kept quiet. They tried to engage him in conversation, but weren't able to learn anything about him or his family. When pressed about his hobbies, Renny's answer was succinct.

"I like rocks. I'm gonna be a geologist when I grow up." He pulled a couple of marble-sized rocks from the pocket of his torn jeans, expounding on their properties and where he'd found them.

A month passed, and while they couldn't really call Renny their friend, he was, at least, an acquaintance.

◉

The smell of grass was overpowering as Matthew's face was pushed into the grassy playground; his arms ached from being pinned behind his back.

"You think you're so smart, don't you?" the school bully growled, tearing up Matthew's sketchbook and letting the pieces fall to the ground.

It had started out as a relatively ordinary school day. Joshua was home sick, and when the recess bell rang, Matthew and Gary found a quiet corner of the playground to re-hash the latest Star Trek episode and draw pictures of the USS Enterprise firing its phasers at the evil Klingons. Like antelopes at a drinking hole watching for predators, the two boys kept an eye out for the schoolyard bullies, who only bothered them if Renny wasn't around. Unfortunately, Renny had been called to the office at the recess break.

The three bullies saw Matthew and Gary alone and sensed weakness; they set upon the pair as soon as the on-duty teacher had disappeared around the side of the school while making her rounds. The ringleader tried to grab Matthew's notebook; his resistance effectively volunteered himself for additional punishment. The last thing he saw as they pushed his face into the wet grass was Gary, running away.

My friend abandoned me!

Other children, eager to see a fight, ran towards them. Matthew struggled, got one arm free and flailed around, hitting one of his tormentors in the side of the head with his elbow. The ringleader, who stood over him, glowering, ordered his accomplices to roll him over.

"You're gonna pay for that, smarty pants," he growled, delivering a kick to Matthew's ribs. He cried out as pain lanced up his side.

The boy wound up to deliver another kick. Matthew closed his eyes, trying in vain to twist out of the way.

The blow never arrived.

He heard an odd crunching sound and cautiously opened his eyes. The ringleader was kneeling on the ground, his hands over his face and blood pouring from his nose. His accomplices released Matthew and scrambled to their feet. Renny Harris was standing there, silent, fists raised and glowering at the bullies. The attackers did a quick calculus and decided the odds weren't enough in their favour; they lifted their bloodied leader and scurried away. Renny reached down, offering Mathew a large hand.

"Er, thanks," Matthew said as Renny effortlessly lifted him to his feet.

"No problem," Renny replied gruffly. "I don't like bullies."

"Neither do I," Matthew chuckled, wincing from the sore ribs.

Just then, they saw Gary running across the field towards him, the on-duty teacher in tow.

He didn't abandon me!

The teacher took in Matthew's dishevelled appearance and concluded that Renny was the aggressor; it took Matthew a few breathless seconds to correct her. She stalked off in search of the real attackers.

After that incident, the schoolyard bullies stopped bothering them, even when Renny *wasn't* around, and Renny warmed up to his new friends. During recesses and lunch breaks, Matthew or Joshua helped him with his arithmetic assignments—he was weak in that subject—and his grades improved.

Matthew gradually learned more of Renny's history. He'd been born in a small mining town in northern British Columbia and raised by his mother. He'd had never known his father, a bear of a man and a field geologist who'd died in a landslide when Renny was two months old. To pay the bills, Renny's mother started working at the town's small Hudson's Bay store. When the mine closed and took the town's primary source of employment with it, she packed up Renny and headed south, landing a job at Penticton's much larger Hudson's Bay department store.

Matthew's assumption that Renny had been "held back" turned out to be wrong. He was nine years old—a year older than Matthew but the normal age for Grade 4 students—and had just inherited his father's "size genes." Coincidentally, he and Matthew shared the same birthdate: July 16th. Renny's ambition was to be a geologist like his dad, which accounted for his fascination with rocks. Having spent his early years in a small northern mining town, Renny's outdoor skills were impressive—he just had trouble with science and arithmetic.

Renny and his mother lived in a small, rented house only a mile from the Barnes family orchard, so he and Matthew soon began playing together. They both loved Hot Wheels toy cars and spent hours in Renny's basement, setting up different racetrack patterns and complicated jumps.

The Barnes house soon became the weekend headquarters for the four boys. When Ann decided they were spending too much time indoors, she'd shoo them outside for fresh air and exercise.

"And don't come back until dinner!"

The foursome explored the foothills of nearby Campbell Mountain. Renny, the outdoorsman of the group, usually took the lead, poking through the dry dirt, looking for interesting rocks.

"We're kind of a club, aren't we?" Matthew observed one hot summer day when they'd stopped for lunch after a hike to the top of the mountain. He got nods of agreement.

"Then we need a club name," Joshua said.

"How about 'Renny and Nerds'?" Renny said, singing it out of tune to Elton John's latest hit, "Benny and the Jets."

"Losers Club?" Gary suggested.

"Fantastic Four?" Joshua offered.

"How about 'The Explorers Society'?" Matthew said.

"The Explorers Society of Canada!" Joshua declared.

"Ooh, that sounds cool," Renny said. Gary and Matthew nodded in agreement. The Explorers Society of Canada (ESOC) was born.

"We're going to need a flag," Gary said. "Every society has a flag. What should we put on it?"

The foursome brainstormed while they ate lunch.

A week later, Gary had sketched a design they all approved of. In the foreground was a green, scaly, serpent-like Ogopogo—the mythical lake monster said to inhabit nearby Okanagan Lake—grinning and cavorting in waves. Hovering just above the Ogopogo's tail was a red Canadian maple leaf, and behind it, three snow-capped mountain peaks. The words "Explorers Society of Canada" framed the Ogopogo and mountains.

July 16th, 1969

The Barnes family, along with Matthew's three friends, gathered in front of the black and white television to watch the massive Saturn V rocket lift off, sending the first men to land on the moon. It was also Matthew and

Renny's birthday, and Ann and Renny's mom organized a joint birthday party around this historic event. The decorations were space-related, the birthday cake three feet long and narrow: a Saturn V rocket.

Matthew's friends agreed nothing was more important than the Americans beating the evil Soviet empire to the moon. Since Matthew had memorized every scrap of information available on the US space program, he gave a running commentary during the broadcast: how fast the rocket was going; what happened at each stage separation; the trajectory to orbit; the entire mission timeline.

"They'll be landing on the moon on July 20th," Matthew said. "The first thing they'll do is plant the American flag."

"It would be neat to walk on the moon," Renny said. "So many rocks."

"Imagine if we could plant our flag," Joshua said, referring to the Explorers Society of Canada's flag Gary had created.

"Matthew should build us a rocket," Gary said, "then *we* can explore the moon!"

◎

Grade 5

Ann Barnes strode through the front doors of Uplands Elementary School, finding Matthew and Renny sitting in the "chairs of shame" outside the principal's office. Ann had just gotten home from the morning's substitute-teaching when the phone rang; it was the Uplands school secretary, asking her to come in and deal with an incident involving her son.

The look on Matthew's face was the one he wore whenever he'd broken or destroyed or blown up something at home. Renny was avoiding her gaze, studiously examining the picture on the wall beside him.

"Matthew, *what* did you do this time?"

"It was just a science experiment, Mom. We talked about it last week."

"Uh huh," she said. Matthew *had* mentioned something about an assignment involving melting ice cubes. "Renny, what's wrong with your face? Look at me, young man!"

Renny reluctantly turned; his dark brown face had a red tinge, as if he'd developed a mild case of sunburn. One of his bushy black eyebrows was missing.

The door to the principal's office opened, and Matthew's Grade 5 teacher waved them in.

"Mrs. Barnes, thanks for coming in," the teacher said. "Mrs. Harris is at work, and her words were, 'Ann will know what to do.'" She sighed. "I don't know what to do with these two."

The science class assignment had been to find the fastest way to melt an ice cube. Some students tried using large amounts of salt; others dropped them into boiling water or crushed them into many tiny pieces. Matthew and Renny had come up with an outside-the-box solution involving homemade pyrotechnics they figured would be a sure winner. However, it resulted in a table top catching fire and the teacher emptying the contents of a fire extinguisher on it.

Ann listened patiently.

"Well, Mrs. Barnes? Any suggestions?" she said.

"I agree that *some* punishment is in order," Ann said. "But first, let's go back to the assignment. Just to be clear, did you specifically tell them they *couldn't* use any flammable liquids?"

"Well, no, but—"

Ann pressed on. "Matthew mentioned this assignment to me last week. He said he'd asked you for clarification on the rules, and your reply was along the lines of, 'Do whatever you want.' Is that correct?"

"Yes, but—"

"So, it sounds to me they followed the rules. The few there were."

The teacher frowned, not happy with the direction this discussion was going.

Ann continued. "Did they melt the ice cube faster than the others?"

"Well, several students used boiling water and melted the ice in five seconds."

"And these two?" Ann prompted.

"Zero point two seconds," Matthew blurted. "Based on the rate of—"

Ann silenced him with a sharp glance. Renny snickered; she shot him the same look.

"So," Ann said. "They followed the rules, and their experiment was fastest, correct?"

"Yes, but—"

"So, they should get top marks, shouldn't they?"

"Yes, but they started a fire!" the teacher said, now backed into a corner. She turned to the principal for help; he was bemused by the exchange.

"Seems that Mrs. Barnes has you there," he said.

"Alright, now that we agree on their mark," Ann said. "Let's discuss an appropriate punishment..."

Matthew glanced at Renny and winked. Renny grinned back.

◎

Grade 7

Matthew's teacher motioned for Ann to take a seat. "Thanks for coming in, Mrs. Barnes."

"No problem," Ann said. "What's up?"

"A couple of weeks ago, Matthew's penmanship took a turn for the worse. At first it was illegible, but it's getting better. It took me a while to realize that he—Matthew's right-handed, isn't he?"

Ann nodded.

"Well, he started writing with his left hand. I asked around the staff room; one of my colleagues said a hand switch can indicate a significant physical or emotional trauma. So, I have to ask, has Matthew recently suffered any head injuries or other traumatic or emotional events?"

Ann shook her head. "No, he's been perfectly normal. Well, normal for Matthew."

"Huh," the teacher said. "Yesterday he handed in a writing assignment that was, well, here, see for yourself."

She slid a piece of paper across the desk to Ann—rows of illegible scribbling.

"This could be serious, Mrs. Barnes. I think you should get him to a doctor. Maybe a neurologist."

Ann stared at the writing for a good thirty seconds, tilting her head this way and that.

Aha!

Ann smiled. "You said this started two weeks ago?"

The teacher nodded.

"That sounds about right," Ann said.

"What do you mean?"

"You don't see it, do you?" Ann said.

The teacher shrugged and shook her head. "See what?"

"Ah, some background is in order. Two weeks ago, I checked out a book on the life of Leonardo da Vinci from the town library. Matthew read it cover to cover the same day."

"I don't see what this has to do with Matthew's writing problem," the teacher said, alarmed by Ann's lack of concern.

Ann looked around the office, spotting a medium-sized mirror on the wall. "Here, let me show you."

Ann held the paper up to the mirror and the two looked at its reflection. It was Matthew's handwriting, now legible.

"da Vinci sometimes switched hands when he wrote," Ann said. "And he often wrote from right to left."

◎

Penticton 1972 Science Fair

The head judge looked uncomfortable.

"Mr. and Mrs. Barnes, given your son's, shall we say, scientific enthusiasm, I think it would be best if he didn't enter the science fair next year," he said. "After all, he *has* won the top award each of the past four years. Perhaps it's time to give another student a chance?"

Matthew's exhibit was advanced for a high school student, let alone a precocious child still in Grade 7: a series of homemade electromagnets that demonstrated the concept of magnetic levitation. He'd built a three-metre-long track and had a model train car hovering a quarter-inch above it; with a few adjustments, he could make the car move silently back and forth. The judge assigned to the Grades 4-7 category had been so impressed that Matthew could fully explain the underlying mathematics and physics he wanted all the judges to see this amazing project.

Unfortunately, the student exhibitor next to Matthew wasn't pleased he was hogging all the attention; when Matthew took a quick trip to the bathroom, she snuck under his table and played with the wiring. When the gaggle of judges returned and Matthew powered up his device, the sabotage, rather than disabling his experiment, sent twice the planned current to the electromagnets. The model train car shot off its rail, crashed through two display panels (just missing a student) and embedded itself in the far wall of the conference centre.

Matthew was devastated to be drummed out of the science fair.

"Cheer up, son," his dad said as they put the remains of his project into the trunk of the family car. "There will always be people jealous of others' success."

◎

June 1972

"Well, we made it through elementary school," Ann whispered to Nathan as Matthew walked across the stage to get his Grade 7 certificate at the school's graduation ceremonies. "Five more and he'll be finished high school."

"Or less, at the rate he's going," Nathan said. "Finding a new riddle every day is exhausting," he added, referring to what was still the favourite part of Matthew's bedtime routine. "And with his memory, I can't re-use old ones. He *never* forgets."

After the ceremonies, they took Matthew out for a celebratory treat. Ann and Nathan sat across from him at the picnic table in the Dairy Queen parking lot as he devoured his favourite dessert: the Peanut Buster Parfait. Ann looked at Nathan, who nodded.

"Son," Nathan said, "for years now, we've watched you struggle with the slow pace at school."

Matthew nodded, wiping a blob of chocolate sauce off his chin.

Ann took her turn. "In the fall, you'll be going to junior high. You'll have a different teacher for each subject—teachers who specialize in their course material."

He grinned. "Yah, I'm really looking forward to that."

"But we don't want the regular school system to slow your progress," Nathan said. "We think it's time we include you in your education planning."

He paused, glancing at Ann. "We see two options. First, we can arrange for you to skip grades. We think you could be in university in a couple of years."

Matthew's eyes lit up.

"But if you skip grades," Ann said, "you'd be leaving your friends behind. You wouldn't see them often. We're not sure you'd like that. And we aren't sure it would be good for you."

He frowned. "What's my other choice?

"Well," Ann said, "You go through school grades *with* your friends, but we arrange it so you can move ahead in math and science as fast as you can."

"I could do that?"

Nathan nodded. "We've met with your junior-high-school principal. He's talked with your elementary school teachers and is aware of your capabilities; he's got his math and science teachers on board and they'll help you go through the course material at *your speed*. You'll still have to take the other core subjects, English, Social Studies, Shop, Phys Ed, and French, though."

"Wow," Matthew said.

"We also talked to the principal at the senior high school. He's on board, so once you've completed Math and Science 8, 9, and 10, he'll get you started on grades 11 and 12."

Matthew grinned at this prospect.

"There's no need to decide right now," Ann said. "Think on it for a while. Talk to your friends. We're happy with whatever decision you make."

"Okay," he said. "I'll think about it." He paused. "One more thing. Matthew is a kid's name. I'm going into high school, so from now on I want to be called Matt."

FOUR

"High school's gonna be great!" Matt gushed to his parents at dinner after his first full day at McNicoll Park Junior Secondary School. He'd come home with an armload of textbooks he couldn't wait to absorb.

"Josh and I have the same homeroom, Division 11, which is for the smartest grade eights. Our teacher is Mr. Fisher, the senior math teacher. Gary's in Div 12, and Renny's in Div 13."

Matt's dad frowned. "Son, there's no need to brag."

"Dad, they assigned us home rooms based on our marks from grade seven. I'm not bragging." He paused. "At least I didn't think I was."

Nathan conceded the point with a nod.

"But we'll all have *some* classes together," Matt said, his eyes lighting up.

"How'd the first meeting with your teachers go?" Ann asked.

Matt grinned. "Mr. Brownell—he's our counsellor—has arranged for me to skip the regular science and math classes and work at my pace. Mrs. Hill—she's one of the science teachers—got me a desk in her office where I can work. She and Mr. Fisher will let me write the math and science exams whenever I'm ready!"

◎

Junior high school posed many challenges for Matt and his friends. Grade 8 students were at the bottom of the social pyramid and subject to unwanted attention from the older students. In the first week, Matt and Gary were targeted for their smaller size and general "nerdiness," while Josh was singled out for his girth and conservative clothing. The three found themselves, on more than one occasion, stuffed into their hall lockers. That bullying ended when Renny intervened, making it clear he'd "knock some heads together" if his friends weren't left alone.

Renny, thanks to his size, was a natural athlete. He tried out for the junior basketball team and the coach assigned him the "power forward" position. He wasn't a great shot, but a force to be reckoned with jockeying for rebounds. He soon led the junior league in rebounds, and his coach promoted him to the senior team, where he more than held his own against the older players. The rugby and track & field coaches also had their eyes on him.

Josh excelled in all the academic subjects but struggled with those requiring physical skill, such as shop and phys ed. Gary and Renny were average students, but excelled in shop class. Renny needed a little help in math and science, which Matt or Josh were always happy to give.

Junior high school offered social opportunities not found in elementary school: dances, social cliques, special-interest clubs, and the trials and tribulations of young boys and girls moving through the early stages of adolescence. Gary's devil-may-care attitude and repertoire of voice impressions during the morning announcements made him popular with the girls. Renny, thanks to his athletic prowess, was the most popular of the four, and got to hang out with the other "jocks." Matt and Josh remained on the social fringes, academic excellence being their only noteworthy attributes.

Grade 8 passed in the blink of an eye, and Matt had completed Grade 9 and 10 math and science. He had perfect scores on all the exams, which, unbeknownst to him, were considerably harder than those given to the rest of the student body.

◎

Summer in Penticton was a welcome diversion. Matt and his friends earned spending money picking fruit—cherries, apricots, apples, and peaches—at local orchards. Fruit picking was "piece work"—the more one picked, the more one earned. The foursome agreed to pool their pickings and split the earnings equally. The summer temperatures in the Okanagan regularly exceeded 100°F, so fruit picking started before sunrise and ended by noon. That left afternoons and weekends free for doing what Penticton teenagers did: floating down the Penticton River Channel on inner tubes, hanging out at the beach and the town's one and only air-conditioned shopping mall, and bicycling around town.

Their aptly named Explorers Society of Canada made several overnight "expeditions" into the local mountains. The first task when arriving at a campsite was the planting of the recently updated ESOC flag—Matt had learned enough Latin to propose an inspirational motto: *Audentes fortuna iuvat* ("May fortune favour the bold"). Once they'd set up camp, Renny would disappear for an hour or two to scout out the area. He'd always return with a bag of rocks; his signature declaration, "Every rock tells a story" elicited groans from his friends.

They established a secret campsite at Crater Lake, near the summit of nearby Okanagan Mountain Provincial Park. Renny, the budding geologist and outdoorsman, was in his glory on these expeditions, leading the six-hour trek up the steep rocky mountainside populated by rattlesnakes and through valleys filled with ten-foot-high devil's club shrubs before reaching the summit of Okanagan Mountain. The lake, known for its remoteness, difficult terrain, circular shape, and seemingly endless supply of rainbow trout, provided them with countless days of adventure.

Renny fell in love with the surrounding terrain; after learning basic map reading and surveying techniques at the local library, he enlisted his friends to help create a geological map of the area. Their survey efforts were thwarted, though, as their magnetic compasses proved unreliable. The foursome pondered this phenomenon during an evening campfire chat.

"According to one of my dad's old textbooks," Renny said, "it's called a 'magnetic anomaly.' It's because of weird chemistry or magnetism in the surrounding rocks. I wonder..."

"I bet it's a crashed UFO," Gary offered. His favourite magazine, not including the many photography and electronics magazines he devoured, was the very popular Paranormal Research Monthly.

"Sure, maybe it's the Ogopogo's underwater lair," Renny said, referring to the mythical sea monster said to inhabit nearby Okanagan Lake. He enjoyed winding Gary up over his interest in cryptozoology.

"Laugh it up, Sasquatch," Gary replied.

Josh, the quietest of the bunch, spoke up. "There was an article on asteroids in the latest issue of Popular Astronomy magazine; some planetary geologists think they might contain iron or other magnetic minerals."

"Maybe an asteroid did crash here ages ago," Renny said. "That would explain why the lake's so round."

"Wow," Gary said. "It'd be cool if there was an asteroid was down there."

"Then it would be a meteorite," Josh corrected.

Renny turned to Matt. "What do you think, Professor?"

Matt was silent for a moment. "If there's something underground interfering with the earth's magnetic field, we should be able to use our compasses to map it out." *Another puzzle to solve!*

"Ooh!" Renny said. "Let's get started on that tomorrow!"

The Explorers Society of Canada had a new mission.

Ann Barnes was cleaning out the basement storage room when she heard Matt come home from his fruit-picking job. He clomped down the stairs to get a bottle of pop from the spare fridge they kept in the basement.

"Whatcha doing, Mom?"

"Just cleaning up, honey. I thought I'd take your old toys to the Thrift Shop."

She pulled out a pile of thin cardboard boxes—jigsaw puzzles. She stared at the dust-covered box on top—a faded image of an early 1960s rocket—and smiled.

I think I'll keep these.

"That was my first jigsaw puzzle," Matt said. "When Dad got home from work that day, you had me show him how fast I could finish it."

"You *remember* that?" she said.

"August 12ᵗʰ, 1962." He shrugged.

Ann's jaw dropped. "You were only two years old!"

"Seems like only yesterday," he quipped.

Ann stared at him. "What else do you remember from that time?"

Another shrug. "I dunno. A lot, I guess."

"What do you mean by 'a lot'?"

Matt was silent for a long time. "Mom, I remember *everything*."

Ann shuddered as a chill ran up her spine. *He's not bragging—just stating a fact.*

Later that afternoon, Ann retrieved her journals—diaries she'd started when Matt was born—then sat down and quizzed him. Not only could he recall every event in her diary—she picked dates at random—he volunteered astonishing details she hadn't documented but could vaguely recall: the weather; what clothes he wore; what he'd had to eat.

Even more curious now, Ann made a trip to the local library's psychology section and learned that research into "photographic memory" was still in its infancy. It was also called "eidetic memory," although there was debate over subtle differences between the two; the former more related to the recall of pages of text or numbers, the latter a perfect recall of visual images. Matthew apparently had both, along with a seemingly total recall of all the episodes in his life.

This boy is going to be a challenge.

Renny looked embarrassed as family and friends belted out a horrendously off-key rendition of the Happy Birthday song. He nodded at Matt, then together they blew out the candles on the two birthday cakes on the dining room table. Renny's vanilla cake was geology-themed: a cross-section of a mountain, complete with several stratigraphic layers and lit with fourteen candles. Matt's cake was chocolate, in the shape of NASA's Apollo lunar lander and sporting thirteen candles.

After they'd consumed many helpings of cake and ice cream, the four teens sat on the living room floor to look at their presents.

"Hey guys, check this out," Matt said, holding up a thin paperback book his parents had given him that morning: *Flatland - A Romance of Many Dimensions*. "It's the story of a fictional character who lives in a two-dimensional world, like on a sheet of paper. He can only move up, down, left, and right, then gets pulled out of his world by a creature from the third dimension."

Matt's voice rose as he started babbling, the words coming faster and faster. Renny's thick eyebrows rose in alarm.

"Just imagine," Matt said, "an apple in three dimensions looks like a circle in two dimensions. Does that mean there's a four-dimensional version of an apple, and we only see the three-dimensional version? And what about wormholes? To get to the other side of an apple, a worm has to crawl half way around. But if it eats through the apple, it can get to the other side quicker. Imagine if we could create wormholes out into space—we could cover vast distances!"

"Don't they do that on Star Trek?" Renny said, trying to bring his friend back to planet Earth. "Warp speed!"

"I think you need a black hole to create a wormhole, don't you?" Josh added cautiously.

Matt was oblivious to his friends' banter, blabbering maniacally about higher dimensions and reference frames and other incomprehensible topics. Renny exchanged several worried glances with Gary and Josh.

Enough is enough, Renny decided.

"Okay, Professor. We get it. Let's go outside and get some fresh air."

Matt's eyes were glazed over; it took Renny and his friends several minutes to calm him down.

For the next two weeks, Renny noticed Matt would occasionally tune out and start mumbling about multiple dimensions. He had no idea what Matt was going on about, but clearly the concepts in that thin book had profoundly affected his best friend.

By the end of Grade 9, Matt, who was not quite fourteen, had completed Grade 12 math, physics, chemistry, and biology, scoring perfect marks in each. He was most interested in math and physics, finding biology to be "rote memorization" and chemistry to be "just cooking, but with physics." Matt's parents had planned for this accelerated progress and arranged for a tutor to start him on university-level courses.

Matt stared at the twenty-something young man who'd driven up from Vancouver the previous day and was now sitting in their living room.

"Hi Matt, I'm Brian Hamilton."

"Hi." They shook hands.

"Brian's working on his doctorate in neuropsychology at UBC," Ann said.

Brian nodded. "I'm doing research into eidetic memory and advanced spatial relationship skills. I heard through the grapevine about your abilities—a colleague works in UBC's Faculty of Education and has been reviewing your IQ tests. And, coincidentally, your parents put out feelers in the math and physics departments for a tutor. So here I am."

"Psychology, huh?" Matt said, not particularly impressed. The look he gave his parents spoke volumes: *I need someone to tutor me in math and physics and you brought me a psychologist?*

Nathan got the message. "Son, Brian has a Bachelor's degree in Honours Physics and Mathematics and a Master's degree in biophysics."

Matt's eyes lit up. "Really?"

Brian nodded. "My research of the brain takes place at the electrical level."

"Why do you want to tutor me?" Matt said.

Brian stared at him for a moment. "I think we can help each other. I'll tutor you in university-level math and physics. Maybe some physical chemistry, too. Based on what I've seen of your work, we should be able to get you through the entire undergraduate curricula in math and physics by the time you're finished high school."

Matthew nodded his approval. "Cool."

Brian continued. "In return, I'd like you to be one of my research subjects. You have an amazing memory, and I want to understand how it's organized, and how you retrieve facts so quickly and accurately. I'll do a series of directed interviews, along with written and visual tests. I'm teaming up with a post-doc from the physics department to develop a next-generation EEG—that's electroencephalograph—to measure the brain's electrical activity. Once that's working, I'd like to get scans of your brain while you're during memory retrieval exercises."

Matt didn't hesitate. "Let's do it!"

Brian smiled. "Great! Here's what I suggest. I'll send you study material by mail, and we'll talk by phone twice a week. Once a month, I'll drive up from Vancouver and we'll work together for a day."

"It's a deal!" Matt said.

◎

Grade 10 was coming to a close; Matt and his friends would soon be "moving up" to senior high school. Those three years in junior high had been formative ones. Renny topped out at six-foot, two inches and one hundred and eighty pounds of solid muscle. He was impatient to start senior high school, having been invited to try out for the football and rugby teams.

Gary had only grown a couple of inches, but, thanks to his hosting the morning announcements on the school's public address system, was one of the most popular kids in school; his repertoire of accents and impersonations proved entertaining to staff and students alike. Josh had somewhat "grown into his weight," but remained on the heavy side. Matt shot past Gary, sprouting from four feet ten inches at the start of Grade 8 to a respectable five feet seven inches by the end of Grade 10. And, since he was just approaching his 15th birthday, his growth spurt wasn't over.

Academically, little had changed with the foursome. Renny and Gary remained average students. Matt followed his own alternate learning track in math and sciences while getting mediocre grades in the subjects that didn't capture his interest. At the Grade 10 graduation ceremony, Josh received the award for top academic student, well-deserved even though Matt was miles ahead in math and science.

Then it was time for summer vacation. Gary was the only one of the four to have reached the milestone 16th birthday, and got a "real" job working at his dad's camera store. Renny, although he wasn't turning sixteen for a couple more weeks, convinced the owner of the local independent grocery store to hire him to stock shelves. Josh and Matt were still fourteen-going-on-fifteen and relegated to picking fruit. But whenever their work schedules aligned, the foursome hung out in the warm Okanagan sun.

◎

The four teenagers looked up at the huge radio telescope dish that blocked out the sun. This was DRAO—the Dominion Radio Astrophysical Observatory, Canada's premiere research facility in radio astronomy. The observatory was nestled in an isolated valley southwest of Penticton, in an electromagnetically "quiet" area ideal for listening to the sounds of the universe. Josh's dad, an electrical engineer, had been working there for over twenty years and arranged an in-depth tour for his son's friends.

"It's a twenty-six-metre dish," Josh said, "with feeds from 400 MHz up to 6 GHz." He'd spent so much time there he knew more than the university undergrads hired to guide tourists. "Let's head inside."

"Uh, if you guys don't mind," Renny said, "I'd rather go exploring." He pointed his lips towards a rocky outcropping half a kilometre to the east. "Looks like some cool stuff over there."

"Suit yourself, big guy," Josh said.

Renny nodded and headed off, his ever-present backpack tinkling with the sounds of a geologist's tools.

Josh, with Matt and Gary in tow, went inside to the main control room. The observatory was busy, but everyone made time for the inquisitive teens. Gary spent most of his time shadowing the electronics technician who was doing various repairs and maintenance on racks of complex equipment. Josh watched over the shoulder of the observatory's lone computer programmer as he typed away, while Matt peppered the research scientists with questions in physics, radio astronomy, and cosmology.

Two hours later, they'd literally exhausted the observatory staff, and went outside to sit at one of the staff picnic tables.

"Here comes Bigfoot," Gary said, nodding to the east; Renny was trudging towards them across the dry, sagebrush-covered ground. When he arrived, he dumped his heavy backpack on the table, which nearly tipped over from its weight.

"You should see the stratigraphy over there!" he gushed. "There's everything from slide deposits to volcanic sandstone, there's lava deposits, basal breccia... the works! I've got tons of samples to look at."

Renny up-ended his backpack, and rocks of various shapes and sizes rolled across the picnic table. He picked one at random.

"Every rock tells a story." In unison, his friends groaned.

◎

"So, how's the boy genius doing?" Stuart Barnes said over the cup of coffee he was having with his uncle and aunt in their living room. He was only seven years older than his cousin Matt but already suffering from a receding hairline, and had recently graduated at the top of his class in the Faculty of Law at the University of British Columbia. He'd landed an articling position in the Vancouver office of a London-based law firm that specialized in intellectual property law—patents, trademarks, and copyrights. They'd snapped up Stuart before graduation, primarily because of an assignment he'd done in his second-year intellectual property law course.

The instructor had given the students a hypothetical scenario involving an inventor looking for funding from a large corporation. The inventor wanted to demonstrate his invention, but first needed the company to sign a non-disclosure agreement: a legally binding agreement often used when parties want to make sure the information exchanged remains confidential.

While Stuart's classmates produced NDAs that were several pages of legalese—to cover every loophole—his was a single page with only *five paragraphs*. And he had the audacity to claim his NDA applied to *any* intellectual property situation. His professor had to read it several times before realizing it was the most elegant combination of simplicity and concise legal language he'd ever seen, and awarded Stuart a 100% mark. When the professor announced he planned to use Stuart's NDA as an example in future courses, Stuart advised him that wasn't possible, as he'd already copyrighted it in both Canada and the US. He'd found a loophole in the law school's regulations—which automatically gave the school copyright on all student work—by registering his copyright in Belize during his spring break vacation. Apparently, Belize was not a signatory to the Universal Copyright Convention Treaty, which UBC's intellectual property regulations (and Canadian law) assumed. Stuart's combination of audacity, legal maneuvering, and utter cheek gained him both accolades and derision from the faculty.

The "Barnes NDA" soon became famous throughout legal circles as the tightest NDA ever written; if a law school wanted to use it in their curriculum, they had to get a licence from Stuart. Only one company—a large, multi-national law office headquartered in New York—was foolish enough to use the Barnes NDA without permission. They suffered the embarrassment of being on the losing side of a copyright infringement lawsuit brought forward by the 3rd-year law student. Stuart settled for a written and public apology, and damages of one hundred thousand dollars.

"Matt's doing just fine," Ann said. "Thanks to his tutor, he's well into university-level math and physics."

"But our boy's also pulling his nose out of textbooks lately and doing more inventing," Nathan added proudly. "Tell Stu about Matt's latest project."

Ann nodded. "Last night we were coming back from dinner in Naramata—you know how dark and windy that road is. Well, we came around the corner by Three Mile Beach Road and almost hit a deer. Luckily, Nathan stopped in time, but it gave us quite a scare and gave Matt an idea. As soon as we got home, he grabbed his notebook and began scribbling away. He's been out in the garage since he woke up, tinkering."

At that moment, the lights in the house dimmed, then flickered as the house's electrical system briefly overloaded. The odour of burnt electrical insulation wafted into the living room.

"Speak of the devil," Stuart said. "I think I'll go see what he's up to."

Matt was leaning over a contraption on the garage workbench, waving smoke away.

"Hey, cuz," Stuart said.

Matt raised his head "Hey, Stu! When did you get into town?"

"Last night—I'm just home for the weekend. Whatcha working on? Your Mom said you came up with another brainstorm—I mean 'Barnes-storm' last night," Stuart said, using the term he'd coined for whenever his cousin came up with a brilliant idea.

Matt nodded enthusiastically. "Well, they told you we nearly hit that deer last night? It got me thinking. A car's headlights are fixed, so when a car turns a corner, they only light up what's directly in front of the car. I figure that if the car's headlights automatically steered *into* the turn, they'd give the driver extra time to react."

"Cool," Stuart said, nodding.

"I'm trying to figure out how to do that. First, I figured the lights should turn whenever the driver turns the steering wheel. That's what this version does. Here, I'll show you," he said, pointing towards the contraption on the bench.

"I mounted the headlight in this bracket with a small electric motor. When you turn this simulated steering wheel, the headlight moves."

Matt connected the battery, then turned the wooden steering wheel. The electric motor whined and the bracket pivoted, the headlight's beam moving in the same direction. When he returned the steering wheel to its centre position, the headlight moved back to point straight ahead.

"I think a better way would be to turn the light based on how fast the car turns—its yaw rate. But I've got nothing to use as a yaw rate sensor." He sniffed the air. "Hand me that voltmeter? I've still got a short somewhere."

"Sure thing, Professor." He grabbed the meter off the bench. There were small rubber clips spaced equally along the red and black leads between the meter and its test probes. "What are these rubber things?"

"Oh, I made those up to keep the leads from getting tangled," Matt said. "That's a universal problem with meter leads."

"Wow, that's a good idea!" Stuart said, trying unsuccessfully to get the leads to tangle. "In fact, that's sort-of the reason I popped by. When you get a moment, could you join me and your parents?"

"I'm done here for the moment," Matt said, wiping off his hands. "I need a drink." He disconnected the battery and followed Stuart into the house.

After refreshing everyone's drinks, Matt sat beside his parents. "So, what's up?"

"Matt, remember when you and your friends helped my dad with his cardboard box supply problem last summer?"

Matt nodded. Uncle Ed's regular order of several hundred cardboard boxes, used to ship fruit to customers, had been misread by the supplier— who sent stacks of cardboard sheets instead. Ed had fruit waiting to ship, so in a panic, he enlisted Matt and his friends to cut and hand-fold the boxes. After folding only a few, Matt had a "Barnes-storm": a fixture made of small pieces of plywood connected by a complex arrangement of hinges that allowed them to fold a cardboard sheet into a box in seconds instead of minutes.

Matt nodded. "Yah, that contraption was pretty cool, but what that made it *interesting* was how it could be adapted to make *any* box shape."

"Exactly," Stuart said. "You've come up with some amazing ideas and inventions; you should profit from them."

Matt shrugged. "I just like solving puzzles."

Stuart nodded. "But that headlight gizmo you're working on—if that were properly marketed, it could save lives."

"I guess..." Matt said.

"I think you should patent that headlight invention, and possibly those meter lead clips as well."

Matt shrugged. "Sure, I guess. How do I do that?"

"I can take care of it," Stuart said. "It's what I do for a living. But let's talk about something else first." He opened his briefcase and extracted a thin folder. "Last fall, and with your parents' permission, I filed patent applications for your cardboard box-folding fixture and its general solution."

Matt turned to his parents with eyebrows raised; they both nodded and smiled.

"Matt," Stuart said, "the Canadian Patent Office approved both applications. You're the proud owner of two patents," he said, handing over official certificates. "Since you're a minor, your parents will have to sign affidavits certifying that you are the inventor."

"We're so proud of you, son!" Nathan said.

"Cool," Matt said. "So, what happens now with these patents?"

"Well, successful patents become public, so anyone can read them. What a patent does is give the inventor exclusive rights to their invention for twenty years. No one can make, sell, or use anything covered by your patent without your written permission. My law firm will field queries from anyone interested in using them and negotiate licencing agreements on your behalf."

"Sure, I guess."

"These are Canadian patents, but Canada has signed the Universal Copyright Convention Treaty, so registering them in the US and other countries is easy. Now let's talk about patenting your turning-headlight gizmo. And maybe those meter lead clips?"

Stuart spent the afternoon tutoring Matt in the language and process of patents. He took copious notes as his brilliant young cousin described his inventions.

Just before dinner, he packed his notes into his briefcase. "I'm heading back to the coast tomorrow night. When I get to work, I'll do what's called a 'prior art search,' where I check to see if there are any similar inventions. If not, then I'll prepare and file the patent applications."

Matt nodded. "Sounds good, Stu."

"Okay, gotta go, cuz. I'll be in touch!"

◎

Renny's sixteenth birthday heralded another step towards teen independence. That morning, he waited outside the town's Motor Vehicle Branch office to be first in when the doors opened. He showed his student id card as proof of age, passed a short knowledge test, then left proudly clutching his learner's licence, which allowed him to drive as long as someone with a full licence was in the car.

That afternoon, Renny stood beside Matt while their friends belted out another off-key rendition of the Happy Birthday song. It was a tradition he looked forward to every year since he and his mother moved to Penticton nine years ago and he'd become friends with this bunch of crazy guys.

Gary, always trying to get under Renny's skin, opted for "alternate" lyrics, which he sang in sync with the others:

Happy birthday to you!
You should live in a zoo.
Like the monkeys and the tigers,
And you look like one, too!

Renny gave Gary the stink-eye, took a deep breath and easily extinguished the sixteen candles on the hot rod racing car-shaped cake. Then he joined in singing for Matt; having the same birthdays meant there were always two birthday cakes.

He opened presents from his friends—mostly gag gifts—then realized a gift from his mother was absent. He glanced at her and raised his eyebrows in question.

I know money's tight, but...?

She smirked. "Your present's outside, son."

Renny charged out the front door, his friends close behind. He stopped short when he saw what was sitting in the driveway; his friends piled into him.

"Whoa..." Matt remarked.

"Holy cow!" Josh said.

"No way," Gary added.

It was a 1955 Chevrolet Bel Air, its black glossy paint glinting in the bright afternoon sun.

"Happy birthday, son," his mom said.

"Mom..." Renny stuttered. "How...? Where...?"

She smiled. "This was your dad's car. It's been in storage up north since he died. I had it shipped here last week. Our neighbours kept it in their garage for me. They pushed it across the street while you were blowing out candles." She handed him the car keys, a twinkle in her eyes. "Try it out."

Renny jumped behind the wheel and turned the key. The overhead-valve, inline V-8 rumbled to life.

"You know," Matt said as Renny revved the engine, "it looks like the Batmobile." Gary and Josh nodded agreement, and the three of them started running around the car singing a famous '60s television show theme song.

"Nana nana nana nana, BATMAN!"

"Get in here, runt" Renny shouted at Gary, who, although the smallest of the four, was five months older and had already had his licence so was an acceptable chaperone. "Road trip!" He was in car heaven as the Chevy lurched out of the driveway and around the block, much to his mother's chagrin.

Renny had to suffer through a set of driving lessons before his mother lengthened his "driving leash," allowing him to cruise around Penticton (but only during daylight hours and only with her or Gary present). Matt found a used Citizen Band radio at the local pawn shop, which he and Gary installed in the Batmobile.

"Your CB handle's gotta to be 'Batman'," Matt declared.

Renny nodded sagely. "Eh. Batman it is. I'll pick yours. I'm thinking... 'The Professor,'" not only an homage to one of their favourite '60s sitcoms, but a nod to Matt's intellectual prowess.

Gary and Josh both declined CB handles, just happy to be part of the crew as they cruised around town in the Batmobile. They chatted with other CB operators, hung out at the local Dairy Queen and consumed foot-long hot dogs and Peanut Buster Parfaits, and cruised Lakeshore Drive and Main Street along with the other teens. Renny was the envy of every car-loving teenager in town, wisely declining all offers to race off-the-line at stop lights.

Mom would kill me if she caught me racing.

It was his best summer ever.

FIVE

In September, Matt and his friends graduated to the town's only senior high school. Penticton Senior Secondary ("Pen-Hi") was the collector school for the town's three junior highs, so the Grade 11 cohort grew to triple what Matt had become accustomed to over the past three years. For reasons he couldn't articulate, he was uncomfortable being around that many unfamiliar faces.

There's just too many strangers.

Grade 11 students had to take a set of core courses, so Matt had some classes with his friends. But while his peers were taking math, physics, and chemistry, Matt sat at a desk in the guidance counsellor's office, working on the latest set of assignments from his tutor. Matt was aware of the rumour circulating around the school—amongst those who came from other junior high schools—that he was deficient in those areas and taking remedial lessons. But he didn't care.

Students were allowed two elective courses from a pool of academic and technical subjects. Matt chose French 11, which meant another class with Josh, and the self-paced Electronics 11/12 with Gary. Matt and Gary planned on completing the entire year's course material as fast as possible so they could start on a "special project." Josh opted for Typing 11 as his second elective, to better hone his keyboarding skills for when he became a computer programmer. Renny chose Geography and Auto Shop, the former because it had a section on geology, the latter so he could save money by working on the Batmobile.

During the first of their mandatory Guidance 11 classes, all students took an "aptitude test" to help guide their career choices. Matt recognized many of the questions from IQ tests he'd been taking regularly since Grade 3. When the test results came back, Matt and his friends huddled at their favourite lunch spot on the lawn in the school's courtyard to compare results.

"According to this," Gary said, waving his test results, "I'm going to be an actor or a pilot."

"Why not both?" Renny suggested.

Gary nodded in agreement. "What did you get, Bigfoot? Crazed loner who lives in the woods and talks to rocks? Bouncer at a strip club?"

"Why not both?" Matt said.

"Professional athlete or auto mechanic," Renny said. "Was hoping it would say 'geologist.'"

"Mine says air traffic controller or computer programmer," Josh volunteered. "I hope it's the latter."

"Why not both?" Gary said.

"What about you, Professor?" Renny said.

Matt paused, his face turning a light shade of red. "Well, mine says, 'Results inconclusive—please see your counsellor.' Seriously." He shrugged.

"Hey!" Renny said. "There's a box at the bottom of mine labelled 'SB-Intel Quot.' I got 117—is that good?"

"Pretty sure it means 'profoundly retarded'," Gary replied, earning a growl in response.

Matt, who had more than a passing familiarity with IQ tests, came to Renny's rescue. "That's the Stanford-Binet scale; a score of 110 to 119 means 'above average.'"

"Let see yours, runt." Renny snatched Gary's printout. "Aha! 119! That means you're only slightly less profoundly retarded than me!"

"Two points is two points," Gary replied. "Second place is the first loser." He looked to Josh.

"138. How about you, Matt?"

Matt shrugged. "Mine doesn't have a number. It just shows asterisks."

Renny hooted. "So, Professor, not only do you *not* have the aptitude for any career, your IQ doesn't even register! Ha ha!"

They all roared with laughter. Matt joined in, as his friends knew the truth: his IQ was so high it was literally off-the-chart.

◎

The school year passed quickly and with no major incidents. Josh was the top Grade 11 student, but his classmates still considered him an oddball for his conservative clothing. Renny's tryout for the football team was a formality; he became a star offensive tackle, feared by quarterbacks up and down the valley. Gary, thanks to Renny's not-so-subtle urging, had started working out in the summer and added some muscle to his diminutive frame. He swapped his thick eyeglasses for contact lenses and honed his repertoire of impersonations during the school's morning announcements, a combination that made him popular with the girls. His change in appearance also made it easier to sneak into local bars that had arcade claw machines, his latest passion. Matt and Josh, while definitely interested in the opposite sex, both found teenage girls incomprehensible. The feelings were mutual; their stereotypical "nerdiness" and being a year younger than other Grade 11s made them undesirable and the butt of many jokes.

They're the first puzzle I can't solve, Matt realized. *At least not yet.*

By Christmas, Matt and Gary completed the Electronics 11 curriculum; with their teacher's blessing (and for extra credit), they starting building circuits for an underwater robot Gary was building in his basement and planning on testing out in the summer, a project he codenamed "Aquarius."

Matt continued powering through the assignments mailed by his tutor, Brian. To fulfill his part of the tutoring arrangement, Matt endured a "Q&A session" each time Brian made the monthly trip from UBC. Brian came prepared with an extensive series of questions intended to help him understand the organizational structure of Matt's phenomenal memory.

When Brian posed a fact-based question such as, "What's the capital of Brazil?" and Matt replied, "Brasilia," Brian was ready with follow-ups.

"How do you know that? Where did you first learn about Brazil?"

"From the World Book encyclopedia series, 1964 edition, Volume A-B, page 207. The first paragraph of that entry lists the capital, population, language, land area, etcetera. They follow the same format for every country."

"Do you see that text in your mind?"

"Uh huh."

Matt's answers to more application-specific questions were also illuminating.

"What colour is the sky?"

"Blue."

"Why is it blue, and not red or green? What makes it blue?"

"Scattering. Fundamentals of Optics, by Jenkins and White. I read that textbook when I was twelve. Chapter 22 - Absorption and Scattering, page 468, has a graph showing the scattering intensity as a function of wavelength according to Rayleigh's Law. The blue component of white light scatters more because of the fine particles in earth's atmosphere. That's why Mars has a red sky—the dust particles in its atmosphere are larger."

"So, you see that graph in your mind?"

"Yup. I see every page of the book."

Brian's line of questioning about personal events was equally fruitful.

"Let's go back to March 13th, 1965."

"That was a Saturday."

"What did you have for lunch?"

"Tomato soup. Crackers and cheese. A glass of milk."

"How did you arrive at that answer? Take me through the steps."

"When you said the date, I 'saw' a calendar for 1965, and March the 13th was the second Saturday. I 'zoomed in' on that date, and a series of images appeared. It's like a filing cabinet in my mind, one cabinet per year and one file folder for each day. The folder has pictures in it, photos of what happened to me that day. What I ate, what I wore, what others around me were doing."

"About those 'photos.' Are you in them, or are they 'taken' from your point of view?"

"My point of view."

"So, it's like you're looking through a camera?"

"Yup."

"Do you recall how you felt that day?"

"Hmm. Good question." Matt paused. "No. Come to think of it, I don't have *any* memories of how I felt that day." He paused again. "On any day, actually."

"Interesting. Do you see a calendar for every year since you were born?"

"Yes."

"Do you see calendars for other years? Like, before you were born? Or in the future?"

"I *can* see a calendar for *any* year you pick, but there's only filing cabinets and folders for the years I've experienced."

Brian made audio recordings of each interview and took copious notes, remarking several times how valuable Matt's contributions were towards his research.

"I'm getting a good feel for the depth and breadth of your memory," Brian said. "My next step is to figure out *how* you retrieve the information, bio-electrically speaking. But that'll have to wait until I finish my dissertation: a next-generation electroencephalograph—a brain scanner— which should take a year to build. I want to get you in it."

"Cool."

◎

June 1976

Matt sat across the table from Brian in the high school's counselling office; Brian pulled a thick sheaf of papers out of his briefcase.

"Matt, we're coming to the end of the school year and I've taught you everything I know about math, physics, and chemistry, so this is a good time to see where you're at. I've got exams here that cover the undergrad curriculum in these subjects. And some graduate-level material just to challenge you. Treat them as you would real exams."

Matt shrugged. "Okay."

"Let's start with differential calculus," Brian said, taking a small stapled set of papers off the top of the stack and sliding it across the table.

Matt felt a thrill as looked at the first question, solving a simple partial differential equation. He stared off into space, seeing an oddly shaped curve floating in front of him. *Ah, separating the variables will work here.* He envisioned a pair of functions that, when combined, made up that curve. He merged those functions in his mind, then wrote down their product. *Easy.*

It took him just over three hours to complete the seventeen exams.

"I'll let you know the results as soon as I can," Brian said, packing up the exams. "Might take a month or so. And I've got plenty of data to collate from our interviews."

◎

With Grade 11 behind them, Matt and his friends enjoyed another hot Okanagan summer. Josh's dad had arranged a summer intern position for his son at the radio observatory, assisting their sole programmer. Renny was stocking shelves at the grocery store, and Gary worked at his dad's camera shop. Matt wangled a job at the town's RadioShack electronics store; he'd impressed the manager with his electronics knowledge, then cinched the job by demonstrating that he'd memorized the company catalogue and the specs for every product. Their jobs all paid the minimum wage of $3.20 per hour, more than double what they could earn picking fruit in the local orchards. Matt and Gary also helped Josh build a microcomputer from a kit he'd ordered from Popular Electronics magazine.

They celebrated Matt's and Renny's joint birthday—16 for Matt and 17 for Renny—then took the traditional cruise around town in the Batmobile, with Matt behind the wheel for the first time now that he had learner's licence. But the highlight of the summer of '76 was "Project Aquarius," an endeavour requiring all hands on deck.

◎

Gary stood at the bow of the 20-foot aluminum skiff that bobbed in the calm morning waters of Okanagan Lake just off the western shore of Rattlesnake Island. The ESOC flag, mounted to the boat's radio antenna, fluttered in the light breeze. The lake bottom here plunged to over four hundred feet and was home to the mythical Ogopogo lake monster. Gary scanned a ninety-degree arc of water with his binoculars; nothing but flat water.

"Anything?" he said, not looking away.

"Nothing here," Josh said, who was watching the port-side quadrant.

"Nada," Matt, to starboard, said.

"Sweet fuck-all back here," Renny added from the stern.

Shit. Gary sighed and lowered the binoculars to give his eyes a break. The boat's owner/skipper—a friend of Gary's dad—lounged behind the wheel, slumped to one side and gently snoring. A reporter from the Penticton Herald newspaper, looking the stereotypical part with two cameras and cassette recorder hanging from his neck, sat in the bridge's shade, waiting for something interesting to happen. Gary stared at the water.

My pride and joy is down there, somewhere...

"PogoBot" was Gary's attempt at an underwater probe. It began life as an oil drum before he added a small plexiglass viewport and mounted a Kodak 126 Instamatic camera, with a four-shot flashcube, facing out. PogoBot's "brains"—a set of handmade circuit boards he and Matt built during Electronics 11—controlled a battery-powered mechanism that pressed the camera's shutter button every thirty seconds, advancing the film winder each time. To survive the pressure at the bottom of the lake, Matt figured out how much reinforcing the drum needed and how much ballast was required to get it to sink.

The test dives of PogoBot, in the shallow and protected waters of the Penticton Marina two weeks ago had gone off without a hitch, resulting in a brief article and a photo of the lakebed in the local newspaper. A reporter from the Vancouver Sun newspaper, who was passing through town on his way to another story, saw the article on "Project Aquarius" while having lunch at a roadside diner. He tracked Gary down at his dad's camera shop, interviewed him, and posted a similar story the following week. The guys, buoyed by their early successes, decided to go-for-broke and deploy PogoBot at full depth.

They made the thirty-minute trip from the marina out to Rattlesnake Island, powered up PogoBot, sealed its lid, then lowered it to the bottom with a yellow poly rope. After waiting five minutes—more than enough time for the camera to activate and hopefully catch a photo of the elusive Ogopogo—they started pulling it up. That's when things went pear-shaped.

Apparently, they'd let out too much rope when they lowered PogoBot and it caught on a rock or overhang. They pulled and pulled and pulled; eventually the rope surfaced with a frayed end. And no PogoBot. Renny had tried to lighten the mood by insisting that it was the Ogopogo that chewed through the rope, angry at having its picture taken. It was a wasted effort.

Gary glanced at Matt. "Time?"

Matt looked at his Casio digital watch. "Twenty-nine minutes, twelve seconds."

"So, Professor," Renny said, "when's your little gizmo, the whatchamacallit, supposed to kick in?"

Matt sighed. "The 'whatchamacallit' is an electromagnet time delay relay ballast failsafe. It'll activate precisely thirty minutes after we powered up PogoBot." The mechanism in question was a backup device that Gary had insisted on: a battery-powered electromagnet on the inside bottom of the drum that held an iron weight to the outside. Gary had sized the PogoBot's battery so it would keep the electromagnet energized only long enough to lower it to the lake bottom and take pictures. Once the battery ran out, the electromagnet would fail, the weight would drop off, and PogoBot would float to the surface. In theory.

"Time?" Gary asked again.

"Thirty minutes, fifteen seconds."

"So the Professor's failsafing gizmo didn't work," Renny said.

"Oh ye of little faith, Batman," Matt said. "Four hundred feet is a long way down—it'll take PogoBot about... sixty seconds to ascend."

"Assuming it didn't flood," Josh, ever the pessimist, added.

Gary shot him a nasty look. "Thanks for the vote of confidence. Back to your lookouts, please."

A minute later, Renny let out a yell. "Thar she blows!" Fifty metres astern, the PogoBot shot out of the water; Gary turned in time to see it land with a large splash.

Renny's shout woke up the boat's skipper; he started the engine, spun the vessel around and cautiously approached the bobbing drum.

"I think it's happy to see us," Renny said.

"Let's get it aboard!" Gary yelled, cranking on the hand-winch to lower the skiff's bow ramp.

It took the four of them several minutes to corral the drum and get it onto the ramp. Gary winched the ramp up and the drum rolled onto the deck. The reporter snapped photos and dictated into his recorder as they tipped the drum upright, then unscrewed the bolts holding the lid on. Gary grabbed a flashlight and stuck his head inside.

"Looks dry!" his voice echoed from inside the drum. After a minute of grunting and groaning, he extricated himself from the drum, holding the Kodak camera.

"Ta da! And it took four pictures!" he exclaimed, pointing at the small transparent window on the camera's back that showed the 126-film cartridge's frame number.

"Woo-hoo!" Matt yelled. "Let's get them developed!"

Gary shot the remaining eight pictures, taking photos of the PogoBot and a couple of group shots, before sealing the camera in a Ziploc bag.

A small crowd (mostly family and friends) was waiting at the marina, eager to hear how the boys had fared; it took Gary a breathless ten minutes to tell the story.

"Now we gotta go develop the film!" he said, waving the camera as his friends wrestled PogoBot onto the dock. A middle-aged man, who'd been standing at the back of the crowd, approached Gary. He sported a crewcut, had the build of a wrestler and the lurching swagger of a sailor.

"Mr. Stocks, can we talk?"

Gary nodded. The man peppered him with questions while his friends stood back and watched. He grilled Gary on details of the drum construction, the electronics, his educational plans, everything.

This feels like one of those mock job interviews we did in Guidance 11 class, Gary thought.

Twenty minutes later, the man ran out of questions. He was silent for a few moments, then nodded.

"Thanks for your time, Mr. Stocks. Here's my business card. If you're looking for a summer job after you graduate, give me a call." He turned and ambled along the dock towards the parking lot. His friends rushed over.

"Who was that?" Josh asked.

Gary handed over the card. "Mike McFarlane, the owner of Canadian Submarine Engineering Ltd., based in North Vancouver. They build remotely operated vehicles for subsea work: oil and natural gas fields, salvage, etc. I read about him in Popular Mechanics—he's a legend in the subsea industry."

"What did he want?" Renny said.

Gary smiled and puffed out his chest. "He read about Project Aquarius in the Vancouver Sun newspaper last week and drove up from the coast to see it in action. He offered me a job after I graduate."

"Nice!" Matt said. "Now, those photos...?"

They rolled the PogoBot in the marina's warehouse, then piled into the Batmobile for the short drive to Stocks Camera Shop on nearby Main Street. Gary headed for the darkroom at the back of the store while his friends waited anxiously out front.

He returned an hour later holding twelve 8x10-inch glossy black and white photos, smiling triumphantly.

"Well, we got four good shots of the lake bottom," he said. "But no Ogopogo."

His friends cheered anyways.

The front page of that Saturday's edition of the Penticton Herald newspaper had a picture of the foursome standing behind PogoBot with the caption, "Lake Monster Hunters." A full-page article followed on page 3, including two of PogoBot's underwater photos.

◎

September 1976

Brian Hamilton sat across from Matt and his parents in the Barnes-family living room. He'd driven up from Vancouver that morning.

"So, Matt, ready for grade twelve?" Brian asked.

Matt shrugged. "Now that you and I are done, I'm going to have lots of spare blocks. It's gonna be a slow year." He sighed.

Brian nodded. "Matt, remember those exams you did just before school ended? I've got the results and wanted your parents here when I go over them."

"Did I do that badly?" Matt said.

Brian chuckled. "Just the opposite. Matt, you scored one hundred percent in all the math exams: linear algebra, geometry, statistics and probability, differential and integral calculus. Likewise, your physics and chemistry scores were perfect."

"Way to go, son!" his dad said.

Matt shrugged; he hadn't found them particularly difficult. "So, what do I do now? I've got another year in high school before I can go to university."

"Let's discuss that in a second," Brian said. "First, I have to come clean about something. Those tests weren't just ones I threw together. They were *real* exams, prepared by professors in UBC's mathematics, physics, and chemistry departments. Those professors were the ones who marked them."

Brian pulled another sheet of paper from his briefcase.

"I've got a letter from the head of UBC's math department—he's impressed with your abilities and they want to offer you a full scholarship in their graduate program."

"Wow," Matt said.

"Oh, Matt," Ann said, "we're so proud of you!"

"One other thing," Brian said. "I don't know if you noticed, but amongst those tests was one that a colleague in the Faculty of Education prepared for me."

Matt nodded. "I remember that one. It was more fun than the math and physics tests. Some questions were actually hard. It was an IQ test, right?"

Brian bobbed his head. "Not *just* an IQ test. I asked her to create the *world's hardest* IQ test. She surveyed professors in several faculties to come up with challenging questions."

Matt nodded. "That explains a lot."

"Creating a test challenging enough for someone with a very high IQ requires input from people who are *more* intelligent. That's why we consulted university professors. The best we can tell from this test is that your IQ is *at least* 180. We'd need an even harder test to find out how much higher." Brian scratched his head. "Not sure how we'd do that." He shrugged. "Anyways, don't let this high score go to your head—pun intended. It's for my longitudinal research—you know, establishing trends."

Matt didn't respond, so Brian continued. "The math department head has prepared a study guide for you—I've got it here—and will ship you their grad-level textbooks as an incentive."

Ann smiled at her son. "And you thought you'd have too much free time this fall."

◎

"Holy shit, Professor," Renny exclaimed, "you've got a lot of stuff here."

He shuffled through the dozen university brochures covering Matt's bed as they hung out at the Barnes household one wintery Saturday afternoon in December. Matt had put his many spare Grade 12 blocks to good use, drawing on the school's counselling office resources to request information from, and apply to, universities around the world.

"Wow," Renny said. "Canada, the US, Europe, and the UK. Even a couple from the Far East." He held up a colourful brochure resplendent with snow-covered mountain peaks. "What the fuck is ETH, and where is it?"

"Eidgenössische Technische Hochschule," Matt said, mangling a German accent. "That's the Swiss Federal Institute of Technology in Zurich. They've got world-class physics and chemistry departments." Matt's voice lowered, his tone turning reverential. "Albert Einstein taught there."

"Do you know what field you're going to study? Math? Physics? All the above?"

Matt shrugged. "I... I dunno..."

Renny stared at the brochures. "Must be nice to have so many options. I'd kill to get into a geology program like at the University of Arizona. Hell, I'd give my left nut just to go to UBC. If I'm lucky, I'll end up at Okanagan College in Kelowna." He sighed. "I hate being poor."

"Cheer up, Batman," Matt said. "OK College has a good first-year science program—you'll need that for any geology program. You'll end up somewhere cool, I just know it."

◎

Ann Barnes sipped her after-dinner coffee and stared across the dining room table at Matt. She glanced at her husband, who gave a barely perceptible shrug and a tilt of the head. *Give it your best shot!*

She cleared her throat. "Matt, honey, it's only two weeks until graduation. Isn't it time you let us in on your plans?"

Matt looked up from his dessert. "You mean, who I'm taking to the grad dinner and dance?" he replied, poker-faced.

Ann smiled. *He knows exactly what I mean. I'm glad he's getting the hang of sarcasm.*

"No, Mr. Smarty-Pants. Your university plans."

Matt had expended significant effort in the past six months researching universities around the world—their academic programs, locations, culture, languages, everything. He'd written countless letters, received stacks of material in the mail, sent out applications, and rung up large long-distance phone bills talking to academic counsellors at various institutions. Early in this process, he'd politely asked his parents to "butt out" and let him do the research himself. They'd reluctantly agreed, and had gleaned little about what he was doing.

"Yes, you've held out long enough," Nathan added.

"Well, as you know," Matt led with, enjoying tormenting them a bit longer, "thanks to my tutor Brian, I mean *Doctor* Hamilton now, UBC's math department has offered me a full scholarship—I mean 'fellowship'— in their graduate mathematics program.

"The other Canadian universities I'm considering—McGill and Waterloo—will also give me full undergrad scholarships in math, physics, or a combination of both. I think Josh is leaning towards computer science at Waterloo, so being at the same university with him would be cool. I considered applying to RMCC—Royal Military College of Canada—as they have an excellent scholastic reputation, but I've got no interest in joining the Canadian Armed Forces. Or wearing a uniform. Or taking orders.

"Several US universities are interested but have been, by comparison, stingy. MIT and Caltech will let me into their graduate math programs, but no scholarship money. Columbia is the only ivy-league school that is even considering my application. Turns out they're partial to American students.

"As for the international universities... Cambridge is interested, as is Oxford. ETH has offered me a year-one scholarship in their applied physics-slash-math program. From the pictures I've seen, Zurich looks like a neat place. And Einstein taught there. If I was going to go overseas, it would be ETH."

Ann was on the edge of her seat, as was her husband. *Switzerland is a long ways away!*

"So?" Nathan said.

Matt couldn't keep his parents in the dark any longer. "UBC," he said. "I'm going to UBC."

"So, math it is?" Ann said.

Matt shook his head.

Ann was thoroughly confused. "Then what...?"

"Well, as much as I love math and physics, I have a feeling I'm going to need a practical, hands-on education. I've decided on Engineering—Engineering Physics." He paused as his decision sunk in.

"That's right, Dad, I'm going to get the Red Jacket and the Iron Ring, same as you!"

"I'm so proud of you, son," Nathan said, almost tearing up.

There was a long silence, which Ann eventually broke.

"So, who *are* you taking to the grad dinner and dance?"

Pen-Hi Class of 1977 Graduation Ceremonies

Renny's mother, sitting in the audience with Matt's parents, dabbed her teary eyes with a Kleenex when her son's name was called and he strode across the stage to receive his diploma from the school principal. Matt, having already received his, was waiting at the side of the stage; Renny grabbed his arm and raised it, turning towards the audience.

Victory!

Once all the diplomas were handed out, a parade of teachers took turns announcing the scholarship and bursary winners. Josh, as top academic student, made three trips up to the stage, winning a total of $3500 from local organizations. And that was in addition to the computer science scholarship the University of Waterloo had awarded him. They had the best computer science department in the country, and he couldn't wait to start. Matt didn't win any scholarships or bursaries because, well, he'd forgotten to apply for them. Renny hadn't come away empty-handed—he won a $250 bursary from the Hudson's Bay Company. But even with the bursary he'd won and the money earned stocking shelves, Renny and his mother couldn't afford the cost of university tuition and living expenses. Following Matt's urging, Renny enrolled in the first-year science program at Okanagan College in nearby Kelowna, a 45-minute drive north. His dream of becoming a geologist like his dad wasn't looking promising. He wasn't going alone, though—Gary enrolled in the college's two-year electronics technology program, and the two planned on car-pooling.

And this was just the first night of Grad Week activities; there were still the grad photos, the formal dinner and dance, bush parties, and a fancy dinner out with friends at the Penticton Golf Club. For many in the Pen-Hi class of '77, graduation signalled the end of their academic journey. But for Matt and his friends, it was just another step in the transition towards adulthood.

◎

The four teenagers had their last summer together, working their jobs, cruising in the Batmobile, camping. As August came to a close, they launched a last expedition to Crater Lake. It took them until mid-afternoon to make the long hike up Okanagan Mountain, and, in keeping with their tradition, they removed any flagging tape and every cairn they found, to make it harder for other hikers to find their secret camp.

They spent the rest of the day fishing, hauling in plenty of lake trout. The next day they explored the rugged shores of the lake, adding data points to Renny's map of the area's magnetic anomalies.

After a dinner feast of pan-fried trout, baked beans, and Pop-Tarts wrapped in foil and heated in the campfire, the foursome relaxed on their sleeping bags in the warm summer evening, looking up at the stars. Gary broke the silence.

"It's a weird feeling, isn't it? We've been together since elementary school. In a week, we're splitting up. Matt and Josh are off to university.

Me and Bigfoot are heading to OK College. I wonder when we'll be able to do *this* again?"

There was another long silence, broken by Josh. "Why don't we make a plan to meet back in Penticton regularly? Say every year? Maybe every couple of years?"

There were murmurs of agreement.

"You've been rather quiet, Professor," Renny said. "What's on your mind?"

It took Matt half a minute to respond. "You guys seem to know where you're headed in life. I don't. There are more puzzles to be solved. I *have* to figure out how things work. How *everything* works. I know *where* I'm going next, but I don't know *where I'm going*." His frustration was obvious.

"Don't sweat it," Renny said. "We all know where you're going, don't we?" More murmurs of agreement.

"Where?" Matt asked, perplexed.

Gary pointed straight up at the bright band of stars that formed the Milky Way. "Somewhere up there," he said in a slow, deep voice.

Matt was silent for a moment. "Well, when I get there, you'll have to join me."

"Deal," Gary said.

"Deal," Josh said.

"Eh," Renny added.

The next day, after a breakfast of cold trout and beans, they broke camp and hiked out to the forestry road where Gary's dad was waiting for them in his pickup truck. It was a somber ride back to town; by the end of the week, Josh had flown east, and Matt was on his way to Vancouver.

SIX

Matt waved goodbye as his parents drove away from Place Vanier, the UBC student residence they'd just helped him move into.

I'm on my own for the first time! he realized.

His first order of business, after unpacking his few possessions, was an appointment with the Director of the Engineering Physics program. Matt headed south along the UBC campus main mall towards the engineering buildings, looking for the landmark his dad had often mentioned.

There, in the middle of the mall's wide, lawn-covered median sat a truncated white pyramid, two metres high, each face adorned with a large, inset, red "E." According to Matt's dad, back in '69 the engineering students constructed "Big E"—the engineering cairn—from high-strength concrete and rebar. There were many rumours about it: it was the tip of an immense underground structure rivalling one of the Great Pyramids of Giza; it contained a full propane tank to discourage physical attacks; and it held the remains of "Omar," the pickup truck mascot of the Forestry faculty. To UBC engineering students, it marked the edge of their campus territory; to students of rival faculties, including Forestry, Arts, and any other group the engineers chose to annoy, it was a focal point for those protesting the engineers' antics. But, thanks to the efforts of a previous generation of engineering students, "Big E" withstood all manner of abuse over the decades: painted with other faculty's colours, lit on fire, and attacked with forklifts and jackhammers.

Matt ran a hand over the pock-marked cairn, thrilled to be joining this elite fraternity of Engineers steeped in tradition: the Red Jacket, the Iron Ring, Engineering Week, the engineering stunts (hanging the shell of a Volkswagen Beetle from various public structures). Then there were the more controversial traditions Matt was not comfortable with: the Lady Godiva Ride and the 40-Beer Club.

I hope I can make Dad proud.

Matt found the building he was looking for, arriving at the Director's office precisely on time. He knocked on the door.

"Come on in!"

Matt pushed the creaky wooden door open. A slight, middle-aged man wearing a ratty cardigan sweater and thick, black-framed glasses sat behind an old wooden desk, partially hidden behind stacks of paper.

"Uh, Doctor Oldman? I'm Matt Barnes."

"Welcome, Mr. Barnes! I'm Bill Oldman. Been looking forward to meeting you. I've heard interesting things about you from my colleagues in the Mathematics Department. Please have a seat and—"

"Wow... that's TRIUMF's main magnet." Matt's attention had strayed to a large black-and-white photo that covered one entire wall of the small office. Matt turned to Professor Oldman. "You designed it." A statement of fact, but delivered with a tone of awe.

"Yes, I did," Oldman said with pride. "It's a sect—"

"A sector-focussed pinwheel electromagnet with a diameter of eighteen metres," Matt blurted out. "It generates a field strength ranging from 3000 to 5700 gauss and weighs 4400 tons."

"Wow, son, you know your stuff."

Matt nodded. "I've read everything I could find about TRIUMF. How did you do the fine-field trimming given the pinwheel shape? Did you use mechanical shims?"

Oldman shook his head. "No, we used circular trim coils pairs and pie-shaped harmonic coil sets. The hardest part was—hang on, we're getting off-track here. We're here to discuss your schedule; we can talk magnetism another time."

"Sorry, sir."

"No problem—I've rarely seen a student with such an interest in magnetism. Alrighty... I've got a letter here from Professor Kennedy, the head of the Mathematics Department, confirming that you've successfully challenged all the courses needed for a bachelor's degree in mathematics—that's quite the accomplishment for someone just out of high school. And a similar letter from Professor Erhardt, head of the Department of Physics. Oh, I see Brian Hamilton was your tutor—that explains a lot. I remember Brian from his undergrad years. Brilliant fellow. I see him around campus occasionally—he's doing interesting research in electrical mapping of the brain."

Including my brain, starting next week, Matt mused.

Oldman stared at Matt. "Mr. Barnes, you clearly have an aptitude for mathematics. Why engineering physics?"

"Sir, I want to learn *everything* about magnetism," Matt said. "Magnets have fascinated me since I was four years old and my mother tacked my first artwork up with fridge magnets. I want to *understand* the underlying physical phenomenon that produces magnetic forces. It's a puzzle I need to solve and I can't do it with *just* mathematics and theoretical physics."

Oldman nodded. "Fair enough. Engineering Physics falls under the jurisdiction of the Faculty of Applied Science but is administered by the Department of Physics, which is part of the Faculty of Science. I've discussed your situation with deans of both faculties, and they're giving me some latitude in setting up your program. Assuming you perform well, that is. The Engineering Physics program is thirty percent each of mathematics and physics courses—which you're exempt from—so that opens up a lot of room in your calendar. So, rather than figure out a multi-year plan today, let's focus on this fall's semester—we'll evaluate your progress in January."

Oldman pulled out a large sheet of paper with a grid drawn on it—five columns by nine rows. Most of the boxes already had notes scribbled in pencil. "This is a standard fall-term course schedule for first-year engineering. Let's remove the courses you're exempt from, then see what other courses you can fit in.

"We expect our first and second-year engineering students to take eight courses per semester. Okay, math courses. You're exempt from Math

150-Calculus of Several Variables, Math 151-Linear Algebra, and Math 165-Differential Equations I." Oldman attacked the sheet with a white eraser.

"For physics, you're exempt from Physics 155-Mechanics, and the theory portion of Physics 156-Thermodynamics. I want you to take the laboratory portion of Thermo—it's important that engineers have good experimental skills."

"That's why I'm here, sir."

More erasing. "Okay, that leaves you with... Introduction to Engineering, Engineering Drawing, Earth Sciences for Engineers, and the Thermo lab.

"In order to graduate in Applied Sciences, you have to pass English 100 and three more humanities courses, one of which has to be an introductory economics course. I suggest you space them out and take one each year.

"That leaves you short three courses for this term. Let's see what we can find." Oldman pulled out a copy of the university's master calendar.

It took them another half-hour to find courses Matt was interested in and fit into the open slots of his unconventional timetable: third-year engineering courses in Fluid Mechanics and Electromagnetism, and an introductory computer science course.

Matt inspected the timetable. "I've still got spare slots."

"Eight courses is already a heavy load, Mr. Barnes—you'll be in class seven hours a day. Maybe stick with that for now?"

"Sir, I came here to learn. I can handle more."

Oldman stared at Matt for a moment. "Okay, but remember, I'm giving you a lot of latitude and don't want to see you fail."

"I can handle it, sir."

After consulting the course calendar, they found a graduate-level mathematics course titled, "Introduction to Algebraic Topology."

Oldman leaned back in his creaking chair and inspected the timetable. "Well, I think that covers it. Good luck, Mr. Barnes. You're enrolled in what many consider the toughest program at UBC, *and* you've added additional courses. Now, what year to place you in? Academic-wise, you're half way between first-year engineering and second-year Eng Fizz, but closer to the latter. When do you plan on graduating?"

Matt stared at the thick course calendar for several seconds. "I think four years ought to do it."

Oldman tilted his head, pondering Matt's cryptic reply.

"Okay, then. We'll put you down as first-year engineering, with a 1981 graduation year. Make sure you mention that when you get your red jacket."

The red jacket!

"Thank you, Professor."

Oldman was silent for a moment, mulling something over.

"One more thing. Your reputation for mathematics is impressive, as is your interest in electromagnetism. Would you care to indulge me?"

Matt shrugged. "Sure."

Oldman went to his blackboard, picked up a piece of chalk and scribbled a long calculus equation. "This is the integral form of the electrostatic energy E of an arbitrary charge distribution that possesses volume density rho and surface density sigma."

Matt stared at the equation, then nodded.

"Can you solve for E, given the special case where we have a dielectric medium wherein all surface densities of charge sigma reside on conductor surfaces?"

"Yes."

"Yes, what?" Oldman said.

"Yes, I can solve for E," Matt said, matter-of-factly. "Do you have a particular geometry in mind?"

Oldman shrugged and handed Matt the chalk. "Assume a sphere."

Matt nodded, his eyes going unfocussed as his brain pushed aside the mathematics and visualized a sphere floating in a dielectric liquid. The electrostatic charge, mitigated by the dielectric, formed a complex pattern on the sphere's surface. He "flew" across the surface of the sphere, making a circumnavigation while noting the minor but periodic fluctuations.

Matt's eyes refocussed. He went to the blackboard, paused, then wrote a short equation.

Oldman stared at the blackboard. "That's... that's correct. How did you do that?"

It's harder for me to explain how I solved it than it is to solve it.

"I, uh, used the divergence theorem and solved for sigma by flying... I mean by using a surface integral over the conductor's surface."

Oldman's jaw dropped. "Well, I see your reputation is well-earned, young man. This type of problem is typically found in a graduate-level electromagnetics course."

Matt shrugged. *Then the next four years should be a cake-walk.*

"Well, Mr. Barnes, perhaps you will be able to handle this course load," Oldman said. "Do stop by sometime and I can tell you stories about the TRIUMF magnet design."

"Deal! Thank you, sir."

"By the way, everyone here calls me 'Uncle Bill'," Oldman replied.

"Okay, thanks, Uncle Bill!"

Matt's next stop was the UBC Bookstore, where he left with an armload of new textbooks that set him back a staggering two hundred and ten dollars. Once back in his room, he cracked open the book at the top of the pile and started reading, his brain absorbing the information like a dry sponge dropped in water.

Matt revelled in the orderliness of the life of a full-time student: awake at seven o'clock, shower, breakfast in the residence cafeteria (where he picked up a bag lunch), eight straight hours of classes, a bland dinner of questionable nutritional value, then evenings reading ahead in the textbooks and completing the simple class assignments.

Having an eidetic memory meant Matt never took notes in class—he focussed on what the professor was saying and writing on the overhead projector or blackboard. The only time he picked up his pen was to jot down a reminder to follow up on a particular topic.

He spent his weekends writing programs for his computer science course and haunting UBCs many libraries, working his way through every textbook and research paper that touched on magnetism. He held to the promise he'd made his mother: every Saturday and Sunday, he took a two-hour walk around campus for exercise and fresh air. And, he spent every second Saturday morning in a musty lab in the bowels of UBC's medical school building, getting his brain scanned by his former mentor, Dr. Brian Hamilton.

Of Matt's nine courses, the only one that gave him trouble was English 100—Literature and Composition. It was a required course for every UBC undergrad and, more often than not, the bane of engineering and science students. Matt's English 100 professor had a penchant for Shakespeare; Matt found the Bard's writing akin to another language, one with few rules and much nuance. A strategic purchase of the "Coles Notes series on Shakespeare" proved to be the Shakespearean equivalent of the Rosetta Stone.

Matt soon became uncomfortable with the level of "socializing" in the residence. Every Friday and Saturday night, there was a party on at least one floor in his building, and sometimes more than one. By late September, the carpeted hallway on every floor smelled faintly of beer. His fellow students tried to get him to participate, but he was too busy reading and thinking. Not to mention his feeling uncomfortable in social groups larger than three or four.

And there were the young women. *Aliens—fascinating to look at, distracting as hell, but seemingly from another planet.*

Mid-term exams were held in October, and Matt found them unexpectedly easy—he'd been hoping for at least *some* challenges. Luckily, none of the math or physics exams required he show intermediate work—a good thing as he tended solve most problems in his head. Word soon got around the residence about Matt's mathematical prowess and he was pestered with requests for help. He was willing to help fellow students learn a concept, but had no time for someone who just wanted the right answer.

One evening in early November, following an uninspiring cafeteria dinner, Matt wandered into the residence's common room to watch television before returning to his room to study. He found the sitcom everyone was watching tedious; a commercial break from an automobile manufacturer caught his attention.

"Steerable headlights," remarked a third-year mechanical engineering student whose room was next to Matt's. "That's so cool. I wish I'd thought of that."

"But.... that's my invention!" Matt muttered.

"What was that?"

"Uh, nothing." In a near panic, Matt sprinted upstairs to the payphone on his floor and called his cousin Stuart, who lived in downtown Vancouver.

Matt recapped the TV ad. "It's exactly what's in my patent!"

"Easy there, cousin," Stuart said. "This happens more often than you'd think. I'll look into it."

◎

December arrived, signalling the end of fall term and the start of the two-week exam period. Matt breezed through all his exams except for the dreaded "English Comp," the English 100 pass/fail composition test that gave students the opportunity to prove they could string together a coherent set of thoughts and put them to paper.

He caught a ride home to Penticton with a floor-mate who was passing through the Okanagan Valley, and spent most of his Christmas vacation catching up with his three pals. Renny was grudgingly enjoying first-year science at Okanagan College. Josh regaled his friends with stories of writing computer programs on an actual IBM mainframe computer at Waterloo. Gary described the cool electronic gizmos he'd built as part of his electronics training.

Matt's second term began just after New Year's Day, when the first-term exam marks were posted. Matt scored 100% on all his engineering, math, and computer science exams, and was relieved to get a "pass" on the English Comp test. This term offered Matt all new courses, including Quantum Mechanics and Applied Electromagnetic Theory. The latter had a significant lab component where the students had to perform several complex experiments. Matt stumbled through the first experiments—his technique was sloppy and his experiments had a tendency to catch fire—but soon found his groove and completed the entire set, then convinced the Teaching Assistant to let him perform more experiments for additional credit to make up for his earlier, less-than-perfect work.

◎

When April arrived, the partying (and general noise) in the residence died down as students started studying for final exams. Matt was in his room one rainy Sunday when the payphone at the end of the hall rang.

"Matt Barnes! Phone!" a floor-mate yelled.

Matt walked the length of the hallway and plunked himself onto the stool in the phone booth, his legs sticking out. He picked up the hanging receiver.

"Uh, hello?"

"Hey, cuz," came Stuart's voice in the receiver, "How're the final exams going?"

"Pretty good, Stu. Two more this week, then I head home. I start work with your dad next week." Matt's uncle Ed had arranged a summer job for him at the phone company. "What's up?"

"I'm calling from Chicago—just got out of court. Remember that TV commercial you told me about last fall, the steerable headlights?

"Oh yah, what ever happened with that?"

"That's why I'm in the Windy City. After you called, I did some digging and realized we had an excellent case for patent infringement, so my firm sued American Motors on your behalf. We just got out of court."

"I didn't know *we* were going to court."

"I didn't want to bother you while you're at school."

"How did *we* do?" Matt asked, expecting the worst.

"We won, Matt. We won *big*."

"How big is big?"

"Matt, are you sitting down?"

"I'm on a stool in a phone booth, Stu. How big?"

"Matt, the judge threw the book at American Motors and its headlight supplier. He awarded us *five hundred thousand dollars* in direct damages."

"Wow, that's some serious money!"

"That's not the best part. The judge also awarded *punitive* damages. This wasn't the first time American Motors poached a patent, and the judge wanted to send a message. The legal term is 'a spanking.'"

"How much?"

"The judge awarded us six *million dollars* in damages. Six million! As per our agreement, my firm's cut is one million, plus expenses and disbursements. The partners at my law firm are thrilled. Matt, you will soon have just over *five million dollars* in your bank account. It'll take a month or so to process the award, so when you get home, I suggest you find a good financial advisor."

Five million dollars? What does a university student do with five million dollars? Stuart rambled on with legal details, but Matt didn't hear a thing.

With the prospect of soon becoming a multi-millionaire, Matt had trouble concentrating on his remaining exams. But he persevered, and, with first year now behind him, he looked forward to a summer at home with family and friends.

◎

A week after returning home, Matt started working alongside his uncle as an apprentice lineman at the BC Telephone Company. After spending the previous eight months with his head in books, Matt had some trepidation about the physical labour required: digging holes to plant telephone poles, climbing those poles, stringing telephone cables, crawling into underground cable vaults. Being a lineman wasn't all grunt work, though—it did require some thinking: setting the pole anchors at the correct angle and reading survey plans to make sure they knew where to dig (and where *not* to dig).

Matt spent Friday and Saturday evenings with his friends in the Batmobile, cruising up and down Penticton's Main Street and Lakeshore Drive. When Renny picked up Matt to start their third weekend of summer, he was uncharacteristically quiet and looking rather glum.

"What's up, Batman?"

Renny let out a long sigh. "Our house is up for sale. The owners offered Mom the first opportunity to buy it, but we just don't have the money. Interest rates are sky-high right now and Mom can't qualify for a mortgage. Luckily, those high rates means there's not many buyers out there. I told Mom I'd skip school in the fall and get a second job, but she nixed that idea. I guess we're going to have to look for another house." He sighed again. "I hate being poor. I'm never getting out of this town."

"Cheer up, big guy. I'm sure things will sort themselves out. Let's hit the Dairy Queen, my treat." Renny nodded silently.

As Matt watched Renny consume his second foot-long hotdog and wash it down with a chocolate milkshake, he began forming a plan to help his best friend.

Working full time, the weeks sped by for Matt. Renny was stocking shelves at the local grocery store, and Josh was working with his dad at the radio observatory. The trio sorely missed Gary, who'd completed his first year in electronics technology at Okanagan College and wangled a summer job in North Vancouver at the subsea engineering company whose owner came to see the PogoBot two summers ago. Weekends were the same: cruising around town in the Batmobile, floating down the river channel, and going on the occasional camping trip. Renny became obsessed with the magnetic anomaly at Crater Lake; he made it his goal to figure out if the lake had been formed by a meteorite strike.

◎

"Well, Mr. Barnes, we are certainly happy to see you," the bank officer gushed. "When Stuart contacted me, I was more than happy to help," he said, thrilled to be on the receiving end of just over five million US dollars. "How can we help you?"

"First, I want to pay off the mortgage on my parent's house." Matt said.

"That's easy," the officer replied. "We hold the mortgage. I assume you'll give them the good news?" he asked.

Matt nodded.

"Anything else?"

"Yes." Matt explained.

The bank officer raised his eyebrows. "That *is* unorthodox, but we *can* do it. You'll need to hire a real estate lawyer to take care of the details. Anything else?"

"No. The rest goes into a high-interest US-dollar savings account."

"Are you sure you don't want to invest it? I can get you a much higher rate of return. Let me give you information on the mutual funds we offer," he pleaded, fumbling in his desk drawer for the brochures and practically salivating at the prospect of investing millions of someone else's money.

"A high-interest savings account," Matt insisted. He had no immediate plans for the money, but knew he'd need it someday and didn't want it tied up. Interest rates were running at close to fifteen percent per year—his windfall would grow at a rate of three quarters of a million dollars a year.

◎

Matt answered the phone on the second ring.

"Professor, I'm coming over to pick you up," Renny said, then hung up.

Minutes later, the Batmobile tore up the Barnes gravel driveway. As soon as Matt got in, Renny was bursting with news.

"You won't believe what happened today! My mom got a call this morning from the real estate agent who's listing our house, saying that someone bought it. That put mom into a real funk. A couple of hours later, they sent over a lawyer. We thought he was coming to give us notice, but guess what? Somebody bought the house and transferred the title to mom! An 'anonymous benefactor,' as the lawyer put it. We went from being homeless this morning to owning our house this afternoon! In-fucking-credible!"

"Whoa, that's amazing!" Matt said, trying to keep a straight face. "Any idea who this benefactor is?"

"Nope. Lawyer-client confidentiality," Renny said. "But that's not all. That same benefactor set up an educational trust fund for me. *Ten thousand dollars*! I can go to university now!"

"No shit?" replied Matt. "That's totally awesome! Sounds like you have a guardian angel. Any idea where you'll go?"

"UBC, you nerd!" He punched Matt playfully in the shoulder. "I already called my counsellor at OK College and told her what happened. She said she'd make a call and get my application fast-tracked. Let's hit the A&W— drinks are on me! Hell, burgers and onion rings, too!"

◎

"I'm really gonna miss her," Renny said, glancing in the car's rear-view mirror; his mom was waving goodbye as they pulled out of the driveway. "I hope she'll be okay on her own."

Matt leaned forward so he could look in the car's side mirror.

"She'll be fine, Batman. Mom and dad will watch out for her."

Renny turned to Matt, momentarily confused. "My mom? No, I'm talking about the Batmobile. I hope I covered her up well enough."

"Jesus, Renny!"

Renny chuckled. "Just making sure you're paying attention, Professor. Seriously, mom will be just fine without me."

"There's a pay phone on each floor in residence," Matt said. "You can check in with her as often as you need to. Your mom, I mean. Besides, we'll be back at Christmas—you'll be able to see *both* of them."

The last two months of summer had passed in a flash. Matt had thoroughly enjoyed working as a phone company lineman, developing a new appreciation for tradesmen. Josh had just left for his second year at the University of Waterloo. With Renny's education costs now covered by the mysterious "benefactor," he and Matt bought a faded red, four-door 1974 Datsun 710 so they'd have wheels at university. Matt, having a bank account balance with seven digits to the left of the decimal point, toyed with the idea of buying them both fancy new cars, but the financial conservativeness his parents had instilled in him won out. Not to mention the unwanted attention they'd attract on campus.

"This is really happening," Renny said. "I'm going to university."

"That's a fact, Batman," Matt said. "I can't believe we got everything in here." The back seat and trunk were packed as tight as a well-played game of three-dimensional Tetris. As Renny pulled onto Highway 97 South, he worked the standard transmission through its gears, the overloaded car grudgingly responding.

Three hours later, they stopped for lunch at Manning Provincial Park, both ordering grilled cheese sandwiches and soup at the park lodge's Pinewoods Restaurant. They arrived at UBC's picturesque Point Grey campus late-afternoon, pulling into the student parking lot at Place Vanier, the residence Matt lived in last year.

They waited in line to register; Matt got the same room as last year and Renny a room on the same floor. It took them ten trips to move the contents of the Datsun into their respective rooms, then Matt took Renny on a tour around campus. Renny was most interested in the Geological Sciences building, which was shared with the Astronomy department.

◎

With Dr. Oldman's blessing, Matt took on another challenging workload: five upper-level physics and electrical engineering courses, a computer science course, and two graduate-level math courses. And, due to his predilection for performing experiments that often caught fire, he had to attend a fire extinguisher refresher course run by the department's safety officer. He had one spare slot in his timetable and opted for Economics, one of the three humanities courses engineers needed to graduate.

"Don't forget to apply for an NSERC grant before the end of fall term," Dr. Oldman said, reminding him of the National Science and Engineering Research Council summer jobs program. "If you do well this year, you might get a position at TRIUMF."

Matt's eyes lit up. *Work at TRIUMF? That would be awesome!*

Oldman pulled a round cloth patch from his desk drawer and slid it across the desk. "Now that you're officially Eng Fizz, you'll be needing this."

It was the official Engineering Physics patch: five inches in diameter and a quarter-inch thick with "ENGINEERING PHYSICS - UBC" stitched around its perimeter. In the middle was the Earth, with a satellite orbiting and a thin gold line representing its launch trajectory. All second-year (and up) engineering students sewed a similar patch on the front of their red engineering jacket, advertising their chosen discipline.

Matt's second year on campus was much more enjoyable now that his best friend was around, even though he and Renny only crossed paths in the evenings and on weekends. Renny was thrilled to be a second-year student in the Faculty of Science's Department of Geology, impressing his instructors with his hands-on knowledge and excelling at the "hard" geology courses. He had trouble with the mandatory second-year math and physical chemistry courses, but Matt was more than happy to help him. Renny found the west coast weather a surprise, often commenting on how much it rained and how rarely the sun came out. They kept in touch with Josh and Gary by mail as often as Canada Post allowed.

Matt heard a commotion in a room near his when he came back from his regular Saturday afternoon walk. He stuck his head in the door to find several students clustered around an object.

"What're you guys up to?" Matt asked.

"Rubik's Cube, Matt. It's totally cool." One of them tossed it to him. "Let's see what the math whiz can do with it!"

Matt examined the cube. It had six faces, each covered by nine coloured squares. An internal pivot mechanism allowed each face to rotate independently.

A new puzzle! Matt felt an almost erotic tingle of excitement.

"The trick is to make each face a solid colour," said the cube's owner. "It's really tough. There must be millions of permutations, eh?"

Matt closed his eyes; the cube in his hand remained stationary while the duplicate in his mind rotated on each of its three axes. The elegance and symmetry of this object, this puzzle, was breathtaking. After ten seconds, he opened his eyes.

"More than a few million."

"Huh?"

It's so obvious—how do I put it into words?

"There's, umm, eight corners and twelve edges. That means there's eight-factorial ways to arrange the corner cubes. Seven of the corners can be independently oriented, because the eighth depends on the other seven. So that's three-to-the-seventh-power combinations. Then there's twelve-factorial-over-two ways to arrange the edges, since an odd permutation of the corners implies an odd permutation of the edges as well. You can flip eleven of the twelve edges independently, with the flip of the twelfth depending on the preceding ones—that gives two-to-the-eleventh power possibilities. Put all that together and you get... four point three times ten to the nineteenth power. Or forty-three quintillion."

A long silence followed, broken by a 4th-year computer science student.

"Yah, but can you *solve* it?"

Matt stared at the cube, imagining its faces making a complex series of rotations in 3-dimensional space. *Ah, that's easy!*

"Sure." Matt rotated one of the cube's faces, then another. "Watch this corner cube here—see how it moves in a back-and-forth three-D spiral pattern?" His rotations increased in speed, and in less than a minute, he handed the cube back, each face now a solid colour. "Done."

"You scare me," said a fourth-year electrical engineering student.

"I'm glad you're on *our* side," added the computer science major. "You *are* on our side, aren't you?"

Matt shrugged.

One of his floor mates grabbed the cube, reshuffled it, and tossed it back to Matt. "Try again."

This time it took Matt only twenty seconds—five to visualize the solution and the rest to manipulate the real cube. For the next week, Matt had to endure students coming to him with their cubes, some to see how fast he could solve them, others just to "reset" theirs to the "solved" state.

◎

"Well, fuck. I guess we're not going home for Christmas tomorrow," Renny said, staring at the TV in the residence common room as they watched the weather segment of the evening news. A large snowstorm, the first of the season, had covered southern BC's mountain passes with over a metre of snow. The only highway into the Okanagan Valley was closed. Indefinitely.

"Or the next day," he added.

"So we'll go with Plan B," Matt said, heading for the payphone on their floor.

Early the next morning, they drove their old Datsun along Marine Drive to Vancouver International Airport. Renny had refused Matt's offer to pay for both plane tickets; he'd already put a serious dent in the "education fund" set up by his anonymous benefactor, but wasn't willing to accept charity from his best friend. He was counting on getting a decent-paying summer job next year to at least partially refill that account.

They parked in the long-term parking lot and caught the shuttle bus to the terminal. After passing through security, they boarded a packed Pacific Western Airlines Boeing 737 flight. Renny had sweet-talked the ticket counter agent into giving them exit row seats over the wing (more legroom); Renny got the window seat and Matt the aisle. As the airplane accelerated down the runway then pitched up, the airflow over the wing condensed, forming a smoky-white tube that snaked back and forth across the wing's top surface.

"Check out the airflow here, Professor," Renny said, leaning back into his seat.

Matt leaned across. "Cool," he said, before going silent.

The silence lasted a full minute, then Matt opened the notebook he always carried and began scribbling notes and mumbling. "Lift vector... perpendicular to two-D surface plane... different reference frame... higher dimensions..."

He's off on another physics tear, Renny thought, watching his friend madly scribbling sketches, notes, and equations. *Last time I saw him do that was when he read that Flatland book. And that fucked him up for weeks...*

◎

The Christmas break gave Matt and Renny the chance to catch up with Josh and Gary, who'd also returned home for the holidays. The foursome hung out as much as they could, given their family social obligations. Maintaining a Christmas Day family tradition started when Matt was five, he accompanied his parents to the town's retirement centre where they helped serve turkey dinners to the seniors.

Second term at UBC started off on an encouraging note for both Renny and Matt. Renny had scored first-class marks in his applied geology courses and scraped by with lower second-class marks in his more theoretical subjects. Matt, of course, had aced all his engineering, physics, and math courses, and received a bare pass in economics.

"That's because my Econ prof knows I've figured out that economics is voodoo science," Matt said. He'd had many spirited in-class discussions with the professor before deciding it was no more a science than psychology was.

"They're both just crude attempts to apply the scientific method to the behaviour of chaotic, random systems," Matt declared.

Matt continued with his gruelling academic schedule, nine hours a day, five days a week, continually challenging his physics and math professors with probing questions that kept *them* on their toes. He spent his weekends in the bowels of UBC's Main Library, continuing his hunt for obscure papers on electromagnetism. He found many written in Russian (Russia had its share of brilliant physicists and mathematicians), so he got permission to audit Russian 110—a.k.a. "Russian for Science Students"—so he could learn the Cyrillic alphabet and basic Russian vocabulary. Matt soon realized that Russian wasn't a "modern" language; most of the technical words and phrases were simply English ones translated into Cyrillic, so once he could sound them out, their meaning usually became clear.

◎

Spring soon arrived, signalling final exams. They were a minor annoyance for Matt but a challenge for Renny, who'd spent many of his Friday and Saturday nights trying to out-drink engineers at the Pit—the only student watering hole on campus. More than once, Matt got a late-night phone call requesting he come pick up his inebriated friend.

They returned home to Penticton in time to watch Gary graduate from Okanagan College at the top of his class. His high marks and talent for robotics helped him land a permanent job with the North Vancouver-based subsea engineering company he'd interned at the previous summer.

Renny was excited about his summer job with the Geological Survey of Canada—the national organization for geoscientific information and research—as a junior field geologist. He'd be spending the summer in northern Alberta assisting with a large-scale field survey. Matt, with the highest marks in second-year Engineering Physics and glowing recommendations from Dr. Oldman and his other professors, won a coveted grant from the Natural Sciences and Engineering Research Council to work at the nearby TRIUMF cyclotron facility. As a junior NSERC fellow, he'd be working in the Magnet Controls group, which maintained the complex devices used to steer the exotic sub-atomic particle beams into various physics and medical experiments. Renny and Matt realized this would be their first summer apart since Grade 4.

SEVEN

Matt's vantage point on the high metal catwalk that ran around the inside perimeter of the massive building gave him a bird's-eye view of the array of massive concrete blocks—all painted bright yellow—that covered the entire floor of the 50,000-square-foot building. This was the Tri-University Meson Facility, or TRIUMF, Canada's national particle accelerator centre. Beneath the concrete blocks lay the world's largest cyclotron—a massive magnet that accelerated a stream of negatively charged hydrogen ions in an outward spiral to three-quarters of the speed of light. At strategic locations on that spiral, the beam struck thin graphite foil "targets," producing high-energy proton streams that were magnetically steered to experiments on the cyclotron's periphery.

This is physics heaven! Matt thought.

Matt's job title was "research associate," the junior member of a small team of physicists, engineers, and medical researchers designing the magnetic beam-steering system for an experimental cancer treatment facility. One of the cyclotron's protons streams was dedicated to this project—it was steered to another carbon-film "target" and generated a shower of sub-atomic particles including positively charged *pi-mesons*. These exotic particles, also known as *pions*, held the promise of treating certain types of rare brain cancers, acting literally as sub-atomic "depth charges."

After only two weeks at work, Matt was already impressing his supervisor—a full professor in physics from the University of Victoria—with his abilities and innate understanding of magnetic fields. When Matt was not putting in long workdays designing the magnetic controls for the fine-focus portion of the cancer treatment system, he lived on campus in the same room he'd occupied during his second year, spending his spare time in UBC's many libraries reading obscure physics papers. And taking his obligatory weekend walks to get exercise and fresh air.

Matt's solitary weeks were punctuated by regular get-togethers with Gary, now living in nearby North Vancouver in a one-bedroom apartment only three blocks from the headquarters of Canadian Submarine Engineering. Every other weekend, they'd meet up for lunch or dinner, usually in downtown Vancouver. Several times during the summer, Matt joined Gary on "sea trials" in nearby Indian Arm where they tested the remotely operated vehicle, or ROV, that his company was building for a Texas-based offshore oil company. Gary loved his job, which married his interests in electronics and robotics. He'd become adept at operating the ROV manipulator arms, partly due to his prowess with arcade claw machines.

Matt kept up correspondence with his other friends as often as Canada Post allowed. Josh had a summer job in Toronto, Ontario, writing software for a telecommunications company. Letters to and from Renny's remote survey camp had a two-week turnaround time. Renny wasn't the best at writing letters, but he said he was enjoying his work, occasionally lamenting that he was more interested in searching for meteorite fragments.

Matt's summer passed in the blink of an eye; it was time to go back to school.

◎

Matt and Renny reunited at UBC on the Labour Day weekend, Renny looking more like the "Bigfoot" moniker Gary had assigned him years ago. The hardships of life at a field camp had put another ten pounds of muscle on him but at the expense of his appearance and vocabulary, the latter now including even more coarse language. They were both assigned the same rooms as last year and were looking forward to their third-year courses (and higher, in Matt's case).

Matt's academic year began with the obligatory course scheduling session with Dr. Oldman. They started with the mandatory third and fourth-year engineering courses he wasn't exempt from, then filled the gaps with graduate-level math and physics courses.

"Don't forget your Humanities course," Oldman cautioned. "You need two more, so I suggest you take one in each of your final two years."

Matt nodded, flipping through the calendar before deciding on Philosophy 155: "Introduction to Rhetoric." With his calendar set, Matt was ready to tackle his forty-five hours per week of classes.

While he enjoyed all his courses, his current favourite was Physics 410—"Techniques of Experimental Physics," where students had to pick ten experiments from a pre-selected pool. Matt made quick work of those, honing his experimental skills, then proposed additional experiments, mostly in electromagnetism, for extra credit.

◎

"Remind me again why we're doing this?" Renny gasped, struggling under the weight of his load. Matt had convinced him to help haul an assortment of equipment down the trail to the cliffs overlooking English Bay.

Jesus, I'm carrying half my body weight. I hope I don't have a frigging heart attack.

"I had a new idea for magnetic field modulation, and I built this gizmo to test it out. If my calculations are correct, there isn't enough room in any of the labs in Hebb Tower. Or Thunderbird Stadium, for that matter."

"But why so many batteries?" Renny wheezed.

"I need the amps. And here I thought you were a tough guy..."

"I'll show you tough guy," he growled.

"This spot here should do," Matt said as they arrived at a viewpoint high above the water, looking down on Wreck Beach and out onto English Bay. Off to the west were the mountains of Vancouver Island, forty kilometres away.

Renny dropped his load onto the ground, then plunked himself down.

"I need a break." He shielded his eyes from the mid-day sun as he scanned the beach below, a known hangout for nude sunbathers. "I wish we'd brought binoculars."

"It'll take me ten minutes or so to set everything up," Matt said as he started organizing the pile of equipment.

"It'll take that long for my heart rate to get below two hundred," Renny said, still hoping for a glimpse of the Swedish bikini team, sunbathing topless, of course.

Fifteen minutes later, Matt announced he was ready. He'd assembled a metre-long aluminum track, decorated with wire coils, cable bundles connected to the batteries, an old-fashioned rheostat, a couple of circuit boards, some large capacitors, and a knife switch. He'd anchored one end of the track to the ground with wooden stakes; the other end was tilted up thirty degrees and aimed west, towards the water.

"So, what the fuck is this thing?" Renny said.

"It's a linear accelerator, but with a twist. The coils are electromagnets and will accelerate those iron slugs along the track."

"So... a high-tech electro-cannon," Renny said, proud to have invented a new word.

"Basically," Matt said. "But the cool part is the magnetic field modulation I came up with—it should be way more efficient. Let's do a test shot at five amps," Matt said. He placed a small iron weight onto the aluminum track, adjusted the rheostat, then turned to Renny. "Care to do the honours? Just close that knife switch."

Renny nodded. "We'll need a countdown."

They chanted in unison. "Five, four, three, two, one, FIRE!"

Renny closed the switch.

The contraption hummed for two seconds as the capacitors charged, then the iron slug disappeared off the track with a loud "crack." Three seconds later, there was a splash in the water just offshore.

"Woo-hoo!" Renny exclaimed.

Matt sighted at the splash through a crude surveyor's transit. "Depression angle is twenty-six degrees—given our height above the water, that's... one hundred and fifty-two metres. Seems about right," he said, jotting his observations in a small notebook. "Let's try ten amps next."

The next shot produced a much louder bang, the splash appearing further offshore.

"That was more than twice the distance," Renny said.

"Yup, the force should be non-linear with respect to input current. Let's do a few more at this setting."

Another five shots; all landed in the same area. "That's good for today," he said, a burnt-insulation smell coming from the contraption. "The coils are getting stressed."

"Come on, let's do one more!" Renny pleaded. "This is just getting fun!"

Matt hesitated. "Okay, maybe one more, at fifteen amps," he said, placing their last slug on the rail, then reaching for the dial.

"Allow me, Professor," Renny said, grinning and stepping between Matt and the controls.

"Five-four-three-two-one-FIRE!" Renny yelled as he jammed the knife switch over. Matt heard a high-pitched whine from the contraption and glanced at the dial; Renny had turned it to maximum.

"NO!" he yelled over the whine, reaching for the knife switch. "It's non-linear! It'll..."

An explosion drowned out Matt's shout. Renny fell backwards five feet, landing on his ass, blinded and deafened.

It was ten or fifteen seconds before his senses returned. The 'electro-cannon' was now a smoking pile of debris, the wires gone, the batteries melted, the surrounding earth scorched. A rapidly dissipating trail of white smoke, high in the air, led off to the west.

"I told you it was non-linear!" The ringing in Renny's ears muted Matt's yelling. Matt pointed at the melted dial on what remained of the rheostat. "Fifty amps! That could have accelerated the slug to... Jesus, twenty-four hundred kilometres per hour! That's almost Mach Two!"

Renny winced as he touched his forehead; one of his eyebrows was partially burnt off. He glanced around. "Professor, it is my professional opinion that we should get the fuck out of here."

"I agree, Batman." They kicked dirt over the melted remains of the batteries, packed up the rest of the equipment, and headed back to the residence.

About half way up the trail, Renny giggled and touched his eyebrow.

"Remember back in grade five when we did that science experiment, melting the ice cube? This kinda reminds me of that."

"Not funny, Batman. We could get into a lot of trouble for this."

"I wonder how far out in the bay that last shot went," Renny said.

"Let's see..." Matt said, as they continued up the trail. "The standard equation for a projectile trajectory, neglecting any drag effects, is R equals V-squared sine two-theta over g. At an angle of thirty degrees, it would have gone... shit... approximately five hundred kilometres. That puts it way past Vancouver Island and out into the Pacific Ocean."

"Fuck me," Renny said.

"But at those speeds, drag dominates, which is one-half rho A vee-squared C-sub-D." Matt paused as they walked along the trail. "That brings it down to... roughly forty kilometres."

"Isn't Vancouver Island about forty kilometres away?"

Matt nodded.

"And you were sort of aiming in that direction, weren't you?"

Matt nodded again. "Shit."

"Double shit," Renny added.

They slunk into residence and maintained a low profile the rest of the day. During dinner, they overheard students discussing the loud noise that morning.

"Maybe we should watch the news," Renny whispered to Matt.

After dinner, they casually slipped into the residence's common room in time for the six o'clock news.

"Our top story tonight. Witnesses report seeing and hearing an unidentified object streak across English Bay this morning that left a smoke trail heading west across Georgia Strait. Reports are coming in of an explosion in the woods just west of Nanaimo on Vancouver Island. We spoke with scientists at UBC's astronomy department—they said it was likely a meteorite. In other news..."

Renny stole a glance at Matt and let out a sign of relief. *I think we dodged a bullet.*

◎

Physics 430 (Applied Electromagnetic Theory) Tutorial Session

"What are you working on there, Mr. Barnes?" asked the professor in charge of the tutorial session. He'd been watching over Matt's shoulder as Matt jotted down a series of partial differential equations.

"Uh, just something I've been thinking about, sir," Matt replied.

"May I?"

Matt nodded as the professor took the sheets of paper off his desk and scrutinized them.

"This looks like a four-dimensional version of the standard wave equation," he said. "That's a very interesting idea you have here, but this is Applied Electromagnetic Theory, not wave mechanics. Best you focus on the task at hand."

"But as you can see on page two, sir, I'm setting up a framework so I can merge Maxwell's Equations into a multi-dimensional topology."

The professor stared at Matt. "Why would you want to do that?"

Matt shrugged.

◎

Matt entered the third-floor teaching lab of the Electrical Engineering building and sat at the bench he'd been occupying since the start of term. This was Mechatronics 300, a brand-new course (and one of Matt's favourites) intended to teach budding engineers how to solve real-world problems through lateral thinking. And today was the mid-term exam. Given the haphazard manner in which the professor taught the course, Matt didn't know what to expect.

Professor Tompkins was already at his desk as other students trickled in, a stack of cardboard boxes neatly arranged beside him. He cleared his throat.

"Today is the mid-term exam, so, like this entire course, we're going to do something unconventional. Each of you, singularly or in pairs, will come up and get one of these boxes. Inside you will find several items, one of which is a billiard ball. Your task, in the next ninety minutes, is to construct a device, machine, or mechanism that moves the ball a distance of at least five metres across the floor at the front of this room. You can only use what's in the box."

Matt joined the orderly queue and retrieved his box. He took it back to his bench and took stock: besides the billiard ball, there were three, 2-inch-diameter rubber wheels; a dozen popsicle sticks; a tube of 5-minute epoxy glue; a box-cutter knife; string; wire; four gears of different sizes; a wooden spoon; a pencil; a large rubber band; a roll of duct tape; and a plastic bag containing an assortment of nuts, bolts, and screws.

As Tompkins meandered around the room, Matt stared at the box's contents while recalling the exam parameters, brainstorming his options. It appeared the professor expected everyone to build some sort of rubber band-powered vehicle.

But this is a class in lateral thinking. What else could I build? A catapult, perhaps? Hmm... let's review the original instructions.

When Tompkins came by Matt's bench, Matt caught his attention.

"Yes, Matt?"

"Sir, I just wanted to clarify a few points. The goal is to move the ball at least five metres, correct?"

"Yes, Matt."

"Using *any* kind of mechanical device?"

"Yes."

"Can I use the cardboard box?"

Tompkins chuckled. "Sure, Matt."

Matt nodded.

Tompkins turned to address the class. "If there are no more questions, time starts now. You have ninety minutes."

Matt started scribbling on the side of the box. *How about a... no, could it be that simple?*

An hour and a half later, the benches were littered with various contraptions and devices. On Matt's bench, the pile of parts was untouched.

One by one, the teams brought their inventions forward for testing. Two groups had made catapults, only one of which worked. Most had made rubber band-powered, self-propelled carts.

"Well, we just have Matt Barnes left," Tompkins prompted.

Matt strode to the front of the class, the billiard ball in one hand and the cardboard box under his arm. He placed the cardboard box on the floor, grabbed one edge, and pulled. The box separated at a precise cut line and folded over onto itself, forming a wedge-shaped ramp. Matt carefully placed the billiard ball at the top of the ramp and released it. It rolled down the ramp, across the floor, then bumped up against the far wall.

There were hoots of laughter from Matt's classmates.

Tompkins looked sternly at Matt. "You didn't follow the instructions."

"Um, I believe I did, sir."

Tompkins shook his head. "The instructions were to build a machine to transport the ball across the room."

"Sir, your exact words were, 'construct a device, machine, or mechanism that transports the ball a distance of at least five metres across the floor at the front of this room.' I constructed an incline plane, one of the six types of 'simple machine' that changes the magnitude or direction of a force. You covered that in our first class. The ball had to be transported at least five metres. It did that."

The room went silent as Tompkins stared at Matt for ten long seconds. *Oh shit,* Matt thought. *This is not going the way I thought it would.*

Tompkins' face broke into a huge grin, followed by a bellowing laugh.

"You're absolutely right, Matt!" he exclaimed. "Full marks to you! Class, this is a fine example of thinking outside the box. Literally!"

Mathematics 506: Advanced Non-Euclidian Geometry

"Well, Mr. Barnes, how did you find last week's assignment?" said Professor Moyles. Matt was the only student in this class, and, although the course had a syllabus, Moyles more-or-less let Matt's interests determine what happened week-to-week.

"Well, sir, I finished the approximation of a four-dimensional framework using hyperspheres. I want to characterize how different four-dimensional force functions can be realized in 3-space."

Moyles nodded—he was familiar with Matt's interest in hyper-dimensional geometry. "I can't see why you'd want to do that, but it sounds like an interesting mathematical exercise. Please continue."

"Well, as you suggested, I started with a four-dimensional manifold with no boundary. I've built a continuous function between its topological spaces, but I'm having trouble closing it, mathematically speaking."

"Is your continuous function homeomorphic?"

"What do you mean by homeomorphic?" Matt asked.

"Oh, that's right. We haven't covered homeomorphism yet. Homeomorphic means the continuous function also has a continuous *inverse* function. If the function is homeomorphic, you can close it using an elastic deformation function."

Matt looked thoughtful for close to a minute. "Yes, my function is homeomorphic."

Moyles chuckled. "And just how do you know that, son?"

Matt scratched his head. "I dunno. It just seems obvious to me."

"Tell you what, Matt. Why don't you come up with a proof for that?"

"Right now?" Matt asked, raising his chalk to the blackboard.

Moyles chuckled again. "No, son. Next week. Prove that every simply connected, closed three-manifold is homeomorphic to the three-sphere. If you can, then closing it should become apparent."

Matt shrugged. "Okay."

"Let's talk more about homeomorphism now," Moyles said, taking the chalk from Matt.

◎

A week later...

"Here's that proof you asked for, sir." Matt handed Moyles four sheets of paper. "I did it in 4-space, 'cause that's what my framework is in. But you can see at the end of page three how the problem reduces in 3-space."

Moyles started reading Matt's work, a smirk on his face. He re-read the pages several times; the smirk faded and his face turned pale.

"Professor, are you okay?" *He looks like he's going to have a heart attack.*

Moyles' voice dropped to a whisper. "Matt, do you know what you've done?"

"Uh, the proof you asked for?"

"Son, when I gave you this assignment last week, I didn't think you'd actually do it. I think you've solved the Poincaré Conjecture!"

Matt shrugged. "I'm not familiar with that one, sir."

"Ah yes, I was going to cover that next week. It's one of the hardest problems known in geometric topology, posed by Henri Poincaré back in 1904. Mathematicians have been trying to prove Poincaré for over eighty years. And you did it in 4-space!"

Matt shrugged. "Solving it in 4-space was easier."

Moyles' mouth hung agape for a good ten seconds. "Matt, could you please sign and date each page? I want to show this to a couple of colleagues in the department."

"Sure thing, sir." *Whatever...*

◎

Another week later...

Matt arrived at his weekly seminar with Dr. Moyles to find Professor Kennedy, the Head of the Department of Mathematics, waiting there.

"Matt, my boy," he gushed. "When Moyles told me you solved Poincaré, I was skeptical. But I reviewed your work, then passed it on to Professor Rosen, who specializes in geometric topology. We've both confirmed your work is correct."

Matt shrugged. *Whatever.*

"Matt, this is big news. Big news! Rosen suggested you write this up for JAMS—the Journal of the American Mathematical Society. Publishing in JAMS would be good for your academic career *and* for our department."

"I wasn't looking to publish," Matt said. "I just needed that framework for my project. But if helps the department, I guess I could do that."

"I understand," Kennedy said, grinning. "But Professor Moyles and I came up with a better idea. Back when you were in high school, we tried enticing you to join us for graduate work—God knows why you chose Engineering Physics! Matt, solving Poincaré is a big deal. A. Really. Big. Deal. I have a proposition for you: if you write up your proof as a thesis, we'll fast-track you through a master's degree program. You're set to graduate in '81, correct?"

"Yes, sir."

"Then all you have to do is register for Mathematics 549 next year and you'll be good to go."

"Sir, I don't know what to say..."

"I know, I know, it's not the traditional way to get a graduate degree, but very little you do is. Our department has a reputation of being rather stodgy, and I want to change that."

Matt shrugged. "Okay." *Whatever gets these guys off my back.*

◎

Matt knocked on Professor Oldman's slightly ajar office door and poked his head in.

"You wanted to see me, Uncle Bill?"

"Ah yes, Matt. Please come in. I know final exams are just around the corner, but I thought we should take a stab at your courses for next year."

"Sure," Matt said.

Oldman shuffled papers. "Let's see... other than Applied Science 450-Professional Engineering Practice, and your last humanities course, you've completed all the required courses for your Engineering Physics degree. I've had discussions with the Professor Jones—the Dean of the Faculty of Science—and the heads of the physics and mathematics departments. The Dean has signed off on you registering for Mathematics 549—Master's Thesis—for your proof of the Poincaré Conjecture. That's pretty amazing. But I was wondering what other courses you're interested in."

Matt nodded. "I'd like to do a directed studies, if that's possible."

"In what area?"

It took Matt ten minutes and two blackboards full of equations to elaborate.

Oldman's eyes widened. "I think that will work. In fact, we can do you one better. During our last department meeting, your name came up."

Matt grimaced. *Uh-oh!*

Oldman chuckled. "No, son, in a good way. Professor Erhardt, our department head, mentioned he was put-off that the math department is fast-tracking you through a master's program for solving Poincaré."

Matt grimaced. "I'm sorry if that's causing problems, sir. Professor Moyles sort-of pressured me to do a formal proof—I had no intention of making a big deal about it."

Oldman shook his head. "Your modesty is amazing, Matt, as is your brilliance. But the subject matter you just proposed for a directed studies would be more in keeping with a master's degree-level of research. I'll discuss this with Erhardt, but I think he'd be willing to go that route."

Wow, two master's degrees next year? I'm going to be busy!

Final exams came and went—easy for Matt but a challenge for Renny, even though he'd significantly dialled back his partying. Then the two best friends parted ways for the summer; Renny was off to northern Canada to do geological surveying, while Matt returned to TRIUMF, continuing his magnetic beam-steering work.

◎

September 1980

It was time for Matt and Renny's fourth and final year at UBC. Renny returned from his summer fieldwork, worn out but with many hilarious stories to tell. He had a full load of courses, opting for two astronomy courses as his science electives.

"I wanna learn more about meteorites and asteroids," he said.

Matt's calendar was beyond daunting: one fourth-year engineering course, his last humanities course (Latin 201), three graduate-level physics courses, directed studies leading to a master's degree, and writing up his Poincaré proof as a thesis for the mathematics department. As in previous years, he only saw Renny in the evenings and on weekends. Matt put his head down and got to work.

◎

March 1981

Matt, along with his fellow fourth-year engineering students wearing their red engineering jackets with "81" on the left sleeve, marched past the

Faculty of Arts building, chanting the UBC Engineers Hymn:

We are, we are, we are the Engineers!
We can, we can, demolish forty beers!
Drink rum, drink rum, drink rum and follow us!
For we don't give a damn for any old man who don't give a damn for us!

They cheered and taunted the arts students staring out the building's windows. Matt and his classmates had just taken part in The Ritual of the Calling of the Engineer in the auditorium of the SUB—the student union building. More commonly known as the Iron Ring Ceremony, it was a private—but not secret—ceremony where candidate engineers recited The Obligation, an inspiring five paragraphs written in 1922 by Nobel laureate Rudyard Kipling, reminding them of their responsibility to practice engineering by professional and ethical standards. Matt didn't care much for its religious references, but recognized the history and tradition behind it. Then they received their iron rings—stainless steel, actually—to be worn on the little finger of the engineer's working hand.

Matt looked at his ring again. *I've got one now, just like my dad.*

The crowd of engineers worked its way back to The Pit for more celebrations. Matt took a detour, returning to his tiny office on the top floor of Hebb Tower. He still had a lot of work to do.

UBC Physics Department - Master's degree thesis defence

Matt paused his presentation and scanned the audience in the large seminar room. After an hour of talking, writing equations, and drawing sketches on the overhead projector, he was glad to see that the three professors on the examination panel were still awake.

Time to wrap this up.

"To summarize, this 4-space geometric model that includes an expansion factor based on the Hubble Constant, correctly, accurately, and independently predicts the existence of magnetic force fields in 3-space."

He paused. "Questions?"

Two of the three professors on the panel took turns peppering Matt with questions to test his general knowledge of physics rather than specifics of his thesis. He fielded them with ease.

The third member of the panel, a senior professor and the department's leading expert in quantum mechanics, jumped in.

"So, Mr. Barnes, you're saying that at the sub-atomic level, all matter in the universe is expanding?"

"No, sir, I'm not saying that."

"Then I'm confused, Mr. Barnes."

"About what, sir?"

He flipped through a few sheets of paper. "Equation 12 on page 3 defines a sub-atomic expansion rate R-sub-E."

Geez, this guy doesn't get it...

"Well, sir, my model, which defines four geometric dimensions, is a mathematical construct. It's a theoretical framework that predicts existing physical phenomena such as magnetic force fields—I never said it was a descriptive model."

The professor scratched his head. "I don't follow."

Wow, for a physics prof, this guy is kind of thick! Well, here I go...

"Let's take quantum string theory, for example," Matt said, purposely wading into dangerous territory, this professor's field of expertise.

"What about string theory?" the professor demanded.

"String theory is a theoretical framework that correctly predicts certain physical phenomena. It does so by modelling the point-like particles of particle physics as one-dimensional objects called 'strings.' Correct?"

The professor nodded. "That's a crude but adequate description."

"Well, no one thinks that those point-like particles are actual strings, do they?"

"Of course not," the professor barked. "That would be ludicrous."

Gotcha!

"Here's another example: quantum kleptodynamics, a cornerstone of quantum physics, includes a conceptual model wherein when sub-atomic particles interact, they 'steal' spin and charge from each other. Its author has stated clearly that there is no actual stealing going on."

The professor nodded. "Continue."

"Well, sir, my n-equals-4-space model is similar in that respect. It correctly predicts magnetic force fields, but I in no way have explicitly or implicitly stated that I think matter is actually expanding."

I do suspect that's the case, but I won't say it out loud. At least not yet.

There was silence in the room as the professor digested Matt's analogies for a good thirty seconds, flipping back and forth through the written version of Matt's thesis. Then he shook his head.

"I don't like it," he declared.

A shiver ran down Matt's spine. *The review panel has to be unanimous!*

"Well, sir, is there any other information or background I can provide?" Matt said, trying to keep the pleading out of his voice.

"Seems more like science fiction than science," the professor grumped.

The room went silent.

"I have some questions," came a voice from the back row. All heads in the audience turned.

The owner of the voice stood up; he was hard to see as he was standing in the shadows at the rear of the hall. He was a slight, middle-aged man with rumpled clothing and tousled hair. Matt's first impression was that this was one of the building's janitors who'd snuck in, then he caught himself. *Appearances are often deceiving,* Matt's parents had drilled into him.

"Yes, sir?"

"Rumour has it you're the M. Barnes who recently solved the Poincaré Conjecture? Did solving that help on this thesis? If so, how?"

"Absolutely," Matt said, bobbing his head. He launched into a five-minute explanation involving hyperspheres, manifolds, and other exotic geometrical concepts.

"Fascinating," the man said. "Fascinating indeed. Next question. Well, more of a request. You mentioned quantum kleptodynamics a minute ago. I know it's not relevant to your thesis, but a master's-level student is expected to have a grounding in all areas of physics. Could you give us a one-minute summary of its key features?"

All heads in the audience swivelled back towards Matt.

Who is this guy?

Matt cleared his throat, took ten seconds to organize his thoughts, then gave what he figured was a reasonably concise summary.

The man was silent for a few seconds. "Couldn't have said it better myself. One last question. What made you think that magnetic force fields are a 3-D effect caused by an expanding hyper-fluid flow through 4-space?"

Again, all heads swivelled back towards Matt. *What's going on here?*

Matt relayed his anecdote about flying home for Christmas three years ago, watching the airflow condensing over the airplane wing.

The man reflected on Matt's answer for a moment, then chuckled. "Brilliant! Absolutely brilliant! That's the kind of out-of-the-box thinking that's missing in physics today! It should be encouraged, not dismissed out of hand," he said, directing his remark at the dissenting professor on the review panel.

Who is this guy?

There were murmurs throughout the crowd as the man sat down. The lead professor on the review panel cleared his throat. His entire demeanor had changed, from antagonism to being cowed. "I suggest the examination panel decide now."

The three professors huddled together, each glancing up several times at the mystery person in the back row. After only two minutes, the head of the panel stood up.

"Mr. Barnes, thank you for your presentation. This examination panel grants you a Master of Science degree in Physics. Congratulations."

A round of applause followed. A few students approached and offered congratulations, and the audience trickled out. Matt gathered up his stack of overhead slides.

"Ahem."

Matt looked up to find the mystery back-row questioner standing in front of him, looking even more rumpled in the full glare of the overhead lights. Most of the department's senior professors were hovering nearby, watching intently.

Who is this guy?

The man held out his hand. "Mr. Barnes, it's a pleasure to meet you. I thought your thesis was brilliant. Absolutely brilliant."

"Thank you," Matt said. "And you are...?"

"Oh, sorry. Feinberg's my name. Dick Feinberg."

Dick Feinberg... Richard Feinberg? THE Richard Feinberg? The Nobel laureate in Physics? The man who created quantum kleptodynamics? Oh, shit...

"I, uh, it's a pleasure to meet you, sir!" Matt stammered.

Feinberg bobbed his head like a bird. "Professor Oldman is an old buddy of mine and sent me a copy of your thesis. When I realized its author was the same student who solved Poincaré, I decided to pop up from Caltech and meet you."

"I'm... I'm honoured, sir."

"Mr. Barnes, do you have time to chat?"

"Of course, sir."

"Good, let's go get lunch. I know a good place near here."

The "good place" turned out to be the Faculty/Alumni Club lounge, an exclusive restaurant overlooking Vancouver's English Bay. A visiting Nobel laureate and his guest were, naturally, given the best table in the place. As soon as they were seated, Matt felt the urge to say something.

"Uh, Dr. Feinberg, I hope I didn't offend you when I said your quantum kleptodynamics was a conceptual model."

Feinberg chuckled. "Not at all, Mr. Barnes. I came up with the term 'kleptodynamics' near the end of a very long pub crawl in Vienna back in 1973." He winked.

"Mr. Barnes, I'm intrigued by your multi-dimensional approach to magnetic fields. Were you planning on taking your research further?"

Matt nodded. "There's an n-equals-five version of my model that could offer a way to increase electromagnet field strength by differentially modulating several 4-space M-fields. I've done some ad hoc experiments that indicate the average current should increase *less* than linearly with respect to the M-field strength." *At least that's what I'm telling everyone...*

"Interesting. Very interesting." Feinberg crunched on a breadstick for a moment, then took a sip of ice water. "Mr. Barnes, I'm in a bit of a bind and I was hoping you could help me out."

Speechless, Matt could only nod. *A Nobel laureate wants my help?*

"The Dean of our physics department expects me to take on a grad studenteveryfiveyears. Downrightinsistent, actually. Problemis, I haven't found a student interesting enough or who can put up with my idiosyncrasies. Untiltoday, thatis. You're exactlythe type ofstudent I want to work with. What do you think?"

Work under Professor Feinberg?

"I... I'd be honoured, sir."

"Great," Feinberg said. "You might have to write the GRE—that's the Graduate Records Examination—but since you're about to have two master's degrees, maybe not. Here's my card—contact my assistant and she'll tell you what administrative nonsense needs to be taken care of."

◎

UBC Graduation week - May 1981

The announcer read the next name on the list. "Renwick Norman Harris, Bachelor of Science degree, major in Geology and minor in Astronomy."

Renny strode acrossthe stagetowardsthe lectern, his graduation gown riding high—almost up to his knees—due to his height and massive shoulders. He reached out a beefy right hand to shake the hand of the dean of the Faculty of Science and accepted his diploma with his left. In the audience, Matt sat with his parents, Gary, and Renny's mom, and cheered. An hour later, Matt walked on-stage to receive his Bachelor of Applied Science degree (honours) in Engineering Physics and Mathematics. After a catered lunch for graduates, family, and friends, Matt returned to the stage in the afternoon session.

"Matthew Edward Barnes, Master of Science degree in Physics. Mr. Barnes' thesis is titled, 'A 4-Space Derivation of Magnetic Force Fields.' The dean of the Faculty of Science shook Matt's hand and handed him his diploma. Matt nodded and turned to head off-stage.

"Not so fast, Mr. Barnes." The dean motioned for Matt to remain. "Ladies and gentlemen, Mr. Barnes has been busy this year! He is also receiving a Master of Science degree in mathematics for his thesis, 'A Solution to the Poincaré Conjecture using an n-Space Manifold Tensor Matrix.'

"Proving the Poincaré Conjecture has been a goal of mathematicians for over eighty years. Accomplishing this feat has placed Mr. Barnes in the running for the prestigious Fields Medal, the highest award available to mathematicians and often described as the mathematician's Nobel Prize. Mr. Barnes is the first student in UBC's history to receive three degrees the same year."

The audience applauded. Renny hooted.

Two days after the graduation ceremonies, Matt and Renny vacated their rooms and drove their fully loaded Datsun back to Penticton. Renny had accepted a full-time job with the Geological Survey of Canada as a Field Geologist, but had three months off before starting. Matt had no plans until September, so the pair spent that time relaxing and enjoying the hot summer weather Penticton offered. They cruised in the Batmobile and made several camping trips up to Crater Lake, refining Renny's map of the area's magnetic anomalies.

"I'm convinced there's a meteorite down there, and I'm going to find it," Renny vowed during their final evening as they camped by the lake's shore.

"You know, that would be a great thesis for a master's degree," Matt observed.

Renny snorted. "Yah, me getting a graduate degree. That'll be the day."

Matt chuckled. "Good point. We're all amazed you made it out of high school, let alone getting a Bachelor's degree."

Renny growled half-heartedly.

"No, seriously, Batman. We've collected lots of data. There's definitely something down deep a few kilometres north of here that's affecting the earth's mag-field."

"I'll think about it," Renny offered.

July came to an end, and it was time for Renny to leave. He'd be flying to Ottawa for two weeks of training before heading to his assigned field camp in the Northwest Territories.

"Josh's meeting me at the airport," Renny said. "I'm going to stay with him for the weekend before moving to the hotel they've got me booked into."

"Say hi from me," Matt said wistfully. After graduating at the top of his class in computer science from the University of Waterloo, Josh had taken a job with Environment Canada in Ottawa, doing weather modelling. It was his dream job, a mix of computer programming and mathematics. Gary remained in the Vancouver area, but spent much of his time working offshore, maintaining and piloting his company's remotely operated vehicles on oil rigs.

Matt was lonely for the rest of the summer; he passed the time working in the family orchard and pondering his hyperspatial model. At the end of August, he hopped a flight to Vancouver, the first leg of his journey to Pasadena, California, to start the next chapter of his education at the prestigious California Institute of Technology.

EIGHT

Matt arrived at Caltech's main lecture hall his customary ten minutes early and took his preferred seat: second row, just left of centre. Other students trickled in, filling the surrounding seats, some offering those awkward nods of acknowledgement strangers often do. Just before the top of the hour, five students came in together; four clustered around a medium-height, dapper young man sporting an expensive suit and shiny gold diamond cufflinks. His black hair was perfectly arranged in an Elvis-style pompadour and he spoke loudly with a nasal, East coast accent. Those around him hung on his every word.

He's their social centre of mass, Matt thought, employing a physics analogy to the mysterious field of social dynamics. *Or moons, orbiting a massive planet.*

Mr. Perfect Hair stopped in front of the first row, scanned the seating and frowned; there wasn't enough room for his group to sit together. A young woman from his entourage took the cue and stepped forward.

"Would y'all mind making room? There's five of us," she said, the tone of her drawl more of an order.

To Matt's surprise, one student in the first row actually got up and moved to a peripheral seat. Still one seat short, she looked at Matt.

"Would you mind?"

Matt stared back at her. "Yes."

"Yes, as in 'yes you'll move'?"

"No," Matt said.

Her eyebrows furrowed. "Well, is it yes or no?"

"Yes, as in 'yes I do mind,' and no, as in 'no, I won't move.' If you wanted to sit together up front, you should have come earlier." He motioned over his shoulder with his thumb. "There's plenty of seats further back."

"How rude!" she remarked. Perfect Hair sniffed the air as if mortally insulted.

Matt's jaw dropped. *Seriously?*

"Well, I guess we'll just have to make do," Perfect Hair said, purposely taking the seat directly in front of Matt and relegating one of his entourage to the third row. He looked over his shoulder and gave Matt the once-over, then muttered something to the young woman next to him. She barely stifled a giggle.

What a tool, Matt thought. *And he smells like Brylcreem.*

Matt was about to fire back a witty retort when a distinguished-looking man entered from the side door and strode to the lectern. The room went silent.

"Welcome—"

Perfect Hair reached out and linked hands with his friends on each side; they bowed their heads.

"Dear Lord, we humbly beseech thee to grant us—"

Geez! They're actually praying!

The speaker was clearly perturbed but waited out the disruption. Luckily, the prayer was a short one.

"—in the Lord's name, Amen."

"As I was saying," said the speaker, "welcome everyone to this year's graduate school orientation. I'm Doctor Owen Hunt, Chair of the Physics, Mathematics, and Astronomy Division. Today I'll walk you through our doctoral program. You're here because you're the best of this year's applicants. Most of you will make it through, but some won't.

"Let's start with introductions. Please stand up, give us your name, tell us where you did your undergraduate degree, and what research area you're most interested in." He nodded at a young woman at the right edge of the front-row group. "Young lady, you first."

She shot to her feet. "Emily Roberts, *magna cum laude* in physics from Princeton. I hope to work on solar plasma dynamics." Hunt nodded, then looked to the small Indian man next to her.

"Nabil Doshi, math and physics from the Indian Institute of Science in Bangalore. I would like to do research in particle physics."

Eventually it was Perfect Hair's turn; he unhurriedly stood up, shot out his cuffs and straightened his suit before speaking. "Charles William Winston the Third, from Boston." He pronounced his name "Chawles" and his town, "Bastan."

"*Summa cum laude* in physics and mathematics, from Harvard," he said proudly, emphasizing the Latin honourific and pronouncing his alma mater, "Ha-vad." "I plan to work in radio astronomy."

The introductions continued into the second row. Then it was Matt's turn.

"Matt Barnes, Engineering Physics from UBC. I'm going to work on superconducting electromagnetism with Dr. Feinberg."

Charles William Winston the Third let out a quiet snort. He leaned over to the young woman next to him—part of his entourage—and muttered, "An engineer? In Caltech physics?"

Matt *had* to defend his alma mater. "Pardon me. Engineering Physics *and* Honours Mathematics. That's the Canadian equivalent to *maxima cum laude* here in the States."

"I bet he doesn't even know what '*maxima cum laude*' means," Winston muttered.

Matt couldn't resist.

"Catapultam home." *I have a catapult.* "Nisi pecuniam omnem mihi dabis, ad caput tuum saxum immane mittam." *Give me all your money or I will fling an enormous rock at your head.*

"I beg your pardon?"

"Vah!" Matt said. "Denuone Latine loquebar?" *Oh, was I speaking Latin again?* "Me ineptum. Interdum modo elabitur." *Silly me. Sometimes it just sort of slips out.*

Professor Hunt chuckled. "It's good to see someone here knows their Latin. Let's continue with our introductions, shall we?"

As the next student stood and introduced himself, Winston turned and glared at Matt.

Matt stared back. *You're a dick.*

Once the introductions were done, Professor Hunt continued. "Let's get back to why you're here. The first hurdle you have to overcome is the 'Basic Requirement'—written exams in Classical Physics and Quantum Mechanics. You have to pass both exams by the end of your first year. We hold these exams twice a year: in October—that's six weeks away—and next June. These are tough exams; if you can't pass them, you don't belong here.

"Next is the Advanced Physics Requirement: you have to complete six quarters of graduate-level physics and math courses from a pool pre-selected by the department. This ensures you have a broad knowledge of physics, and you're expected to start taking them right away. These have to be completed by the end of your second year. While you're doing that, you have to find a supervising professor and plan your area of research.

"Once you've completed your Advanced Physics Requirement, you take the oral candidacy exam. This is a one-to-two-hour presentation describing your project, why it's worthy of research, what questions it answers, and so on. A faculty committee determines whether you're suitable for the area of research you've selected, in other words, approving your thesis topic and making sure you're ready to tackle it. You get to select which faculty members are on your committee, but there are *some* restrictions. For example, if your research area is experimental, you should include one theoretical physicist, and vice versa. You've got four years to take the oral candidacy exam; once you've passed it, you're admitted into PhD candidacy. That's when you focus on your research.

"After you've completed your research comes the dissertation defence. Similar to the oral candidacy exam, a committee examines the results of your research and passes judgment on whether you've succeeded.

"You're also required to attend the weekly department seminars—these will help you learn what research is going on in the department. And finally, you're expected to, at least once per semester, lead a tutorial for your fellow students in an area you're familiar with."

Hunt stared at the crowd, then shrugged. "Well, that's it. You've got five years to complete the program. Any longer and you'll need permission for an extension. Questions?"

Matt waited while his fellow students posed the obvious questions. Then he put up his hand.

"Yes, Mr. Barnes, isn't it?"

"Yes, sir. The Advanced Physics Requirement—is it possible to challenge the course work and just write the exams?"

The surrounding students started whispering. Hunt shook his head. "I doubt any student could manage that." Winston chuckled at Matt's audacity.

Matt paused before answering. "I'm sorry, sir, I should have been more specific. I wasn't asking if it is *possible*, but whether it is *allowed*."

The room was silent as the professor stared at Matt.

"Come see me after." There were more snickers from Winston and his entourage.

Once the session was over, Winston intercepted Matt.

"So, you think you're going to work with Dr. Feinberg, the Nobel Laureate? You do know you don't get to choose your faculty advisor, right? And you know Feinberg doesn't do research in electromagnetism? Professor Clarke is the department's leading magnetician—he's an old friend of the family, by the way. And how did an engineer—a *Canadian* engineer—get into Caltech?"

Matt stared at his antagonist for a few seconds. "That's none of your business," he said, sidestepping Winston and moving towards Dr. Hunt.

"Ah yes, Mr. Barnes," Hunt said. "You're here on Professor Feinberg's fellowship." He stared at Matt. "You weren't totally honest earlier, were you?"

"I... I beg your pardon, sir?" Matt said.

"You neglected to mention a couple of important details, didn't you? Your two master's degrees, in physics and mathematics, and that you are *the* M. Barnes who solved the Poincaré Conjecture two years ago. I hear you're in the running for the Fields Medal, young man."

Matt fidgeted. "Uh, yes, sir, that's correct. But you *did* ask us to state what our *undergraduate* degree was. I try to be concise when answering questions." He shrugged. "Sometimes I over-do it."

Hunt stared at Matt for a few seconds before nodding acceptance.

"Based on what Professor Feinberg has told me about you, I think we can accommodate your request. But be warned, you'll be taking on a considerable workload."

"I can handle it."

Hunt pondered Matt's reply. "Given what you accomplished in four years at UBC, I think maybe you can, son."

Hunt glanced over at Winston and his entourage, clustered at the edge of earshot, intently watching them. "Mr. Barnes, may I offer you a piece of advice?"

Matt nodded.

Hunt lowered his voice. "Getting a doctoral degree at Caltech can be like navigating a boat in shallow waters. While the process *is* primarily academic, there are certain... shall we say... political reefs one must steer around."

"I'm not sure I follow you, sir," Matt said.

Hunt lowered his voice another notch. "I see that you and Mr. Winston didn't exactly hit it off. He comes from a wealthy and influential family. Very influential. I suggest you watch your step around him. Just a friendly piece of advice." Hunt turned and left.

Great, Matt thought. *Day One and I've already found the class bully.*

It took Matt the better part of his first week to get the administrative paperwork sorted out for his PhD program—being an "alien" meant several additional forms to fill out. Dr. Feinberg backed Matt's request to challenge the courses for the Advanced Physics Requirement, and Professor Hunt signed off on it.

Matt got to work. He bought all the textbooks he needed, then hunkered down in his small on-campus apartment. While his classmates were studying for the Basic Requirement exams, Matt was absorbing the material for the Advanced Physics Requirement.

In mid-October, he, along with the eleven other doctoral candidates, wrote the two Basic Requirement exams: Classical Physics and Quantum Mechanics. Thanks to his past schooling and eidetic memory, he scored one hundred percent on both. Only five of his eleven classmates made the cut, including Charles William Winston the Third.

With that hurdle cleared, Matt returned to studying for the Advanced Physics Requirement exams and planning his research with Dr. Feinberg.

◎

Matt looked around the small conference room at his fellow grad students. It was his turn to lead a seminar, and he'd chosen to speak on one aspect of the advanced geometry he often used. He arrived his customary ten minutes early to prepare his overhead slides, then waited until the clock on the wall ticked to the top of the hour. He waited an additional minute in case any faculty member showed up, which they often did.

Matt cleared his throat. "Welcome everyone. Today I'm going to talk about—"

"Dear Lord, we humbly beseech thee to grant us—"

Winston was holding hands with his colleagues and praying. Out loud. *Enough of this bullshit.*

"Excuse me! I'd appreciate it if you wouldn't interrupt my lecture. Why don't you do your praying before class, or at least do it silently? Then those who want to listen to my seminar can do so without interruption."

Winston's face cycled from anger to disgust. "How dare you interrupt us! We pray at the start of every class. Our religion demands it!"

No backing down now. "Huh. Which religion is that?"

Winston looked mortally insulted. "Christianity, of course!"

"Then you follow the Bible?"

"Of course!"

"Where in the Bible does it tell you to pray before every class?"

"It doesn't specifically say that, but—"

"You must be familiar with the book of Matthew," Matt said. *I wonder if he'll catch the irony here.*

"I know the Bible inside and out!" Winston barked.

"Do you now?" Matt said. *I memorized it when I was nine years old.* "Then you know Matthew 6:5?"

Winston stared at Matt, his face turning a shade of pink.

I thought not...

"Allow me," Matt said. "Matthew 6:5. *And when you pray, do not be like the hypocrites, for they love to pray standing in the synagogues and on the street corners to be seen by others. Truly I tell you, they have received their reward in full."*

"Don't you quote the bible to me!" Charles barked.

"How about Matthew 6:6? *But when you pray, go into your room, close the door and pray to your Father, who is unseen. Then your Father, who sees what is done in secret, will reward you."*

"You're taking it out of context!" Winston shouted.

Matt shrugged. "If you need more context, I can quote the verses before *and* after. I think the interpretation is clear."

"Don't tell me how to interpret the Bible!"

"*Mister* Winston," Matt said. "If you continue disrupting my seminar, I'm going to ask you to leave. Then I'll file a complaint of academic misconduct with the department."

Winston turned red and spluttered.

The door opened; Professor Hunt entered and took a seat at the back. He noticed the tension in the room.

"Okay, what did I miss?"

"Just some housekeeping items, sir," Matt said cheerily. "Thank you for joining us."

"Well, let's get started, then."

Matt nodded, ignoring Winston. "Today I'm going to talk about an interesting trick in my mathematical toolbox." He launched into a tutorial on geometric topology, manifolds, metric spaces, and other esoteric mathematics.

An hour later, he'd completed his presentation.

"In summary," he said, "the reanimate tensor manifold method is a useful tool in arriving at force field solutions, by first extending the vectors into n-space. This has applications in plasma dynamics, electromagnetics, particle physics, cosmology, and quantum gravity, to name but a few."

He paused. "Questions?"

"That's a brilliant construct," Emily Roberts said. "It may be helpful in my modelling of plasma spin vortices."

Matt nodded his thanks.

"Fascinating," Nabil Doshi added. "I would like to discuss this further with you."

"Any time," Matt said. "Any more questions?"

Charles Winston launched into a series of questions, thinly veiled attacks on Matt's mathematics. Each time Matt answered or refuted one of Winston's arguments, there was another. This continued for almost twenty minutes.

"I have one more question," Winston said. "Your approach assumes the n-manifold is homeomorphic."

He's no slouch at geometric topology. Just a bit out of date.

"Yes, it does," Matt said. "Every simply connected, closed n-manifold *is* homeomorphic to an n-sphere."

"I see," Winston said. "I guess that's where I disagree."

"And what's the basis of your disagreement?"

"You have not proven your homeomorphism assertion."

Oh, this is going to be fun...

Professor Hunt, who'd been silent the entire hour, cleared his throat. Loudly.

"*Mister* Winston," Hunt said. "Do you realize that the young man you're arguing with, and losing badly to I might add, is *the* M. Barnes who *solved* the Poincaré Conjecture while an undergrad at UBC? *The* M. Barnes who is in the running for the Fields Medal?"

Winston's face cycled through several shades of red.

There's a non-zero probability Winston's head will explode. Here's hoping...

"So we can safely assume Mr. Barnes is an expert on this topic," Hunt added.

Winston composed himself then turned to Matt. "I stand corrected, Mr. Barnes."

News of Winston's "spanking" made the rounds of the Caltech physics department faster than a speeding tachyon. To Matt's chagrin, that raised his popularity, something he never wanted. It also brought Winston down a few pegs, an added benefit.

By Christmas, Matt had written and passed—aced, actually—four of the Advanced Physics Requirement exams. He'd been ready to write all six, but the professors assigned to teach the remaining two courses, which weren't scheduled to start until January, hadn't submitted their course plans yet, let alone prepared exams.

Matt flew home for the holidays to spend time with his family, but it wasn't the same without his friends in town. Renny was somewhere in an Arizona desert, doing fieldwork. Gary was in Costa Rica with his girlfriend Nadia, an archeologist from the University of Toronto. He'd met her six months ago while on shore leave following a stint working at an offshore oil rig in the Gulf of Mexico. He'd fallen madly for her and taken an indefinite leave of absence from his subsea job to tramp through the jungles of Central America, helping her explore submerged Mayan tombs with a small, balky, robotic underwater vehicle she'd inherited from her thesis advisor. Josh did come home for Christmas, but he only had time for one brief visit because of the demands placed on him by his very religious family. Matt spent most of the holidays thinking about getting back to Caltech and planning his upcoming research.

◎

January 1982

Matt took a seat in the back row of the physics department's largest lecture hall. This was the weekly department seminar, where professors and post-docs gave presentations on their research. The official purpose of these seminars was to make sure that grad students kept abreast of the myriad of ongoing research projects. But after being a spectator for one semester, Matt realized their true purpose was to allow the professors to show off and try to one-up each other.

There was a strict pecking order in the seminar's seating arrangements. The senior faculty members sat at the front, associate professors and post-docs in the middle, and grad students in the back. Undergrads stood against the back wall. Dr. Feinberg usually arrived late and sat wherever he wanted to, often planting himself on the steps if no seats were available. Matt enjoyed these seminars; this one, the first in the spring term, included a spirited debate between two senior professors on the half-life of the proton, resulting in a round of bets being wagered.

Professor Hunt, as chair of the department, moderated.

"Well, that concludes this week's seminar," Hunt said. "Next week, Professor Singh will give an update on his condensed matter research."

Attendees rose to leave.

"Oh, one more thing. I have a special announcement." Everyone returned to their seats.

"This morning I received a fax from the President of the International Mathematical Union, headquartered in Berlin. The fax was a courtesy 'heads-up' for a press release about to hit the newswires. The reason they faxed me is that the press release pertains to someone in our department."

Hunt shielded his eyes, peering into the seminar room's dark back rows. "Is Mr. Barnes here today?"

A murmur ran through the crowd. Heads turned towards the back of the room.

What the hell? Matt thought.

"Mr. Barnes, please come down here."

Oh shit, what did I do?

Matt navigated past several sets of legs, then down the steps to the front of the room, painfully aware of all the eyes on him. Hunt motioned for him to stand beside him at the lectern.

"Mr. Barnes is in his second term as a prospective doctoral candidate in our department, and doing quite well, I might add, demonstrating his prowess at geometric topology. What some of you may not know is that, during his third year of undergrad engineering physics at the University of British Columbia, he solved the Poincaré Conjecture, a problem that has stumped mathematicians for over eighty years. UBC awarded him a Master of Science degree in Mathematics for this accomplishment. Well, I'm pleased to announce that the International Mathematical Union has awarded Mr. Barnes the 1982 Fields Medal. It's one of the highest honors that can be bestowed on a mathematician, and is often referred to as the 'mathematician's Nobel Prize.' Mr. Barnes will receive his medal at the IMU's International Congress of Mathematicians, which is being held this summer just up the coast in Berkeley. Please stand and congratulate him on this amazing accomplishment!"

The room erupted in applause, and Matt's face turned bright red. Everyone clapped, except for Charles William Winston the Third and his followers.

◎

Matt was uncomfortable with the attention he received over the Fields Medal announcement. That attention tapered off after a couple of weeks, and by April, he'd written (and aced) his two remaining exams for the Advanced Physics Requirement. That was when Dean Hunt told him he was only the second Caltech student ever to accomplish this feat—Dr. Feinberg being the first.

I'm in good company!

A month later, Matt took his Oral Candidacy Exam. His ninety-minute-long presentation had several of the professors on the committee baffled by the advanced, multi-dimensional mathematics he proposed using to design a high-powered electromagnet. "I think you should include a faculty member from the Applied Mathematics department," one of the panel members suggested.

The committee conferred in private for only ten minutes before calling him back.

"Mr. Barnes, you are now officially a PhD candidate. Congratulations, you're only the second student in the history of Caltech to be granted candidacy after one year. The other one is sitting in the back row, I believe." Dr. Feinberg waved and grinned from ear-to-ear.

◎

Matt's research goal was audacious: create a superconducting electromagnet an order of magnitude stronger than those currently in existence. He'd already solved the problem in his mind, visualizing the 5-dimensional geometry that allowed for the complex interplay of 4-dimensional magnetic force fields. It was a puzzle, but one in five dimensions. Now he had to draw on his engineering skills, developed in his teens as a garage inventor and honed by four years in UBC's engineering physics program, to turn theory into reality.

At least that was his *advertised* goal. Higher dimensions were calling, poking at the edges of his consciousness, promising even more wondrous discoveries. But those realms, what Matt called "n-space," had to wait. For the next six months, he toiled away in his lab in the basement of the physics building, taking only Saturdays off.

In late summer, Matt reluctantly interrupted his research to attend the International Conference on Mathematics at the University of California, Berkeley in San Francisco. The ICM was held every four years, and host to several other award presentations. Matt happily shared the limelight with the Fields Medal winners from the previous three years, along with those for the Nevanlinna Prize (for mathematical aspects of Information Sciences), the Gauss Prize (for mathematical contributions outside the field of mathematics), and the Chern Medal (lifelong achievement in mathematics). The awards were presented immediately following the opening ceremonies; Matt was the first Canadian to receive the Fields Medal, a 14-carat gold medal and modest "reward" of $12,000. In his brief acceptance speech, he acknowledged the award's namesake—noted Canadian mathematician John Charles Fields—then graciously donated his reward back to the Fields Trust, managed by the University of Toronto. As soon as he could extricate himself from the mandatory social events, Matt ducked out and caught the train back to Pasadena. He had a big puzzle to solve.

◎

Four months later...

Dr. Feinberg tapped lightly on the meter sitting on the bench next to the humming assembly. Wisps of steam wafted off the curved cylindrical housing that formed a nine-inch diameter toroid, a superconducting electromagnet cooled with liquid helium to just above absolute zero.

"Thirty-five-point three Tesla!" he said with awe in his voice. "And continuously! Fabulous, my boy! You've done it."

Matt nodded. "Overcoming the dielectric heating was tough. I took the best mechanical aspects of a Bitter air-core non-superconducting electromagnet and combined them with those of a conventional superconducting magnet. But it's the pulsed, tri-axial, multiphasic modulation in the coils that produces the intense M-field."

"And you only needed five geometric dimensions to figure that out," Feinberg said. "And a baker's dozen of fire extinguishers, according to the department's safety officer." He paused. "I think this is worthy of its own name." He stood up and made the sign of a cross with his hand over the electromagnet assembly. "I dub thee the Barnes Superconducting Electromagnet."

"I'm honoured, sir." Matt smiled and bowed deeply. Dr. F. appreciated it when his students indulged his idiosyncracies.

Feinberg cautiously leaned over and peered into the centre of the toroid, making sure he kept his arms behind his back.

"The air in the centre is blurry—do you know what causes that?" *If this was a science fiction novel,* he thought, *I'd say that the concentrated M-field was tearing apart the structure of space-time. Or something cool like that.*

Matt muttered something.

"Sorry, what was that?" Feinberg said.

"I think it's a, umm... chaotic turbulent effect," Matt said. "I do plan on looking into it."

Feinberg looked up and grinned. "Uh huh." *He's up to something.*

"Matt, what's that thing?" he said, pointing to a contraption sitting on a bench in the corner. It was a pair of aluminum rings, each the size of a basketball, held two inches apart with a hefty structure. There were permanent magnets bolted to each ring, spaced equally around their circumference, with tight coils of wire between the magnets.

Matt's face turned red. "Oh... it's, uh, just a test fixture. Nothing important."

Feinberg stared at Matt. "Uh huh." *He's definitely up to something.*

He clapped his hands together once. "Now comes the *really* hard part: writing it up," referring to the penultimate hoop Matt had to jump through.

◎

Matt spent the next two months struggling with the arduous task of writing up his dissertation. It was a comprehensive report: his predictions;

his experimental setup and results; how his empirical data matched his predictions; and how he'd contributed something new to the physics body of knowledge. He assumed that having two successful master's-level theses under his belt would help, but Caltech had its own documentation standards. Fortunately, the department had several talented writers on staff whose sole function was to turn the unorganized thoughts and experimental results generated by brilliant minds into coherent documents.

Dr. F. was right—this is harder than the research!

Matt forwarded a draft copy to Dr. F., whose only comment was to elaborate on how he derived some of his base mathematic formulae; Matt often skipped steps that were obvious to him.

Two revisions later, Feinberg signed off. "I guess it'll do. Have you decided who you're nominating for your thesis review committee?"

Matt nodded. "Besides yourself, the same as on my candidacy examination panel: Professors Singh, Chen, and Clarke. Since the panel recommended I include someone from the Applied Mathematics department, I nominated Professor Anton."

Feinberg mulled over Matt's choices. "I only know Professor Anton by reputation—she's a stickler for wanting to see *all* intermediate work. Good choices otherwise, although I should warn you—Professor Clarke will be a tough sell. He considers magnetism to be his turf. He hasn't published in ages, but is still highly regarded by his peers."

"He is the department's senior magnetician," Matt said. "I figured it would be bad form *not* to include him."

A pained expression appeared on Feinberg's face. "You're right, but he and I haven't gotten along since I brought you on." He lowered his voice. "Frankly, I think he's miffed, and a bit jealous, that you've upstaged him on his home turf."

Matt grimaced. "Should I choose someone else?"

"Well, it's tradition to have the same panel members on both review committees. At this late stage, you'd have to convince Professor Hunt you have a valid reason to change your nominations. Just make sure your ducks are in a row and you should be okay. He may not like me much, and by extension, you, but he's gotta be impressed by thirty-five Tesla. Who wouldn't be?"

Matt hand-delivered copies of his thesis to the faculty members he'd nominated, then invited them to his lab for a demonstration. All were impressed, except for Professor Clarke. He hummed and hawed and grumped, seemed uninterested, and asked several irrelevant questions.

Just like Dr. F. predicted. Well, as long as he gives my work a fair shake.

The committee members had sixty days to review the thesis and give comments. All the feedback he received was positive, just several requests to elaborate on his mathematics. Then it was time for his thesis defence.

◎

The department's main seminar room was standing room only; the review committee members, including Dr. Feinberg, sat in the front row. Other faculty sat immediately behind them, with many of the department's grad students filling the remaining seats at the back.

Professor Hunt walked up to the lectern. "Welcome, everyone. Today we have a dissertation defence in applied physics by Mr. Matt Barnes. His thesis is titled, 'Realizing a 35-Tesla Electromagnetic Field Strength via an n-Space Closed Manifold.' I'll ask you to hold your questions until after his presentation."

He turned to Matt. "Mr. Barnes?"

Matt stepped up to the lectern.

"Thank you, Professor Hunt." He nodded at the undergrad student operating the overhead projector; his first slide appeared on the screen.

Matt gave a brief introduction, then did his best to walk the audience through his complex multi-dimensional equations. Next, he described his experimental setup and test results. That took close to an hour. He took a sip of water.

"In summary," Matt said, "a 5-space geometric framework allows for a 4-space solution that predicts a significantly larger M-field than with conventional electromagnets. By combining a conventional superconducting electromagnet with certain mechanical aspects of a Bitter air-core non-superconducting electromagnet, and using a pulsed, tri-axial multiphasic modulation of the M-field, a continuous 35.3-Tesla field was realized."

Matt paused. "Questions?"

The room was silent.

Not surprising, given how complicated my math is!

A few questions trickled in, but they were requests for elaboration on his mathematics. He wasn't expecting any surprises; he'd been thorough in his theoretical work and research, and his experimental results were solid. The review committee members peppered him with pro forma questions on classical and quantum physics, ensuring he had a thorough understanding of "the basics."

Once the question period was over, Professor Hunt stepped up to the lectern.

"Thank you, Mr. Barnes. Please step out into the hallway while the committee confers."

Matt spent the next twenty minutes pacing back and forth in the empty hallway. Then the door opened, and a student came out; she had a strange look on her face.

"Uh, you might as well get comfortable. They're... going to be awhile."

Why so long? Matt thought. *Did I miss something?*

Another twenty minutes passed. Matt paced. Then another twenty. Then another. He thought (imagined?) he heard the occasional yelling coming from the seminar room.

Just when he figured he couldn't take any more delay, the door opened, and the student beckoned him in. The room was quiet enough to hear a proverbial pin drop. Dean Hunt motioned for him to stand beside the lectern. Matt turned to look at the review committee members.

Professors Singh and Chen looked sheepish, while Professor Anton was staring at the ceiling. Feinberg was glaring at Dr. Clarke; Matt had never seen him look so angry.

What's going on?

Dean Hunt cleared his throat. "Mr. Barnes, we find ourselves in a bit of a pickle here. As you're aware, each member of the committee selects one of four grades: pass with no revisions, pass with minor revisions, pass with major revisions, and fail. Your overall grade is the lowest of the five individual grades."

He paused.

"You received three 'pass with no revisions' and one 'pass with minor revisions.' Unfortunately, one of the committee members decided your thesis does not pass muster, and gave you a 'fail'."

Matt turned white, and it took every ounce of self-control to keep his knees from buckling. *Holy shit!*

"Um, can—can I offer any further clarification?"

"No, the candidate cannot," Professor Clarke growled.

"But my theory is sound, and my experimental results solid."

Clarke addressed Professor Hunt, refusing to respond to Matt. "The candidate's mathematics are gibberish."

Feinberg jumped out of his seat, motioning towards Professor Anton. "The committee member from the mathematics department doesn't have any issues with the math—why should you? And how do you account for *the fact* that there's a superconducting magnet in his lab that produces a continuous thirty-five Tesla? You saw it yourself!"

Clarke shrugged. "Yes, yes, yes. I think he just tinkered enough and got lucky. You know, monkeys, typewriters, and Shakespeare."

Fuck you, Matt thought.

"Then give him a 'pass with major revisions' until he can clean up his math to your satisfaction!" Feinberg thundered.

Clarke folded his arms across his chest. "That isn't going to happen."

Feinberg and Clarke glared at each other for thirty seconds. Hunt broke the silence.

"Faculty rules are clear. Doctoral candidate Barnes receives a fail on his dissertation defence." He addressed the audience. "This session is concluded. Thank you for coming."

The audience filed out, all staring at Matt and whispering to each other. Matt sat down on the edge of the low stage. Feinberg came over; Matt looked up at him.

"So, what do I do now?"

"I don't know, son. Nothing like this has ever happened. Clarke *is* within his right to give the grade he thinks is appropriate, even though he was way out of line. I'll talk to the Dean."

NINE

The fallout from Matt's failed dissertation defence rocked the department and, to a lesser extent, the entire Caltech institution. Everyone, faculty, staff, and students had expected Dr. Feinberg's *wunderkind* to breeze through. Questions were being asked. Feinberg threatened to resign unless the department investigated Dr. Clarke's behaviour. To add insult to injury, the department offered Matt a *master's* degree for his doctoral work.

"Do you think I should accept?" Matt asked his mentor, no longer sure of anything.

"Well, outside the US, a master's is considered a bona fide degree, a necessary rung on the academic ladder. But in the US, it doesn't have the same cachet; in fact, it's viewed as a consolation prize. Announcing you have a master's degree is like saying, 'I wasn't good enough to get a PhD.'"

A dark cloud passed over Matt's face.

"Sorry, son," Feinberg said, "no offence intended. But if you accept, Caltech *will* publish your thesis, so the physics community will get to see your experimental results. A lot of researchers will benefit from your super-strong electromagnets."

"And if I refuse?"

"Your thesis becomes an unpublished manuscript, Caltech has no rights to it, and you withdraw from the program."

It took Matt only a day to decide. He penned a brief note to Professor

Hunt, thanking him for the offer but respectfully declining. Reading between the lines, Matt's message was clear: *Take your master's degree and shove it up your departmental ass.*

Most of Matt's fellow doctoral candidates sympathized with his situation. They were all on edge now, worried that one misstep might land them in a similar predicament. The only ones not concerned were Charles William Winston the Third and his entourage; they found Matt's situation amusing. Whenever one of them saw Matt in a hallway or the cafeteria, they'd nod, smile, and say, "Hello, *Mister* Barnes."

Things became crystal a week later when fellow doctoral candidate Nabil Doshi, whose lab was next to Matt's, sat down at the table when Matt was having lunch in the cafeteria.

"Matt, there's something I need to tell you. I'm not sure how you'll take it."

"What's up?"

Nabil glanced around the room before replying.

"Yesterday, I overheard Charles Winston chatting with one of his friends in the hallway. They were discussing your situation. I clearly heard him say, 'And that's what happens when you cross a Winston.'"

Ah, that was the last piece of the puzzle, Matt realized. *Professor Hunt's warning about Winston coming from an influential family. Winston mentioning that Professor Clarke was an "old friend of the family." Feinberg's caution about Clarke being miffed for taking on a grad student doing magnetism research.*

"So, Matt, what are your plans now?"

Matt shrugged. "Gonna spend the summer back home in Canada. Dr. F. got me a teaching assistant position for the fall term. I'll teach a few courses and that'll give me time to wrap up my affairs here. After that, I honestly don't know."

◎

Matt's return home was bittersweet. He was ashamed to be returning without the expected doctorate, but his parents understood and gave him lots of space. He spent many days sitting in the backyard, pondering his future. From the moment he'd started documenting his multi-dimensional mathematics back in his third year at UBC, there was a whisper coming from his subconscious. Something he couldn't quite put his finger on. Something more. The realm of higher dimensions—"n-space"—was beckoning. He'd hoped that Caltech's academic environment and resources would have facilitated that exploration. *Alas...*

One sunny morning he decided to go for a walk and clear his mind, to see if he could turn that whisper into something more substantial. He threw an assortment of snacks and a water bottle in his daypack, yelled "Going for a hike, be back later," to his mom, then trudged up the hill behind their house. He followed a game trail up the slope of Campbell Mountain until he reached an intersecting hiking trail that circled the mountain. He followed that meandering trail clockwise for several hours before stopping at a natural viewpoint on the mountain's southern slope. Below was a small lake, the Penticton reservoir, which was the town's primary water supply. It was at its highest level of the year, the remnants of the winter snow pack melt now just a trickle in the many creeks that fed it. He scanned the surrounding topography, breathing in the warm summer air; a large, dark, circular shape in the water just above the reservoir's small dam caught his attention.

That looks like it's worth checking out.

He scrambled down a narrow single-track trail that brought him to the reservoir's edge. That circular shape he'd spotted from above turned out to be the mouth of a perfectly round concrete spillway—the city engineering department's solution to prevent high water from overflowing the wooden dam during the spring melt. Around its perimeter, water flowed smoothly over the rim, disappearing into the bowels of the earth with a muted roar.

Wow! It looks like Einstein's general relativity visualization of a mass deforming the fabric of space-time—a flat rubber sheet with a heavy weight in the middle. Or one end of a Schwarzschild wormhole.

He sat on a boulder, pushed down the analytical side of his mind, and willed himself to relax and enjoy the beauty of the surroundings and the warm sun on his face. That lasted less than a minute. Fluid dynamics equations describing how the water flowed into the spillway clamoured for his attention. Matt's mind jumped to four geometric dimensions; he "saw" a 4-dimensional shape that, when intersecting with the 3-dimensional world, matched the smooth geometry of the spillway's flow.

Matt couldn't help but follow that dimensional train of thought: *what 5-dimensional shape could produce such an object when looked at from 4-D space?*

A family of complex shapes appeared in his mind, fantastical objects that could only exist in the realm of mathematics: N-manifolds, handles, knot invariants, and Klein bottles. The four-dimensional magnetic force field equations he'd developed for his UBC master's thesis then extended to five dimensions for his failed doctoral dissertation appeared, overlaying themselves on the beautiful symmetry of the flowing water. He tried moving up to six dimensions, but his body's senses were an unwanted distraction. He took a deep breath and pushed them aside; his vision faded, he no longer heard the rush of water, and the feeling of the warm sun on his face melted away.

Free of those distractions, his mind turned inward.

Where was I? Oh yes, 6-space...

The elegant topology of this realm allowed his 5-dimensional magnetic force fields to disappear and "magically" reappear elsewhere in 5-space.

Matt continued riding this multi-dimensional train: *what 6-dimensional object would produce these shapes in 5-D?* Even more complex equations and elegant objects swirled in his mind.

Seven dimensions?

He iterated dimensionally upwards; the hyper-dimensional shapes becoming more fantastic at each step. Matt intuitively knew that each dimensional step mapped directly to an aspect of the physical world: electromagnetism, light, sub-atomic particles, and quantum mechanics.

Time was meaningless in Matt's journey through the dimensions, the shapes becoming even more exotic and the equations increasingly complex. His voyage came to an abrupt halt at the eleventh dimension—11-space—as there was no mathematical way to go any further.

There is no further.

Could it be that simple?

Apparently so!

It's all there... everything!

The entire universe...

Then, a disturbance. Something distant. Matt reluctantly pushed the images and equations aside and climbed down through the many dimensions to allow his other senses to return.

Matt felt something poking his shoulder. He shook his head and blinked his eyes until they re-focussed as he crashed back into the three-dimensional world.

A teen-age boy was standing in front of him; three similar-aged boys stood close behind.

"Hey, are you okay? Hey mister, are you okay?"

Matt gave his head another shake. "Uh... uh... yah."

"Figured you were high, or maybe having a stroke," the teenager said.

"No... I'm okay. I was just... just deep in thought."

The teen shrugged, then joined his friends as they headed up the trail.

Matt took a deep breath and looked around. Something was different. The lighting had changed; the sun was now close to the mountains on the west side of the valley. A quick estimate of then-and-now sun angles and basic trig gave the answer. *I was out of it for almost five hours!* Matt shuddered as a chill ran up his spine. He had a blinding headache.

Holy crap! I really zoned out. He shuddered again, reviewing the multi-dimensional images he'd just envisioned. *I gotta write this down!*

Matt reached into his pack and pulled out a pen and brand-new notebook he'd tossed in as an afterthought. He scribbled and scribbled, slowly at first, then more maniacally, frustrated that his hand couldn't put ink to paper as fast as his mind willed it. The sun was about to set, and the fading light made it impossible for him to continue.

It took every ounce of Matt's determination to stand up and get his legs moving. The hike back to his house was a struggle; equations and complex shapes swirled in his head and clamoured for attention, forcing him to concentrate on putting one foot in front of the other and not trip or sprain an ankle. It was dark when he stumbled into the backyard; his mom saw him through the kitchen window and came outside.

"We were getting worried, honey," she said. "Your dad was about to go looking for you."

Matt just stared at his mom.

"Honey, are you okay? You look sort of—"

"I figured it out," he whispered.

"What did you figure out, honey?"

He paused, then gave her an odd look.

"*Everything.*"

Ann shivered at the tone of his voice.

Matt looked around his bedroom—the floor was littered with hundreds of sheets of paper covered with equations, mind-boggling sketches, and notes. The geometry of the 11-space he'd envisioned during his hike was literally mind-boggling. It had taken him days of uninterrupted thinking to lay down a set of consistent, 11-dimensional equations that defined the realm that formed, no, *was,* the foundation of the universe. A foundation that popped into existence at the Big Bang, when time began, and instantly began expanding. And would continue expanding until the end of time.

Matt's complex yet elegant 11-dimensional equations offered a discrete number of solutions in its neighbouring dimension, 10-space, the realm that "defined" gravity, mass, and inertia. In other words, Einstein's general relativity. Other 10-space equations offered solutions in 9-space, where quantum mechanics—wave functions and probability distributions—forced quantities like energy and momentum to be restricted to discrete values and allowed particles to behave as waves and waves as particles.

Ah, there's Dr. F.'s quantum kleptodynamics equations!

Solutions in 8-space hinted at explanations for the strong and weak nuclear forces, and defined quantum wave functions which, in different combinations, were the building blocks for the elementary sub-atomic particles: electrons, fermions, bosons.

In 7-space, there was something similar to light, but was orthogonal to "regular" light, a.k.a. photons. In this dimension, electricity, magnetism, and electromagnetism were the same thing, depending on the reference frame; each fell out as separate phenomena/solutions in 6-space.

Also in 6-space, there were shortcuts that allowed electromagnetic energy to pass through lower dimensions seemingly undetected.

Like the fictional wormhole, but for magnetic force fields.

Maybe for all electromagnetic energy?

Is there an equivalent one for mass?

Other, more well-known phenomena such as magnetic and electric fields, sub-atomic particles, and electromagnetic energy, were, by comparison to those in the higher dimensions, trivial solutions in the relatively simple 5-, 4-, and 3-space.

Another week passed, then two. Matt hardly slept and barely ate as he maniacally scribbled and sketched and solved equations. His mom brought him meals, which he barely touched. Her attempts to get him to take a shower, at least every couple of days, were ignored.

Matt travelled up and down through the dimensions, adjusting his equations until they coalesced. Eventually, he lowered his pen and let out a long sigh as his mind returned to the simplicity of the 3-dimensional world. He shakily got to his feet and shuffled to the bathroom. A stranger stared back in the mirror: pale skin, gaunt, baggy eyes, greasy brown hair.

He showered, put on clean clothes, and headed downstairs. His mom had heard him moving around and prepared a proper meal.

"Are you back in the real world now, honey?"

Matt simply nodded. He proceeded to devour her home cooking, comforted to know his mother accepted without question his behavior, what Renny referred to as "going on a physics tear."

Many thoughts ran through his head as he came to terms with what he'd just accomplished.

It's all there. Everything. Because the universe, at its most basic level, is an eleven-dimensional expanding fabric of, well, universe-stuff! I think I just solved the biggest puzzle there is: The Universe.

Does that make me "God"?

Matt was mentally exhausted from those weeks of intense thinking and occupied himself with activities requiring very little brainpower. He helped with chores around the house, watched hours of mindless television shows, and wandered through the family orchard, picking fruit as the summer harvest progressed: cherries, apricots, peaches, apples.

Apples. Huh.

Newton had an apple tree for inspiration.

I got a spillway in a murky reservoir.

With his friends scattered around the globe, Matt felt... lost. He wanted to talk to them and explain what he'd just accomplished. He was coming to terms with the staggering implications of his "11-space expanding universe" theory. But he also knew that a scientific theory was just that, a theory, unless it was *testable*. And, in physics, "testable" meant it had to do two things: explain known facts; and make falsifiable predictions about phenomena not yet observed.

How does one test a Theory of Everything?

Matt was already convinced his theory met the first criteria. Solutions to the equation sets from 10-space down to 3-space described known phenomena, from gravity to quantum mechanics to particle physics to electromagnetism. For the second criteria—making falsifiable predictions—Matt penned an appendix to his work with a few predictions. He started with 10-space.

Conventional wisdom (and Einstein's theory of general relativity) said that gravity was a deformation of space-time, a point source originating at an object's centre of mass. Matt's theory stated that all matter (including the Earth) expanded at a rate proportional to its mass, so gravity was not a point source. A well-known thought experiment came to mind: imagine a hole drilled through the centre of the earth, from the surface on one side to the surface on the other. Conventional gravitational theory said that if a rock was dropped down the hole, it would accelerate at a constant 9.8 m/s² to the centre of the Earth, then decelerate as it continued "up" on the other side, stopping just when it reached the surface. Matt's theory predicted that the acceleration should drop off linearly as the rock got closer to the centre of the Earth. It would still arrive at the surface on the other side of the earth, but just take longer. *Not a feasible experiment, but still...*

Two of Matt's 9-space solutions included quantum wave functions not yet theorized. These functions corresponded to a low-energy neutrino originating in 8-space, and an energetic but short-lived meson coming from 7-space. He deduced that the latter's signature (what he called the H-meson) should be buried in the massive data dumps already collected at high-energy particle colliders like CERN and Fermilab. *If one knows what to look for.*

8-space offered a solution allowing for matter to be made, not of atoms, but of free quarks—elementary particles and a fundamental constituent of matter. But the temperature and pressure required to produce "quark matter" could only be found at the centre of a neutron star. *Not exactly testable!*

7-space predicted a form of light orthogonal to existing light—if one knew where and how to look for it.

One of the 6-space solutions predicted magnetostatic wormholes—transferring magnetic energy along an undetectable path. That was likely a special case of a more general solution set: wormholes able to pass any form of electromagnetic energy.

Now convinced his theory was more than just hyper-dimensional nonsense, he took his original notebook to the town's lone stationery store and made two sets of photocopies; he buried one set in a Tupperware container in the back yard, gave the notebook to his parents to store in their safety-deposit box, and took the other set with him when he returned to Caltech in time for the fall term.

Good thing Dr. F. arranged for me to keep my lab until Christmas. Got some tinkering to do.

◎

Matt truly enjoyed teaching at Caltech, watching for that look of enlightenment when a student suddenly understood a new concept. He approached teaching as a problem, a puzzle to be solved: *how to get the information from my brain into theirs?* He received positive feedback from his students, likely because of his casual demeanour and outside-the-box thinking, traits honed from working with Dr. Feinberg.

No longer a doctoral candidate but "just a teaching assistant," Matt had dropped several rungs on the academic ladder. Most of his former doctoral colleagues treated him the same as before, but Charles Winston and his followers were still trying to make his life miserable.

"Oh, how the mighty have fallen," Winston muttered whenever within hearing distance.

Matt always replied with an appropriate insult (in Latin), that flew right over Winston's head.

"Foetorem extremae latrinae." *You are the stench of a low-life latrine.* Or, "Odiosus mihis." *You're just a foul smell, as far as I'm concerned.* And so on...

But Matt had a higher priority: Dr. Feinberg had arranged for Matt to keep his research lab, and he was putting it to good use.

◎

Nabil Doshi, Caltech doctoral candidate, turned off his equipment for the night, frustrated with the neutrino detector he was banking his PhD hopes on. His work was based on a theory proposed in 1974 by physicist Daniel Freedman, who postulated that low-energy neutrinos, which had an annoying habit of not interacting with almost every form of matter, *should* interact with an entire atomic nucleus. Nabil's "Coherent Recoil Detector" was a compact device that would, in theory, detect an increase in the neutron count of the nuclei in a dense crystal lattice whenever a low-energy neutrino "wandered into the room" and gave it a subtle "kick."

Nabil spent months wringing the bugs out of his detector, finding more electrical noise problems than he'd ever thought possible. But the last time he did a five-day data collection run, his detector reported three low-energy neutrino bursts several orders of magnitude stronger than expected from cosmic background levels.

There's either a supernova in the solar system, a fusion reactor in the neighbourhood, or I've discovered a new type of neutrino. Or I've still got electrical problems. Occam's Razor says it's the latter.

He sighed, flipped off the lights and locked the door behind him. As he walked along the dusty basement corridor towards the staircase, light filtered through the frosted window of the adjacent lab's door.

I wonder what Matt's up to? He's not "officially" doing research anymore... maybe he's working on something for Dr. Feinberg?

Matt and Nabil had started in the Caltech graduate program together; initially Matt had moved ahead faster until his academic career suffered an ignominious end earlier that year. They were not exactly friends, just fellow researchers who often collaborated, acting as a sounding board and loaning each other equipment when needed. On one occasion, Matt had used one of his n-dimensional mathematical tools to help Nabil solve a maddeningly complex set of partial differential equations. In return, Nabil had shown Matt how to improve an electrical design he'd been struggling with.

Nabil considered knocking on Matt's lab door, but Caltech had an unwritten rule: *you never, ever bother another researcher in their lab.* Nabil curbed his curiosity even after hearing a muffled shout from Matt's lab.

"Holy shit!" Then, a few seconds later, "Woo-hoo!"

◎

Nabil looked up from the circuit diagram laying over his tray of half-eaten food in the student cafeteria.

"Hey, Nabil, mind if I join you?" Matt Barnes was standing there, holding a tray.

Nabil nodded.

Matt sat down across from him and dug into his meal. Nabil was staring back and forth between the circuit diagram and a long piece of graph paper. He sighed.

"Still having noise problems?" Matt said.

Nabil nodded. "I'm getting neutrino bursts I can't account for. Just when I think I've got the detector tuned, I let it run for a week to measure the background flux, and I get these seemingly random events. It *has* to be electrical noise, but I can't figure out where it's coming from."

"May I?" Matt said, motioning at the graph paper.

"Sure." Nabil turned the plot around and slid it across the table. "I had another spike last night. I think you were working then, weren't you?"

"Umm... yah. Just tinkering," Matt said.

"No worries," Nabil said, "unless your electromagnets are producing neutrinos. Now *that* would be interesting."

Matt stared at the plot. "What's the y-axis units here—keV?"

"No, electron-volts. I'm looking for low-energy neutrinos."

Matt traced his finger along the x-axis (time), mumbling to himself for nearly a minute.

"Uh, Nabil? I think your detector is working properly."

Nabil stared at Matt. "How could you know that? It reports a 1.05eV spike that lasts 900 milliseconds. If that's real, it could only come from a nearby fusion reactor with a short time constant or an otherwise undetectable supernova in the solar system. Both are, well, highly unlikely, but there's no other known source of that type of neutrino flux. It *has* to be an electrical noise problem."

Matt paused; he was choosing his next words carefully. "You and I have had a good working relationship here, even with the political bullshit going on. I trust you'll keep what I'm about to say between us?"

Nabil nodded. "Absolutely." *What does he know?*

Matt looked around to make sure no one was listening. "Okay. Let's say I've got something in my lab that might produce such a neutrino burst," he said, pointing at the peaks on the graph.

Nabil shook his head vigorously. "You are, or were, working on high-strength superconducting electromagnets. There's no way that could generate neutrinos!"

Matt blushed.

"I *was* working on electromagnets—but that's ancient history. Now I'm tinkering with... something else. It just occurred to me that one of its side effects may be a burst of low-energy neutrinos. I'd have to run the numbers, but 1.05eV sounds right, and your time plot correlates with the times my... er... project was running."

"Are you sure?" Nabil whispered.

"Ninety-nine percent sure. Let's do a test to confirm. How long do you need to capture baseline data?"

"Five days."

"Okay, I won't touch my... experiment until next week. Then we'll do a controlled test—I'll power up my gear and you can see if you detect it."

"Sounds good." Nabil was relieved that his noise problem might not be a problem after all.

Matt was true to his word. After a five-day data collection run, Nabil's noise problem failed to reappear. Then, one night, at an agreed-upon time, Matt fired up his "secret" experiment next door; the pen on Nabil's chart plotter peaked, dropping off a fraction of a second later. Matt wouldn't divulge what he was doing, but clearly Nabil's detector was working.

◎

December 21, 1983

Matt walked out of the physics building to a waiting taxi, carrying the cliché cardboard box with his few belongings. His last few days at Caltech had been draining; on the morning of his penultimate day, he discovered that someone had cleaned out his lab, including the "other experiment" he'd been tinkering with. He made the rounds, saying his goodbyes, including a long one with Dr. Feinberg.

"Thanks for everything you've done for me," Matt said.

"The pleasure's been all mine, son. Sorry things worked out the way they did. I'm not giving up on getting Professor Clarke sacked. He done you wrong. I've filed an official complaint against him for academic misconduct. Apparently, he's the one who ordered your lab emptied—I heard through the grapevine he's looking to restart your work."

Matt sighed. "Figures."

Feinberg shook his head. "But that's not going to happen. The Feinberg Publishing Company—that's me, by the way—took the liberty of mailing a copy of your thesis, I mean your 'unpublished manuscript,' to everyone in the physics community I know. And that's a lot of people! Clarke will *not* get credit for any of your work, so help me me. No matter how long it takes."

Matt nodded his thanks.

"So," Feinberg said, "what are your plans now?"

Matt shrugged. "I think it's time for a vacation. Maybe I'll see if there's any research opportunities in Europe."

Feinberg nodded. "I've got contacts all over the continent. Hell, all over the world. Say the word and I'll make some calls."

Matt reached out his hand. "Thanks for everything you've done for me, sir. I couldn't have asked for a better mentor." He turned to leave.

"Oh, one more thing," Feinberg said, winking. "I mailed you a Christmas present. It should be waiting for you when you get home."

◎

Matt flew home to Penticton to spend the holidays with his family. It was great to be around friendly faces, but still depressing as none of his friends could make it home. Dr. F.'s "Christmas present" was waiting for him at the Greyhound bus depot: a wooden crate two feet on each side and weighing nearly one hundred pounds. Matt and his dad wrestled it into the trunk of the family car. When they got home, they put it in the garage.

Matt attacked the wooden lid with a crowbar, prying it back. There was a handwritten note on top of the contents, which were buried in bubble wrap and Styrofoam peanuts.

```
Matt:

I don't know what this is, but I think it's best you have
it.

Warmest Regards,
Dr. F.

P.S. I told our shipping agent it was "miscellaneous test
equipment. Value: $10" ha ha ha

P.P.S. Can't wait for you to explain what this is.
```

"What the heck is this?" his dad said, pulling away the bubble wrap and exposing a pair of aluminum rings bolted together and decorated with coils of wire.

My experiment!

Matt smiled. "Just a going away present from Dr. F. It's a little something I was working on in my last months at Caltech."

◎

New Year's Day, 1984

Matt packed a few personal items and clothes in his backpack and caught a flight to Vancouver International Airport. He followed the crowds from the domestic arrivals terminal to international departures, stopping to scan the large electronic board showing outgoing flights. It took him only a few minutes to decide; he approached the nearest Air Canada ticket counter.

"One-way ticket to Rome, Italy, please. First class." He handed over his Canadian passport and gold Visa credit card.

I have a bank account with nearly ten million US dollars. I can afford it!

Matt spent the next four months travelling through Europe, sometimes staying in youth hostels, other times in five-star hotels. He saw the tourist sights and visited academic institutions and physics-centric research facilities. He'd started in Italy, at the Dipartimento di Fisica at the University of Rome. Then on to Switzerland and the Grenoble Institute of Technology. Next was ETH Zurich, where Einstein did some of his ground-breaking work. Then CERN—the largest particle physics lab in the world, straddling the French/Swiss border. Under the border, technically. Next stop, Germany. Then France. A dozen universities and research labs in total. Matt was welcomed at every facility, in part because of his Fields Medal and two master's degrees, and part because of his failed doctoral thesis that Dr. Feinberg had circulated. Matt was treated as a VIP and invited to give impromptu lectures in electromagnetism or advanced mathematics. Everyone knew what had happened to Matt (at least the broad strokes); several institutions offered senior lecturing positions or immediate entry into their doctoral programs. But that was as far as the offers went, the apologetic remarks variations on the same theme:

"Sorry, that's the best we can do. If you had a PhD, we'd hire you on the spot."

As Matt worked his way across Europe, he weighed the pros and cons of his meagre offers. But there were way more cons than pros. He wrapped up his quest across the English Channel, first visiting the University of Oxford, then ending up at the University of Cambridge.

◎

Matt sat on a wooden bench on the edge of the Cambridge Lawn Tennis Club's grass courts, munching on a Cornish pasty and sipping a can of Diet

Coke. *They call it fizzy pop here.* The grey, overcast skies somehow enhanced the mystical aura of the centuries-old, ivy-covered stone buildings.

The University of Cambridge—the birthplace of modern physics! All the giants of physics—Maxwell, Stokes, Rutherford, Rayleigh, Thomson, Wilson, Chadwick, Bragg—walked these grounds and corridors.

Matt had spent the last two hours getting a VIP tour of "The Cavendish"—the famed Cavendish Laboratory run by Cambridge's department of physics. Dr. Edward Samuelson, the current Head of the Department and the lab's director, walked him through the facilities, then convinced him to give an impromptu lecture on his hyperspatial model and how it allowed him to create his ultra-high-powered electromagnets.

"I hear through the grapevine you've been checking out the big players on the Continent," Samuelson said. "Everyone here has read your doctoral thesis; Feinberg sent it to me and I circulated amongst the faculty. Fascinating stuff. I called him and he explained what happened at your dissertation defence. What Professor Clarke did to you was unconscionable. If you ever decide to go for a doctorate again, we'd be happy to accommodate you here. I'm sure we could fast-track you through in a year or so."

"Thanks for the offer, but that ship has sailed."

Samuelson nodded. "While your academic reputation is impressive, as much as I'd like to have you on our faculty, we can only hire post-docs. The only position open right now is for a part-time lecturer—not a position befitting someone with your CV."

"No problem, sir," Matt said. "Thanks for taking the time to show me around."

Matt finished his lunch and tilted his head back, absorbing the vibe of the campus. *Yes, this is where I want to be. Aw, what the hell...*

He tossed his garbage into a nearby garbage can—correction, dustbin—and headed back to the Cavendish. He ran into Dr. Samuelson, who was leaving the building.

"Mr. Barnes, fancy meeting you again! Did you forget something?"

"No. Sir, that lecturer position—can I apply for it?"

Samuelson's eyebrows shot up. "As I mentioned, that position is beneath someone with two master's degrees *and* a Fields Medal. It's not even full time, just two classes: a second-year electromagnetism course, and an introductory physics course. The salary isn't great, either, only ten thousand pounds for the year. Why would you want that?"

Matt shrugged. "Well, sir, that's hard to say. I enjoy teaching, and I get a fantastic vibe off this campus. I've decided this is where I want to be right now. And money isn't a concern."

Samuelson paused, then nodded. "Okay, you're hired."

"Thank you, sir. I appreciate it. Oh, one other thing. Are Lecturers here allowed to publish? I've been toying with some ideas on the theoretical side that I might want to write up."

"Well, Mr. Barnes, I'm pretty sure that no lecturer here has *ever* published, but there aren't any rules preventing it. Of course, it has to pass our peer review process."

Matt nodded. "Of course, sir. Good to know."

By the end of the day, Samuelson's administrative assistant had prepared the paperwork for an international work visa for one Matthew Barnes (B.A.Sc., M.Sc. M.Sc.) as an Unaffiliated Lecturer in the Physics Department.

Matt flew home to pick up his few belongings. Two weeks later he was back in Cambridge, living in a small, two-bedroom rental apartment—called a 'flat'—on the north end of Cambridge and overlooking the River Cam.

The Cambridge academic year didn't start until October 1st, which gave Matt several months of free time. If one had followed Matt around, they would have seen him lead an odd and solitary life. He spent his first month driving around the town's outskirts in a faded green 1973 Vauxhall he'd purchased, visiting abandoned industrial sites. He spent the rest of his time doing business with local machine shops and industrial supply stores, ordering parts and equipment.

When the Cambridge fall term, known as "Michaelmas," began, Matt started in on his new role as Lecturer in the Department of Applied Mathematics and Theoretical Physics. That role placed him near the bottom of the department's academic food chain, so he was assigned a windowless, stuffy office in the basement of the department's Old Press Site building. As he was "only a Lecturer," even grad students and newly minted post-docs looked down on him. Even his two master's degrees and a Fields Medal weren't enough to get him access to the faculty lounge, unless invited. But Matt cared little for the trappings of power or prestige.

Tuesday and Thursday mornings he taught a second-year course on Electromagnetism, a subject he was overqualified for. Those same afternoons was "Introductory Physics," an entry-level course for students from outside the department who needed a basic understanding of physics—a prerequisite for higher-level science courses. This course was much-debated amongst the professors in the physics department, with those less-progressive referring to it as "Physics for Dummies." Matt didn't mind; he found the perspectives of the scientifically uninformed students quite refreshing.

Introductory Physics had one unique student: the young man listed in the class roll as "Edward W." turned out to be His Royal Highness Prince Edward, Duke of Cambridge, elder son of the Prince and Princess of Wales and grandson of Her Royal Majesty Queen Elizabeth II. Second in the line of succession for the throne of England. The Prince was majoring in geography, but had a keen interest in astronomy and Matt's course was a prerequisite. Not only did Matt have to contend with many of his students being more interested in royalty than physics (especially the young women), he also had to deal with the presence of a small security detail that accompanied the Prince everywhere. Prior to the semester start, Matt had to endure a tedious security briefing from a pair of nameless, humourless agents from MI-6, the British Secret Intelligence Service.

Matt soon fell into a comfortable, if not unusual, routine. On days he wasn't fulfilling his on-campus duties, he drove to an abandoned industrial area northeast of Cambridge town, spending long days there, and sometimes staying overnight. Communications with his family and friends slowed to a trickle, letters becoming less and less frequent. Matt even skipped coming home for Christmas that year, explaining to his parents in a brief letter: "Too busy on a new project. Have a good Christmas. Talk to you in the New Year."

TEN

Five months later...

The Cavendish Lab's courier dropped off the daily bin of letters and packages at the FedEx depot in downtown Cambridge. Buried in that pile were three prepaid express letter envelopes. When those envelopes arrived at FedEx's London Heathrow sorting facility that night, one was put on the next cargo flight to Egypt, the other two onto a transatlantic flight. The Egypt-bound envelope, after arriving at Cairo International Airport, was transferred to a smaller cargo plane destined for the tourist mecca of Luxor. It sat at Luxor's FedEx depot until picked up by a local worker, who transported it across the Nile by ferry, then to an archeological site in the rocky hills to the west. The other two envelopes arrived in Toronto, Canada, then their paths diverged. One was delivered to a federal government office in nearby Ottawa, the other continued west for several thousand kilometres, then north by floatplane to a geological field camp in a remote corner of northern Canada.

Renny Harris squeezed his burly frame through the mess tent's narrow doorway and waited for his eyes to adjust to the dim light.

"Hey Renny, you got mail!" the camp cook said, pointing at a pile of envelopes and packages on the table. Renny's eyes lit up—mail was a morale booster when working far from civilization.

"Fuck, yah," he said, grinning. He rifled through the stack of mail, found the FedEx mailer addressed to him, tore it open, and pulled out a letter-sized envelope. It had no return address, just the University of Cambridge's logo in the top left corner.

Huh. Must be from Matt. Haven't heard from him in over six months! I wonder what he's been up to?

He opened the envelope and pulled out airline tickets with a note attached by a paper clip.

```
To:   Mr. Josh Allen
      Mr. Renny Harris
      Mr. Gary Stocks

Gentlemen (and I use the term loosely):

Greetings from Cambridge, England! You are cordially
invited to attend a meeting of The Explorers Society of
Canada in Cambridge in June. Attendance is not optional.
Details and travel arrangements are attached.

Matt
```

Excellent! Renny thought. *I was going to take some time off this summer. Wonder what adventure Matt has in store for us...*

"I'm sorry sir," came a voice off to Renny's right as the large oak door silently closed behind him. "This is British Airways executive lounge. It's for first class and business class passengers only."

Renny turned toward the receptionist; her eyes widened.

I don't blame her—I look like I just crawled out of the woods.
Actually, I did.

His journey had started twelve long hours ago. A pre-dawn floatplane took him from his survey camp in northern Canada to Yellowknife, Northwest Territories. Then a Twin Otter south to Edmonton, Alberta, where a Boeing 737 brought him to his current location: Toronto's Pearson International Airport. He was still wearing his "camp clothes," his possessions stuffed into his large backpack.

His smiling at the receptionist didn't help; Renny had yet to realize that, given his normal appearance and demeanour, smiling at strangers more often than not elicited a fight-or-flight response. As it did from some wildlife.

"Umm, the ticket agent told me to come here after I got through security," he rumbled, handing over his boarding pass. "Am I in the wrong place?" She carefully took it from his massive, hairy hand, then scrutinized it.

"Ah, yes! My apologies, Mr. Harris! Welcome to British Airways," she said, checking his name off a list. "Your flight to London Heathrow leaves in two hours—I'll notify you when it's ready for boarding. Please enjoy your stay here."

"Thanks," he said, his knees weakening at her seductive British accent and hint of expensive perfume.

I've been away from civilization for too long!

Renny proceeded into the lounge. Floor-to-ceiling windows offered a panoramic view of one of Pearson's several runways. He felt out of place amongst the well-dressed travellers sitting in black leather sofas and chairs, sipping drinks and conversing in quiet, business-like tones. He'd spent most of the past year living at remote field camps where "normal" things such as manners, behaviour, appearance, and hygiene were, well, optional. The aroma of food caused his stomach to remind him how long it had been since he'd had a decent meal; he spotted a long buffet table with a self-serve bar in the centre of the lounge.

Bet I can make a big dent in that!

He dropped his pack into an unoccupied seat and headed towards the buffet, then heard a loud and familiar voice coming from the far side of the lounge.

"So the bartender says, 'The Klingon can stay, but the Vulcan in the gorilla costume has to go!'"

Renny grabbed his pack and wove his way through the labyrinth of chairs, his appearance alarming several travellers. The other two members of the Explorers Society of Canada were seated at a marble coffee table in the corner; Josh was trying unsuccessfully to corral several empty beer bottles that were rolling across the table. Gary spotted him first.

"Hey, look everyone!" he said, raucously. "It's Bigfoot! Get over here and sit down before someone calls a game warden!" Since Josh didn't drink alcohol, clearly it was Gary who'd consumed the contents of those errant bottles. His friends rose to greet him. Josh had his usual "deer in the headlights" worried look, aware that other travellers were now staring at the trio. Renny smiled and shook his hand.

Josh sniffed the air. "Geez, Renny, you smell like you just crawled out of the woods." He made a show of wiping his hand on his shirt.

"Actually, I did just come out of the woods," Renny deadpanned. He poked Josh's ample stomach with a large finger. "And I see you're not getting any exercise. Still flying a desk?"

Josh blushed. "Well, since you brought—"

"I've seen more intelligent-looking grizzly bears," Gary said, offering his hand. He had a good buzz on.

Renny shook Gary's hand, then held on and effortlessly raised his massive arm until Gary's feet were six inches off the carpeted floor.

"And I've had meals bigger than you," Renny growled, slowly turning his friend and examining him the way a bear might inspect a fresh kill. Being friends since elementary school meant Gary was one of the few people in the world who could twist Renny's tail and survive unscathed.

"Guys, we're making a scene," Josh said, glancing nervously at the other lounge visitors.

Gary sniffed the air and made a face. "You do know, Grizzly Adams, they have bathrooms here? Toilets, running water, soap, all the modern conveniences..."

"Yah, I guess I should go clean up."

"Yah, you should," Gary said, his feet still dangling in the air. "And put me down—you're frightening the locals."

Renny noticed several travellers were staring at him. He let out another growl, then slowly lowered Gary. "I'll be baaack," he said in his best Schwarzenegger.

"Bring more beers," Gary yelled at him.

Renny nodded. "Eh."

Twenty minutes later he returned, showered, clean shaven, and wearing clean clothes. He had four bottles of beer in one massive hand, the other balancing an enormous plate of food.

"Talk about luxury!" he gushed, the leather chair groaning as he lowered his gigantic frame into it. "They even have showers here!"

"Leave it to Matt to have the Explorers Society travel in style," Josh said, raising his glass of diet Coke in a toast.

"Speaking of Matt," Renny said as he dug into his food, "do either of you know what he's up to? I haven't heard from him since before Christmas, then, out of the blue, I get a letter and plane tickets."

"Same here," Gary said. "Since he left Caltech, he's gone off-grid."

They both stared at Josh; he had the world's worst poker face and could not lie if his life depended on it.

"*You* know something," Renny stated.

Josh nodded reluctantly. "Well, I *have* been in touch with him."

"C'mon, spill it," Gary said.

"You know he got a part-time job lecturing in the physics department at Cambridge?"

Both friends nodded.

"Well, I get letters from him once a month or so—just technical questions."

"Like what?" Renny said.

Josh shrugged. "Really weird stuff. Once it was a question about how to find the numerical solution for a complicated fourth-order differential equation. Another time, it was a bunch of questions about computer networking. Then I got three pages of questions on low-level Unix programming. Stuff like that."

"You'd think there'd be people at the university who could help him," Renny said. He paused. "The Professor's up to something."

They all contemplated that for a moment before Gary spoke.

"He's *building* something." Even half-drunk, Gary was still perceptive. Renny and Josh nodded in agreement.

"Well, we can speculate 'till the cows come home," Josh said, "but I imagine we'll find out when we get to London, huh?"

"So, runt, what have you been up to?" Renny asked Gary. "Last Christmas you said you and your anthropologist girlfriend were going to

Central America to play with that little robot you built... what do you call it?"

"TombCrawler," Gary said proudly. He'd built a small, eight-legged crawling robot that could change shape and navigate narrow passages, and even climb walls. A small video camera with pan-and-tilt capabilities fed its image back to a control console over a thin umbilical cable. "And Nadia's an archeologist, not an anthropologist. Her doctoral thesis is that there was actual contact between the Mayans and Egyptians. We used the TombCrawler to explore a couple of unopened Mayan burial chambers in southern Belize—that was back in January. We found the evidence she was looking for, or at least clues leading in that direction. For the past three months, she's been working a dig in the Valley of the Kings outside Luxor."

Gary's eyes lit up as he continued the story. "I had TombCrawler over one hundred metres along a previously buried tunnel in an early-dynasty Egyptian tomb. Frescoes on the walls made it easy to date and revealed Mayan influences. We showed the video and photos to officials from the Egyptian Ministry of Tourism and Antiquities, and they've agreed to issue an excavation permit. Her thesis will re-write the history books!"

"That's way cool," Josh said.

"Wow," Renny added.

"She's still got a couple of months of field work to do. I came back to Toronto last month to check on our apartment. I go back to Luxor in two weeks."

Renny turned to Josh. "So, what's up with you? Still figuring out how to predict the weather?"

Josh shrugged and his face turned red. "How's your field work going?" he said, changing the subject.

Renny took the hint. "We're doing a multi-year, large-scale, geological and lithographic survey of the region north of Great Slave Lake. It's kind-of interesting, but I'm having more fun hunting for meteorites in my spare time. I've found four this year, including one I'm pretty sure came from Mars. Here, look." Renny extracted a small canvas bag from his backpack and dumped its contents onto the marble table.

"Every rock tells a story."

The trio spent the next hour theorizing about why Matt had organized this trip. Then a gentle hand touched Renny's shoulder; it was the British Airways receptionist.

"Gentlemen, your flight is ready to board now," she said. "Gate B-14."

Renny watched her walk away and sighed. *I think I'm in love...*

The trio headed to their gate. They were assigned, not coincidentally, three seats side-by-side in the upstairs, first-class cabin of the Boeing 747 taking them to London.

After their plane reached cruising altitude, they settled in for the seven-hour flight. Renny produced a dog-eared novel from an inside pocket of his jacket, Josh tilted his seat back and pulled a sleep mask down over his eyes, and Gary pulled a magazine from his backpack.

"You still reading that crap?" Renny said, referring to the Paranormal Monthly magazine Gary was reading. Renny thought all that stuff about aliens, Bigfoot, and the Loch Ness monster was just a waste of time, and he took every opportunity to rib Gary about it.

Gary nodded, happily taking the bait. "Actually, the latest issue's got a really interesting story. For the past three months, there've been reports of unexplained radio signals coming from high altitude and out towards the moon. The scientists at SETI have tracked some of those signals."

Renny smirked. "Yah, and I'll bet they'll find that Bigfoot is behind it. Or the Loch Ness Monster, maybe."

"No," Gary said, "this is for real! Several non-government ground stations have tracked the signals. The sources aren't even in orbit—they're almost stationary. And they don't appear to be natural."

Renny snorted.

Josh pulled his mask up onto his forehead. "I was talking to my dad last week. His observatory provided some of the interferometric measurements for a couple of those signals. He said they're real, and they have an unusual polarization."

"Aliens, man. Aliens," Gary said.

"Bullshit," Renny said, returning to his novel.

◎

London Heathrow Airport

After clearing British customs and retrieving their luggage, the trio passed through frosted glass doors into the international arrivals hall, where a large crowd waited for arriving passengers.

"Matt's letter didn't mention anything about anyone picking us up, did it?" Josh asked, scanning the many signs held up by limousine drivers and tour operators.

"Nope," Gary said.

Renny pointed to the back of the crowd. "Uh, I think that's for us." A pair of arms held up a white flag sporting a red maple leaf, a mountain range and a grinning green sea serpent cavorting in the waves—the official logo of the Explorers Society of Canada.

"Follow me, ladies," he said, using his bulk to bulldoze a path through the crowd; his friends followed closely in his wake. Once Renny got through the mass of people, he saw who was holding the flag.

"Professorrr!" Renny roared.

"Renny!"

Renny wrapped his enormous arms around his best friend and picked him up in a bone-cracking bear hug before depositing him back on his feet.

"Jeez, Renny!" Matt exclaimed, holding his ribs. "Have you been wrestling bears or something?"

"Well, last month, there was this grizzly that kept hanging around the camp, so rather than shoot it, the camp supervisor sent me out to—"

"I don't think I want to know," Matt said, wincing. Gary and Josh were more restrained, each slapping Matt on the back and shaking his hand.

Renny took a step back and got a good look at his best friend. Matt's skin was pasty white, his hair greasy. He had dark bags under his eyes, and his clothing looked like he'd slept in them for several weeks.

"Professor, it's my professional opinion that you look like shit." Gary and Josh nodded in agreement.

Matt shrugged. "Guys, I've been busy the past couple of months preparing for your visit. Really busy. Come on, I've got a cab waiting."

Matt led his friends outside to the taxi queue; he waved to a driver leaning on his taxi's bonnet and reading a tabloid newspaper. They piled into the taxi while the driver loaded their luggage into the taxi's boot.

"Off to King's Cross, Guv'na?" the driver said.

Matt nodded. They pulled away from the curb and were soon on the M4, heading east to London.

"So, Matt, what's the scoop?" Gary said.

"Yah, what are you up to?" Josh added.

Matt shook his head. "Not here. Let's just enjoy the ride. I'll tell you everything once we get to Cambridge. Damn, I'm glad to see you guys." He grinned.

Renny found the first few minutes of the drive terrifying, as his brain could not accept the fact they were travelling more than one hundred kilometers per hour on the wrong side of the highway. An hour later, they arrived at King's Cross Station in the heart of downtown London.

"I've already got our tickets," Matt said, paying their driver then leading them inside the station. After only a brief wait, they boarded their train, the porter showing them to a comfortable and private first-class cabin.

"Matt, we can't take the suspense any longer. What *are* you up to?" Gary pleaded.

"I've been working on something. Something big. Something *amazing*. But it's easier to show you than tell you."

"Then tell us about what you're doing at the university," Josh said.

Matt shrugged. "It's a lecturer position—nothing fancy—just part-time, teaching a couple of first and second-year courses. But the introductory physics course I taught last term? One of my students was Prince Edward, the Duke of Cambridge."

"Wow, he's second in line to the throne, isn't he?" Josh said.

Matt nodded. "And a pretty bright student. He's doing a degree in geography but is interested in astronomy and my course was a prerequisite. A security team accompanies him everywhere on campus. I had to go through a background check and endure two lengthy security briefings. They even gave me a code phrase to use in case of trouble."

"Cool," Gary said.

"A part-time lecturer?" Renny said. "That seems beneath you..."

Matt shrugged. "It's more than I need to live. Besides, I'm rather busy with my other... er, work." Attempts to extract further details from Matt were fruitless, so they spent the rest of the train ride enjoying the passing scenery.

After disembarking at the Cambridge train station, Matt hailed another taxi.

"We'll drop off the luggage at your hotel, then head to my, er, lab. I'll explain everything there."

"My body isn't sure what time of day it is," Gary grumbled.

After a brief stop at the Regent Hotel, they headed northeast, the taxi following a little-used road to a deserted industrial complex covering several square kilometres. The area had seen better days, with most of the buildings run down or falling apart.

They pulled up in front of a dingy old factory building. Matt paid the taxi driver, confirmed he'd return to pick them up in three hours, then led his friends to the building's rusty front door.

He bowed. "Gentlemen, welcome to AdAstra Enterprises. Matt Barnes, Owner and President, at your service." He unlocked the door, then quickly went inside and over to the now-beeping panel of a very modern security system. He entered a long code to silence it.

"This is *your* company, Matt?" Renny said, looking around at the dingy old building.

"Yup."

"And what does AdAstra Enterprises do?" Gary said.

"You'll soon see," Matt said with a grin.

"AdAstra—wait, I know that phrase," Josh said. "It's... Latin. Isn't it part of NASA's motto? *Ad Astra per Aspera*—A rough road leads to the stars."

"Close," Matt said. "Hollywood claims it belongs to NASA, but that's an urban myth. It actually comes from the Royal Air Force's motto: '*Per Ardua Ad Astra*—through struggle to the stars.'"

"Your company name means 'To the stars'?" Renny said.

Matt nodded and grinned. He locked the door behind them, then led them further inside, turning on lights along the way. They passed through a dusty, unused reception area, through another locked door and down a long hallway. Renny poked his head into each doorway. Kitchen. Bathroom. A small room with a cot. All recently used.

"Matt, do you *live* here?" Renny asked.

"Uh, sometimes, yah." Seeing the questioning look on his friends' faces, he elaborated.

"I do have a flat in town, but it's easier to stay here when I'm doing my, uh, experiments."

"What kind of experiments?" Josh said.

Matt grinned. *"Now* I'll explain everything."

ELEVEN

Matt led his friends into another room with a large, oval table surrounded by comfortable but dusty office chairs. Blackboards covered the walls, all filled with complex mathematical equations, graphs, and strange geometric sketches. In the middle of the table, there was something the size of a basketball covered by a large cloth.

"Have a seat, guys. I'll explain what I've been up to the past year." He paused, not sure where to start.

"Hang on," Renny said, "I'm starving. Mind if I raid your kitchen?"

"Knock yourself out, Batman."

"Anyone else want something?" Renny said. Gary and Josh shook their heads.

Renny returned a minute later with several bags of potato chips, half a loaf of bread, and a bottle of orange juice.

"Your pickings are slim, Professor. Not sure about this bread, either," he added, picking off a few bits of mould.

Matt shrugged, then looked around the table. "Okay, you know that since I was a kid, I've been interested in magnets, right?"

"Interested?" Renny snorted. "More like obsessed." Gary and Josh chuckled.

"Ever since mom stuck my first kindergarten artwork on the fridge, I wanted to know how magnets work. In school, I read every science book I could get my hands on—they all talked about 'magnetic lines of force' and so on, but there was no explanation of how magnets *actually* worked. I couldn't figure out where the energy comes from to hold a magnet to the fridge. The best I could find were pathetic explanations like, 'there's no energy required because there's no work being done,' or, 'it's potential energy stored in the magnet.' I couldn't accept those answers. It was a puzzle I had to solve: what's the physical mechanism that produces magnetic force?

"By the time I was half-way through my second year at UBC, I'd read every physics, math, and engineering textbook that touched on magnetism: Maxwell's Equations, the Biot-Savart Law, Laplace and Lorentz forces, Faraday's Law, even relativistic electromagnetism. By the end of my third year, I'd read *every* technical paper in *every* physics journal *ever* published that even remotely touched on magnetism. There's plenty of fascinating and elegant mathematical models and theories that describe how magnetic forces act, but none explained how magnets really worked. I got the feeling this was one of those 'dirty little secrets' in physics—no one knows the answer, but everyone's too embarrassed to admit it.

"Renny, remember when we flew home for Christmas in our second year at UBC?"

Renny shrugged, his mouth full. "Vaguely. By the way, these chips are stale."

"I think they call them 'crisps' over here," Josh said.

Matt continued. "You had the window seat, and as we took off, you pointed out the condensed airflow over the wing."

"Oh, yah," Renny said, "now I remember. You stared out the window for a while, mumbled a bunch of math shit, then zoned out for the rest of the flight, scribbling in your notebook."

Matt nodded. "Seeing that got me thinking about how airflow over the wing's surface resulted in a force vector—lift—at right angles to the surface. That's when I made the leap: what if magnetic force is actually an *effect* caused by something happening in a higher dimension?"

Josh raised a hand. "Hang on—the difference in air speeds over the upper and lower surfaces is what generates lift. The lift vector is in a plane corresponding to the wing's cross-section."

Matt nodded—Josh rarely missed a thing. "You're right, of course. But it's what I *saw* that got me thinking. From *my* reference frame, the air was flowing over the two-dimensional top wing surface, but the lift vector was rising perpendicularly out of that surface, into the third dimension.

"That concept of reference frames and multiple dimensions got me thinking. Einstein's 1905 paper on relativity showed that magnetic and electric fields were, when viewed from different reference frames, the same thing. Then, in his 1915 paper, 'The Field Equations of Gravitation,' he simplified gravity in our three-dimensional world by adding a fourth dimension: time. Four years later, the German mathematician Theodor Kaluza unified Einstein's space-time with Maxwell's equations for electromagnetism by adding a *fifth* dimension.

"To explain magnetic force fields in terms of higher dimensions, I needed something similar—a mathematical framework that described the universe with more than the three geometric dimensions we perceive. To keep it simple, I started with four dimensions."

"Hang on," Gary interjected. "Didn't Einstein say that time was the fourth dimension?"

"Yes and no. In Einstein's space-time construct, time is an *intrinsic property* of three-dimensional space. I'm talking about four *geometric* dimensions. You guys with me so far?"

Matt received cautious nods.

"I used a mathematical tool called 'tensor math' and created a four-dimensional representation of geometric space—I called it my 'Hyperspatial Model.' But those equations didn't provide a solution that resulted in magnetic forces—something was missing. Just like the airplane wing requires air flow to generate lift, my model needed something moving. Some source of energy."

Matt paused. "You all know that the universe is expanding, right?"

"Edwin Hubble proved that," Josh said.

"Exactly. I hypothesized that, if our three-dimensional universe is expanding in all directions, any higher geometric dimensions that might exist would also be expanding. So I thought, what would a four-dimensional, expanding universe look like? Mathematically speaking, I mean. I took a four-dimensional version of the Navier-Stokes equations—

that's a set of differential equations that describe the motion of viscous fluids—and added them to my hyperspatial model, then added a four-dimensional factor for the expansion rate that Hubble calculated."

Gary put up his hand to stop Matt. "So, let me get this straight—you're saying that our universe consists of a four-dimensional, expanding fluid? What's this fluid made of?"

"Well, it's not really a fluid, like water. In my hyperspatial model, it's the *fabric* of 4-D space that's expanding in all directions—I just model it as a fluid."

"So, how did that help you figure out how magnets work?" Renny asked.

"At the end of my third year at UBC, when I was scheduling my fourth-year courses with Dr. Oldman, I told him I wanted to do directed studies in magnetism based on my hyperspatial model. It didn't take much convincing. When the head of the Physics department read my proposal, he decided it was better suited to a master's thesis. The math department was already fast-tracking me through their master's program because I'd solved the Poincaré Conjecture, and the physics department didn't want to be left out.

"So, for my thesis, I postulated that when a magnetic field is created, electrons—technically a four-dimensional version of electrons—flow *through* the fourth geometric dimension, not one of our three regular dimensions. The difference between the flow in the fourth dimension and the lack of flow in the lower three dimensions results in a flow differential. And in physics, when you've got a differential, there's energy potential. That differential produces the magnetic force we can perceive and measure in our three-dimensional world!

"The review panel for my thesis defence agreed it was an innovative and unique approach, as it predicted magnetic force using a non-conventional method. But one professor on the panel thought it was more science fiction than science and was reluctant to give his approval. That's when a visiting professor stood up and quizzed me."

"That was Dr. Feinberg, right?" Josh said.

Matt nodded. "He won the Nobel Prize for Physics in 1975 for his theory of Quantum Kleptodynamics. He's quite the mathematician; when he heard through the academic grapevine that the student who solved Poincaré was defending a master's thesis in physics, he flew up from Caltech. After peppering me with questions, he pronounced my thesis 'brilliant.' And when a Nobel laureate says that, *no one* disagrees—at least no one who wants to keep their career—so that holdout professor on the review panel changed his vote.

"Afterwards, Dr. Feinberg—he prefers to be called 'Dr. F.'—took me to lunch. We talked shop, and he invited me to come to Caltech to do a PhD.

"So off I went. I had an inkling that my hyperspatial model could—with additional work and maybe another dimension or two—explain more than just magnetism. But I didn't think Caltech was ready for something that audacious. One of the solutions in my hyperspatial model predicted a way to create electromagnets with much higher field strength than ever before. So I made *that* my thesis."

"Hang on," Gary interjected. "You're saying that your doctoral thesis was camouflage for what you were *really* doing?"

"Uh, well, kind of. Yah, I guess," Matt said, shrugging. His friends chuckled.

"Jesus Christ, Matt," Renny said. "Only *you* could pull that off."

Matt shrugged again. "So, fast forward—I did my research and created a superconducting electromagnet that was an order of magnitude stronger than any in existence. Then I did my thesis defence—that's when things went pear-shaped. I wrote to you guys with the details—basically I got caught in the middle of some nasty intra-departmental politics and got screwed over."

"Yah, so sorry to hear that, Matt," Josh said.

"You must have been pissed," Renny said. "I'd a torn someone a new asshole."

Matt shrugged. "I was at first, then I got over it. I don't need their degree anyways—I only enrolled in the doctoral program so I'd have access to Caltech's research facilities. I'm on to way more interesting things now. Dr. F. arranged a teaching assistant job for me starting in the fall, so I had the summer off and went home. That's when I had my *real* breakthrough."

"Jeez, there's more?" Gary said.

Matt smiled. "We're just getting to the good stuff," he said, relaying the story about his fugue while watching the water flow into the spillway at the Penticton reservoir. His multi-dimensional journey through n-space.

"What I envisioned during those five hours took me another two weeks of almost non-stop work to get down on paper in terms of mathematics and geometry. That was without a doubt the hardest, most complicated and challenging work I've ever done.

"What I came up with was this: the universe consists of eleven geometric dimensions. The first three are the ones we can perceive with our five senses. The remaining eight are, well... weird. As you step up through dimensions four to eleven, the geometry, or scale, gets smaller, and the energies involved get proportionally larger.

"The eleventh dimension, or what I call '11-space,' is the foundation, or base dimension, of the universe. My guess is that when the universe came into existence—you know, the singularity called the 'Big Bang'—it was just one dimension. One extremely hot, dense dimension. It quickly expanded and cooled, and more dimensions came into existence, each with its own features, like gravity, electromagnetic radiation, sub-atomic particles, and so on. Since the eleventh dimension is the foundation of these lower dimensions, whatever happens in 11-space affects them all. And since 11-space is expanding, the lower dimensions are, too."

"Ah," Josh said, "so that's why we see our three-dimensional universe expanding."

Matt nodded. "Because it actually *is* expanding, but it's happening way below the sub-atomic level."

Matt paused. "Now, I won't bore you with details about the other dimensions, but here's the Reader's Digest version. The set of equations I came up with to describe 11-space has a finite set of solutions, all of which are in 10-space. Those, in turn, have solutions in 9-space, and so on, all the way down to 3-space. 10-space is the realm of gravity, mass, and inertia. Physicists have been trying to figure out what gravity is for over a century. Einstein described it as being the curvature and deformation of space-time. Turns out, it's a lot simpler than that."

"So, you're saying Einstein was *wrong*?" Renny said, barely keeping up.

"Not wrong, but only correct in the context of three dimensions plus time. Since 11-space is expanding, inertial and gravitational mass, which is defined in 10-space, is also expanding. All matter, from the smallest sub-atomic particle to planets and suns, expands at a rate proportional to its mass. That's why the chair you're each sitting in stays on the floor—the building underneath the chairs, and the planet underneath that, are expanding at different rates."

"And since we're expanding," Josh said, "we don't feel it, right?"

Matt nodded. "But it would be more correct to say we *can't* feel it.

"Moving downward. The 9-space solutions yield quantum mechanics, wave functions, probability density functions, and so on.

"One of the 8-space solutions describes what's known as *strong interaction*, the force that confines quarks into protons, neutrons, and certain other sub-atomic particles. Another 8-space solution yields *weak interaction* or weak nuclear force—which governs the decay of unstable sub-atomic particles."

"You mean radioactivity?" Gary said.

"Yup. 7-space is the realm of sub-atomic particles like quarks, leptons, and bosons. What's cool about the solutions in this dimension is that it predicts three sub-atomic particles already predicted by other theories but not yet found: the top quark, the Higgs boson, and the tau neutrino. It *also* predicts several other particles not yet theorized: I call them the H-neutrino, the H-meson, and the H-electron. I know, boring names—I'll come up with better ones later.

"In 6-space, we have electricity, magnetism, electromagnetism. Turns out they're the same thing, depending on the reference frame chosen. Just like what Einstein and Kaluza said.

"5-space is what I think is the most interesting of the eleven dimensions. There's a solution there that allows for propagation of electromagnetic energy through lower dimensions along an undetectable path—basically, wormholes, but for electromagnetic energy only. We'll circle back to that in a minute.

"In 4-space, the aforementioned hyper-electron, or H-electron, can move through 3-space and produce magnetic force fields. That was the basis of my master's degree thesis at UBC.

Matt paused. "I wrote up the equations for my 11-space geometry.

That's when I realized that I'd found it."

"Found what?" Renny said.

Matt's voice got quieter, almost reverential. "A coherent theoretical framework that fully explains and links *all* physical aspects of the universe, from the infinitesimally tiny realm described by quantum mechanics to the vast scale of stars, galaxies, and clusters of galaxies explained by Einstein's General Theory of Relativity. You see, up until now, there's been an incompatibility between quantum mechanics and the General Theory of Relativity—their domains are vastly different, both in scale and makeup. My 11-space model links the two, and is consistent with the Standard Model."

"What's that?" Josh said.

"The Standard Model of Particle Physics is an existing theory that describes three of the four known fundamental forces in the universe: electromagnetic force, weak nuclear force, and strong nuclear force. For a theory, any theory, to be consistent with the Standard Model, it must predict the existence of all known sub-atomic particles: quarks, leptons, and bosons."

"And I'm guessing yours does that," Gary said.

Matt nodded enthusiastically. "And more. Okay, let's switch tracks for a moment. You guys remember back to my thirteenth birthday, when my parents gave me the book 'Flatland'?"

"How could we forget?" Josh said. "You ranted about it for days."

"We thought you might be going crazy," Gary added.

"Right," Matt said, "so a quick refresher." He leapt out of his chair and went to the blackboard, grabbed a piece of chalk and drew a circle with a line through its middle. "As you know, pi is the ratio of a circle's circumference to its diameter. Let's assume this circle has a diameter of one metre. That means its circumference is pi times the diameter, or three point one-four metres. If you're on one side of the circle and you want to get to the opposite side, you have to go around the circle, travelling half the circumference, roughly one point five metres.

"But if you could go through the middle of the circle, you would only need to travel a distance equal to the diameter—one metre. You'd save half a metre of travel—50%. A shortcut.

"The same thing applies for a three-dimensional object, like an apple. A worm on the surface of an apple has two choices to get to the other side: travel around the outside of the apple, or go through the apple, a shortcut through the third dimension. You guys with me so far?"

Josh spoke up. "Sure, but the worm first has to eat its way through."

"That's correct," Matt said. "But once it has, it can travel back and forth."

"So could other worms," Renny said, trying hard to contribute.

Matt nodded. "Now comes the *really* neat part! In my hyperspatial model, the higher geometric dimensions have more compact geometry than our 3-space. The model includes a value that describes the curvature of each dimension—basically what pi does for three dimensions, so I call it 'hyper-pi.' The geometry of those higher dimensions is more compact than the lower dimensions. Incredibly compact, so hyper-pi is *very* large. Let's say it's a billion—it isn't a constant like in our three-dimensional world, but that doesn't matter right now. So, if you can imagine a circle, in two dimensions, but pi was not 3.14, but a billion, then...?"

It was Josh who answered. "Then... the diameter of the circle would be... much smaller in relation to the circumference. A billion times smaller." He paused. "Aw, that doesn't make any sense."

"My brain hurts," Renny added.

"But it is mathematically correct," Matt said. "So, imagine an apple with a diameter that is a billion times smaller than its circumference..."

Josh stared at the blackboard for a few seconds. "The apple is smaller on the inside than on the outside," he said, shaking his head at the absurdity of his statement.

Matt nodded. "Okay, let's put that aside for a moment. Now, my hyperspatial model says that in 10-space—the realm of gravity and mass—every object with mass is a multi-dimensional hypersphere that exists along with other hyperspheres in the 11-space 'sea.' Our senses only work in three dimensions, so we can't perceive any aspects of those higher dimensions. Besides, they're incredibly compact."

"That's very interesting and theoretical," Josh noted, "but what does it have to do with magnetism?"

"Remember what I said earlier about electromagnetic wormholes in 5-

space? I built a device in my lab at Caltech that transported a magnetic force field over a distance of twenty-five centimetres, and there was *zero* measurable magnetic field anywhere along that gap. I call it a *magnetostatic wormhole*. That experiment alone was worth publishing, but I was onto something bigger. My model predicts that if two magnetostatic wormholes with the same polarity are aimed at each other, their magnetic force fields would generate a force vector into 10-space. And 10-space is...?"

"The realm of gravity, mass, and inertia," Josh said. He'd been paying attention.

"Bingo," Matt said. "The math for a 10-dimensional force vector is incredibly complex, but suffice to say that such a vector would create a 'tunnel' through 10-space. In other words, a wormhole. A mass-traversable wormhole."

"But what good is a wormhole in 10-space?" Josh said.

Matt smiled. "Even though the wormhole exists in, or through, 10-space, its two endpoints will be in whichever dimension the force fields that created it originate in."

Matt let that sink in.

"Now, remember I said earlier that in the geometry of hyperspace, hyper-pi is really large? Well, the larger the masses involved, the larger hyper-pi is. And in 10-space, it's a lot larger than a billion. For example, the distance between the Earth and Moon, in our standard three-dimensional space, is, on average, 385,000 kilometres. According to my model, hyper-pi for 10-space in the Earth-Moon neighbourhood is roughly ten to the twelfth power. So, if one could create a 10-space wormhole between the Earth and the Moon, it would only be *seven one-thousandths of a millimetre* long!"

The room was silent for a full minute as Matt's friends digested everything he'd said.

"When I realized that, I started tinkering with this." Matt reached forward and, with a flourish, pulled the cloth off the object in the middle of the table. It was a pair of ring-shaped electromagnets, a foot in diameter, clamped together inside a robust mechanical frame. Coils of thin insulated pipes wrapped around both rings. A nest of wiring came off into several bundles.

"This is a pair of high-intensity superconducting electromagnets based on the design from my doctoral research. When I circulate liquid nitrogen through those pipes, the coil temperatures drop to 77 degrees above absolute zero and each generates a magnetic field of 10 Tesla. If I modulate the amplitude, frequency, and phase of each one's magnetic field, it becomes a magnetostatic wormhole generator. Since both have the same polarity, they push against each other and generate a force vector that is at a right angle to our three-dimensional universe."

"Uh, what do you mean 'at a right angle'?" Gary said.

"Into 10-space." Matt gave them a moment.

"You mean that stuff you just talked about isn't theoretical?" Josh said, staring at the assembly.

"No. It's real. When I finally got this working, it created what I figured was a semi-stable micro-wormhole only a couple of millimetres wide. I wasn't sure where it went, but it was making a whistling sound—when I blew some blackboard chalk dust towards it, the dust disappeared. I figured it went somewhere into space, so I borrowed a fibre-optic imager and a high-end spectrometer from a colleague, stuck the fibre-optic strand into the wormhole and recorded some images. They were just coloured streaks of light, which I hypothesized was star light. It took me several weeks to analyze each streak's colour and match it to known star spectra. Then it was a simple exercise in triangulation. Turns out I'd created a wormhole into space, two hundred kilometres up."

"And the stars were streaks because...?" Josh asked.

"Because the wormhole's far end wasn't in a fixed position—it was moving. It's hard to explain, but the Earth is a hypersphere and although it's rotating in 3-space, there's a hyper-dimensional component to that rotation."

"Holy shit, Matt," Gary said. "That's incredible!"

"Fuck me," Renny added. "The Professor can create wormholes." He started laughing.

Matt nodded his thanks. "I got this working in the fall of last year; I experimented with it for a couple of months until my teaching contract expired."

"How did you get it out of Caltech?" Gary asked.

Matt smiled. "That's a story for another time. But let's just say it was an inside job."

"What happened to your doctoral thesis? Did it ever get published?" Josh said. "And the follow-on work you did, your... 11-space expanding universe theory, did you publish that?"

"Eventually, yes. When I rejected Caltech's offer of a master's degree 'consolation prize,' my thesis became an unpublished manuscript and Caltech had no rights to it. Dr. F. was so pissed at the way the department handled my situation he sent copies to colleagues around the world, not only so they'd know that much higher strength electromagnets were available, but to prevent anyone at Caltech from claiming my work as theirs. He's amazing.

"When I started teaching at Cambridge, I submitted my doctoral thesis and my 11-space paper to them for peer review, got their blessing, then sent abstracts to the two top physics journals in the world. To my surprise, the journals rejected both submissions. I'm positive it was political, as they're both based in the US. I submitted them to a physics journal here in the UK—it's called 'The Physics Journal B'—they published them two months ago in back-to-back issues."

Matt paused. "Haven't got any real feedback yet, but these things take time." He shrugged.

"Speaking of Cambridge," Gary said, "how'd you end up here? And by 'here,' I'm referring to this building."

"Since last fall, I've been working here in my spare time, building a larger version of this thing on the table."

Matt grinned. "Who wants to see it?"

TWELVE

Matt led his stunned friends further down the hallway, which ended at a heavy metal door sporting a large yellow and black sign: "Caution: Radiation Hazard!"

Josh stopped short as Matt pulled the door open, its rusty hinges screeching in protest. "Whoa! What've you got behind there?"

"I'm not worried," Gary said. "When there's someone as dense as Bigfoot around, lead shielding isn't necessary." Renny growled and made a half-hearted attempt to cuff him upside the head.

"Children..." Matt said, smiling, clearly having missed his friends' banter. "I put that there as a joke. Wait here while I get the lights," Matt said over his shoulder as he disappeared into the darkness, his footsteps echoing in what was undoubtedly a large room.

A few seconds later, there was the distinct "click" of a switch being thrown; Matt's friends cautiously entered and looked around. Fluorescent overhead lights buzzed and brightened, their harsh glare illuminating only a small portion of the immense room that had a concrete floor and a girdered-steel roof; the rest was cloaked in darkness.

Matt motioned his friends in. They passed through a workshop area, complete with drafting tables and mechanical, electrical, and woodworking tools and equipment. Everything an inventor needed.

"Looks like your garage back home," Renny said.

Gary pointed at a dozen red cylinders lined up along one wall. "What's with all the fire extinguishers?"

"Well, sometimes my electromagnets explode and their power supplies catch fire," he said. "I push them pretty hard."

Renny snickered. "Yup, this *is* like your garage."

Mounted to the nearest wall was a large electrical panel, a mix of modern circuit breakers and old-fashioned fuses and knife switches.

"This used to be a metal foundry," Matt said. "The owners went out of business fifteen years ago. All the buildings here are vacant. I rent this building from a holding company for one thousand pounds per year, and I get free electrical power. I need *lots* of power."

"For what?" Josh asked.

"We're getting there."

Next to the electrical panel were several racks of complicated-looking electronics, some commercial and others obviously handmade, with a myriad of cables feeding into three rack-mounted minicomputers.

Josh inspected the computers and the magnetic tape drive next to them. "PDP-11s?"

Matt nodded. "I got them free from the University—they were surplus."

Opposite the computers was a long table with several computer monitors and keyboards, nestled up against a cinder-block wall one-and-a-half metres high. A bank of video monitors sat along the top of the wall.

"Where do these go?" Gary asked, pointing at a thick bundle of cables coming out of the electrical rack and snaking across the floor towards the middle of the room, still cloaked in darkness.

"To this," Matt said as he reached for a wall switch and dramatically flipped it up. More overhead lights came on with a loud buzz.

Gary let out a low whistle.

Josh's jaw dropped.

"Fuck me," Renny whispered as Matt motioned them forward.

It was a larger, more complex version of the device on the meeting room table: a pair of aluminum rings, two metres in diameter, standing upright on their edges, half a metre apart. The rings were in the centre of a support structure resembling a man-made spider web, its symmetry broken by the odd brace that appeared to be added as an afterthought. The structure's members were a mix of metal and wood, anchored to the concrete floor and the ceiling's girders. Spaced evenly around each ring's circumference were what looked like stainless steel, toroidal vacuum bottles; each bottle had a pair of insulated pipes connected to a tall insulated tank in the far corner. A rectangular black object was bolted to the rings between each pair of bottles.

"This," Matt said proudly, "is HYDRA—the Hyperspatial Drill Assembly. Since it's my second prototype, I call it the HYDRA Mark II, or just 'Mark II.' The two rings are mounts for the permanent magnets—those big black rectangles—and the superconducting electromagnets. Each ring creates a magnetostatic wormhole aimed at the other ring. The magnetic force fields push against each other; the computer controls the amplitude, frequency, and phase of the force field coming out of each magnetostatic wormhole, creating a force vector that's at right angles to our three-dimensional space. That force vector literally drills into 10-space, creating a traversable wormhole."

"Holy shit," Renny said.

Gary walked around the massive structure. "You built this all by yourself?"

Matt shrugged. "Mostly. I got a local machine shop to fabricate the more complex parts, then hired a couple of their guys to help me assemble the stuff I couldn't do on my own."

"They must have wondered what you were building?" Renny said.

"I told them it was a science project for the university, and to keep it 'hush-hush.' The economy here's in a mild depression—many are willing to work for cash, no questions asked."

"What's with all the dents?" Josh said, pointing at a shrapnel-like pattern on one wall.

"If I push the electromagnets too hard, sometimes they explode..."

"Hang on," Josh said, holding his hands up in protest. "You mean this thing actually works? You can create wormholes? How big? How far away?"

Matt smiled. "The Mark II can create a wormhole twenty-five centimetres in diameter. So far, I've opened wormholes out to two hundred thousand kilometres away."

"Geez! That's more than halfway to the moon!" Renny said.

"Can you open a wormhole anywhere—like on Earth?" Josh asked.

"Nope. I can't open a wormhole less than one hundred kilometres above the earth's surface. It's hard to explain why, but it's related to the Earth's hyper-mass in four dimensions. Sort of."

"That's…. that's just freaking incredible," Josh muttered, shaking his head.

"What's with the hot tub?" Gary had followed thick cables from the HYDRA to a vat of oily water on the far side of the cavernous room.

"That's the load dump," Matt said. "If I have to shut the HYDRA down quickly, say, because of a fire or exploding magnet, the collapsing magnetic fields generate huge back-currents which will back-flush into my power systems. I shunt them into power resistors submerged in the vat—the water absorbs the heat generated by the high current."

"How much current are we talking about?" Josh asked.

"Several hundred thousand amps."

Gary let out a low whistle.

"But only for a fraction of a second," Matt added.

"And what's this for?" Gary was pointing at a yellow line, hand-painted on the concrete floor, that went around the HYDRA's perimeter in an odd pattern.

"That's the 'Caution' line. You want to be outside it when the HYDRA's running."

"Curious how you figured that out," Renny said.

"Trial and error," was Matt's cryptic reply.

Matt gave his friends a few minutes to wander around and ask more questions.

"Who wants to see it in action?" They were too stunned to answer, but all nodded.

Matt went over to a workbench and pulled an object the size of a softball out of a large crate. He tossed it to Renny.

"What's this?" Renny asked, hefting it in his hands. It was a couple of small circuit boards and a battery crammed inside what originally had been a kid's plastic toy ball.

"I use these to calibrate the HYDRA. It's a ten-watt omnidirectional radio transmitter and a small battery. I paid one of my students to design them, and a local electronics shop builds them. When I do a hyperspatial drill, my math predicts where the wormhole will exit back in 3-D space, but there are a lot of variables introduced by the HYDRA's physical mechanism, by the rotation of the earth, and by variations in magnetic field strength. Every time I do a drill, I toss one of these through. The transmitter uses a rotating polarization so it's not mistaken for any natural source; I have a small radio telescope dish up on the roof to track them. I compare the transmitter's location to where I wanted it to go, then tweak the control system."

"But that will give you only one line of bearing," Josh said. "How do you triangulate?"

Matt grinned. "The SETI network—the group looking for signs of extraterrestrial life in space. They're tracking lots of anomalous radio signals these days."

"Wait a minute!" Gary exclaimed. "Those signals that SETI has been reporting in the past few months!" He pulled his copy of Paranormal Monthly magazine out of his pack, then looked back and forth from the magazine to the HYDRA. "That's you?" The light bulb came on. "That's you!"

Matt grinned. "Guilty as charged. SETI reports their observations through the Arpanet and I can access that data through the university's network. That's one of the few perks of working there."

Matt took the transmitter from Renny and put it on a wooden stand that was bolted to the floor two metres from the HYDRA's nearest ring, then secured it with a spring-loaded latch. A thin rope, tied to the latch, snaked back along the floor to the concrete wall. Matt checked his watch then flicked a switch on the transmitter; it emitted a 'beep' every five seconds.

"It has a thirty-minute countdown timer, then starts transmitting."

Matt went over to the racks of equipment up against the wall. He closed a large knife switch; it arced like a special effect from a B-rated horror movie and the equipment started humming. He flicked several other switches, causing more equipment to power up. Next, he moved to the computer rack, turning each one on with the flick of a toggle switch; rows of red and green LEDs blinked on and off. He sat at the control console, turned on the computer monitors, and started typing. Josh, the computer geek of the bunch, watched the text scroll by.

"Looks like you're running an old version of Unix," he said as the boot-up messages scrolled by. The LEDs on the computers blinked in complex patterns.

"Renny, could you grab the mag tape from my backpack?" Matt asked.

Renny handed Matt the 8-inch tape reel; he mounted it on the tape drive, threaded it through the reader head and onto a blank pickup reel, then closed the drive door. He flicked the drive's power switch; there was a sucking sound as the drive tensioned the tape in a pair of vacuum columns. Matt moved back to the console and typed in a couple of commands.

"You're loading the application?" Josh said.

"Yup. I don't leave any software here. Way too valuable."

While the tape drive rotated jerkily—reading the data on the magnetic tape—Matt turned on each of the video monitors sitting atop the concrete wall; each showed a different view of the HYDRA.

"What's the deal with all the monitors?" Renny said; they were all tilted to the right.

Matt grinned. "A little trick I picked up at TRIUMF. HYDRA's magnetic fields affect all the video monitors in the room. So, like in TRIUMF's control room, I pre-tilt the monitors—when HYDRA is at full power, the images are level."

Two minutes later, the console beeped and the tape drive stopped turning. Matt typed in another command; two more displays lit up, and columns of numbers scrolled rapidly by.

A series of sharp "clacks" came from the electrical rack, the unmistakable sound of high-current relays closing. The HYDRA started emitting a low-frequency hum.

"Where are you sending the transmitter?" Gary asked.

"Tonight, the moon is almost directly overhead, so I'm aiming for L1, the Lagrange point where the Earth and the Moon's gravity cancel each other. It's only 61,000 kilometres away."

Josh's eyes widened. "Hang on! You're going to open a wormhole into space? That'll suck all the air out!"

Matt smiled—nothing got past Josh. "Yes and no. The wormhole diameter is twenty-five centimetres. The pressure differential between here and the hard vacuum of space is only one atmosphere, so the flow rate is only around nine hundred cubic feet per minute. Besides, I use the pressure differential to suck the transmitter in and only leave the wormhole open until the transmitter's gone through."

"What if the wormhole doesn't close?" Josh asked. "Aren't you worried you might suck all the Earth's atmosphere into space?"

Matt shook his head. "Can't happen. While the drilling takes a lot of energy, holding the wormhole open requires a small, but non-zero amount. If I cut power, the wormhole collapses. Don't worry, I've done lots of tests to make sure the system is failsafe. Any loss of power or control system failure and the wormhole closes."

The worry on Josh's face vanished; he trusted in his friend's abilities. Matt consulted the monitors. "Okay, everything's powered up and the diagnostic tests are complete. Next, the electromagnets. Please bear with me—I have to cool them with liquid nitrogen so they become superconducting, and this part is all manual."

His friends watched as Matt scurried around the HYDRA, opening valves fed by insulated pipes that came from the large insulated steel tank in the far corner of the room. The electromagnets on the rim of each ring hissed as they rapidly cooled. Then he came back to the console.

"Next is the calibration procedure. Now remember, I've put this whole thing together by myself, so it probably seems like a giant kludge. Especially the software..."

Matt typed in several commands, and the rest of the monitors came to life. More columns of numbers scrolled by, and the electronics rack emitted more clicks as relays opened and closed. Matt stared intently at the monitors for a minute, then nodded.

"Okay. System calibration is complete. Now I have to set the targeting parameters. Gary, can you hand me that red book?" Matt pointed to a nearby bookshelf.

Gary read the cover out loud: "Astronomical Almanac—US Naval Observatory." Matt opened it to a bookmarked page, found a series of numbers and typed them in.

"This almanac gives me the lunar polynomials—coefficients for the moon's right ascension and declination—that define its position relative to the Earth. The targeting software will calculate L1's position based on the current date and time."

One monitor displayed a crude graphical diagram of the Earth and the Moon. "Now we start the drill." Matt typed in one more command and leaned back in his chair. His friends peered around the wall at the HYDRA.

The humming coming from the HYDRA became more pronounced, shifting to several low-frequency harmonics. The support structure started creaking.

"Drilling is mostly automatic," Matt said. "The control system is increasing the magnetic field strength; the sound you're hearing is the increased stress in the two rings holding the magnets. Once the magnetic field strength is high enough, the control system will begin modulating the two opposing fields. That creates the magnetostatic wormholes, and the resulting force vector is redirected into 10-space."

As Matt continued his running commentary, he had to keep raising his voice as the hum from the HYDRA got louder. The lights in the building dimmed and several analog panel meters crept towards their red lines. As Matt had predicted, the video monitor images slowly rotated back to level. Every few minutes, he leapt out of his chair and ran to the electrical panel on the wall to throw a switch.

"Still needs some automation," he said sheepishly.

Matt pointed at a number on one of the computer monitors. "This is the overall stress on the support structure. Once the drill moves into 10-space, the stress will level off."

The humming increased in volume for another minute. Then it took on a deeper, almost melodious tone as the stress reading stabilized.

"Okay, the magnetic fields are modulating. The drill is now moving through 10-space."

"Can we get a closer look?" Renny asked, pointing his lips towards the HYDRA.

"Sure, come with me. Just stay behind the caution line." Matt led his friends towards the humming HYDRA, its structure groaning. "Josh, you're not coming?"

Josh shook his head vigorously. "I'll stay over here, thanks."

The three stopped at the yellow line in front of the HYDRA.

"What's that between the two rings?" Gary yelled. The air was taking on a blurry appearance. "If I stare right at it, it looks like fog. If I turn my head, it almost looks like water going down a drain. It's.... it's not right!" he exclaimed, shaking his head as if trying to purge a bad image.

Renny was cradling his head in his hands, as if recovering from a hangover. "The more I look at it, the more my brain hurts," he exclaimed. "It reminds me of watching a toilet flush. A blurry toilet."

Matt nodded. "Some of my equations that describe the interaction of the magnetic fields with the hyperspace topology resemble a four-dimensional rotating fluid. I figure that's how the brain interprets it."

"You're telling us that right now, this thing is drilling through hyperspace?" Renny asked.

Matt nodded.

"What are you guys talking about?" Josh yelled from his chair, safe behind the concrete wall. "There's nothing on the monitors!"

Matt smiled. "The electromagnetic energy coming out of hyperspace isn't light as we know it—it's orthogonal to light. It doesn't appear on the monitors because the video cameras are designed for the visible spectrum. I discovered that the human optic system can detect some aspects of this 'hyper-light,' but the brain doesn't know how to interpret it. I think there's an entire field of research on just that."

Matt watched as his friends struggled to process what they were seeing. The humming emanating from the HYDRA got louder and deeper.

"Let's return to the console," Matt said. "It'll only be another minute."

As they watched, the swirling, blurry phenomenon became more defined, looking more like an out-of-focus toilet being flushed.

"Okay, get ready! The drill's almost there!" Matt yelled over the din.

The stress reading on the monitor suddenly dropped off, and the HYDRA emitted a horrible shriek, an unnatural sound that made their skin crawl and the hair on the back of their necks stand up. There was a loud "pop" followed by the roar of air being sucked into vacuum. A liquid-like sphere, the size of a basketball, hovered between the HYDRA's two rings.

"Congratulations!" Matt yelled over the roar. "You're the first humans, besides me, to have seen an artificial wormhole. Renny, release the transmitter!"

Renny reached down, grabbed the line by his feet and gave it a tug. The spring-loaded arm rotated up and hit a stop; the transmitter catapulted in a perfect arc towards the vortex. It paused at the edge of the liquid sphere as suction fought gravity, then disappeared with a loud sucking sound. Matt waited a few seconds, then typed in another command. The hum coming from the HYDRA died down, the wormhole vanished, and the roar of rushing air stopped. The large room was silent except for support structure, which creaked as the multi-dimensional forces vanished.

Matt broke the stunned silence. "That, gentlemen, was that." He looked at his digital wristwatch. "The transmitter will start in... two minutes."

They followed him to another equipment rack against the wall. "This is the receiver for a 1-metre radio telescope dish on the roof. I'll slew it to what should be the correct elevation and azimuth." He flicked the power switch, adjusted a pair of knobs, then punched a button that started a paper plotter, the pen tracing a flat blue line.

Matt checked his watch. "Three, two, one, now."

"There it is!" Josh said. The plotter pen shot to the right as the paper formed a snaking pile on the floor.

"Right on time," Matt said, adjusting the controls to get a maximum signal. He checked the setting on the knobs. "Okay, looks like an azimuth of zero-nine-three and an elevation of eighty-seven degrees. That sounds about right. Hopefully, SETI will detect this and start tracking. When they post their observations, I'll be able to triangulate."

He looked at his watch. "Well guys, that's the show for tonight! The taxi will be here shortly. Let's lock up, head back to your hotel, have dinner, and talk more."

◎

After his friends got settled in their hotel rooms, they re-convened at a small pub next door.

"It must have cost a fortune to build the HYDRA," Josh said after Matt returned to the table with the first round of drinks.

Matt shrugged. "I rent the building for one thousand pounds a year—a steal, actually. The HYDRA cost me around two million pounds—four million Canadian dollars at the current exchange rate."

"Where'd you get that kind of money?" Gary asked. "Private investors? The British government? Sell your soul to the devil?"

Matt smiled. "None of the above. Remember that invention I made when I was fifteen—you know, the headlights that automatically pivot when the car turns?" Nods. Matt narrated the entire story: the patent, the lawsuit, and the resulting settlement.

Renny stared at Matt. "When was that?"

"At the end of my first year at UBC."

"You were sitting on five million dollars while we were at UBC?" Renny asked.

Matt nodded. "Interest rates were approaching eighteen percent back then, so by the time I moved here, it was almost ten million."

Renny remained silent, still staring at Matt.

Josh, always the perceptive one, cut right to the point. "Matt, this has all been amazing. What's next?"

Matt paused. "Guys, I've proved that hyperspatial drilling works—the physics *and* the engineering. The HYDRA Mark II is just for experimenting. I'm using it to learn more about the physics of drilling through hyperspace. My biggest problem is motion compensation."

"Uh, that means what to us dummies?" Renny said.

"When I open a wormhole in space, the far end—I call it the 'tail'—is in the same inertial reference frame as its mouth, where the HYDRA is. On the surface of the earth, at this latitude, the mouth has a velocity vector of about three hundred metres per second, west-to-east. So that transmitter we deployed isn't going anywhere near orbital velocity."

Gary nodded. "It's gonna burn up pretty quick."

"Unless I put it way far from earth, like we just did. It'll float around at L1 until its battery dies."

Josh scratched his head. "If you wanted to open a wormhole onto, say, the surface of the moon, you'd have to match relative velocities."

"Bingo," Matt said. "I think I've figured out how to give the wormhole's tail a different velocity vector. That's why I've been sending out those probes."

He took a long pull on his ale. "There are engineering limitations on how far the Mark II can drill. Also, the diameter of the rings more or less determines the wormhole's diameter, although diameter is not exactly the right term to use when working with hyperspatial mathematics. So that limits what can we can put through.

"I have plans for a HYDRA Mark III. It'll be bigger and have way more powerful superconducting electromagnets. It should be able to open a wormhole roughly a metre in diameter and have a longer range. It'll have a more powerful control system with motion compensation. And I want to build it inside a large pressure vessel, so we can safely open wormholes into vacuum, and maybe other atmospheres."

"Other atmospheres?" Gary said.

"Well, besides the moon—which doesn't have any significant atmosphere—Mars and Venus are theoretically within range. But to build the Mark III, I'm going to need money. A lot more money." He paused. "Have you guys heard of the Columbus Space Prizes?"

Josh nodded. "That's the Columbus Group, run by Alastair Columbus, the wealthy British industrialist. He owns a chain of luxury hotels here and in Europe. Claims his lineage goes back to Christopher Columbus."

"I've read about him, too," Gary said. "He's quite the adventurer, and into many extreme sports, including cave diving and high-altitude skydiving. He holds the world record for the highest sky dive by a civilian. Just over forty-nine thousand feet. He did that from a balloon."

Matt nodded. "Columbus is a big fan of space exploration, and created a series of challenge prizes for private industry to spur the commercial development of space. First company to orbit a satellite. First to send back live video from the moon. First to return moon rocks to Earth. That kind of thing."

"Serious money, too," Josh said. "Tens of millions of pounds, I recall."

Matt nodded. "I want to go after those prizes."

"Which ones?" Josh said.

"All of them. Winning them will give me enough money to build the Mark III." Matt paused while his friends digested his plan.

"But I can't do it alone. I'm worn out juggling my teaching at the university and getting the Mark II running. Keeping it running and winning the Columbus Prizes... well, I need help. *Your* help."

"But how could we help?" Renny replied. "What you've done is like science fiction. Way past science fiction, actually."

"For once, I agree with Bigfoot," Gary said. "This stuff is so far beyond us..."

Matt shook his head. "The key to winning those prizes is the motion compensation. I've got the math figured out, but I've done a real hack job on the software and don't have enough computing power; my code needs to be tightened up. I've also got some ideas on drilling through higher dimensions, but that math is way more complex. It'll require a massive processing effort."

Renny stared at Josh. "Gee, do we know anyone with those skills?"

"Exactly what I was thinking," Matt said. "If we can solve the motion compensation problem, we'll be able to open wormholes at orbital speeds, and all the way to the moon. Then we'll need robotic vehicles to win the lunar prizes. Gary, that's right up your alley. Also, there's a lot of abandoned hardware on the moon from American and Soviet lunar missions—if we can retrieve some of that stuff, we could make a fortune selling it."

Matt turned to Renny. "With a more powerful HYDRA, we can explore our closest neighbours in the solar system. From right here. We'll be able to get our hands on rocks from the moon. Probably from Mars and Venus. Maybe some asteroids. Maybe even further out and further in. Interested?"

"Mars rocks? Asteroids?" Renny said, incredulously. He grabbed his crotch. "Geez, I'm getting a woody."

Matt looked at each of his friends. "Don't you see, guys? After high school, we took different paths, yet here we are, with just the right skills to make this work. We can be the first humans to explore the solar system. From right here."

Gary spoke up. "Um, Matt, have you considered sending a person through the wormhole? Do you think it would be safe?"

Matt shrugged. "There's no technical reason we couldn't. There's no radiation hazard, and there's a large null in the magnetic field that extends along HYDRA's longitudinal axis. Assuming we have a large enough wormhole, there's no reason we couldn't push someone through in a spacesuit. It's more a question of logistics and safety. We wouldn't want to put someone on the moon without a backup plan. Anyone want to walk on the moon? Be the first person on Mars?"

Gary and Renny put up their hands. Josh didn't. "I prefer to stay on *this* planet, thank you very much," he said.

"I don't expect an answer from any of you right now. It's late and you must be jet-lagged, so let's call it a night. Tomorrow, the Explorers Society of Canada is going on a road trip."

◎

The next day, with his friends now somewhat refreshed, Matt took them on a five-day tour around southern England in a rented passenger van. Matt acted as tour guide, taking in the sights: the white cliffs of Dover; the 1800s-era sailing vessels at Portsmouth; Stonehenge; the historic tin mines of Cornwall; Dartmoor; the rocky cliffs of Land's End. They stayed at bed-and-breakfasts, ate proper English breakfasts and pub lunches and dinners. Never once did Matt pressure his friends—he just answered their many, many questions.

The night before Matt's friends were scheduled to fly home, they met him in their hotel's restaurant. After the first round of drinks arrived, Renny cleared his throat.

"Professor, the three of us had a long talk this morning. You'll be happy to know we've decided to join your little venture."

Gary nodded. "Ad-venture, we hope."

Matt closed his eyes. "Guys, I can't tell you what this means to me."

Josh was next to speak. "Uh, I didn't know how to tell you guys, but remember that federal election we had back home a few months ago? Well, the new conservative Prime Minister is quite the Luddite. Really anti-science. Last month, our department's budget got slashed by half. Last week I got laid off. I'm unemployed." His voice took on a melancholy tone.

"Not anymore, you're not," Matt said, holding out his hand. "Welcome to AdAstra." Josh grinned as they shook on it.

The foursome put their heads together and came up with a plan. Josh would tie up his affairs in Canada and move to Cambridge. Gary's first allegiance was to his girlfriend and her research, but he'd start thinking about the Columbus prizes—building robotic moon vehicles and how to do some snatch-and-grabs of lunar rock samples for Renny.

"I've got some spare time coming up after Christmas," Gary said. "Nadia comes home in January to write her doctoral dissertation. Given what we found in the tomb outside Luxor, her faculty advisor said her thesis is on such solid ground she could write it in crayon on a sheet of papyrus and still get her PhD."

Gary paused. "That leaves Bigfoot here."

Renny shrugged. "You know, I've kinda had my fill of field work. I got accepted into the graduate program in Planetary Science at the University of Arizona. I start in September!"

His friends congratulated him.

"Any ideas for your thesis?" Josh said.

Renny nodded. "I showed my advisor the magnetic anomaly data we collected at Crater Lake over the years. He agreed the lake was likely formed by a meteorite impact and figured it was a worthwhile project."

"Were you able to make any financial arrangements?" Matt asked.

"Well, yes and no. I can go on paid leave and they'll pay for tuition, but I have to commit to working for at least five years after I graduate. Or I can take an unpaid leave of absence, pay for everything myself and hope my job is still available when I graduate."

Renny paused, thinking about the HYDRA demonstration five days ago. "You know, I have this funny feeling I won't be going back to government work once I graduate..."

He paused again. "Aw, fuck it. This little venture of yours sounds like fun. I'll just put in my notice. The government's been cutting back in our department, and it's no fun anymore."

Matt's eyes went misty, touched by his best friend's loyalty. "AdAstra will cover all your school expenses."

Renny shook his head. "No way, pal. You've already done plenty for me and my mom, haven't you?"

Matt's jaw dropped. "How long have you known?"

"About five days now." Renny said. "When you told us about winning that big patent lawsuit and sitting on five million dollars throughout university. That's when I figured out who the 'anonymous benefactor' was."

Neither Josh nor Gary pressed for further information—it was a matter between Matt and Renny.

"Busted," Matt said. "So, do you guys want talk money? Salaries, benefits and so forth?"

They all shook their heads in unison; Gary spoke up first. "Matt, you've offered us the opportunity of a lifetime. Money's not an issue. Let's worry about that later."

"Josh's going to be employee #1," Renny said. "Whatever you work out with him will be fine with us." Matt opened his mouth to protest, but Renny cut him off. "Subject's closed, Professor."

Matt looked around and lowered his voice. "And guys, let's keep this to ourselves, okay? This is ground-breaking stuff, so absolutely no mention of it in letters or telephone calls. What do you say we meet at Christmas and see where we're at?"

He received nods all around.

The next morning, he accompanied his friends on the train back to London, then to Heathrow. He returned to Cambridge alone, sad to see his friends go, but thrilled he'd soon have some help.

THIRTEEN

Four weeks later...

Josh arrived at Heathrow Airport with two large suitcases; he'd moved out of his Ottawa apartment, sold his furniture, and shipped the rest of his belongings home to his parents. Matt was waiting for him in the international arrivals hall, then they did the taxi-train-taxi trip back to Matt's flat in Cambridge. He stayed in Matt's spare bedroom for a few weeks until a flat in the building became vacant.

Josh agreed to a yearly salary of twenty thousand British pounds (equivalent to roughly forty thousand Canadian dollars). Matt offered more, but Josh refused—he'd been working for less when he got laid off from his government job. Matt pressed, and Josh countered with a profit-sharing arrangement: he (and eventually Renny and Gary) would each receive five percent of the company's annual profits (once there were any), as long as Matt agreed to ten percent. Matt had a corporate accountant in Cambridge on retainer, advising on relevant employment and tax laws; she recommended that AdAstra hire Josh as a consultant. A local immigration lawyer helped Josh apply for a Skilled Worker Visa, valid for five years.

Josh immediately got to work. Five days a week, he sat in "math class" each morning while Matt tutored him in hyperspatial mathematics, the foundation of HYDRA's operation. Even though Josh had an honours degree in computer science and mathematics, had spent four years doing weather modelling and was a wiz at calculus, Matt's mathematics were in a different league. It took them a week just to figure out how much Josh needed to understand so he could work effectively on the HYDRA software. Usually, after two hours in math class, he'd end the tutorial by putting up his hands in a show of defeat, claiming "my brain hurts." They'd break for coffee, then he'd spend the rest of the day reading code while Matt tinkered with the HYDRA, worked in his private "Math Room" on hyperspatial mathematics, or sat at a drafting table, sketching subsystems and components for the Mark III.

Josh had spent little time around Matt since high school, so he wasn't aware of some of his brilliant friend's quirks. One day, Josh was taking a morning break from his code reviews and walked past the Math Room. Matt was standing at a blackboard, back to the open door, chalk in hand, his arm frozen in the middle of a complex equation.

"Matt, I'm making coffee. Want some?"

No response.

"Matt?"

Nothing.

Josh shrugged and headed into the kitchen. Ten minutes later, he walked past the Math Room with a fresh cup of coffee—Matt was still there, in the same position, staring at the blackboard. He left Matt alone through lunch and afternoon coffee break, and when it was time to go home, Matt still hadn't moved a muscle.

Josh cleared his throat. No response.

He cautiously approached Matt and was about to give him a gentle nudge. Matt stirred and his hand began moving fast, chalk bits flying as he scratched out a long equation that soon filled the entire blackboard. He let out a long sigh and turned; his eyes were unfocussed, almost glazed over.

"Earth to Matt!"

Matt blinked several times, his eyes slowly coming into focus. "Oh, hey."

"Geez, Matt. You spent all day on that one equation? What is it?"

"I... I solved the motion compensation problem. That one was *hard*. I'll need a few days to come up with a numerical solution you can code, but we've cleared a big hurdle."

"Are you okay now? You were right out of it."

Matt shrugged. "Time flies in higher dimensions."

◎

By September, Josh had a sufficient understanding of hyperspatial mathematics he was ready to start modifying the HYDRA software. He'd already identified several areas for optimization, so he tackled the simple ones first. Unlike most software geeks, he didn't follow the "Not Invented Here" method—re-writing everything from scratch—he only changed code where necessary. And he also took great pleasure in pointing out Matt's abysmal software skills.

"See this?" Josh said, waving a printout. "You've duplicated this code eleven times! Eleven! That's a maintenance nightmare! No wonder you're running out of memory! And look here—you used the Linear Shooting method to solve these partial differential equations. The Rayleigh-Ritz method uses an order of magnitude less processing power. And don't get me started on your inefficient memory organization!"

Matt took Josh's rants in stride, and not personally. "That's why you're getting paid the big bucks," he'd say, grinning.

◎

September passed quickly, and it was time for Matt to report to the university to begin his lecturing role. The fall term, known as "Michaelmas," ran from the first week in October until Christmas.

"Why do they call it that?" Josh asked.

"The name comes from the Feast of Saint Michael and All Angels," Matt replied. "It's a Christian festival that occurs every year on September 29th. The UK has lots of events like that."

This term, the department wanted Matt to teach another course, "Physics 203: Physics of Astronomy," as its regular professor was on sabbatical. Luckily, all three of Matt's courses were scheduled for the same two days, minimizing his time away from AdAstra.

The class roster for "Astro 203" included Prince Edward, who was now in his second year of studies. Even though the Prince attended classes with a two-man security detail, Matt had to sit through another security briefing held by a stern-looking Scotland Yard Inspector. The briefing was the same as the previous year, from how to address the Prince to a code phrase to use in case of an emergency.

◎

Over the next month, Josh methodically updated the HYDRA software, making regular backups on magnetic tape in case he had to "walk back" his changes. By early November he'd finished and completed the testing Matt had suggested.

"Wow!" Matt exclaimed as Josh shut the HYDRA down following a successful drill to low-earth orbit. "The control software's running thirty-five percent faster, so the computer hardware is no longer the bottleneck. Drilling time has decreased by sixteen percent. Well done!"

Josh shrugged. "I just got rid of all that crappy code you wrote. And that was a *lot* of code."

Matt grinned. "Next week I want to try the motion compensation." Josh had converted Matt's equations into working software that would, in theory, allow them to pre-select what speed and direction the wormhole's tail appeared at. But something about that feature bothered him.

"I understand that to speed up the wormhole's tail relative to its mouth, we have to add extra energy during the drilling process. What I don't get is how the amount of energy correlates with the desired velocity. Your equations look similar to a kinetic energy relationship, you know, one-half mass times velocity squared. But what's the mass of a wormhole tail?"

Matt gave a lop-sided grin. "Yah, hyperspatial math can seem downright weird. The tail doesn't have any mass in the real-world sense, but has a 'hyper-mass' that is somewhat analogous to the relativistic mass defined in special relativity. The tail's hyper-mass is based on several factors, including its velocity relative to the wormhole's mouth and its distance from the mouth in 3-space. We have to speed up the tail's hyper-mass during the drilling, then, after it's open, continue pumping in energy to maintain that velocity. But there are still limits on how long we can keep the wormhole open."

Josh pondered Matt's explanation for a moment, then nodded. "Okay, I can accept that, at least for now. But that brings up another question."

"Shoot."

"Scenario: we open a wormhole four hundred kilometres up and we give its tail orbital speed, which is around twenty-six thousand kilometres per hour. That is do-able, right?"

Matt thought for a moment, then nodded. "Should be. At least for a short period. We'll need to pump in a lot of energy during drilling. About... one hundred and fifty megajoules. But, yah."

"Okay, so in that scenario, the wormhole's mouth here is moving at the earth rate, roughly three hundred metres per second due east, but the tail is moving at orbital speed. What happens when we put something, like one of your radio probes, through the wormhole? It gets instantly accelerated to twenty-six thousand kilometres per hour. It'll get destroyed!"

Matt chuckled. "I was wondering when you'd ask. The short answer is no, it won't." He paused. "You want the long answer?"

Josh nodded.

Matt grinned. "Okay, but don't say I didn't warn you. It's all about inertial reference frames. When we open a wormhole, we're creating a hyperspatial manifold through 10-space. A shortcut. That's only possible if a local, *non-inertial* reference frame exists, one that is independent of other inertial reference frames. From our reference frame here on Earth, the tail is moving at twenty-six thousand kilometres per hour. But in the wormhole's non-inertial reference frame, both ends are stationary with respect to each other."

Josh scratched his head. "So the transmitter we toss through—either it's going twenty-six thousand kilometres per hour or it isn't. Which is it?"

"Both. Neither. Depends on your reference frame. To paraphrase Einstein, 'it's all relative'."

Josh was not yet willing to admit defeat. "So, if we stuck, say, a long pole through the wormhole, one end would be stationary here while the other end would be going twenty-six thousand kilometres per hour. That doesn't make sense. It can't be doing both!"

"You're right—it can't, but you can't look at it that way. The fact that we *can* open a wormhole and push stuff through means there has to be an answer that doesn't involve such a contradiction. The instant we open a wormhole, earth-centric and orbit-centric reference frames are no longer relevant—we have to use a wormhole-centric one. In *that* reference frame, the wormhole, and that wooden pole, are stationary."

Matt paused. "Think of it this way: we're using a lot of energy to make a bridge, or shortcut, between reference frames with different velocity vectors."

Josh was only partially convinced. "If we push a mass through a wormhole that has an accelerated tail, aren't we violating the law of conservation of energy?"

"What do you mean?"

"Let's say we push through something with a mass of ten kilograms. You can't tell me that once it comes out the other side, it's *not* moving at orbital speed? It started here on the Earth, with zero kinetic energy, to..."

"Two hundred and sixty megajoules," Matt said, having done the math in his head.

"So, where did that energy come from?"

"When we created the wormhole with the moving tail. Moving mass through an accelerated wormhole tail doesn't violate the First Law of Thermodynamics. There is, however, a limit to how much mass can pass through the wormhole—exceed that and the wormhole will destabilize. I think there's a way to compensate—I want to experiment with that in the coming weeks."

"Huh," Josh said, not fully comfortable with Matt's explanation but willing to give him the benefit of the doubt. "I guess I'll have to see it with my own eyes."

Matt nodded. "Having created wormholes for almost a year now, I've found it's best just to go with it. If nature lets us do something, then our inability to understand it doesn't negate that reality."

Josh soon got his wish. In the following weeks, they opened several wormholes a day, increasing the tail's speed each time while keeping the altitude constant at four hundred kilometres. By the seventh drill, they were up to orbital speed, just over twenty-seven thousand kilometres per hour. Matt's estimate on how much additional energy was required during drilling was amazingly accurate; each time they tossed a radio probe through, the Doppler shift measured by the radio antenna on the building's roof read exactly what Matt predicted. They also tossed heavy lead ingots through non-accelerated wormholes while Josh monitored the HYDRA's response to the large mass transfer (this produced a brilliant meteor shower that baffled astronomers for weeks). Based on these experiments, Josh added software that displayed a "mass remaining" counter on one of the computer monitors.

Josh had mostly accepted Matt's explanation about local non-inertial reference frames and conservation of energy, but still suspected that Matt was somehow beating the universe at its own game. Then he remembered Matt's aphorism: *If the universe lets you do something bizarre, don't waste time pondering the 'why'—just work backwards and figure out the 'how.'*

Josh was also struggling with another, more personal issue. He'd been raised in a staunch Baptist family that literally believed in the End Times and the Second Coming of Jesus Christ. Those beliefs had shaped the young man he'd become, but his interest in science and math had caused those beliefs to waver as he moved from childhood to adulthood. And Matt's revolutionary merging of physics, mathematics, and engineering made his problem worse.

If Matt is beating the universe at its own game, does that mean he's beating God at His game? Is that a sin? Is that evil?

Matt's theory may explain the entirety of the physical universe—does that mean Matt knows what God knows?

Does that make God redundant?

It was enough to make his head spin and lose sleep over. He took some comfort in knowing that in just over three months, he'd mastered the HYDRA software, even though he was just scratching the surface of the underlying multi-dimensional mathematics. He was already thinking of the improvements he could make to the HYDRA control system if he could get his hands on the new computer technology coming onto the market. The computer revolution was underway, and the first generation of 32-bit minicomputers were coming on the market, from companies like Digital Equipment Corporation and Data General.

Josh's presence also meant Matt had another pair of hands around. With Josh manning the controls, Matt was able to make detailed measurements around the HYDRA while it was operating. He spent hours moving around the periphery of open wormholes, probing with various magnetic and electronic sensors while wearing a climbing harness anchored by rope to the concrete floor. During these tests, Josh's hand always hovered near the emergency stop button he'd insisted Matt wire up. Josh was, on a primitive level, horrified that his friend was so close to something unnatural that created a direct path to the cold, dark vacuum of space.

By the end of November, they'd tested all Josh's software changes. "What's next?" he said on their drive back to Cambridge one night. Matt told him.

Josh whistled. "That's audacious."

"Everything ready?"

Josh scanned his monitors, then nodded. "Power-up tests have passed. Calibration is complete. I've input the latest astronomical ephemeris. Our target's orbital parameters—the latest numbers from NASA—are loaded." He checked a couple of readouts on his monitor. "It will take just over forty-five megajoules to open the wormhole at the desired velocity vector, and another... five megajoules per second to keep it open. The target will be above the horizon in... six minutes."

"Perfect," Matt said. "Program it so the drill is complete when the target is thirty degrees above the horizon. That should give us a good ten minutes to track it, if my math is right."

Josh typed in a few commands; the HYDRA software mulled the problem over for a few thousand milliseconds. "It says the drill should start in four minutes, thirty-two seconds."

"Okay," Matt said. "Let's do it."

Josh nodded. He hit a couple of keys on his keyboard and one of his monitors displayed "4:32" in large block letters, then started counting down.

When the counter reached zero, Josh's software took over. Relays closed, power supplies hummed, valves opened to pump liquid nitrogen into the electromagnets. Crude bar graphs displayed key values better than the columns of number that used to scroll by. The HYDRA creaked and groaned as it began its fantastical tunnelling through the fifth and tenth dimensions to its destination: four hundred kilometres into space.

Josh rolled his chair over to a nearby table that had eight Betamax video recorders—one connected to each of the video cameras strategically aimed at the HYDRA—and punched their record buttons. He rolled back and checked his monitors.

"One minute to go!" he yelled over the HYDRA's din.

On schedule, the HYDRA let loose its characteristic shriek. The milky-lens wormhole appeared in the middle of the structure, accompanied by the roar of air rushing out of the cavernous room.

Josh scanned the numbers on the monitors. "Looks good! We're at the right altitude. Velocity vector looks correct. Stresses are within limits." He turned to Matt. "You're up!"

"Okay, I'm ready," Matt said, checking the climbing harness he was wearing before clipping it to a rope tied to an anchor on the concrete floor. He picked up a three-metre-long wooden pole—an inch in diameter—that had a video camera mounted on one end, its cable trailing back along the concrete floor to a video monitor in front of Josh. The image on that monitor jerked around as Matt cautiously approached the HYDRA along its centerline, staying in the null of its intense magnetic fields.

"I still think this is a dumb idea," Josh muttered.

Matt reached the limit of his safety rope, two metres from the wormhole mouth that hovered magically between the HYDRA's rings. The supports creaked and groaned.

"Ready?" Matt yelled over the roar of air.

"Ready!" Josh yelled back, making a mental note: *We should have an intercom and headsets, so it's easier to communicate.*

The video feed from the "pole-cam" briefly turned to static as Matt pushed it towards the wormhole. The image cleared as the camera passed through and into the vacuum of space.

"Keep it steady!" Josh yelled.

"It's like trying to hold an umbrella on a windy day!" Matt yelled back.

The image cleared as Matt pushed the camera further in.

"Okay, that's better!" Josh yelled. "Give me a slow clockwise rotation."

Matt complied, and the image shifted. Matt had rotated the pole a quarter-turn when the Earth came into view.

"Stop turning! No, back ten degrees! There! Stop there!"

Matt held the pole as steady as he could.

Josh squinted at the monitor, trying to get his bearings. The Earth's terminator was a sharp line separating the blackness of space from the blue-white marble turning below. It took him a few seconds to pick out familiar geographical features. The camera was pointing down and to the southwest; he could see the coastline of Greenland, its glacial whiteness contrasted by the vivid blue ocean.

"Okay, do a slow rotation to the right," Josh yelled, glancing at the video recorder connected to Matt's camera, making sure it was still running.

Matt's calculations were bang on. From the corner of the monitor, a silver object crept into view.

"Stop! Stop right there!" Josh yelled. The American space station Liberty appeared, the sun reflecting off its solar panels and silver-white hull sections. "You got it, dead centre! It's about... a kilometre away!"

"Excellent!" Matt yelled. "Any relative motion?"

Josh watched the monitor for ten seconds. "I'd say it's moving slightly faster!"

"Okay, let's keep on it."

Ten minutes later, a combination of hyperspatial stress and Matt's tired arms put an end to the experiment. Matt withdrew the pole-cam, then backed away from the HYDRA before Josh typed in the shutdown command. The wormhole winked out of existence; the cavernous room was silent but for the creaking of the HYDRA's structure.

"Woo-hoo!" Matt yelled as he laid the pole-cam on the concrete floor and shrugged off his harness. He went over to the bank of recorders, hit the stop button on each and ejected the tape cartridges. "Movie night!"

They reconvened in the meeting room with two bowls of buttered popcorn, a case of soda pop (what the British called "fizzy drink"), and a stack of Betamax cartridges. The video from the pole-cam was the first one they watched on the meeting room's larger monitor.

"Looks like your calculations were bang on," Josh said. "Imagine that, getting video from a wormhole moving at 26,000 kilometres per hour!"

"Yah, not bad for a first attempt. The wormhole tail was slightly slower than the station, but that's likely a round-off error in the calculations. Hmm... don't think we can improve on that."

"I wonder if the astronauts on the space station saw anything," Josh wondered.

Matt moved closer to the monitor. "We need a better camera. Two hundred and fifty lines of resolution aren't enough. I want more detail."

Josh nodded. "I'll get Gary on it."

They replayed the tape several times, at normal and slow-motion speeds. "I still can't get over the fact that you were holding onto a pole whose far end was moving at orbital speed."

Matt grinned. "I know. But today's accomplishment means our next drill should be *much* easier. Way further out, but significantly lower relative velocity."

◎

Josh scanned his computer monitors when the HYDRA shuddered uncharacteristically. Nothing was amiss, other than some slightly higher than normal stress readings on the structure.

"I expected those," Matt said, sitting beside him. "They're well within our safety tolerances. Oh, nice hat, by the way."

Josh smiled. "Same to you. Gary did a good job." Shortly after Gary had returned to Canada after their Cambridge reunion, he decided to design the company's logo. The "official" AdAstra baseball caps were bright orange and sported a futuristic double-A symbol based on the Starfleet insignia from Star Trek.

Josh glanced at the monitor showing the pole-cam's video; Matt had jury-rigged a bracket and wooden stand to hold it in place so he could set it up then move back to the console. The monitor showed the pole-cam "flying" slowly about a kilometre above a pockmarked, barren, grey-brown terrain.

That's the surface of the moon!

Josh glanced at another monitor that showed the HYDRA and the pole shoved into the wormhole's mouth.

The video camera at the end of that three-metre-long pole is 380,000 kilometres away!

"Nice to be tracking something that's tidally locked, eh?" Matt said, reading Josh's mind.

Josh nodded. The moon rotated on its axis in almost the same time it took to orbit the Earth, so the relative velocity of any location on the lunar surface was only 3,600 kilometres per hour, a fraction of low-earth orbital speed. The drilling distance (in 3-space) was three orders of magnitude further than their previous orbital efforts; they needed more energy to drill that far, but less to keep the wormhole open, so the stress on the HYDRA's support structure was significantly lower.

"Ready," Matt said.

"It's all yours," Josh replied, sliding his keyboard over. He monitored the readouts as Matt typed a command to execute an interactive script he and Josh had written and debugged over the past week. Another monitor, blank until now, lit up; several columns of numbers began scrolling by.

"Here we go," Matt said. "Watch the hyperspatial stress and shear numbers."

"Got it." Josh knew, at least in principle, what those numbers represented, but still had trouble reconciling them with the esoteric mathematics of hyperspatial drilling.

"Okay," Matt said, "I'll try to null the relative motion one axis at a time." He typed in a few numbers, his head swivelling between the pole-cam monitor and the scrolling columns of numbers. In response, the HYDRA structure let out a groan.

"It's working," Josh said. "The landscape is going by slower now. Stress is up ten percent, shear is up thirty-two percent."

Matt didn't respond—he was off in his "mathematical hyperspace."

After a minute of typing, the video image stabilized; the wormhole's tail was now moving at the same speed as the moon's rotation.

"Everything looking good?" Matt asked.

"Yup," Josh replied.

Matt nodded. "Okay, let's see if we can get closer." He tapped at the keyboard; the HYDRA let out another groan and the video image jumped—the tail had increased altitude.

"Oops," Matt said. "I forgot—the reference frame on the far-side is inverted. Let's make that a minus sign." *Tap tap tap.*

The HYDRA let out another groan and the image shifted, the view now only a hundred metres above the lunar surface. Several massive boulders were perched on the edge of an enormous impact crater.

"Whoa!" he exclaimed. "We're so close!" He looked over at the video recorder bank to make sure they were recording this historic event.

"Maybe we can get closer," Matt said. *Tap tap tap.*

The image shifted again. Fifty metres.

Tap tap tap. Twenty-five metres.

Tap tap tap. Ten metres.

Tap tap tap. Five metres. The air rushing out of the wormhole's tail began kicking up lunar dust, obscuring their view.

"We're so close, we could practically reach out and grab rocks!" Josh exclaimed. He glanced at his monitor. "Stress and shear are approaching safety limits."

Matt nodded. "I'm going to back off."

Tap tap tap. Ten metres. The dust settled.

"Let's leave it here and see what happens," Matt said. "Get ready to hit the panic button if I call for an abort."

Josh nodded, glancing over at the large red button mounted on the console.

The HYDRA creaked and groaned for several minutes; Matt stared at the numbers scrolling by, mumbling to himself, and jotting notes on a legal pad.

"Stress is over-limit," Josh reported. "Shear is climbing rapidly."

"It should destabilize any time now," Matt said.

Seconds later, the HYDRA let out a horrible shriek and the wormhole disappeared with a loud "pop." The control system responded, initiating a controlled shutdown.

"Well, I'd call that a win," Matt said.

"Darn, that was cool," Josh said. "Renny's going to be *so* jealous." He rolled his chair over to the video recorders, hit all the stop buttons, and extracted the Betamax tapes.

"Yup," Matt agreed. "We've got three weeks before Christmas. Today's test gave me some insights into tweaks for the motion compensator. I'd like to make those changes, then do a few drills to low-Earth orbit."

Josh nodded. "Let's keep it simple. It'd be nice to go home for the holidays on a high note."

FOURTEEN

Matt was woken from a deep sleep by a persistent banging on the door to his flat. He stumbled from his bedroom in the dark, stubbing his toe on the sofa. Josh burst in.

"You gotta see this," he said, turning Matt's television to BBC One. Matt shook his head to clear the cobwebs.

They had to wait a minute for the commercial break to end. "And for those of you who just joined us, here's a recap of our top story. Two hours ago, NASA reported a mishap on the American space station Liberty. An astronaut was performing a routine spacewalk to replace an external camera, and somehow his tether came loose. When he used his emergency jetpack, it malfunctioned, and the astronaut is now drifting away from the station. According to NASA, the stranded astronaut has only four hours of oxygen left. The remaining astronauts on the space station are attempting to mount a rescue operation, but it will take hours to prepare. NASA has not released the name of the stranded astronaut, but our sources have confirmed it is Scott 'Red' Hansen. Known for his flaming red hair, Hansen is an experienced NASA astronaut on his second rotation at Liberty."

The announcer paused. "This could be a major blow to the American space program, which has suffered many problems in the past year. They've been struggling to keep their space station operational amidst budget cuts and a less-than-reliable space shuttle fleet. Critics claim NASA is moving too fast, sacrificing safety for cost and schedule. We'll update you when we learn more."

Matt stared at the screen. "They can't mount a rescue that quick," he said. "It takes six hours of pre-breathing oxygen just to get into a spacesuit. Then there's the decompression phase, which takes another seven hours." Matt knew every published fact about the American space program.

"And just last week we spied on them with the pole-cam," Josh said. "Isn't there anything we can do?"

Matt was already working the problem, the puzzle, looking for a way to use the HYDRA to help the stricken astronaut. Thanks to Josh's hard work in the past four months, they'd improved the motion compensation system, so keeping pace with the space station wouldn't be a problem, at least for a few minutes. They could now hold a wormhole in low-earth orbit open for eleven minutes, but its diameter was only twenty-five centimetres.

There's no way we can get the astronaut through the wormhole.

"We've put the pole-cam through before," Josh said. "Can we get close enough to reach through and just push him back to the station?"

Matt had already considered and rejected that idea, along with another eight possibilities that came to mind. "Not enough delta-vee. If we could position the wormhole behind him... the out-rushing air would push him back. Let me think..."

Josh was silent as Matt mumbled, solving a set of complex fluid dynamics equations faster than most computers. He shook his head.

"Nope. Thrust from the air would be miniscule. It would take hours just to cancel his velocity, and we can only keep the wormhole open for eleven minutes, tops."

"There's gotta be something we can do," Josh pleaded.

Matt stared at the wall, his mind racing.

Come on, Barnes! Think laterally!

We can't get the astronaut through the wormhole.

What can we put through the wormhole that would help him?

The astronaut's malfunctioning jetpack was the problem, but AdAstra didn't have a spare jetpack lying around. Even if they did, it wouldn't fit through a twenty-five-centimetre-wide wormhole. He stared at the nearest wall.

What do we have that could help the astronaut?

His eidetic memory came to the rescue as he mentally reviewed literally every item in the building, looking for something, anything, that could help.

"Ah, that might work..." he muttered. He turned to Josh. "Let's get going—I'll explain on the way."

Matt threw on some clothes, donning his bright orange AdAstra baseball cap as they rushed out the door. He started the ancient Vauxhall and pulled out of his parking spot, almost squealing his tires. He explained his idea as they headed northeast.

"You're not serious!" Josh said. "It's metal. What makes you think it won't explode when you get it near the HYDRA?"

"Can't happen. It's made of aluminum, the handle is stainless steel, and the rest is rubber and plastic. All non-ferromagnetic materials."

"You're going to have to stand a lot closer to the HYDRA that when we used the pole-cam. It's too dangerous!" Josh's voice was tinged with fear.

"I've considered *all* other possibilities—this is the only one that has a chance," Matt said. "The worst that could happen is it doesn't work." He drove faster, hoping the local constabulary wasn't out on this isolated stretch of road.

Josh shook his head. "No, the worst is you getting sucked through a wormhole only twenty-five centimetres wide. You'll have to be less than a metre from it, and there's a hard vacuum on the other side!"

"I know. But it's our only option."

They arrived at AdAstra in record time. The pair rushed inside the old industrial building and headed straight for the main hall, where the HYDRA waited like a sleeping dragon.

"Okay, first things first," Matt said. "You get the HYDRA powered up and run the diagnostics."

Matt paused, solving a complex three-dimensional orbital trigonometry problem then, extrapolating for the current date and time. "Ah, good. The ground track of the station's current and next orbits is just west and just east of us. That means we've got two shots at this, ninety minutes apart. I need to find some stuff." He started rummaging through the workshop while Josh threw switches on the electrical panels.

◎

Twenty minutes later...

Josh's heart pounded against his chest wall, and his breathing was reduced to gasps as he tried to watch the HYDRA's readouts, keep an eye on Matt, and watch the monitor showing the video feed from the pole-cam. He fought down the urge to throw up as he uttered a silent prayer to a God he was starting to question.

"There! Stop turning!" he yelled over the roar of air being sucked into the wormhole. "Go back to your left. I see him! He's twenty metres away! He's... he's waving at us. In-freaking credible!" Josh stood up to peer over the concrete wall.

Matt was standing less than a metre from the HYDRA, looking like St. George, the Roman soldier and priest, battling an enormous dragon while armed with only a small sword. Air was roaring past him into the mouth of the wormhole as he struggled to hold the pole-cam steady. He'd secured his climbing harness with two ropes: one to a bracket bolted to the concrete floor, the other around an overhead beam. The camera's cable, crossing the floor to the video monitor at Josh's console, whipped back and forth in the wind.

"What are the numbers?" Josh yelled. "I need the new numbers!"

To implement Matt's daring plan, they had to position the wormhole tail perfectly, and from the image coming from the pole-cam, they weren't close enough.

"Hang on, calculating..." Matt yelled.

Josh waited a long three seconds while Matt solved a complex series of five-dimensional geometrical calculations in his head, then yelled out four numbers. Josh typed in the numbers and hit the Enter key. The HYDRA's support structure groaned in protest.

The astronaut's image on the monitor suddenly got smaller.

"No! No! Wrong way! Wrong way!" Josh yelled over the howling wind. "He's further away!"

"Shit!" Matt yelled, looking over his shoulder at Josh. "Those numbers should be right!"

Josh checked to make sure he'd input the numbers correctly. Yes, he had.

Hang on, Matt keeps forgetting the reference frame on the far side of the wormhole is inverted.

"Matt, what about the—"

His friend realized his mistake at the same instant. "The numbers should be negative!" Matt yelled. "Make all the numbers NEGATIVE!"

Josh rapidly re-typed the numbers, this time with minus signs, and hit the Enter key. He turned his attention to the pole-cam monitor as the HYDRA let out another groan. The view changed. The US flag on the astronaut's backpack filled the monitor.

"It's working! It's working!" Josh yelled. "We're right behind him! About a metre away! Hurry, Matt!"

Matt pushed the pole as far in as he could, felt it hit something, then pulled it all the way out and tossed it behind him. The pole-cam video turned to static briefly before showing a sideways view as it lay on the concrete floor, facing the HYDRA. Josh held his breath as Matt reached for the red cylinder he'd loosely tied to his leg.

This is the moment of truth!

"What's happening?" Josh yelled. He'd lost the video feed when Matt pulled the camera out of the wormhole. His bladder was about to let loose as he stood up and looked over the wall.

"I think he's got it," Matt yelled, holding onto a climbing rope that disappeared into the wormhole. "It's hard to tell for sure 'cause it's so blurry!"

The next ten seconds seemed to take forever. The rope jerked, then fell slack. He gave it a light tug, then pulled more; the rope came out with a carabiner on its end, bouncing in the breeze.

"He's got it!" Matt yelled.

The odour of burning electrical insulation stung Josh's nose; behind him, smoke poured from a power supply on the equipment rack.

"We've got a problem here! I've got to shut it down!"

"I'm clear!" Matt said, stepping back.

Josh slammed his hand down on the red emergency stop button. The HYDRA let out a mighty shriek, and the wormhole winked out of existence. With the intense magnetic forces now gone, the HYDRA's support structure groaned as the stresses from holding open the inter-dimensional conduit vanished. The intense magnetic fields collapsed, sending hundreds of thousands of amps of back-current into the load dump in a fraction of a second. The water in the tank flash-boiled, sending a mushroom cloud of oily steam up to the girdered ceiling.

As the out-rushing air instantly abated, the rope Matt was holding whipped across his forehead, knocking him backwards onto the concrete floor. He stared up at the ceiling, watching the steam cloud dissipate amongst the girders overhead. The odour of burnt power resistors filled the air.

"We're gonna need a bigger load dump," he muttered.

Josh was standing over him. "Are you ok? Still got the right number of fingers?"

Matt nodded, then sat up and gingerly touched a carabiner-shaped welt on his forehead. "All systems operating," he said, mimicking Lt. Commander Data from the new Star Trek TV series. He looked around. "Umm, do you see my hat anywhere?"

Josh helped Matt get shakily to his feet, then they went over to the electrical panel to inspect the damage. Matt wanted to fire up the HYDRA and use the pole-cam to see whether their plan had worked. Unfortunately, two high-voltage power supplies were now a pile of stinking, melted metal and plastic, and they didn't have any spares.

"It'll take at least a couple of days to replace them," Matt said forlornly.

Josh shut off the video recorders that had captured the entire event, extracted the tapes, then they went back to the kitchen. Matt turned the TV on to the BBC news, hoping for an update. They dropped into chairs, exhausted.

"I can't believe we just did that, Matt. I can't believe *you* just did that."

"Okay, so it wasn't the smartest thing I've done," he replied, wincing as he rubbed the welt on his forehead. "I sure hope it worked."

They had to wait almost an hour for the early morning news. The announcer came on with an image of the NASA logo displayed beside her.

"We have an update on our top news story. NASA just announced that tragedy at the American space station Liberty has been averted. The spacewalking astronaut, feared dead after drifting away from the station, has been rescued. NASA hasn't provided any details other than he's safe and back inside the station. He'll be returning to earth next month when the space shuttle arrives with the regular replacement crew."

Matt let out a whoop. "We did it!"

"Those finks!" Josh exclaimed. "They didn't say anything about us!"

Matt shrugged. "I didn't expect them to. Not easy explaining that a fire extinguisher appeared literally out of nowhere."

◎

It took a week to replace the blown power supplies, melted cables, and the big resistors cooked in the load dump tank. Three drills later into low-earth orbit confirmed that the HYDRA Mark II was back in working order. Their final drill of the year (#65) was back to the moon—the wormhole's tail hovering ten metres above the lunar surface. Just for fun, they lobbed one of Matt's radio transmitters in, then watched on the pole-cam as it gently touched down and rolled a few metres before coming to a stop in a small boulder field.

"That'll give the SETI guys something to ponder, at least until its battery dies," Josh quipped. "I'll check with my dad when we get home."

Matt spent his last week before the Christmas holidays at the university, setting the final exams for his courses while Josh took care of several housekeeping tasks. He took the stack of videotapes from their drills to an electronics shop they dealt with and had copies made, then secured the originals in AdAstra's safe.

Three days before Christmas, they locked up AdAstra, caught the train to London, then another to Heathrow, where Matt had booked them first-class tickets on a British Airways Boeing 747 to Vancouver. After a short layover, they boarded a Pacific Western Boeing 737 that got them into Penticton mid-afternoon on December 23rd.

The next morning, the four friends met in Matt's basement.

"We've made tons of progress in the past four months," Matt said. "Josh's done an awesome job optimizing the HYDRA software. Drilling times have dropped by sixteen percent. He found one nasty software bug that's been plaguing me for over a year, and we haven't had a magnet explode since. We added another computer and PLCs to automate the electrical and power controls, so there's no more manually closing relays. The motion compensation software is working—we opened a stationary wormhole in low-earth orbit for almost eleven minutes, and we're now able to hover just above the lunar surface for eight minutes."

Gary whistled. "That's so cool."

Renny scowled. "Damn, I want in on this now." He'd finished his first term in the master's degree program for planetary geology at the University of Arizona.

"Don't worry, Batman," Matt said. "There'll be lots of cool stuff for you to do."

"Uh, Matt?" Josh interjected. "That's it? What about the space station? And the astronaut?"

"What space station?" Renny said.

"What astronaut?" Gary said at the same instant.

"As usual, Matt's being modest," Josh said. "Remember that incident three weeks ago at NASA's space station? When the astronaut floated away but got rescued?" Both friends nodded.

"We rescued him! Matt and me!" Josh told the entire story.

"Come to think of it," Gary said, "NASA never did explain how he made it back."

"Show them the video," Josh urged.

Matt put the first of several video cassettes into the family's Betamax recorder, and the four watched the events unfold from several camera angles. It wasn't production-quality video by any means, but it captured what had taken place.

"Holy shit!" Renny exclaimed. "You were that close to a wormhole opened into space?"

Matt nodded.

"And you weren't worried you'd get sucked in?"

"Of course I was," Matt said. "But it was a risk I was willing to take. I had a safety line. Two, actually—I'm not suicidal."

Renny chuckled. "A fire extinguisher. You save him with a fucking fire extinguisher. Matt, only you could have thought that up."

"It looks like you broke a few things," Gary added, referring to the load dump flash-boil and other small fires visible in the videos.

"It took us a week to repair the damage, but we got the HYDRA running again," Josh said.

"Why can you only open a wormhole for such a short period?" Renny asked.

"Hyperspatial manifold torsional shear," Matt replied.

"Say what?" Gary said.

Josh shook his head. "Get used to it. He says stuff like that a lot. Best to just nod and move on."

Matt shrugged. "There's... there's no easy way to describe it. It's not that I don't want to explain it. The English language just doesn't have words to describe many of the things we do. Josh and I have started a lexicon to describe what we're doing in hyperspace."

Josh nodded. "I coded his equations for the planetary motion compensation, but I don't actually understand them. But you can't deny that they do work."

"Damn," Renny said. "You two are having all the fun." Gary nodded in agreement.

"Don't worry, guys," Matt said. "There's still lots of work for everyone. But enough about our end. Gary, what's your status?"

"Nadia did her thesis defence two weeks ago and passed. She'll get her PhD at the spring convocation!"

"When you two get married, you'll be Doctor and *Mister* Stocks." Renny never passed up a chance at a cheap shot. "Your kids will come from a mixed marriage."

"Screw you, Ape-Man. At least I mate within my species," he shot back. Ignoring Renny further, he continued. "And it gets better—we've signed a contract with National Geographic magazine. She's going to write an article about her discoveries, accompanied by my photographs!"

His friends applauded.

"Has she decided where she's going to do her post-doc work?" Matt asked. "Is she going to stay at the University of Toronto?"

Gary shook his head. "No, she accepted a position at another university—she starts in September."

"Wow," Josh said. "Where?"

"You might have heard of the place..." Gary said. "She's going to be an

Associate Professor in the Department of Archeology at a little school called the... University of Cambridge."

The room went silent.

Gary nodded. "Yup, we're gonna be neighbours!"

"That's three out of four," Josh said. "The band is getting back together."

Gary nodded. "Yup, now all we have to do is get Bigfoot here ed-u-cated and it'll be like old times!"

Renny growled.

"Gary, have you looked into the Columbus Prizes?" Matt said. "Josh and I have been so busy the past months we haven't given it any thought."

Gary nodded. "I've been working on it in my spare time. Orbiting a satellite is possible, depends on what the criteria are, you know, size, payload, number of orbits, etcetera. That's worth *ten million* British pounds. I sent a query letter to them a couple of months ago—got a boilerplate reply. They said they needed to know more about our company, want to meet us, blah, blah, blah, before they'll release any more information. My guess is they're filtering out the backyard inventors and lunatic fringe."

Renny snickered. "Which ones are we?"

Gary ignored him. "I've gone over the basic rules for the Lunar prizes— those will give us the best bang for our buck. Landing a vehicle on the moon and transmitting back video is worth a cool ten million pounds! That one's pretty easy—in fact, 'vehicle' is a misnomer, since there's nothing in the rules that says it has to move. We have to get something onto the surface of the moon that can transmit video back to earth."

"We could do that right now," Matt said. "We left a radio transmitter on the lunar surface a couple of weeks ago."

Josh chuckled. "Yah, according to my dad, it drove the SETI people crazy until it stopped transmitting."

Gary nodded. "Next: landing a robotic vehicle and getting it to travel five hundred metres or more while transmitting video. That's worth another ten million. I figure I can build a modified version of the TombCrawler—it's already small enough to fit through the wormhole."

"That would make it 'MoonCrawler,'" Renny noted.

"Good point," Gary said. "It'll need a video camera, radio transmitter, directional antenna, and smarts so it knows where to point the antenna. I figure you rocket scientists can figure that out. The real problem is making it work in a vacuum, in one-sixth gravity, and in the presence of cosmic radiation."

"You know," Josh said, "It doesn't have to be robust—it only has to travel five hundred metres."

"Good point," Matt said, thrilled to see the ideas flowing. "Just long enough to survive in vacuum for a while."

"We should land it somewhere on the moon that's flat, no obstacles," Renny said.

"I've got just the place," Matt said. He elaborated.

"Ooh, that's going to annoy the Americans," Josh said.

Renny raised his arms. "Bonus points!"

Gary continued. "Next: returning moon rocks, that's worth another ten million. Then there are several 'bonus' prizes for achieving other lunar objectives, each worth five million: travelling over five kilometres; doing a precision 'landing' near any of the Apollo landing sites; and operating through two lunar nights. Not sure how long that is."

"A lunar night is about two weeks," Renny said, partway through his master's degree courses in planetary geology and becoming AdAstra's expert on the subject.

"The precision landing should be do-able now that we've fine-tuned the motion compensation software," Josh said.

"Matt, you know that if we win these prizes, your little secret's going to get out, don't you?" Gary said.

"What do you mean?"

"If you pull this off, I mean *when we* pull this off, AdAstra will be in the news. Everywhere. You'll have reporters nosing around your facilities. They'll go through all your old research papers, talk to your professors, bug you and your parents, and so on."

Josh nodded. "I'll bet certain governments will be *very* interested."

Matt turned pale. "I never thought of that—I was hoping we could keep this under wraps."

Josh shook his head. "Not going to happen. This will be news. Big news."

"You're going to need security," Renny said. "Physical security. You know, to keep the lookie-loos away from the building."

Matt looked deflated, then remained silent for a minute, thinking. "You know, it's time we got some legal advice. Uncle Ed said Stuart will be spending most of his time in his law firm's head office in London for the next couple of years."

"Maybe he can contact the Columbus Group and start the ball rolling?" Josh said. "If anyone can get us those prizes without giving away too much information, it'll be Stuart."

◎

The foursome spent most of their Christmas vacation in Matt's basement, planning for the coming year and only interrupting their work for obligatory family gatherings. At the first opportunity, Matt invited Stuart over and brought him down to the basement, where his three friends were waiting. It took them an hour to fill him in. He was skeptical until he saw the videos, including the dramatic rescue of the NASA astronaut.

"Matt, I'm amazed," Stuart said. "Not surprised, mind you, but amazed. You really can open—you call it a 'wormhole'—into space?"

"We sure can!" Josh said. "I've been working with him for four months now. We've done sixty-five drills so far," he added with pride.

Matt described their plans to go after the Columbus Prizes. "So, given what we're about to attempt, it's time AdAstra retained legal counsel. You interested?"

Stuart nodded enthusiastically. "You betcha. I'm licensed as a solicitor in the UK now, and my employment contract permits me to take outside work as long as there's no conflict of interest. Tell me again how you helped that NASA astronaut?"

Matt went over the details again, showing the video twice. Stuart was quiet the whole time.

"Stu, I know that look," Matt said. "What's going on that devious legal mind of yours?"

"Well, you guys saved that astronaut from certain death, right?"

Matt nodded.

"When your operation becomes public, and it will, that rescue could be worth something. Maybe a reward? What's the life of an astronaut worth? It might be something you could use as leverage. Or a bargaining chip. Something to keep in your back pocket."

"I never considered that," Matt said.

"Well, here's something else to ponder. If you win those prizes, you're looking at what, thirty million pounds?"

"At least."

"What are you going to do with the money? Put it in the bank? You said you want to build a bigger... HYDRA, you call it? What's that going to cost?"

Matt shrugged. "I dunno—maybe... ten million pounds?"

"I'm no engineer," Stuart said, "But that sounds like an enormous project. You're going to need project managers, engineers, construction workers, tradespeople, etcetera. Your company is going to have to grow exponentially to handle the workers and logistics. You'll need to hire lots of staff."

Matt looked dejected. "I never thought of that. You're right, though."

"Let's worry about that *after* you win the prizes," Stuart said.

FIFTEEN

The New Year began with the guys implementing their grand plan. Renny returned to Arizona to continue his master's degree courses, reluctant to be missing out on the Columbus Prize preparations but looking forward to continuing his education. Stuart accompanied Matt, Gary, and Josh to the UK, then stopped off in London to contact the Columbus Group. Gary stayed with Josh until a vacancy opened up in the building—a flat big enough for him and Nadia. With all of them living in the same building, they car-pooled to AdAstra's headquarters in Matt's old Vauxhall.

The trio fell into a comfortable routine: whenever Matt wasn't teaching at Cambridge, he was at AdAstra, advancing his design of the HYDRA Mark III; Josh was tweaking the HYDRA's software to improve the motion compensation; and Gary was working on his MoonCrawler Mark I. Matt spent his evenings marking assignments while Gary and Josh stayed up late playing video games on the just-released Nintendo Entertainment System. The trio had adopted a local Cambridge pub—"public houses" in England— called The Eagle for their off-site meetings. Besides boasting a delicious food menu, The Eagle was where, in 1953, biologists Watson and Crick announced their discovery of the structure of DNA (which earned them the Nobel Prize). It also had the oldest version of an arcade claw machine Gary had ever seen. It took him two hours and several pocketfuls of fifty-pence coins, but eventually he prevailed over the ancient Taito-brand machine.

"Who's the Claw Master?" he yelled, returning to the table clutching a faded stuffed animal.

"You're the Claw Master!" his friends roared in unison.

"I made *that* machine my bitch," Gary said. "Just think, there's a country full of pubs with claw machines... I think I'm going to like it here."

With each successful "drill," the trio gained experience, refining the art and science of creating a shortcut through hyperspace. They had one goal: win the Columbus Prizes. To do that, not only did they need to open a stationary wormhole metres above the lunar surface, they had to figure out how to deploy the MoonCrawler and a video transmitter.

◎

Stuart gazed out the large window of the compartment as his train pulled into the Cambridge train station. The eighty-minute ride from London King's Cross Station had been pleasant, allowing him time to enjoy the late spring scenery north of London. Matt was waiting for him on the platform.

"Hey, cuz."

"Hey, Stu. How'd things go with the Columbus Group?" Matt asked as he pulled away from the kerb in his old Vauxhall.

"Good. It'd be easier if I briefed everyone at once, though."

Matt shrugged.

"How are things going?" Stuart said.

"Great! Having another pair of hands around is improving efficiency. You picked a good day to visit—we're doing a test drill this afternoon."

"Awesome. Ever since I saw those videos at Christmas, I've been dying to seeing the HYDRA in action."

Matt stopped at a pub—correction, public house—to pick up sandwiches and drinks. Twenty minutes later, he parked in front of a dilapidated old building in the middle of a deserted industrial area northeast of town.

What a dump, Stuart thought.

"Welcome to AdAstra," Matt said as he unlocked the door.

Stuart pointed at the sign beside the door sporting a stylized double-A symbol. "Is that your corporate logo? It looks familiar."

Matt smiled. "Yup, Gary came up with it. It's based on the Starfleet insignia, you know, from Star Trek?"

"Ah, now I remember." *A bunch of nerds. Brilliant, but still nerds.*

Matt ushered Stuart in, then down the hallway and through a large metal door into a cavernous room. Josh was at the main computer console, head down, typing away and oblivious to everything around him. Gary was in the far corner, winching something up to the ceiling.

Matt waved his arms wide. "Welcome to Chaos Central!"

Stuart's eyes were drawn to the fantastic assembly in the middle of the hall. He let out a low whistle.

"So, this is it," he said, circling the HYDRA and stepping over the cable bundles snaking across the floor. "It looks much bigger than in the videos."

"Wait 'till you see it in action," Matt said, smiling as they returned to the main console.

Josh finally looked up. "Hi, Stuart!"

"How'd the bug hunt go?" Matt said.

"Good. Found it first thing this morning in your original code. You may be a mathematical genius, but you suck at programming. All the tests have passed, so we're ready to go anytime."

"Great. Let's have lunch so Stu can update us, then we'll do the test drill." Josh nodded. They went over to where Gary was attaching a rope to a contraption on the shop floor. The rope went up through a pulley hanging from an overhead beam.

"Hey, Gary. Whatcha up to?"

"Hi, Stuart! Testing out the MoonCrawler. Matt showed me how to modify that pulley up there to simulate one-sixth lunar gravity. When the MoonCrawler lands, the rope will release and the MoonCrawler will automatically activate. Watch."

Gary pulled on the rope, hoisting the MoonCrawler up to the ceiling ten metres above. "Ladies, I need a countdown."

Stuart joined in as they chimed, "Five, four, three, two, one, LAUNCH!"

Gary let go of the rope.

The MoonCrawler fell unnaturally slow, just like it would on the moon. It gently hit the floor, bounced once, and the rope automatically released.

It remained motionless for five seconds, then came to life, its four wheels extending one at a time. A small dish antenna unfolded and swivelled around before settling on a particular orientation. They applauded. Gary bowed.

One of the MoonCrawler's wheel assemblies jerked, and the vehicle tipped over onto its back, its four wheels twitching like a beetle stuck upside down, its antenna now folded over. Matt snickered.

Gary frowned. "Hmm, still got a few bugs to fix."

"It looks like a bug," Josh said.

"Guys, let's break for lunch," Matt said.

The four headed back to the meeting room, got comfortable in their usual seats, and dug into their food.

Stuart downed half a sandwich, then cleared his throat. "I contacted the Columbus Group and spoke with their head of legal affairs. I told them I represented a private company that was interested in going for their prizes. As you requested, I told them my client has developed an unconventional method of space transportation and wants to keep his proprietary information under wraps. They gave me a package containing the legal terms, along with an application form." He dropped a thick manila envelope on the table.

"Has anyone else applied?" Josh asked.

Stuart shook his head. "As of last week, no. But I have good news and bad news. The bad news: the rules are clear—to win *any* of the prizes, Columbus Group representatives *must* inspect your facilities and observe the 'launch' and 'landing' on the moon."

"I don't want any strangers in here," Matt protested.

"Matt, you can't expect Columbus to give you tens of millions of pounds without them seeing your facilities. You'll have to *prove* that your operation works."

"I guess a live video feed from the moon won't be good enough?" Gary grumped.

Stuart shook his head. "No. They need to see how you get the vehicle to the moon. If you want their prize money, you have to play by *their* rules."

Matt sighed. "You mentioned good news?"

Stuart nodded. "My comment about an 'unconventional method of space transportation' piqued their interest. They pressed me for details, and I re-iterated that my client has a great deal of intellectual property they want protected. So, they agreed to sign a non-disclosure agreement."

He grinned from ear-to-ear.

"The Barnes NDA?" Matt asked hopefully.

"Yup. Tweaked for British law, of course." Stuart chuckled. "They don't yet realize that NDA will govern any future contracts they might sign with you." He paused. "You know, I thought their legal team would be smarter, given who they work for."

"Won't Columbus be pissed when they figure that out?" Gary said. "Maybe we shouldn't bite the hand that's going to feed us..."

Stuart held up a hand. "Not to worry. Legal maneuvering like this is normal in contract negotiations. For now, read over the contest details. Oh, there's one more thing..."

"What's that?" Matt asked.

"The rules refer to the 'Outer Space Treaty,' so I did some digging. Its real name is the 'United Nations Treaty on Principles Governing the Activities of States in the Exploration and Use of Outer Space, including the Moon and Other Celestial Bodies,' and came into effect in 1967 when it was signed by the US, the Soviet Union, the UK, Canada, and a bunch of other countries. It says that space, and any other celestial body, is free for exploration and is not subject to any national claim of sovereignty. No nukes, peaceful purposes only, etc."

"Well, we don't plan on putting nukes on the moon or claiming sovereignty, so why does it concern us?" Matt said warily.

"Every signatory state of the treaty, including the UK, is responsible for activities carried out by non-governmental agencies on its soil. Like AdAstra."

"Seriously? We'll have to report to some government bureaucrats?"

Stuart put up his hands. "Easy there, cuz. It's not as bad as you think. I dug deeper. While the UK was a signatory, they never ratified the treaty. That means they never legally accepted or approved it. That gives us *some* wriggle room. Several years ago, the UK government started up the British National Space Centre—an agency to coordinate civil space activities on its soil. But that agency appears to be defunct. I made some calls, but hit dead ends at every turn."

Matt sighed. "Stu, one more thing. Could you look into the legal status of hardware left on the moon from the American and Soviet lunar missions? And stuff in orbit around the Earth? Does it still belong to those countries or is it fair game for salvage? Gary has an idea for a remote-controlled grappling claw we could use not only to pick up moon rocks but also other smaller stuff lying around."

Stuart chuckled. *Gary is the undisputed world champion at arcade claw games.* "Way ahead of you, cuz. Article VIII of the treaty basically says that whoever launches an object into space or onto a celestial body retains jurisdiction over it."

"So we're screwed," Gary said.

"Again, no," Stuart said. "The way that clause is written means it doesn't apply to *abandoned* equipment. If you were to, say, grab someone's working satellite, you'd be in a world of trouble. I'm fairly confident anything in orbit or on the moon that doesn't work is fair game. Let me worry about that for now."

Matt let out a sigh of relief.

"Now, about that demonstration?" Stuart said.

Matt nodded. "Okay, here's today's plan. Drill number 89: the moon's in a suitable position today, so we're going to open a wormhole one hundred metres above the lunar surface, then nudge it down to two metres. As usual, Josh will operate the HYDRA. Gary will deploy the pole-cam to get us a video feed, and I'll watch the video so I can tweak the motion compensator. Once the tail is stable, Gary will deploy a transmitter. This transmitter has an extra-large battery pack because I want to leave it on the moon's surface so we can confirm relative rotation through the Doppler shift." Stuart ate his lunch and listened as Matt walked them through the plan, using technical phrases that were way beyond him.

"And if we have any problems?" Matt asked.

"HIT THE RED BUTTON!" his friends yelled in unison, laughing.

Once they'd finished lunch, they returned to the main hall. Stuart sat behind Josh and Matt at the console as they prepared for the drill. Once Gary had the pole-cam ready, Matt helped him into his safety harness.

"Everyone ready?" Matt asked, getting nods in return. "Ok, Josh. I've entered the coordinates. Start drilling!"

Josh typed in a sequence of commands. Columns of numbers started scrolling on the monitors. Stuart shivered as unworldly sounds emanated from the HYDRA. He watched the video monitors carefully, their images slowly rotating as the HYDRA's magnetic fields increased. Every few minutes, he got up and peeked over the wall, shaking his head at the scene.

"This thing's actually drilling through... hyperspace right now?" he asked over the whine.

Josh nodded. "Still amazes me, too."

The HYDRA emitted a shriek as the wormhole opened, the sound sending a shiver up Stuart's spine. A roar filled the large room as the air rushed into the wormhole's maw.

Matt keyed his mike and his voice boomed from a loudspeaker mounted to the ceiling. "Okay, Gary. Camera in!"

Gary moved cautiously towards the HYDRA until his safety lines were taut, then carefully fed the video camera through.

"We've got video," Josh shouted over the roar of air as they watched the monitor, just a grey blur. For ten seconds, Matt stared at the dozens of numbers scrolling by on his computer monitor, then began typing madly.

The HYDRA let out a groan. The grey blur on the monitor jerked and slowed, the lunar surface now visible, moving slowly left-to-right.

"Lateral motion looks minimal," Josh observed. "We're high, though. Maybe a hundred metres or so."

"I can fix that," Matt said, typing away. "We need a range-finder on that video camera so we know our altitude," he muttered. Josh scribbled on a notepad he kept beside his keyboard.

The HYDRA groaned again, this time not as loud; the lunar surface got closer. Matt watched it for a few moments. "That's the best I can do," he yelled. "Okay, Gary! Camera out! Probe in!"

Gary pulled the radio probe from a fanny pack around his waist and underhanded it into the wormhole, where it vanished with an obscene, sucking sound.

"Steeeee-rike!" he yelled. "Bomb's away!"

"Shutting down now," Josh said, typing in a command. The wormhole closed with a loud "pop" and the HYDRA's structure groaned as the hyperspatial forces it was fighting against vanished.

Stuart was silent for a moment, processing what he'd just seen. "In-freaking-credible!" he exclaimed.

Josh helped Gary out of his safety harnesses while Stuart followed Matt over to an equipment rack that controlled a radio antenna dish on the roof.

"See this?" Matt pointed at an oscilloscope as a paper plotter spit out a graph. "This is the signal from the transmitter we deployed. We'll leave it on auto-record, and then I can figure out the Doppler shift and correlate our readings with those from SETI."

With the demonstration complete, Matt drove Stuart to the train station so he could catch the five o'clock to London. On the short drive, Stuart rambled on about what he'd just seen.

"I'll let you know as soon as I hear from Columbus," he said as Matt pulled up to the train station.

"Sounds good, Stu. Glad to have you aboard."

As Stuart settled into his seat on the train, he reflected on the day's happenings.

I'm the fifth person in the history of mankind to have witnessed the creation of an artificial wormhole. Matt and his friends are on their way to great things, and I'm part of it!

◎

Stuart returned to AdAstra a month later to find many changes. Josh had cleaned up his normally messy control console. The wiring between the electronics racks had been dressed. The haphazard mess of thick power cables running to the HYDRA had been bundled tightly. They'd even cleaned up the kitchen, bathroom, and workshop. They convened in the meeting and Stuart updated them on his legal maneuvering with the Columbus Group.

"There was minor fall-out from their signing the Barnes NDA; when Columbus realized what his company had committed to, he threatened to fire his lead counsel. Then he calmed down and we talked business."

"What's your impression of him?" Matt asked.

"Brilliant man. Lives for adventure. Definitely a type-A personality. Possibly double-A. He strikes me as someone whose good side we want to be on. He wants to meet you. As for the NDA, we should be ready to throw him a bone."

"What did you have in mind?"

"I'm not sure yet," Stuart replied. "He's got his fingers in a lot of different pies—should we give him preferred access to the HYDRA? I don't know... maybe he wants to launch his own satellite network?"

Matt nodded. "Okay, let's think more on that."

Stuart took the evening train back to London. In the weeks that followed, he had trouble concentrating on his "real" job at his London law firm; he was more interested in the goings-on at AdAstra.

A month later, he got a short fax from Matt: *Tell Columbus we're ready.*

SIXTEEN

The business world was abuzz when Alastair Columbus, the multi-millionaire hotel tycoon and adventurer, called a press conference at his flagship London hotel. Journalists, business reporters, and writers from around the world crowded into the hotel's largest conference room, which was reduced to standing room only. Columbus hadn't provided any advance details, so the rumour mill was working overtime: he was expanding his already huge hotel empire; he was going to break his own record for the highest skydive by a civilian; he was dying of cancer and giving all his money to charity.

The crowd whispered and murmured as hotel employees set up a pair of large TV monitors, flanking the lectern on the raised floor at the front of the room. Another employee wheeled a commercial-grade videocassette recorder in on a cart and played the first minute of a Columbus Group promotional video to ensure everything was working. Following a sound check on the lectern's microphone, the employees disappeared out a side door.

Several minutes passed before Columbus, wearing his trademark khaki brown pants, pink LL Bean polo shirt, white trainers, brilliant smile and tousled hair, burst through the door and strode to the lectern. Four young men followed close behind, taking seats to one side. Columbus looked around the now-silent room and smiled.

"Ladies and gentlemen, thanks for coming today. Many of you have press deadlines, so I'll get right to it. Four years ago, I created the Columbus Prizes, a contest intended to spur the commercial development of space. Each prize has specific criteria and comes with a substantial cash award. The first launch of a satellite into orbit. First sub-orbital flight of a human. First orbital flight with a human. First robotic vehicle to land on the moon and send back live video, and so on."

He paused for effect. "Today I'm *very* pleased to announce that we have our first winner!" He motioned to the young men sitting beside him. The crowd was abuzz, and Columbus waited for the noise to subside before continuing.

"AdAstra Enterprises LLC—a private British company I'm delighted to add—has not only put a satellite into orbit but landed a pair of robotic vehicles on the surface of the moon and also recovered some moon rocks. I, along with my team of technical and legal advisors, observed AdAstra's, shall we say... deployment of these vehicles. We have confirmed that AdAstra has met the terms laid out in our contest rules."

The BBC's head science reporter couldn't wait for Columbus to finish.

"Sir! I'm sure there've been no rocket launches in the past several months, anywhere in the world. And definitely none from British soil! Could you please explain how this... AdAstra accomplished this?"

Columbus paused, glancing again at the young men beside him.

"The purpose of the Columbus Prizes was to encourage commercial development of space, and it has succeeded. The technology AdAstra used to win these prizes is proprietary, and the disclosure agreement we signed prevents us from divulging details about their operations."

"You mean they've won the prizes, but you can't tell us anything?" the BBC reporter said.

"I can tell you *what* they did, just not *how* they did it." Columbus shrugged. "Representatives from AdAstra have agreed to take part in this press conference and provide *some* details. Now I'd like to introduce Mr. Matt Barnes, president of AdAstra Enterprises."

The crowd buzzed. *Barnes? Who's that?*

Matt stood up and moved to the lectern as Columbus took a seat. He cleared his throat nervously.

"Thank you, Alastair. Good morning, everyone. I'm Matt Barnes. I have a prepared statement to read, after which I will entertain *a few* questions."

He paused, smoothing out a sheet of paper he held in shaky hands. "Monday last week—May 12th, at 1344 Greenwich Mean Time—we deployed a miniature satellite into earth orbit at an altitude of two hundred and fifty kilometres. We gave it enough velocity for a fast-decay orbit, and it transmitted low-resolution video for eight orbits—approximately twelve hours. That video was received by AdAstra's satellite ground station in Cambridge, and by several independent ground stations around the world chosen by Columbus's team. Last Thursday—the 15th, at 0930 GMT—we deployed a stationary transmitter onto the lunar surface that sent real-time video back to Earth. Next, we recovered approximately half a kilogram of moon rocks and dust. Finally, we deployed a robotic vehicle onto the lunar surface—it travelled over five hundred metres while transmitting video. Mr. Columbus and his team have inspected our facilities, our satellite and our lunar vehicles, witnessed the deployments, and recorded all video transmissions. They have confirmed we satisfied the relevant rules for several of the Columbus Prizes."

Matt paused. "Questions?"

There was a small uproar as every journalist tried to get the first question in.

"Mr. Barnes! Whose rockets did you use and where did you launch from? Did you use NASA facilities? You didn't use the Soviet's, did you? Or do you have a private launch pad somewhere?"

"Our transportation mode is proprietary technology, and I will not discuss that today." Matt paused. "But to partially answer your question, we did not use any conventional launch facilities."

"Mr. Barnes! How did you get the moon rocks back to Earth? Where are they now?"

"We returned the samples using the same proprietary transportation method we used to deploy the satellite and lunar vehicles. The samples are in a secure location and are the property of Mr. Columbus."

The roomful of reporters spent the next thirty minutes trying numerous circumlocutions to get more information from Matt about

AdAstra's "launch" facilities, but to no avail.

"Mr. Barnes, you said the satellite was in a fast-decay orbit," asked a French business reporter. "What is that, and where is the satellite now?"

"The rules for this Columbus Prize were specific: the satellite had to transmit for at least six orbits from an altitude of at least two hundred kilometres. We designed the satellite to meet those requirements; nothing more, nothing less. It ran on battery power and did not have any solar panels, a common feature on most satellites. A fast-decay orbit is one where the satellite has just enough velocity to complete a few orbits. Our satellite's orbit decayed rapidly after its ninth orbit, and it burned up shortly thereafter."

"What about your vehicles on the moon? Are they still working?"

"No. Like the satellite, we didn't harden them to survive the harsh environment of space. They have since stopped functioning due to high solar flux and cosmic radiation, but survived long enough to meet the conditions set forth in the Columbus Prize rules."

"Mr. Columbus mentioned there was video recorded?" said a reporter from a leading American economics magazine. "I assume that's what the TVs are for?"

"Yes," Matt replied. He turned to Columbus, who nodded at his staff. The room lights faded, and an employee inserted a cassette into the video recorder.

The TV monitors lit up. First up was a short video tour of the satellite itself, prior to "launch." Matt provided the commentary.

"Our satellite was very simple: a battery-powered, gyro-stabilized, fixed-focus, wide-angle camera feeding a fifty-watt directional video transmitter. We fitted all the components into a package twenty centimetres in diameter and fifty centimetres long."

The image switched, a grainy colour image showing a blue ocean and a brown land mass with a partial cloud cover.

"This is a video feed from the satellite shortly after deployment, received by one of the ground stations selected by Columbus," Matt said. "You're looking at the western coastline of Spain."

Over the course of the next five minutes, the image changed as the miniature satellite sped east across Europe.

"As I mentioned, there's twelve hours of this video—we're just showing you a small portion today."

There were murmurs from the audience.

"Okay, we'll show you the lunar video next. That's much more interesting."

The hotel employee switched tapes.

The static on the screen cleared, showing a wide-angle view, a camera on the lunar surface. The Earth—a pale blue marble—hung in the black sky.

Matt provided a running commentary. "This is the video feed from the stationary transmitter we deployed on the lunar surface. There was no video of its arrival, since it couldn't transmit until it touched down and deployed its directional antenna. Shortly you will see how we recovered the moon rocks and dust."

After thirty seconds, an object appeared at the top of the image, inching downward. It was a small clamshell scoop, larger than a child's toy, but smaller than the ones used for excavation, locked in the open position and hanging from the end of a climbing rope. When it hit the lunar surface, it snapped closed, capturing some rock and dust. Then it slowly ascended and disappeared off-screen.

"Next, you will see the robotic vehicle—we call it 'MoonCrawler'— arrive."

It was a small, metallic object, the size of a toaster, also hanging from the end of a climbing rope. It descended slowly, swaying back and forth as if in a light breeze. As it touched down, it threw up a cloud of dust that settled unnaturally slowly due to the moon's low gravity. The rope released and disappeared up and out of the picture. The object cautiously unfolded into the form of an insect-like vehicle with wire wheels. It paused for a moment, as if taking stock, then crawled towards, then past, the stationary transmitter, disappearing from view.

"What happened to the vehicle?" asked the BBC reporter. "Where did it go?"

Matt nodded at the staff to switch video tapes.

"Here's the video feed from the MoonCrawler."

The video image bounced around as the little vehicle crawled past several medium-sized boulders and climbed up a small rise. It continued in a straight line for several minutes before coming to a stop.

"Where on the moon is this, Mr. Barnes?"

"A large basaltic plain in the Tranquillitatis basin, eight degrees north of the moon's equator."

When the vehicle stopped, its image stabilized, showing a man-made object fifty metres away: a large metal box sitting on four legs wrapped in faded gold foil, heavily burnished from exposure to harsh solar radiation for almost two decades.

"Is... is that what I think it is?" asked a writer from a leading American science journal.

Matt nodded. "Yes, it's the descent module from the Apollo 11 lunar lander. One of the Columbus 'bonus' prizes was to make a precision deployment on the moon. We—Alastair and ourselves—agreed on the Sea of Tranquility, because of its well-known, er, landmarks."

After a few minutes, static on the video increased, then the recording stopped.

"What happened there?" asked another reporter.

"As I mentioned earlier, we built the stationary video transmitter and the MoonCrawler with commercial, off-the-shelf components. The MoonCrawler's sole purpose was to travel at least five hundred metres and transmit video back to earth. Both it and the stationary transmitter are no longer functional."

"That vehicle looks familiar," observed a reporter in the second row.

Matt nodded, glancing over at the other three young men on stage. "Now would be a good time to introduce the AdAstra team."

"To my immediate left is Gary Stocks, who designed and built the MoonCrawler. Gary is also the inventor of the TombCrawler vehicle that was featured in last month's National Geographic magazine."

Gary stood up and nodded to the audience.

"Next to Gary is Joshua Allen, in charge of our computing systems."

Josh stood up, looking as uncomfortable as a deer caught in a vehicle's headlights on a dark country road.

"Beside Josh is Stuart Barnes, our legal counsel."

Stuart stood up and nodded.

"The fifth member of our team—our planetary geologist—was

unavailable for today's press conference."

"Mr. Barnes! What are your qualifications? Where did you go to school?"

"I have two master of science degrees from the University of British Columbia, Canada. One is in mathematics, the other in physics. I also have a bachelor of applied science degree in engineering physics and honours mathematics from UBC. I currently work part time as a lecturer in the department of physics at Cambridge University." Matt looked to Columbus. "Well, that's all I have to say. Alastair?"

Columbus stepped up to the microphone. "Thank you for your presentation, Mr. Barnes. As I mentioned earlier, the rules for these prizes were specific, and the team from AdAstra has met them all."

A pair of assistants magically appeared at Columbus's side, each holding several ornate, carved-glass trophies with a wooden base and engraved brass plaque. Columbus took the first trophy, then turned to Matt.

"Mr. Barnes, on behalf of the Columbus Group, I'd like to award AdAstra a Columbus Prize for deploying the first commercial satellite in orbit. That comes with a cash reward of ten million British pounds."

Another assistant appeared, holding a large ceremonial cheque with many zeroes. Every in the audience applauded while photographers snapped away. Columbus continued.

"Next is the Columbus Prize for deploying a video transmitter onto the lunar surface and sending video back to earth." Another trophy, another cheque for ten million pounds, and more photos.

"Next, you returned moon rocks and dust to earth." A third trophy and another cheque for ten million pounds.

"Then you deployed a robotic vehicle that travelled at least five hundred metres whilst transmitting video." A fourth trophy, another ten million pounds.

"And, finally, you did a precision 'landing' near one of the Apollo landing sites." Trophy and five million pounds.

"Mr. Barnes, you and your team have more than earned your money today. I look forward to your continued successes as we enter a new era of commercial space exploration."

"Thank you, Alastair," Matt said, shaking Columbus's hand. Camera flashes lit up the room.

Columbus returned to the lectern. "Ladies and gentlemen, thank you for coming. This concludes our press conference. We have copies of the video for everyone—you can pick one up on your way out."

Matt and his friends followed Columbus off the small stage and through the side door leading to a hallway, leaving behind a room full of shocked reporters still bursting with questions.

"Well, that went well as could be expected," Alastair said cheerily. "I wish I'd been able to give them more information. Perhaps I can convince you to hold a follow-on press conference and provide more details?"

Matt winced. "We'll see what we can do," he said, weakly.

"I'm guessing that you'd rather *not* exit via the hotel lobby?" Columbus said.

Matt bobbed his head.

Columbus motioned to one of his security team, a burly man with a 'don't-fuck-with-me' look. "Mr. Andrews will show you out another way."

Matt shook Columbus's hand. "Thanks for your help today, Alastair. And I won't forget our deal."

Columbus grinned. "Counting on it."

The security guard motioned for them to follow.

"Well, the cat's out of the bag now," Stuart said as the waitress deposited a round of drinks on their table in a dark corner of the pub. After the hotel security guard escorted them out an unmarked side door, Stuart got his bearings and led them two blocks east and one block north to a pub he frequented when working in London.

"No shit," Gary replied, pointing to the television screen on a shelf behind the bar—it showed a replay of the press conference they'd just left. "We're friggin' celebrities now. Too bad Bigfoot couldn't be here."

"He's writing exams for the next two weeks," Matt said. "I called him last night, and he's quite happy being out of the limelight for now."

Josh nodded. "Yup, and it's a good thing we put up The Wall last week," he said, referring to the security fence now surrounding AdAstra's compound. "That cost a few bucks. I mean pounds."

"Speaking of money, guys," Matt said, "I know we agreed on a fixed salary of twenty thousand pounds for each of us, but we just made *forty-five million* pounds. When we started this little venture, we agreed on a profit-sharing arrangement. Do you guys want your cut now?"

There was a long silence. Josh spoke first.

"Part of that should go to replenish the funds you spent building the Mark II—after all, that's what let us win the Columbus Prizes. And there's the Mark III still to build. I propose we table any discussion about sharing this windfall."

Matt looked around the table, getting nods of agreement from everyone.

"Okay, then. I had to ask."

Stuart took a long pull on his ale. "Matt, one more thing. I think you should seriously consider Columbus's suggestion—holding your own press conference. He dropped a real PR bomb today, and I suspect in the coming weeks the press will do lots of digging. The longer you maintain radio silence, the harder it'll be to control the narrative."

Matt nodded, dreading the idea of standing up in front of those reporters again. They brainstormed, debating what to tell the press, what *not* to tell them, and when.

Stuart's prediction about the media was bang on. The consensus was that AdAstra's claims were bogus, the videos fake, and Columbus had been swindled on a massive scale. Talking heads on the news interviewed actual rocket scientists who claimed there'd been no launches, American, Soviet, or elsewhere in the past six months. The court of public opinion swung back and forth: it was either a scientific breakthrough or the biggest con job of the year.

"Look closely at that video of the MoonCrawler deployment," said a popular American science pundit who claimed the original moon landings never happened. "It's hanging from a climbing rope. Seriously? This is obviously fake—probably done on a movie set."

After a week, part of that debate came to an abrupt halt as astronomers, from both SETI and academic observatories, confirmed they *had* picked up signals coming from low earth orbit and the surface of the moon at the dates and times Matt mentioned during the press conference. With that issue settled, the speculation turned to *how* AdAstra had accomplished such a monumental task in total secrecy. The consensus was that they'd used an as-yet-unknown country with launch capabilities, possibly a small equatorial island nation. Then they'd deployed some type of hovering vehicle to lower the scoop and vehicles to the surface. And returned it to earth. Somehow.

Only one reporter glommed to a key point of Matt's prepared statement.

"Notice that he never said 'launch,' he said 'deployed.' Maybe they didn't use rockets?" He left his train of thought unspoken: *then how did they do it?*

The media quickly discovered AdAstra's operations and converged on their compound northeast of Cambridge, the building now surrounded by a twelve-foot-high security fence topped with barbed wire and "PRIVATE PROPERTY—KEEP OUT" signs every twenty-five metres. A sour-faced security guard blocked the only entrance, and he wasn't giving out *any* information.

"Sod off," was all the reporters could get out of him.

Others in the media dug into Matt's background, combing through his university records and the papers he'd published. His "failed" doctoral dissertation and his 11-space treatise garnered extra attention and were forwarded to scientific advisors kept on retainer. His current and former colleagues and professors at UBC, Caltech, and Cambridge were cornered and pestered into coughing up some tidbit of information. Or dirt. Anything. Many of those interviewed went on camera, or at least allowed their testimonials to be quoted.

"A brilliant mathematician," said the head of UBC's mathematics department.

"A good colleague," said an unnamed Caltech post-doc.

"My best student yet. A brilliant, out-of-the-box thinker," stated Nobel Laureate Dr. Richard Feinberg.

One interviewee wasn't quite so impressed.

"During his short time at Caltech, Matt Barnes was arrogant and troublesome," stated Dr. Charles William Winston the Third, a recently hooded graduate from Caltech's physics department and now a deputy to the President's Scientific Advisor. "His doctoral dissertation was a miserable failure, and he left Caltech under a cloud of controversy. Clearly, he's duped Columbus on a monumental scale, and I trust the media and the scientific community will work together to expose this con job."

"Dr. Winston! Last year Barnes published a paper titled '11-Space: An Expansion Theory of the Universe' in the British Journal of Physics B. In that paper he makes bold predictions: several undiscovered sub-atomic particles, magnetic monopoles, and wormholes, to name but a few. Do you think that paper has anything to do with Columbus's recent announcement?"

"I read that paper. It's nothing but science fiction—just a bunch of meaningless equations."

◎

Two weeks after the press conference, Matt got a disturbing phone call from Stuart.

"I just got a call from someone from the British government. He wants to meet with us to discuss AdAstra's recent activities."

"Which part of the government?" Matt said.

"I don't know. He didn't leave any details other than a name and a phone number. I called the number; it was the switchboard at the Ministry for Business, Innovation and Skills. The receptionist said that 'the Mr. Williams' who called me was out, and she asked me to leave a message. I've arranged to meet with him at our London office next Monday morning at ten o'clock, if that's okay with you."

Matt shrugged. "I'll be there."

SEVENTEEN

Matt glanced at the clock on the wall in the conference room at Stuart's London law firm.

"Almost ten," he said nervously.

The phone rang; Stuart answered it.

"Okay," he said, "send them up to Room C."

Two minutes later, the receptionist ushered in a middle-aged man wearing a rumpled grey business suit. He had beady eyes and moved furtively.

Like a ferret, Matt thought. *Or a rat.*

"Mister Barnes, Mister Barnes," the man wheezed, nodding at each of them. "Thank you for taking the time to meet with me." He handed each of them his business card. "I'm Mr. Williams, managing director of the British National Space Centre."

Matt scrutinized the card. "Never heard of it."

Stuart was more diplomatic. "A pleasure. I came across a mention of the BNSC while doing background research. I tried contacting your organization, but no one knew anything about it."

Williams nodded. "Not surprised. Not surprised. The BNSC's mandate is to coordinate civilian space activities here in the UK. Given the dearth of such activities, at least until recently, our agency has been mostly idling, consisting entirely of myself and one assistant. But we *are* hosted by the

Ministry for Business, Innovation and Skills."

"What can we do for you?" Stuart asked, motioning for him to sit.

"The BNSC exists because the UK is a signatory to an international agreement titled, 'Treaty on Principles Governing the Activities of States in the Exploration and use of Outer Space, including the Moon and other Celestial Bodies.' That's a mouthful, so it's more commonly referred to as the 'Outer Space Treaty.' This 1967 treaty forms the basis for international space law, but is mostly a non-armament treaty, and vague in other areas such as mining the moon, asteroids, etcetera. The UK never ratified this treaty, but being a signatory places certain obligations on us, hence the reason for the BNSC's existence. AdAstra wasn't even on our radar until Columbus's press conference a fortnight ago. I thought we should have an initial meeting and start a dialogue."

"What type of dialogue?" Matt said. Stuart shot him a warning glance.

"Well, it would have been helpful if you'd contacted us *before* you began your, shall we say, extraterrestrial activities. We've had press inquiries but haven't responded—that makes us appear to be either uninformed or hiding something. Water under the bridge. Water under the bridge. Moving forward, though, you'll have to work *with* us."

"What does that mean, exactly?" Matt said. "I don't want or need some government bureaucracy interfering with my *private* operations."

Stuart put his hand on Matt's arm. *Calm down.*

"As I said," Williams wheezed, "the UK *is* a signatory to the Outer Space Treaty, but we never ratified it, so that gives us *some* latitude. Article VI of the treaty states, 'The activities of non-governmental entities in outer space, including the Moon and other celestial bodies, shall require authorization and continuing supervision by the appropriate State Party to the Treaty.' It further says, 'State Parties shall bear international responsibility for national space activities, whether carried out by governmental or non-governmental entities.' Just so we're clear, the British government—and by extension, the BNSC—is the 'State Party' and AdAstra the 'non-governmental entity.'"

Matt was about to speak; Stuart silenced him with a glance. *I'll handle this.*

Williams continued. "Then there's a document called the 'Agreement on the Rescue of Astronauts, the Return of Astronauts and the Return of Objects Launched into Outer Space,' more commonly known as the 'Rescue Agreement.' Since AdAstra's operations are on British soil, Great Britain is now technically a space-faring nation and obligated to render all possible assistance to any personnel or spacecraft in distress. From what little we've gleaned about your 'unconventional' method of space travel, we're not sure this applies. But we have to understand AdAstra's capabilities and limitations insofar as such rescues might be required."

Matt glanced at Stuart and raised his eyebrows. *If they only knew about the NASA astronaut we saved!*

"Anything else?" Matt said, anger in his voice. "Our first-borns?"

Williams stood and backed away from the table. "Gentlemen, I, er, think that is sufficient for a first meeting," he stammered. He pulled a thin binder from his briefcase and slid it across the table. "This is the full text of both the Outer Space Treaty and the Rescue Agreement. There's not much to either, but I suggest you familiarize yourselves with them, then we can talk again. In the meantime, I insist you refrain from any further extraterrestrial activities."

Stuart's firm hand on Matt's arm was the only thing preventing him from leaping across the table and strangling this little man, who was now making a hasty retreat out of the room.

Matt was still seething when Stuart returned after escorting Williams back to the reception area.

"Goddamn government bureaucrats!" Matt roared.

Matt and Stuart caught the next train to Cambridge and convened an emergency meeting of AdAstra's "board of directors" at The Eagle pub. Stuart filled them in on what had transpired during the meeting with the BNSC representative, downplaying Matt's outbursts.

Renny, who'd just returned after successfully completing his master's-level courses at the University of Arizona, shook his head.

"Professor, I'm surprised you didn't choke out that little fucker. I would have."

Matt shrugged.

"Well, now you're up to speed," Stuart said. "This is not unexpected; some government agency was bound to stick their nose in our business. I recommend we tread cautiously and respond strategically. If we're not careful, we could drown in bureaucratic red tape."

Matt looked around the table at his friends. "We're in this together— it's not just up to me now." He looked at Renny. "What do you think, Batman?"

"I say fuck 'em. We're so close to being able to grab moon rocks I can practically taste them. Then there's all the Apollo shit lying around. I say we go for it and let the chips fall where they may."

"Gary?"

Gary shrugged. "We could pull up stakes and move to another... more 'friendly' country? One that didn't sign the treaty? It shouldn't be hard to find a new home now that we're famous." Gary's support was both surprising and touching, given that his girlfriend had just settled into her post-doc position in Cambridge's archeology department.

Risk-averse Josh was last. "We should work with the BNSC. Maybe it won't be as bad as we think."

There was silence for a moment.

"Looks like we have three options," Matt said.

"Before we go off half-cocked," Stuart said, "or full-cocked, for that matter, let's dissect the Outer Space Treaty and that Rescue Agreement to see if there are any loopholes we can exploit."

"If there are, you'll find them," Matt said hopefully.

◎

Dr. Charles William Winston the Third, PhD, gazed out the window of his third-floor office in the Eisenhower Executive Office Building. He stared longingly across the street at the magnificent grey sandstone structure—the West Wing of the White House, where the Leader of the Free World worked.

He sighed. *Someday I'll be working there.*

Winston's boss was the Director of the Office of Science and Technology Policy (OSTP), more commonly known as the "President's Science Advisor." Winston was one of five deputy assistants to the Director (and the most junior), but he considered himself to be "the Deputy Science Advisor to the President."

Thanks to his finally earning his PhD in astrophysics from Caltech and solid family connections (the latter helping more than the former), Winston immediately moved into his current role, one of the top positions at the OSTP. He was being groomed as its next Director, one step closer to the President's inner circle.

The desk phone buzzed; Winston tapped a button. "Yes?"

"Your ten o'clock is here," his assistant said.

"And that is...?"

"The only note you have says, 'the British problem,'" she replied.

"Yes, send him in," Winston commanded. He enjoyed commanding people.

The door opened and a middle-aged, nondescript man walked in and sat in the one guest chair; his assistant closed the door to give them privacy.

"What have you got for me?" Winston demanded.

The man opened a file folder; Winston frowned at how thin it was.

"Not much. I've got a transcript and video of the press conference, and a copy of the videos they released. Everyone I've talked to says this is not a scam—it's the real thing. My source has a source inside the Columbus Group, and they've confirmed there were video transmissions from that satellite and from the moon. Columbus and his key people were present at AdAstra's facilities when they put that equipment on the moon, but no one is talking."

"Why not? Didn't you offer enough money?" One axiom that Winston's father—Charles William Winston the Second—had taught him early in life was: *Everyone has a price.*

The man shook his head. "Columbus's inner circle is tight. Very loyal. I also have it on good authority that Columbus signed an airtight non-disclosure agreement with AdAstra."

Winston frowned. "So, we've ruled out the Columbus Group then. Any intel on how they pulled this off?"

"Nothing I'd call solid. Just a few educated guesses. No one knows for sure how he did it, but that Matt Barnes seems to have pulled off the scientific coup of the year. Possibly the decade."

Winston scowled upon hearing that name. *Matt Barnes. An engineer. A Canadian engineer. A thorn in my side since I arrived at Caltech. Talking down to me during his math lectures—the nerve. A non-believer who quoted scripture at me. Working under Dr. Feinberg. Well, at least I got him kicked out of Caltech.*

"How do we get our hands on this technology?" *Whatever Barnes has developed, it's the intellectual property of the United States government. I know it is. And it's my job—no, my solemn duty—to get it back.*

"Barnes keeps their facilities locked down tight. We've tried getting people inside, but their physical security is formidable. Our best bet is the bureaucratic approach. We've got someone inside the BNSC—that's the British National Space Centre. He's pretty sure he can get Barnes and his merry band of misfits shut down, at least temporarily. If Barnes wants to continue what he's doing, he'll have to play ball with the BNSC. Then our man should be able to get more information."

Winston nodded approval, then motioned at the surrounding office and out the window at the White House. "None of this can be traced back here," he cautioned.

The man bobbed his head. "Not to worry. I've got two degrees of separation between me and the ones doing the legwork. That means three degrees for you."

Winston nodded again. "You may proceed with the plan. Keep me apprised."

◎

The second meeting between AdAstra and the British National Space Centre went as well as the first. Mr. Williams brought along reinforcements in the form of the other fifty percent of the BNSC staff: a younger man named Mr. Brown, who also wore a rumpled suit.

"Mister Barnes," Williams wheezed at Matt. "During our last meeting, I sensed a certain amount of reticence, dare I say hostility, to our involvement?"

Stuart jumped in before Matt could say something he'd regret.

"Gentlemen, let's agree to put the last meeting behind us and move forward, shall we?"

"Bygones," Mr. Brown replied, cutting off his boss.

"Agreed," Stuart said. "We've thoroughly reviewed the documents you provided—thank you for those. We also looked into other space-related international agreements, specifically the Space Liability Convention of 1972, the Registration Convention of 1976, and the Moon Treaty of 1979. While most of these agreements haven't been ratified by space-faring nations, they do provide additional context to the overall legal framework as it pertains to outer space. That's what we'd like to discuss today."

Williams started shaking his head, not liking where Stuart was taking the discussion, but it was Mr. Brown who spoke first. "Please do."

Stuart nodded his thanks to Brown, while Matt glared at Williams.

"We did find one thread common to these documents that *is* relevant to this discussion," Stuart said.

"What's that?" Williams asked warily.

"The root verb used in these documents as it pertains to outer space activities is the word 'launch,' as in 'launching objects into outer space.'"

"So?" Williams said.

"The definition of the word 'launch,' in this context, is: 'the forced expulsion of a propellant, causing a reaction force that propels an object, such as a rocket, upwards against the force of gravity.'"

"I don't see how this is relevant," Williams said brusquely.

Stuart maintained a poker face. "AdAstra's unique capability to *transport* objects into space cannot, by any means, be considered 'launching.' There are *no* rockets involved. The satellite and the lunar vehicles we transported to win the Columbus prizes did not move through three-dimensional space from our facilities to their destination."

"That's splitting hairs," Williams said. "The intent of these documents is clear."

"I'm a lawyer, Mr. Williams, both in the UK and in Canada. Are you?"

Williams glared at Stuart. *No.*

"Law is *all* about splitting hairs," Stuart said. "When it comes to interpreting law, intent does not factor in—only the written words matter. And case law, of course. Of which there is none. AdAstra's position is that the Outer Space Treaty does not apply."

"I think Mr. Barnes has a point," Brown added, agreeably. "At least a point worth discussing further?"

Williams shook his head. "Absolutely not," he said testily, "As outlined in Article VI of the Outer Space Treaty, the BNSC, as representative of Her Majesty's Government, bears responsibility for AdAstra's extraterrestrial activities. We expect AdAstra to fully comply with BNSC directives."

Stuart shrugged. "I guess that's where our positions differ, Mr. Williams."

Williams' pasty-white face had turned red. "You're under the impression this is open to debate."

There was silence for thirty seconds while Williams and Matt glared at each other.

Mr. Brown broke the silence. "If I may? Article VI of the Outer Space Treaty calls for 'authorization and continuing supervision.' Perhaps we could discuss how the BNSC could meet its treaty obligations with only minimal involvement and/or interference in AdAstra's operations?"

Stuart nodded. "That's an excellent suggestion, Mr. Brown." He turned to Mr. Williams. "How do you see this 'authorization and continuing supervision' being realized?"

"First off," Williams said, with a gleam in his eye, "we'd need to perform an audit of AdAstra's facilities and operations to see where they intersect with our treaty obligations. As I mentioned earlier, the treaty is primarily a non-armament treaty, so we'll first want to confirm you're not deploying weapons of mass destruction in orbit or on the moon. I'm hoping *that* step is a formality."

"Yah, no nukes here," Matt said, glaring at Williams.

"Good to know, good to know," Williams said. "Next, to ensure there are no national security issues, we'll need a complete technical disclosure of AdAstra's technology. We've received a query from the US State Department; they're concerned this technology may be *their* property."

Matt couldn't hold it any longer. "There's zero chance in hell I'm ever going to release details on our intellectual property!" he shouted. "The US has no claim on it, either!"

Williams continued, ignoring Matt's outburst and now speaking to Stuart. "Finally, we'll need to develop a framework, that is, policies and procedures, wherein the BNSC first authorizes, then monitors, AdAstra's future activities, including planning and operations. A BNSC representative will need to be present at *all* future extraterrestrial operations."

Matt stood up. "A babysitter?" he barked. "No fuc—"

Stuart cut him off. "Mister Williams, Mr. Brown, thank you for coming in today. We'd like time to consider what you've said. Can we meet again, say, in a week?"

"I see no point in meeting again unless AdAstra changes its position," Williams said. "In fact—"

"A jolly good idea," Brown said. "Thank you for meeting with us today."

Matt glared at the two BNSC representatives as Stuart ushered them out of the room.

Fuck that guy and his organization, Matt thought. *I'd like to toss a big rock through a wormhole and de-orbit it onto his house...*

◎

Two days later...

Matt nodded to Josh, who was sitting beside him at the control console. Josh typed in a command, and the HYDRA executed its orderly shutdown, closing the wormhole that had given them a four-hundred-thousand-kilometre-long shortcut through space. The roar of air ceased and the cavernous room was eerily silent but for the creaking of the HYDRA's support structure. They went around the concrete wall.

Renny, who was standing next to Gary in front of the HYDRA, broke the silence. "WOO-HOO! Fuck yah!"

Gary returned Renny's high-five. "That was freakin' awesome!" he yelled as he unclipped his safety harness from the floor anchor.

"Let's get this shit bagged up and into the freezer," Renny said, referring to the small collection of fist-sized rocks that lay in a haphazard pile on the concrete floor between them. Moon rocks.

After that second, less-than-productive meeting with the BNSC, the foursome agreed to throw caution to the wind. At least for now. For the past few weeks, Renny had been helping Gary build "MoonClaw"—a three-fingered device that, when attached to a climbing rope then pushed through the wormhole, allowed them to grab rocks off the lunar surface more selectively than the crude method they'd used to win one of the Columbus prizes. They'd tested it at the Apollo 11 landing site, and the rock pile was their reward. And something more.

"Funny you should use the word 'shit,' Bigfoot," Gary snorted. He prodded a faded canvas bag, lying amongst the pile of rocks, with his shoe. They'd spotted the bag with the video camera attached to the MoonClaw's tether; Matt had nudged the wormhole's tail over the object, and Gary snagged it on his fourth attempt. After all, his prowess with claw arcade games was unmatched. "The astronauts did leave bags of shit behind."

"Maybe we should triple bag that one," Josh said. They put on N95 respirator masks and rubber gloves, then double (or triple) bagged everything into industrial-grade zip-lock bags which they stored in an industrial deep-freeze unit Matt had installed for just this purpose.

"Great work, guys!" Matt said. "Time to call it a week. Let's regroup on Monday morning and figure out what else we can salvage!"

◎

Matt's hoped-for Saturday-morning sleep-in was interrupted by a 6am phone call—it was the security guard manning the gate at AdAstra's headquarters. Matt couldn't understand what the problem was—there was a lot of shouting in the background—but it was clear Matt's presence was required. Now. Stuart was still in town, having stayed at Matt's the previous night, so the pair jumped into Matt's old Vauxhall and headed northeast at a moderately high speed.

They arrived at AdAstra to find several vehicles parked outside the gate, including a nondescript brown sedan, a police car from the Cambridgeshire Constabulary, and a white utility van bearing the Cambridge and North Dumfries Hydro logo on its sides. There was a four-way argument underway between the security guard, the Hydro worker, and a pair of men wearing rumpled business suits. The police constable was trying unsuccessfully to de-escalate the situation.

Matt got out of the car; one of the suits turned around. It was the BNSC's Mr. Williams, accompanied by his associate, Mr. Brown.

Oh shit!

"Ah, Mr. Barnes! Mr. Barnes! Glad you're here," Williams said. "We recently learned that you continued performing operations from these facilities even after being cautioned not to."

He handed Stuart a sheet of official-looking paper. "By order of the British National Space Centre, the Ministry for Business, Innovation and Skills, and Her Majesty the Queen, I have a Cease-and-Desist order signed by His Honour Judge Allan P. Smythe of Southeastern Circuit Court. This order requires that AdAstra and its employees cease operations and immediately vacate the premises. It further states that electrical power is to be disconnected from these facilities until further notice."

Stuart took the document and retreated to huddle with Matt. They returned a few minutes later, and Stuart addressed the Constable.

"I am Stuart Barnes, Barrister and Solicitor, and AdAstra's legal counsel. We will file an emergency appeal of this order first thing Monday morning. Furthermore, my client has advised me that there's high-voltage electrical equipment in these facilities—there could be significant damage or fire if power is cut off. I suggest a compromise: we agree not to use the facilities until we've had time to file the appeal, and the BNSC refrains from cutting off the power."

"I think that's fair," said Mr. Brown. That earned him a withering stare from his boss.

"I want in there now!" Williams hissed, closing his suit jacket to hide a camera hanging around his neck.

The Constable knew a suitable compromise when he saw one. "Agreed." He turned to the hydro employee. "We won't be needing your services today, mate." The worker got into his van and drove away.

Williams couldn't resist one last dig at Matt. "Mr. Barnes. You do realize this wouldn't have been necessary had you chosen to work *with* us." He and Brown returned to their vehicle.

The media soon got wind of the government's actions at AdAstra, thanks to an "anonymous" phone tip (it was Williams). By that evening, the various new outlets had chosen their headlines:

"*AdAstra shut down!*"

"*Government pulls plug on space ops on outskirts of Cambridge!*"

"*Aliens hidden at secret Cambridge lab!*"

EIGHTEEN

The following Monday morning, Stuart paid a visit to the Southeastern Circuit Court building in Cambridge and was granted an interim stay of the BNSC order; that gave them seven days to figure out their next step. They spent the entire week brainstorming their options, careful not to do anything other than turn the lights on and run the coffee machine.

"I'm sure that BNSC asshole Williams is monitoring our electrical usage," Matt grumped.

None of the options he and his friends came up with were appealing. The consensus swung back and forth, from Renny's "fuck 'em" strategy to packing up and moving to another country. Matt returned to his flat every night angry, frustrated at being mired in bureaucracy instead of doing HYDRA operations.

By noon on the Friday, they'd had enough.

"Fuck it," Renny said, "let's go drinking." No one disagreed.

They locked up the building, piled into Matt and Stuart's cars, waved to the security guard at the gate and drove towards town. They arrived at The Eagle pub well before Happy Hour; the pub was almost empty and not too noisy so their regular corner booth was quiet enough. They nursed their first round, not saying much that hadn't already been discussed many times that week.

"Next round's on me," Matt said.

He weaved through the tables to the bar, got the barman's attention, and placed his order. As Matt waited, a young man approached, wearing a Cambridge college blazer and a ratty old baseball cap pulled down almost to his eyes. Since Matt taught at the university, he was naturally curious whether it was one of his students. The young man was trying to appear inconspicuous, which made Matt look closer.

"A pint of ale and two sparkling waters, please," the young man said. The barman nodded. Matt recognized the cultured accent.

He sounds very familiar...

"Mr., uh, Windsor?" Matt whispered, "Is that you?"

"Drat," replied His Royal Highness, Prince Edward, the Duke of Cambridge. His cover was blown.

"Hello, Mr. Barnes," he whispered back. "Just having a pint with my detail." He tilted his head toward a table in the other corner of the pub, where two of his security detail sat, now eyeing Matt.

"I understand," Matt whispered back. "I'd invite you to join us, um, your Royal Highness, but you're clearly trying to keep a low profile."

"I appreciate the offer, but my detail wants us where they can keep an eye on things. We'll be leaving as soon as it gets busy. Cheers," he said, heading back to his table.

Matt returned to his booth, carefully balancing the tray with five drinks of various shapes, sizes, and colour, from hard liquor for Renny to soda water for Josh. He motioned for his friends to lean in.

"See those three over in the corner?" Everyone looked. "The one with the baseball cap is Prince Edward."

Josh's eyes widened. "The Duke of Cambridge? The royal you taught last year? And again this year?"

Matt nodded.

Renny watched them for a few seconds. "The other two are clearly his bodyguards."

"You nailed that one, Batman."

Both men, aware of Renny's interest, gave him a hard look back. The Prince leaned over and spoke to his detail and they both visibly relaxed; clearly the Prince had told them who Matt and his friends were.

"I gotta take a whiz," Renny announced, tossing back his whiskey shot. "British ale goes through me like drain cleaner." He maneuvered his bulky form through the tables to the back of the pub, entering a semi-secluded area that had a payphone on the wall next to the bathroom doors. A scruffy-looking man wearing a faded khaki army jacket was using the phone; he glanced at Renny, then turned away, covering the phone's mouthpiece with his hand.

Yah, that's not suspicious, Renny thought. He walked past him into the rest room, overhearing a small part of one side of the phone call, the man's Irish accent strong.

"Are the boys outside yet?" A pause. "Good."

An alarm bell rang in Renny's head. He waited until the bathroom door closed, then turned and put his ear against the door so he could keep listening in.

"He's at the table in the corner on the right. Yes, only two minders. Give me two minutes to get into position, then move in."

Fuck me, they're after the Prince!

Renny skipped taking a whiz, flushed the urinal, then opened the bathroom door, purposely ignoring the guy on the phone as he headed back to his table.

"That was quick," Gary said.

Renny relayed what he'd just heard.

"Let's get out of here," Josh said.

"Call the police?" Gary offered.

"No time," Renny countered. "This is all going down now!"

"We have to let the Prince's security detail know," Matt said. "I'll go— they know me, sort of."

Renny stood. "I'll watch the phone guy," he said, as the man came out of the back room and moved to the bar.

Matt headed towards the Prince's table. The Prince's two 'minders' eyed Matt suspiciously as he approached the table and sat down.

"*Mister* Barnes, can we help you?" said the one with shocking red hair, his overly polite tone clearly sending the message: *We know who you are. Go away!*

"Listen! My friend Renny just overheard someone on the payphone in the back. They were talking about the Prince."

"Beg yer pardon?"

"The guy at the bar wearing the khaki jacket! My friend Renny is standing right beside him! Renny overhead him talking about the Prince to some people waiting outside. I think they're after him!"

Both bodyguards looked towards the bar. Matt leaned in and whispered the code phrase he'd been given during his security briefings.

The red-haired bodyguard instantly reached into his jacket, tilted his head forward, and spoke into a hidden radio microphone. "Danny Collins. Code Red. Eagle Pub. Code Red."

The pub's front door opened and two serious-looking men entered. They spotted their associate at the bar; he nodded and tilted his head towards the Prince's table. Both bodyguards rose, but the two arrivals drew handguns first. One of them shook his head.

"Sit down and show us your hands. NOW!"

The nearly empty pub went silent as the two bodyguards reluctantly complied. A young couple who'd just come in turned and bolted. The few other patrons froze or dove under their tables.

"Okay now, he's coming with us," one assailant said, motioning with his gun at the Prince.

"Not going to happen," both bodyguards said, shaking their heads.

"One way or another, he is."

There was a brief stand-off as the four men traded stares.

The scout—the one Renny encountered at the back of the pub—moved towards them from his vantage point near the bar.

"Let's wrap this up," he said to his men, smirking as he pulled a submachine gun from inside his jacket.

He stopped mid-step as a pair of burly arms appeared from behind, wrapping him in a bear hug. With his arms pinned, he struggled briefly but didn't have the strength to wriggle free. He stamped his foot against his assailant's in-step, then snapped his head back, attempting a head-butt. That just made Renny, the owner of those massive arms, angry. He let out a roar that would frighten a grizzly bear (and probably had), lifted the man off his feet and flexed his arms. The sound of the man's arm bones shattering and ribs cracking echoed through the now silent pub; he went limp and his weapon clattered to the floor. The nearest assailant swung his handgun towards Renny while the other shifted his aim back and forth between the Prince's bodyguards.

Then many things happened at once. Renny bellowed and tossed the broken man in his arms like a rag-doll at the two other assailants; the one closest got off a single round in Renny's direction as he fell to the floor under the deadweight of his broken accomplice. Renny lurched forward, roaring like a wild animal, stomping on the now pinned assailant's gun hand, turning it to hamburger. He collapsed on top of the pair, blood spurting from the side of his head as he pummelled the bottom man in the face with his massive fists. Both of the Prince's bodyguards leapt into action; the red-haired one, who was closest, launched himself at the remaining assailant while the other drew his handgun and put himself between the Prince and danger. Matt, who was sitting beside the Prince, instinctively threw himself at the heir to the throne; they fell to the floor under the table, Matt's head clipping the table edge as a bullet struck the wall where his head had just been. Matt landed on top of the Prince, dazed, then felt a heavy weight on his back.

The red-haired bodyguard engaged in a violent hand-to-hand struggle with the remaining assailant, the latter's gun clattering to the floor. The other bodyguard, kneeling on Matt's back, had a clear shot; he fired two rounds into the assailant's chest, who dropped to the floor with a thump.

A bitter odour of gunpowder wafted through the air of the now deathly quiet pub; the silence broken by approaching sirens. The bodyguard kneeling on Matt yanked him off the Prince to make sure his charge was unharmed. His partner, hand bleeding profusely from a bullet hole, rolled the bloodied and dazed Renny off the two assailants. The one suffering from Renny's bear-hug was still unconscious; the bottom one, with a bloody face and mangled hand, stirred. The bodyguard kicked their weapons away, expertly flipped his gun to his uninjured hand and calmly shot the assailant in both legs.

Armed police officers burst in and whisked the Prince away to safety. More security personnel soon appeared, trying to make sense of the situation. Paramedics hustled Renny and Matt into an ambulance, accompanied by the injured bodyguard.

◎

Addenbrooke's Hospital, Cambridge

Matt lay on coarse, starched sheets in a hospital bed, the overhead fluorescent lights glaringly bright. He gingerly touched the bandage on his forehead that covered a gash expertly stitched closed by the emergency room attending physician. His head throbbed from the concussion he'd received when his head hit the table. His memory of the events immediately after the failed kidnapping attempt was foggy; he remembered only snippets of the ambulance ride, his best friend on the stretcher beside him, suffering from a gunshot to the head.

Gary, Josh, and Stuart sat in visitor chairs along the wall of the small room, the concern on their faces clear. Renny was in the adjacent bed, a wide bandage wrapped around his head from the 7.62mm bullet that had taken a chunk out of his left ear. He was regaling his friends with his version of the events.

"Don't you get it?" Renny roared, high on pain meds. "I started a new sport: Terrorist Tossing! I was bowling for bad guys! Ha ha ha!" Matt winced at the outburst.

The door opened and two men entered. The first one was an older, distinguished-looking man wearing a well-tailored suit, followed by one of the Prince's bodyguards from the pub—the red-haired one who was now sporting a heavy bandage on his right hand.

"Gentlemen, I'm Inspector McTee. Scotland Yard." He scanned the room. Not seeing any threats, he nodded towards the open door.

Prince Edward, the Duke of Cambridge, entered, followed by another bodyguard. The Prince looked around the room and smiled.

"Well, Mr. Barnes, Mr. Harris. I owe you a debt of gratitude. You literally saved my life yesterday."

Renny and Matt both shrugged. "Uh, I'm just glad we were there, your Highness," Matt offered weakly.

"Perhaps you could introduce me to your friends?"

Matt made the introductions, his attempts to follow the proper protocol hindered by his blinding headache. Then he turned to the guard with the bandaged hand. "We never formally met. I'm Matt Barnes. How's your hand?"

The guard, surprised that anyone was concerned about his welfare, held up his hand and gave a lop-sided grin. "O'Donnell. Seamus O'Donnell. Bullet went clean through. I'll live, but it's my gun hand, so I won't be popping bad guys for a while."

Matt nodded, then turned to the Prince. "I trust you are okay, your Highness?"

Prince Edward nodded. "Not a scratch, thanks to you two. The Palace isn't happy this happened, even though *I* was the one who insisted we visit the pub."

An awkward silence followed, broken by Renny.

"Uh, this may be a dumb question, but am I in trouble? I mean, like, legal trouble?" He turned to Stuart. "I put a pretty good beat-down on those two terrorist assholes. Do I need to get a lawyer, or solicitor, or barrister, or whatever the fuck you call them here?" Then he blushed, realizing he'd just used foul language in the presence of royalty.

Stuart opened his mouth to answer; not having one, he closed it and looked over at Inspector McTee, who smiled and chuckled. "I think not. In fact, I'm fairly certain that should I attempt to pursue charges against *anyone* in this room, I'd soon be looking for alternative employment."

One of the security detail touched his earpiece with his finger. He turned to the Prince.

"She's here."

The Prince nodded, then turned to Matt and his friends.

"Gentlemen, my grandmother is here and would like to meet you, if that's okay?"

Matt shrugged. "Sure." *Why would his grandmother be here?* he wondered, foggy from his pain meds.

One of the security detail opened the door.

An elderly lady wearing an off-yellow dress, a flowery bonnet and matching purse came in. She scanned the room with an alertness that belied her advanced age.

The Prince's grandmother? Oh shit!

Renny came to the same realization, pulling the sheets up to cover his hairy body. Matt tried to sit up straighter and was rewarded with another blinding headache.

Even the Prince straightened up. "Your Royal Majesty, may I introduce the young men who helped save me yesterday. Mr. Matthew Barnes and Mr. Renny Harris. And their colleagues Mr. Gary Stocks, Mr. Joshua Allen, and Mr. Stuart Barnes, Solicitor."

The Queen of England calmly looked each of them in the eye before turning her attention back to Matt and Renny.

"Well, Mr. Barnes. Mr. Harris. Mere words cannot describe how grateful I am that you two came to the aid of my grandson."

Matt shrugged. "Right place at the wrong time, your Majesty." Renny nodded in agreement.

"I understand that you'll both make a full recovery?" she said, turning to Inspector McTee for confirmation. He nodded.

"That's excellent," she said. "My grandson has told me about the fine job of teaching you're doing at Cambridge."

"He's an excellent student, Your Majesty."

She smiled the way only a proud grandmother would.

"I understand from my daily briefings that you five have been up to some... shall we say... extraterrestrial shenanigans lately?"

"Well... uh... we..." Matt stammered, blushing.

"Fascinating things you're doing at AdAstra," she added. "And I'm told you've recently run afoul of one of our government bureaucracies."

Matt gulped. *I think I might throw up. In front of the Queen.*

The Queen smiled, her eyes twinkling. "Relax, Mr. Barnes. Contrary to popular opinion, the Crown *does* possess a sense of humour."

That deflated the tension in the room. The Queen made small talk for several minutes—she excelled at it.

"Well," she said, finally. "There remains only one more issue to deal with."

"Your Majesty?" Matt said warily.

"I told you we were in trouble," Renny whispered.

The Queen smiled. "Quite the contrary, Mr. Harris. Where the Crown is concerned, even a sincere 'thank you' isn't sufficient."

"I'm... er... not sure we follow you, Your Majesty," Matt said.

"The Crown is expected to recognize acts of bravery such as yours. It has been decided that you two will receive the George Medal for conspicuous gallantry and courage in the face of danger."

"Um, you really don't need to do that," Renny offered. "Uh, ma'am. I mean, uh, your Highness."

"Agreed," Matt added, "uh, your Majesty."

The Queen smiled again. "Somehow I thought you'd say that. But it *has* been decided."

Matt tried one final protest. "Your Majesty, we are trying to keep our work at AdAstra out of the public eye as much as possible."

The Queen nodded. "Not to worry, Mr. Barnes. There is a provision in our protocols for keeping such decorations... confidential."

"Really, your Majesty, there's no need," Matt pleaded.

"Mr. Barnes, you and Mr. Harris have done the Crown a service, and even though you are citizens of the Commonwealth, your decorations are *not* optional. But I believe I should be able to smooth out your bureaucratic difficulties. So long as you promise not to do anything that might embarrass the British government?"

Matt nodded. "Thank you, your Majesty. We will endeavour to... behave."

I feel like I'm being chastised by my grandmother.

"No, thank you, Mr. Barnes, Mr. Harris. It was a pleasure meeting you." She looked at the others in the room. "All of you." And with that, she swept out of the room.

Renny waited until the door had closed. "Well, fuck me."

Matt nodded. "Well said, Batman. Well said."

"I got a question," Renny said. "Who the fuck is George, and why does he have a medal named after him?"

Matt and Renny were discharged the next day, glad to be out but sad to no longer be on the receiving end of attention from the pretty nurses. They were surprised to learn that the hospital wing they'd been in had been emptied for "security reasons." There was no mention of the incident in the media.

As soon as Renny's head wound healed, he returned to Canada to start the field research for his graduate degree. His thesis supervisor had agreed with Renny's hypothesis that a buried meteorite caused the magnetic anomalies around Crater Lake. Drawing from AdAstra's large bank account, he hired a local helicopter company to perform a low-altitude geophysical survey in a twenty-kilometre radius of Crater Lake. They flew an expanding grid pattern while towing a magnetometer, a device sensitive enough to detect minute fluctuations in the Earth's magnetic field. It was a standard, but high-tech, meteor hunt.

Meanwhile, back in the UK, Stuart got a call from the BNSC, requesting another meeting.

◎

Stuart's receptionist ushered the BNSC's Mr. Brown, along with a jovial-looking, nearly bald man, into the meeting room.

"Where's Mr. Williams?" Matt asked.

Brown grimaced. "Mr. Williams is... I'm the acting head of the BNSC now and have full authority over your file. This is my new assistant, Mr. Byrd."

"That's an interesting turn of events," Stuart said. "Well, let's get started. I'm preparing a formal court brief to challenge your cease-and-desist order, so—"

Brown raised his hand. "May I?"

Stuart frowned at the interruption, but nodded.

"I'd like to start off with an apology," Brown said. "Our marching orders as they pertain to AdAstra have... changed recently."

Matt and Stuart leaned forward slightly.

"Mr. Williams is no longer in the employ of Her Majesty's government. It appears he was being influenced by, shall we say, an 'external' agency? The cabinet minister responsible for the BNSC has been instructed to provide AdAstra with *whatever* government assistance you might need."

"Instructed? By whom?" Matt said.

"Our minister answers *directly* to the Prime Minister," Brown said. "The Prime Minister's directions on this matter, as I understand it, come from Buckingham Palace. So, I dare say, should anyone in our modest agency introduce any further impediments to your operation, or fail to remove existing ones, I expect they would find themselves made redundant rather quickly."

"More like getting the Spanish Archer," Byrd added, speaking up for the first time. He and Brown chuckled.

Jeez, Matt thought, *the Brits sure have some odd expressions.* But he got the point.

"So, I propose we move forward?" Brown said.

"Agreed," Stuart said.

"Great Britain *is* a signatory to the Outer Space Treaty, but never ratified it, so that gives us some latitude. But we *are* expected to hold to the spirit of the treaty. Our new mandate is to help you navigate those treaty obligations so your operation can run smoothly. We're here to talk about how *we* can help *you.*"

Matt and Stuart stared at each other for a few seconds, each processing this plot twist. They smiled and nodded. Stuart started off by having Brown and Byrd sign a non-disclosure agreement (the Barnes NDA), then they got to work.

Two hours later, they'd agreed on a set of action items. The BNSC would use its connections in the Foreign and Commonwealth Office to address international concerns—specifically the Americans, who were applying not-so-subtle pressure on the British government to access AdAstra's technology. In other words, the BNSC was going to run interference. They would also arrange for generous government tax relief in exchange for AdAstra providing local employment. In addition, the BNSC would use their government access to the World Court to get clarification rulings related to the Outer Space Treaty. In return, AdAstra agreed to include a BNSC representative—Mr. Byrd—in their high-level planning meetings and allow him limited "observer" access during future missions that fell under the treaty's scope.

"You know," Stuart said as the visitors left the building, "if they can help with half of the items on this list, things will be much easier moving forward."

"I guess having a friend in high places helps," Matt said, silently thanking the Queen.

Stuart nodded. "You're learning, cousin. You're learning."

◎

Matt looked around the large table in their main meeting room. In addition to the regulars—Gary, Renny, Josh, Stuart—was AdAstra's newest employee.

"Guys, please welcome Nigella Lomberg," Matt said, motioning towards a severe-looking, slightly overweight middle-aged woman sitting next to Matt. "AdAstra's interim Financial Director."

A round of applause.

"Nigella comes highly recommended by several of Stuart's corporate clients. She specializes in helping high-tech companies get off the ground. We're counting on her to guide us through our growing pains."

"That's my plan," she said, her gravelly voice reflecting decades of chain smoking.

"Nigella is here on contract for six months—if things work out, I'm hoping she'll join us permanently."

She shrugged. "We'll see how things go."

"Next up," Matt said, "welcome back to Renny, who's completed his field work for his master's degree."

Another round of applause.

"What'd you find?" Gary said. "A flying saucer?"

Renny smiled. "No such luck. My geophysical scans showed a ferromagnetic body two kilometres underground, northeast of Crater Lake, so I hired a drilling company and flew them in. The second core we drilled showed definite signs of non-terrestrial compounds. And by that, I mean a meteorite. I got several more samples over a one-hundred metre radius. I just gotta do my analysis, write it up, and submit it."

"Woo-hoo!" Josh said.

"I'll buy you new crayons for your field trip report," Gary added. Renny growled and chucked his pen across the table; Gary deftly dodged it, allowing it to bounce harmlessly off the wall. Nigella was taken aback at this informal, bordering on childish, behaviour.

"Okay, moving on," Matt said. "AdAstra has grown a lot in the past year, and will grow more as we start construction of the HYDRA Mark III. We're projecting significant revenue in the coming months, so I want to run an efficient organization. I'd like to hand over many of the business-level activities to Nigella so I can concentrate on the more technical stuff."

"I'll do my best," she promised.

"So, Nigella's first task is to come up with an appropriate corporate structure."

Matt paused. "Next item. Once the Mark III is up and running, we're effectively opening the door to commercial access to space. I expect we'll get inquiries from everyone from academia to private research centres to military organizations. We need to develop guidelines—a corporate code of ethics—for what we will and won't transport."

"No weapons in space," Josh suggested.

Stuart nodded. "That's already covered by the Outer Space Treaty."

"No contracting to *any* military organization," Renny added.

"No dangerous goods," Gary said.

"No intentional contamination," Josh offered. "I'll bet some organizations or governments would pay a fortune to have us dump garbage or radioactive waste on the Moon."

"That's also covered by the Outer Space Treaty," Stuart noted.

Matt smiled as the ideas flowed. "Stu, this is where you come in. I'd like you and Nigella to figure out how we should structure customer contracts. I propose that everything we transport should be based on the 'no-cure, no-pay' approach—the customer doesn't pay us until whatever we transport arrives at its destination. Comments?"

Everyone in the room agreed.

"What about people?" Josh said. "The Mark III will be big enough to transport people. What if someone wants to pay us bags of money to set up their own private space station, or moon base? You know, transporting equipment, supplies, people?"

Matt nodded. "We don't yet know whether it'll be safe to use the Mark III to move people, but that is a likely scenario. Unless we build our own moon base first."

"That would be fucking cool," Renny said.

"This brings up an interesting legal issue," Stuart said. "Let's say someone hires us to put people on the moon. What if we transport them there but can't get them back?"

Matt nodded. "I've thought a lot about this. That's why I want our contracts structured solely for one-way transport, payable upon arrival at the destination. In Stuart's scenario, the contract would be complete and we'd get paid as soon as we transport everything and/or everyone specified in the contract to their destination."

"The legal term is 'executed,'" Stuart added, "but I get your drift."

"You'd leave people stranded on the moon?" Nigella asked. The others bristled at the suggestion that Matt, or any of them, would be so callous.

Matt put up his hands to calm his friends. "Guys, it's a fair question. Nigella doesn't know us, and I'm glad she posed it."

Stuart jumped in. "Under the terms of the Outer Space Treaty and the Rescue Agreement, we'd be obligated to assist where possible in any rescue."

Matt nodded. "Of course. But my point is, this is new technology—a paradigm shift in space transportation. It'll have its problems. Let's play out a hypothetical scenario. We transport some people and their supplies to the moon so they can build their own moon base. All goes well for a while—days, weeks, months, whatever—then they have some catastrophic problem and need evacuation. But then *we* have an unexpected problem that prevents us from helping them right away. Maybe we lose power. Maybe everyone here falls sick and can't come to work. Maybe aliens attack. Who knows what? Of course we'd help if we could, but what if we can't? I want airtight contracts, consistent with the existing treaties, so customers understand what they're getting *and* what they're *not* getting."

Stuart nodded. "From a legal perspective, what Matt's proposing is the same as a hiker who hires a helicopter to drop them off in the wilderness, then plans to hike out or stay and live off the land. The contract is for a one-way trip, nothing more. If the hiker runs into trouble, that's their problem. If they radio for help, the helicopter company, or someone else, would probably rescue him. Then perhaps they'd sort out a fee-for-rescue, but only after the hiker was safe."

"Except that in this scenario," Nigella said, "we've got the only helicopter in town."

"Good point," Stuart said, making notes. "But what if our 'helicopter' is broken?"

"And our contracts have to reflect that a customer's delivery might be delayed if we have to assist in a rescue," she added.

Stuart nodded. "Good point. That's an easy clause to include." He jotted down another note.

"Umm, Matt?" Josh said. "Now might be a good time to bring Nigella up-to-speed on Operation Red Jet."

Matt nodded, then spent the next ten minutes explaining how, the previous year, he and Josh had saved the stranded NASA astronaut. With a fire extinguisher.

Nigella was silent for a few moments as she digested this revelation.

"Wow. And you did that because it was the right thing to do. Kudos. But, speaking as your Financial Director, have you considered approaching NASA and asking for recompense? Saving the life of an astronaut could be worth serious money."

Stuart smiled. "We've already discussed that at length, and decided to keep this in our back pocket for now, in case we need leverage or a favour in the future."

Nigella shrugged. "Fair enough. Probably a good call. Thanks for reading me in on that. Oh, and I like the multifaceted meaning in the operation's name."

Matt continued. "Our contracts need to be written so the customer knows that, not only are they one hundred percent responsible once their equipment, supplies and/or personnel get to the agreed-upon destination, our liability ends at the same time."

"Sounds like you're asking for a contract that's as tight as the famous Barnes NDA," Gary said.

"That would be ideal."

"I think we can handle that," Stuart said, looking at Nigella. She nodded back.

"One last item on our agenda," Matt said. "Our financial model."

"I assume you have preliminary thoughts on that?" Nigella said.

Matt nodded. "I propose that all income goes into general revenue. Sixty-five percent of our gross is used to cover salaries, operations, taxes, etcetera. Everything needed to keep the lights on, the employees paid and happy, and the drilling going."

"That makes sense," Nigella said.

"Next, profit sharing. When we started this little venture, we decided that Gary, Josh, and Renny each receive five percent. I get ten percent, and Stuart, two-and-a-half percent."

Nigella nodded. "That leaves seven and a half percent."

"That goes to the foundation," Matt said.

"And what foundation is that?"

Matt explained.

"Wow, you continue to amaze me," she said. "I recognize that you're funding this foundation for altruistic reasons, but those donations will reduce our corporate taxes. Once I've seen our revenue stream for a few months, I can advise on whether to tweak the percentage going to the foundation so AdAstra doesn't pay *any* taxes."

Matt shrugged. "Sure, I guess. But we're not using the foundation to avoid paying taxes." Matt said.

"Understood," Nigella said.

"And last, employee pay. I propose something unconventional, if not radical. In most places, employees are paid on a sliding scale, depending on the job title and qualifications. The more 'important' your role is, the more you make. What if, instead, we pay everyone the same? From us in this room to the technicians, the security guards, the people who sweep the floors and clean the toilets."

"That is rather unconventional," Nigella said. "Any thoughts on what the salary might be?"

Matt shrugged. "We can't, and shouldn't, pay less than whatever the minimum needed to live is."

"Some countries have a mandated minimum wage—the UK doesn't," Nigella said.

Matt shook his head. "I'm not talking about a minimum wage like in Canada, which right now I think is around eight bucks an hour. You can't *live* on that. I'm talking about a 'living wage,' what's needed to meet basic expenses—food, housing, child care, transportation, taxes, etcetera. I don't know what that number is, but I guess it's on the order of ten or fifteen thousand pounds per year. What do you guys think?"

"We're good with that, Matt," Josh said on behalf of his friends.

"The one downside I see," Nigella said, "is that it might be hard to hire people at the higher end of the pay scale, such as senior executives or engineers."

"First off," Matt said, "I refuse to hire anyone who's just in it for the money. Second, I acknowledge your concern, so we'd have to set the number high enough that those senior people would *want* to work here for that amount."

Nigella nodded. "Let me get cost-of-living data from the government then run a few financial forecasting models so I can figure out what we can afford."

Matt looked around the table. "Well, unless there's anything else, let's adjourn. We have to get our ducks in a row so we can grab stuff off the moon!"

NINETEEN

Two weeks later...

Stuart looked around the table in AdAstra's meeting room. All were present save for Renny, who'd returned to the University of Arizona to finish his master's degree thesis.

"I got an update from our friends at the British National Space Centre," Stuart said.

"I hope it's good news," boomed Renny's voice over the speakerphone in the middle of the table.

"Well, it's not bad news," Stuart said. "Mr. Wood reported that the BNSC filed a petition with the World Court, asking for an expedited ruling on the status of non-operational US and Soviet hardware in orbit and on the Moon. Staff in the BNSC's host ministry—the Ministry for Business, Innovation and Skills—have experience with the court's bureaucracy and helped draft the petition. Wood says they hope to pull this off without tipping off the Americans or the Soviets. There's a lull in the court's calendar right now, so we might get a ruling soon."

"I'd call that good news," Matt said. "Let's proceed assuming we can legally salvage anything that's non-functional. I can't see any advantage in salvaging defunct satellites in orbit, so let's focus on the Moon. First, we need a shopping list: what's there, what'll fit through a twenty-five-

254

centimetre wormhole, and where each item is."

"I'll take the lead on that," Josh offered.

"I can help," Renny's disembodied voice said. "There's a couple of guys here who worked at NASA's Lunar Receiving Lab in the early '70s, analyzing moon rocks from the Apollo program. They might have useful intel."

"Good idea," Josh said.

Gary spoke up. "Once we think we know what's there and where everything should be, let's do a video survey to verify the exact positions. That way, when we do go for them, we won't waste time looking."

"Good point," Matt said. "Okay, next. How do we get stuff off the Moon? The MoonClaw worked okay, but we could only steer it by moving the wormhole, and even with Gary's prowess, it took too long for each grab."

"I have a couple of ideas," Gary said.

"Keep us in the loop," Matt said. "Next: recovery. All that stuff has been sitting in a vacuum for at least fifteen years, and subjected to thermal cycles, solar flux, and cosmic radiation. We should assume everything is fragile—we don't want stuff to crumble when we bring it back. How do we protect them during retrieval, and how do we store them here?"

"I'm on it," Gary said.

Renny's voice came through the speakerphone. "Why don't we transport containers to the lunar surface, load them there, *then* retrieve them? Not sure how we do that, though."

"Good idea," Matt said. "If anyone has a suggestion, bring it to Gary."

"Uh, Matt?" Josh said. "Remember when we did those first drills close to the lunar surface? The out-rushing air from our side of the wormhole blew moon dust everywhere. That's why we had to lower the video transmitter and MoonCrawler from ten metres up when we went for the Columbus prizes."

"What's your point?" Gary said.

"Whatever we grab will get blasted by our atmosphere as we bring it through the wormhole. Anything fragile will get destroyed. We need to deflect the out-rushing air away from where we're working."

"I already have a solution for that," Gary said.

"Okay," Matt said. "Last item: selling the stuff. Do we do it ourselves or hire an auction company?"

"I'll take that one," Stuart said. "Our firm does a lot of work executing wills for wealthy clients; we have associates who specialize in estate sales."

"As long as we make bags of money," Renny said.

Matt smiled. "Well, that covers everything I had. Questions?"

"Yup," Gary said. "The HYDRA Mark III will give us a bigger wormhole, right?"

Matt nodded. "My latest calculations show we should get a diameter of around one point seven metres. Best case, two metres, but I won't know for sure until it's operational."

Gary nodded. "When Josh and Bigfoot prepare our lunar shopping list, they should identify any bigger, high-value items we can get with the Mark III. When we do the survey, we should locate those as well, along with larger items that might not show up in our research."

"Good point," Matt said. "Anything else?"

"Rocks!" Renny said. "I want moon rocks! Lotsa moon rocks! Every rock tells a story." Everyone groaned.

"Of course we'll get you moon rocks," Matt said. "Anything else?" His four friends shook their heads and there was a "Nope" from Renny.

"Alrighty then, let's get to work!"

A month later...

Stuart returned to AdAstra, this time bringing a guest. They convened in the meeting room, again with Renny present via speakerphone as he was still in Arizona, putting the final touches on his thesis.

Stuart kicked off the meeting. "I'd like to welcome our BNSC liaison, Mr. Byrd. Hopefully his presence during this and future planning meetings will make things run smoother, government bureaucracy-wise."

"Thank you, Mr. Barnes," Byrd said. "I share your optimism."

Matt nodded. "So, what news do you bring?"

Byrd cleared his throat. "We got a ruling from the World Court. They confirmed that, as per Article VIII of the Outer Space Treaty, whoever launches an object into space or onto a celestial body retains absolute jurisdiction over it."

Matt sighed. "So we're screwed."

Byrd shook his head. "You'd think so, but no. There's a sub-clause to that article that limits said jurisdiction to functional objects only."

"Hang on," Josh said. "What does 'absolute jurisdiction' mean?"

Stuart fielded that. "That's one of the few legal terms that actually means what it says: total ownership and/or control. However, in legislation, treaties, etcetera, it's used exclusively in reverse, like a corollary. In the context of the Outer Space Treaty, it means that, by default, a country's jurisdiction over the hardware they left on the Moon does *not* apply to *non-functional* objects."

"Does that mean what I think it means?" Matt said.

Byrd nodded. "The BNSC, and by extension the UK government, feels comfortable taking the position that everything non-functional *is* fair game for salvage."

"Is anything there still functional?" Gary said.

Renny answered. "Just the retroreflectors, mirror assemblies left behind by Apollo 11, 14, and 15, so NASA could make accurate Earth-Moon distance measurements. Pretty sure the Soviets left one or two behind during their lunar rover program, too. I asked around—universities and research labs around the world occasionally bounce lasers off them. They've degraded, though, from solar radiation or a buildup of moon dust."

"We should charge NASA to clean them off," Gary said. "A low pass with the HYDRA oughta do it."

"That's a fantastic idea," Matt said. "Let's add that to our to-do list. So, other than the retroreflectors, everything is fair game?"

Byrd nodded. "Yes. However, I recommend you tread carefully and consider national pride. Many in the US consider the Apollo landing sites to be historical sites, and off limits."

"How do we get around that?" Josh wondered.

"Well," Byrd said, "Article VIII of the treaty also says, more or less, 'if you find something, you have to return it to the owner.' But then there's the Lunar Treaty, which has an article that basically says 'don't litter.'"

"Where does that leave us?" Josh said.

"Two options come to mind," Stuart said. "One: after we retrieve an item, we offer to return it to the country that put it there, in exchange for a 'reasonable' salvage fee."

"We could call it a 'garbage collection fee,'" Renny said.

"Our electricity costs to do a drill is only a few thousand pounds," Matt said. "I hope we'll get way more than that from an auction."

"Matt, don't underestimate your costs," Stuart said. "You spent a lot of time, and a small fortune, developing the HYDRA Mark II. It would be reasonable to factor your research and development costs into any salvage fees, not to mention operational costs. But you might have to produce financial information to justify the fees."

"Good point," Matt said. "I'm not keen on divulging *anything* we don't have to. What's Plan B?"

"We auction each item, but give the original owner the option of the last bid. The advantage of that approach is the bidding process establishes a fair market value. If the owners want their stuff bad enough, they'll have to pay what the market dictates."

"Ooh, I like that idea," Josh said. Everyone agreed.

Another month passed, and things were falling into place. Nigella hired an administrative assistant, and the two were well on their way to organizing AdAstra as a bona fide business with a proper management structure, not just some brilliant guys horsing around the solar system. Josh pre-programmed the HYDRA control system with the coordinates of the Apollo and Soviet landing sites. With help from Renny's sources at the university, they'd identified approximate locations at each site where "high-value targets" were most likely to be.

Gary had taken what he'd learned with his original MoonClaw to build MoonClaw 2.0, which had several new features. The three-fingered, rubber-coated grabber claw now opened and closed via a small electric motor, allowing for finer remote control. He replaced the tether—previously a climbing rope—with a small-diameter marine-grade umbilical ordered from a subsea company in Edinburgh. It was strong enough to hold all the MoonClaw's components (and whatever they grabbed off the lunar surface), and had electrical conductors for power and video. He wound the umbilical onto a small electrically operated drum placed near the HYDRA—no more manual feeding the claw in and out.

Three metres up the umbilical from the claw—just above its video camera—was Gary's novel steering mechanism: a Plexiglas cone, its vertex pointing up and attached to the umbilical by a two-axis hinge controlled by a pair of small electric motors.

"The cone acts like a sail," he said. "When it's tilted off-centre, the out-rushing air will force it, and everything below it, to move laterally. This'll give me limited ability to steer the claw and grab specific objects and rocks."

"Asymmetrical cross-section generates a lateral drag vector," Matt said. "Brilliant!"

Gary controlled everything—the winch, the steering cone, the claw—from a "bellypack" remote control box he strapped around his waist.

"Just like we used when I worked on ROVs," he said, referring to his time in the subsea industry.

Josh was increasingly concerned for the safety of those working near the HYDRA. "We need better communications—yelling back and forth is crazy. I want to see some type of guardrail in place—I have nightmares about one of you getting sucked in."

Everyone agreed. Gary found headsets with microphones at a local electronics supply store and wired up an intercom between the HYDRA control console and his bellypack. Matt had a local machine shop fabricate a three-metre-diameter Plexiglas hemisphere with a twenty-five-centimetre hole in its centre. They mounted this "shield" on a wooden frame directly in front of the HYDRA; from behind it, Gary could deploy the MoonClaw with much less buffeting from out-rushing air.

Months ago, Josh had updated the HYDRA software so the wormhole's tail could be shifted a few metres *after* the wormhole was open. That feature turned out to be key in their rescue of the NASA astronaut, and possible only because Matt had solved some complex geometric equations in his head in mere seconds. For the upcoming salvage operations, Josh turned those equations into software, their inputs now coming from a Nintendo video game joystick he wired into the HYDRA control console. But as he coded those complex equations, he was again awestruck by Matt's mathematical abilities while simultaneously worried that the Almighty God would soon tire of their intrusion into His universe's higher dimensions.

◎

It was time for their first video survey—a hunt for "high-value targets." Renny wouldn't be missing out this time—he'd just returned from the University of Arizona, having submitted the final version of his thesis and thrilled to be "back in the trenches."

"It's in my supervisor's hands now," Renny said. "He says it's a done deal."

"Seems like the bar's pretty low there, eh?" Gary replied, always looking for an opportunity to twist Renny's tail. "Sounds like a chicken-shit outfit to me."

Renny growled.

"Okay, children," Matt said, "back to business. It's time for the first drill: the Sea of Tranquility. Today we have two modest goals. Number one: complete a three-hundred-and-sixty-degree survey, centred at the Apollo 11 lunar lander and working outwards for at least twenty metres. Number two: exercise the steering cone, winch, and grabber claw. And, if the opportunity arises, Gary will try to grab some stuff. Questions? No? Okay, let's do it!"

Matt and Josh took their places at the control console; interim Financial Director Nigella and the BNSC's Mr. Byrd sat behind them, thrilled to be witnessing their first wormhole. Once the HYDRA was powered up and had passed the initial checks and calibrations, Josh started the drilling procedure, now fully automated. On schedule, the wormhole opened with its characteristic shriek, causing Nigella and Byrd to shiver.

"You get used to it," Josh said sympathetically.

Matt scanned the monitors; finding nothing amiss, he nodded at Gary and Renny. They went around the wall towards the HYDRA, clipping their safety harnesses to a floor anchor. Gary buckled the bellypack around his waist and donned a headset.

"Testing, one, two, three. Is this thing on?"

"Loud and clear," Matt replied into his microphone.

"Wow, it's much quieter now, and calmer," Gary said, referring to the plexiglass shield that deflected much of the out-rushing air.

"Okay, deploy the MoonClaw," Matt said, as he punched the record button on the Betamax recorder connected to the MoonClaw's video camera.

Renny fed the claw mechanism and umbilical through the hole in the shield; the claw was sucked into the wormhole and the umbilical went taut. Gary flicked a switch on his bellypack and the winch drum slowly rotated, unspooling umbilical while Renny guided the video camera, then the steering cone, into the wormhole's mouth.

"We're through, and have video," Josh reported seconds after the camera disappeared. A monitor at the control console showed a bird's-eye view of the lunar surface from twenty metres up, looking down on a large metal box wrapped in gold foil: the descent stage of the Apollo 11 lunar lander. "There's the Eagle, right below us!"

"Nice aiming, Josh," Matt said. "Gary, the camera's bouncing around like crazy. Can you let out two metres?"

Gary moved a joystick forward for a couple of seconds; the winch rotated two revolutions.

"That's better," Josh said. "Okay, I see a debris field at four o'clock, and something at ten o'clock. Over to you, Matt."

Matt nodded. "I'm zeroing our coordinates and starting the survey," he said, typing in a command to activate the joystick interface. "Tracking right towards that debris field." He nudged the joystick.

The HYDRA structure groaned as the wormhole's tail moved, the image on the video monitor changing as the MoonClaw umbilical dutifully followed. A small dust cloud billowed up from the lunar surface as the out-rushing air blew away moon dust accumulated since 1969, exposing more artifacts. Matt made a running commentary into a tape recorder each time they spotted something man-made.

"Three o'clock, six metres: large white object. Looks like a backpack from a spacesuit."

"Four o'clock, five metres: two small white objects. Possibly boots."

"Six o'clock, five metres: small brown rectangular object."

"Ten o'clock: four metres: the American flag, lying flat."

Eleven minutes later, a combination of orbital mechanics and hyperspatial torsion forced them to shut the HYDRA down. Gary had plenty of time to test the MoonClaw—other than the steering cone controls being backwards, it worked well—he could move the grabber claw laterally up to two metres from the wormhole's tail.

They re-grouped in the meeting room, reviewing the video footage as Josh sketched a large hand-drawn map on the wall. Renny called it their "treasure map."

"Okay," Matt said. "We've located fifteen man-made objects: two life support backpacks, two cameras, three boots, the faded American flag, one scoop, two penetrometers, and four unknown objects."

"Those backpacks are too big," Gary said. "We'll have to leave them for the Mark III. But I think we can go for everything else."

"I strongly urge you to leave the flag where it is," Mr. Byrd said. "Bringing that back could provoke an international incident. The yanks are pretty twitchy about the old stars and stripes—we wouldn't want jolly old England to go to war over this."

Everyone at the table nodded; everyone except for Renny. "Fuck 'em! Finders keepers."

Mr. Byrd shot Renny a warning look, which he shrugged off.

"I'd call this first survey a success," Matt said.

"When can we go grab stuff?" Renny grumbled. He really wanted moon rocks.

"Hang on," Gary cautioned. "There's a few things need fixing. The controls for the steering cone are backwards. There's too much electrical noise on the intercom. And there were glitches in the umbilical winch motor control when I was winching in."

"Can we take care of those *after* we finish our video survey?" Josh said.

Gary shrugged. "Sure."

By the end of the following week, they'd surveyed the other five Apollo landing sites and identified almost one hundred possible "targets of value," many small enough to be recovered with the Mark II. Not limiting themselves to American artifacts, they located, with considerable effort, the remains of several Soviet Luna-series landers.

Now it was up to Gary to fix his MoonClaw.

◎

A week later, Stuart, who was back in London, got a phone call from Matt.

"We're ready."

The next day, Stuart and the BNSC's Mr. Byrd took the morning train up from London. They arrived by cab at AdAstra's headquarters just before ten o'clock; Matt convened a "pre-drill" meeting.

Gary had completed his repairs and modifications. The steering cone now moved in the right direction. He found a corroded connector at the umbilical winch motor; it was now glitch-free and even ran slightly faster. He'd eliminated the static on the intercom by running a shielded cable back to the HYDRA control console. He wanted wireless headsets, but the ones he'd bought from a local electronics supply store didn't work in the presence of the HYDRA's intense magnetic fields.

"Thanks to Gary for his hard work," Matt said. "Okay, today we're going back to the Apollo 11 landing site with a modest goal: recover Target #1." He pointed to the treasure map on the wall.

Stuart raised his hand. "Would you mind explaining, for me and Mr. Byrd, how you're going to retrieve stuff without damaging it?"

Gary chuckled. "It'll be easier to show you than to explain it. But if you're that interested, there's a flowchart in the other room—it takes up an entire blackboard."

"Okay, maybe we'll just watch."

"Gentlemen," Matt said, "to your stations, please."

Stuart followed Gary and Renny into the HYDRA main hall, Renny making a detour through the machine shop area to grab a plexiglass cylinder from a collection of several dozen sitting on a workbench. They'd positioned a long wooden table in front of the HYDRA, nestled between the umbilical drum and the plexiglass hemisphere Gary had nicknamed "The Deflector Shield." On top of the table, at the end nearest the HYDRA, was a metre-long, narrow, fibreglass trough. At the other end lay Gary's remote control bellypack and a small video monitor strapped to the tabletop. Laid out on the table was the first three metres of the MoonClaw umbilical, with steering cone, video camera, and three-fingered grabber claw.

"What's with the trough?" Stuart said.

"Makes it easier to slide everything in and out of the wormhole," Gary said as Renny placed the plexiglass canister on the table.

"Ah, this is what you'll store each item in."

"Eh," Renny said. "Pretty fucking cool design, if I do say so."

The canister had a circular lid, spring-hinged on one edge and with a thick face seal. A thin metal rod ran down the inside, connecting the hinge to a pressure plate on the canister's bottom. Renny pried the lid open just past ninety degrees, fighting against the hinge's heavy spring that was trying to pull the lid closed. The rod locked the lid in the open position, and he gently laid the canister in the fibreglass trough.

Gary strapped the bellypack to his waist, donned a headset, then cycled the bellypack's controls: the claw opened and closed; the cone tilted on two axes; the tether winch rotated in and out; the video monitor displayed the image from the video camera—a sideways, table-top view of the HYDRA.

"MoonClaw checks complete," he said into his headset. "Setting the claw now."

Renny took the now-closed claw and inserted it into the canister. Gary toggled a switch on his bellypack and the claw opened, jamming its rubber-coated fingers against the canister walls. Then he inspected the umbilical on the tabletop.

"Ok, Matt," Gary said. "We're locked and loaded."

"Copy that," Matt replied. "Come on back and we'll start the drill."

Gary took off the bellypack and headset, and Stuart followed him and Renny back behind the concrete wall.

"Here we go," Josh said. He typed in a few commands.

The HYDRA emitted its now familiar creaks, groans, and hums as current coursed through the powerful electromagnets; drilling through hyperspace had begun.

On schedule, the wormhole opened with its customary shriek and roar of disappearing air.

"Drill complete," Josh said, scanning his monitors. "Everything looks nominal. You're clear to deploy."

"Roger that," Gary said.

He and Renny went around the wall and clipped their safety harnesses to a floor anchor. While Gary donned the bellypack, Renny pushed the trough through the hole in the shield until it was inches from the wormhole. After getting a nod from Gary, he slid the canister into the wormhole's mouth; the suction caused the umbilical to go taut. Gary winched out and the video camera and steering cone followed the canister into the wormhole.

"We've got good video," Josh reported soon after the video camera disappeared. "Wow! The Apollo 11 descent module is directly below us. Looks like about ten metres altitude. I'm really getting good at this!"

"Okay," Matt said, "I'm tracking right to the first debris field." He gave the joystick a gentle nudge; the HYDRA assembly groaned as the wormhole's tail, 380,000 kilometres away, drifted away from the Eagle.

"Those mods to the steering cone are working great," Gary reported. "Not only is the whole assembly way more stable, it's deflecting air away from the area underneath the claw."

"Okay guys, we're right over Target #1," Josh said, referring to a rectangular, man-made object lying on the lunar surface.

"Got it," Gary said, staring at the monitor beside him. "Winching out."

As the video camera and claw-plus-canister inched towards the lunar surface, the image of the rectangular object got larger. Gary lowered the canister while making deft adjustments with the steering cone; when the canister touched down, he thumbed a control to close the claw.

"Okay, canister is down. Winching up a metre."

The claw withdrew from the canister, which now sat upright on the lunar surface.

"Target is at your nine-o'clock," Josh said over the intercom.

"I see it," Gary said. "Tracking left." He adjusted his joystick; the whole assembly swung lazily to the left as Gary opened the claw.

Stuart held his breath as Gary showed why he could beat any arcade claw game ever built. He waited patiently for the claw to stop swinging, then winched out. The claw's fingers draped over the object. Gary thumbed a control.

"Got it!" he exclaimed as the three fingers closed. "Winching up. Shifting right."

Gary positioned the claw directly over the canister. "Bomb's away!"

The object (Stuart was still not sure what it was) fell unnaturally slow in the Moon's low gravity. When it hit the pressure plate at the bottom of the canister, the spring-loaded lid snapped shut.

"Gotcha!" Gary yelled.

"Confirmed!" Josh said, watching the same video feed.

Gary winched up a few inches, then back down and grabbed the canister's wire handle.

"Got it! Winching up and bringing it home now!"

As the steering cone and video camera emerged from the wormhole, Renny guided them along the trough and onto the table. The claw and canister came through last.

Josh shut the HYDRA down; the room went silent.

"FUCK YAH!" Renny shouted, his voice echoing throughout the cavernous room.

Josh, Matt, and Stuart rushed around the concrete wall, eager to see what they'd recovered.

Matt leaned in next to Gary, who'd pressed his face against the canister.

"Gentlemen, looks like we caught ourselves a camera!" Matt said.

"Not just *any* camera," Gary said. "That's a Hasselblad EL with a Zeiss lens!"

"Holy cow!" Josh exclaimed, checking his notes. "That's Neil Armstrong's camera!"

They whooped, hollered, and slapped each other on the back.

Gary raised his arms in victory. "Who the Claw Master?" he bellowed.

In unison, they all yelled back, "You're the Claw Master!"

"Let's get this into storage," Josh said. "It's worth a small fortune." He and Matt carefully walked the canister to the antechamber of their recently installed industrial deep-freeze unit. They placed it inside another, larger plexiglass canister that had a hinged lid and a vacuum port. Matt closed the lid, attached a hose from a nearby vacuum pump to the canister's port, then flicked the pump's power switch. It chugged away while Matt watched its pressure gauge.

"We want redundancy in our vacuum canisters," he said to Stuart. "We pump the outer one down to slightly less vacuum than on the Moon. That keeps the inner one sealed and the outer one as a backup."

Once the pump's gauge had reached the desired pressure, Matt closed the valve and disconnected the pump, then stowed their prize in the freezer, now dubbed the "treasure room."

AdAstra's salvaging of the Moon was underway.

After two more weeks of intense effort, they'd visited the remaining Apollo sites and three Soviet sites, refining their recovery procedure and sometimes recovering multiple artifacts during a single drill. As expected, they had several minor setbacks. One canister failed to close, forcing them to leave behind a fist-size, multi-coloured moon rock Renny lamented over. Gary dropped one canister onto the lunar surface from too high; even in the one-sixth gravity, it landed with enough force that its pressure plate activated, prematurely snapping its lid shut. And one artifact they'd recovered had been too light—when Gary dropped it into the canister, it failed to trigger the pressure plate. He decided the only way to recover it was to jam the grabber claw inside and pull it back with its lid still open.

After twenty-three drills, the "treasure room" now had a collection of double-sealed vacuum canisters, each containing moon rocks, moon dust, or an American or Soviet artifact.

"Time to make some money!" Gary said.

TWENTY

A half-hour before the auction's start time, the largest room at Somerville's—the oldest and most prestigious auction house in the world—was packed. Those occupying the two hundred seats had to pass a vetting before receiving a coveted invitation to this historic event. Somerville's executives initially thought attendance might be low; the US government's recent public denouncement of AdAstra's lunar salvaging activities included a not-so-veiled threat towards anyone taking part in the auction. Alas, those concerns were for naught. And, as was the custom for events of this nature, a dozen seats had been reserved for media, what AdAstra's interim Financial Director Nigella Lomberg called "free advertising."

At precisely at ten o'clock, Sir Jonathan Smythe-Jones, the head of Somerville's London office, appeared through a side door and strode to the lectern. Matt and Stuart followed close behind, taking seats beside him. The room went quiet.

"Welcome," Smythe-Jones said with a smile and a thick Welsh accent. "Today we're proud to be hosting the world's first lunar auction! AdAstra Enterprises has, in addition to recovering moon rocks and moon dust, salvaged several non-functioning pieces of lunar exploration equipment left behind in the '60s and '70s by the US and the Soviets. AdAstra preserved each item by placing it inside a plexiglass vacuum canister already on the lunar surface, sealed each canister *in situ*, recovered it, then placed it inside another vacuum canister which was stored in a darkened industrial freezer at minus twenty degrees Celsius. A month ago, we released a list of all available items; last week, registered bidders had the opportunity to view them at our secure facility."

The room buzzed with excitement. Smythe-Jones glanced to his left.

"We have two representatives from AdAstra here today: Mr. Matt Barnes, President, and Mr. Stuart Barnes, legal counsel. They are ready to field questions our staff can't answer."

Matt and Stuart nodded to the audience.

"The winning bidder for each item receives a video of its salvage and a certificate listing the date, time, and its coordinates on the moon. In addition, —"

A man sitting in the second row, wearing an expensive double-breasted suit, stood up.

"Excuse me! I am James Ryan, legal attaché to the US embassy here in London. The US government objects to the salvage of our equipment. We claim rights to those artifacts, and will prosecute anyone who purchases them here today." He turned and glowered at the crowd.

Smythe-Jones, with decades of experience as an auctioneer, knew how to deal with this.

"*Mister* Ryan, have you no manners? The World Court has ruled that *every* piece of non-functioning equipment on the moon is fair game for salvage. The US is a signatory to the World Court treaty and must abide by its rulings. I find your behaviour insulting, and will not stand for your crude attempts to bully our staff or clients. I'm going to have to ask you to leave. Now!" He snapped his fingers; a pair of ushers, standing against the side wall, moved in and escorted the American from the room.

Smythe-Jones turned back to the audience. "Well, wasn't that exciting? As I was saying before I was so rudely interrupted, each artifact comes with a framed copy of the World Court's recent ruling that confirms any non-functional lunar artifact is considered abandoned."

The room erupted in laughter.

"Great Britain signed but did not ratify the 1967 Outer Space Treaty. If they had, AdAstra would be obliged to return everything recovered to the country that left them there. For a reasonable salvage fee, of course. So, in keeping with the spirit of maritime salvage law and Article VIII of the Outer Space Treaty, for items auctioned today we will allow the country that put them on the moon the option of last bid; the bidding process determines fair market value. We have representatives from the US and the Soviet Union here today."

That revelation sent a murmur through the crowd.

Smythe-Jones put up his hands. "I know, I know. It's unusual, but treaties are treaties, and everyone here today was apprised in advance of the bidding terms."

The room went silent; everyone was eager for the auction to begin.

"I will now hand the microphone over to our head auctioneer, Mr. Radcliffe. He will first auction the moon rock and dust samples, then the man-made artifacts. Mr. Radcliffe?"

Radcliffe was a portly man with a balding pate, an enormous handlebar moustache, and a heavy wool suit. He stepped up to the lectern and adjusted a couple of controls; the room lights dimmed and a large image appeared on the projection screen behind him, showing several dozen double-walled vacuum canisters sitting in a freezer.

Radcliffe cleared his throat. "AdAstra collected twenty-five canisters of moon rocks and dust samples from various locations on the moon, those locations coincident with where they recovered the man-made artifacts to be auctioned later. AdAstra is keeping five for their own research and will donate five to various non-profit research laboratories and academic institutions in Canada, Europe, the UK, and Asia. We will now auction the remaining fifteen. I ask you to refer to your auction package for details."

Radcliffe paused as the audience shuffled through their documentation.

"Item one." A close-up photo of a vacuum canister within a vacuum canister appeared on the screen. "One-point-three kilograms of moon rocks and dust, recovered from the region known as Oceanus Procellarum. Position 2.5° South latitude, 43.2° West longitude, near where the US Surveyor I landed in 1966. Bidding will start at ten thousand pounds. Do I hear ten thousand?"

Several bidders raised their numbered paddles.

"Twenty thousand." More paddles.

When the bidding reached one hundred thousand pounds and was still going strong, Radcliffe increased the bidding in fifty-thousand-pound increments. Then by one hundred thousand pounds.

Eventually, Radcliffe rapped his gavel. "Sold to bidder number seven for one million, one hundred thousand pounds!" He made a note in a ledger.

Matt turned to Stuart, mouthing, *Holy shit!*

A new photo appeared on the screen. "Item two: a canister containing one moon rock, fifteen centimetres across and weighing zero-point-nine kilograms. AdAstra recovered this from the Mare Imbrium region, position 29° North latitude, 0° East longitude, which is near where the Soviet Luna 2 probe crashed in 1959. Bidding will start at fifty thousand pounds. Do I hear fifty thousand?"

Item two sold for an even one million pounds to a German private collector. The remaining thirteen canisters of rocks each sold for, on average, *a million pounds*.

"That's over fifteen million pounds," Matt whispered to Stuart.

"We will now move on to the Soviet-made artifacts," Radcliffe said. The screen behind him switched to show a close-up of a canister containing several lumps of metal.

"Item sixteen: five metal fragments recovered from 29° North latitude, 0° East longitude. These are confirmed to be the remains of the Soviet Luna 2 probe. On September 13th, 1959, Luna 2 was the first spacecraft to reach the surface of the moon, and the first human-made object to make contact with another celestial body. Its crash site is near where the Americans landed Apollo 15 twelve years later. We have confirmed the authenticity of these fragments, as one is a pentagonal element that bears the Cyrillic text 'СССР ЯНВАРб 1959,' which, when translated into English, is 'USSR January 1959'. This element is from one of the two spherical metal pennants stored onboard the Luna 2.

"I'll start the bidding at one hundred thousand pounds." Again, bidding was fierce; a Saudi private collector was the last bidder, offering a staggering two million four hundred thousand pounds.

Radcliffe turned his attention to the Soviet representative sitting in the front row. "Last bid option to the Soviets."

The Soviet nodded vigorously. *Da.*

Radcliffe banged his gavel. "Sold to the Soviet Union for two million, four hundred thousand and one pounds!"

The representative for the Saudi collector who'd just lost out was not happy.

Stuart leaned over to Matt. "This is going really well," he whispered.

Matt could only nod, amazed at the magnitude of the winning bids.

"Item seventeen: a misshapen lump of metal assumed to be the remains of the Soviet Luna 7 lander. AdAstra located it at 9.8° North, 47.4° West. We'll start the bidding at fifty thousand pounds."

Because of its questionable state, this lump sold for a mere three hundred and fifty thousand pounds, again to the Soviets.

"Item eighteen: this object was lying one metre from the Soviet Luna 13 lander, at coordinates 18.9° North, 62° West. We have confirmed it to be one of the lander's two stereo cameras."

Bidding moved fast, stopping when the Saudi bidder who'd lost out on the Luna 2 remains offered a staggering three million, two hundred thousand pounds. The room went quiet as the Soviet representative made a frantic phone call.

He returned to his seat, then shook his head. *Nyet.* The Saudi bidder was thrilled.

The final Soviet item was part of an antenna found next to the Luna 13 probe, which had successfully landed in December 1966. It sold to an anonymous bidder for seven hundred and fifty thousand pounds.

Mr. Smythe-Jones stepped up to the lectern. "We'll take a ninety-minute break, then auction items left behind by American astronauts."

As the bidders filed out, Matt and Stuart rose and stretched.

"Geez, that's a lot of money," Stuart said.

Matt nodded. "Almost twenty-two *million* pounds," he muttered.

"And the big-ticket items are still to come."

"Welcome back," Smythe-Jones said after the audience settled in following the lunch break. "We're going to continue with items recovered from the six Apollo landing sites. In order for the Apollo astronauts to bring back moon rocks, they had to leave behind an equivalent mass—some were items of scientific and historic nature, while others were... more personal.

"According to NASA records, their astronauts left behind ninety-six bags of urine and/or feces. AdAstra recovered twenty of those, and has donated ten to medical research institutions around the world. Mr. Radcliffe?"

Radcliffe took to the lectern; a new photo appeared.

"Item twenty: an Apollo 11 urine bag, left on the lunar surface on the 21st of July, 1969. Just think, this bag contains, or contained, the urine of Neil Armstrong or Buzz Aldrin! We'll start the bidding at ten thousand pounds."

The price increased rapidly, stopping at eight hundred and fifty thousand pounds.

"As per the rules Mr. Smythe-Jones laid out," Radcliffe said, "this item will go to bidder number forty-two unless the US representative wishes to exercise their final-bid option." He turned to the American in the front row.

"Sir, do you wish to exercise your final-bid option?"

The American nodded.

"Very well, item twenty sold to the United States for eight hundred and fifty thousand and one pounds." Radcliff rapped his gavel.

Bidder number forty-two wasn't happy, but there were plenty more opportunities. Of the remaining nine bags of bodily waste, the Americans exercised their final-bid option only once more; private bidders got the rest. Each sold for, on average, two hundred thousand pounds. Interestingly, the bags of feces sold for more than the urine bags.

"Well, that was rather interesting!" Mr. Radcliffe exclaimed. "Next up are space boots—overshoes, technically—that the astronauts wore over their regular spacesuit boots when walking on the lunar surface. After their final moonwalks, they removed the boots and tossed them away in order to save mass for their return flight. We have one pair from each of the six Apollo missions. Note that we are selling these boots in pairs."

"Item thirty: a pair of space boots worn by Apollo 17 astronaut Harrison Schmitt. We'll start the bidding at twenty thousand pounds. Do I hear twenty thousand?"

Schmidt's boots sold to a South African industrialist for an incredible five hundred and ten thousand pounds. The next four pairs sold for the same price, the Americans opting out each time.

"And finally, in the space-boot category, we have item thirty-five: the boots worn by Apollo 11 astronaut Buzz Aldrin, the second man to walk on the moon. Do I hear one hundred thousand pounds?"

Bidding for these was fast and furious; the Americans hadn't exercised their final-bid option yet on space boots, but every well-informed bidder knew astronaut Eugene Cernan's were sitting in the Smithsonian Air & Space Museum in Washington, DC.

Buzz's boots sold for an amazing eight hundred thousand pounds to an anonymous Japanese bidder.

"Moving on," Radcliffe said. "The Apollo astronauts used Hasselblad still cameras with removable film magazines so they could leave the cameras behind to save weight. Item thirty-six: a Hasselblad Electric Data camera left behind by the Apollo 14 astronauts. We'll start the bidding at one hundred thousand pounds."

That camera, and similar ones from the Apollo 15 and 16 missions, each sold for one point five million pounds.

"And the last camera we have is very special. Item thirty-nine is Apollo 17 astronaut Gene Cernan's Hasselblad. He left it pointing straight up as a long-term experiment to see how much the glass lens would deteriorate from solar radiation. Bidding starts at one hundred thousand pounds!"

The price quickly reached, then passed, the benchmark set for the other cameras. Bidding stopped when a British venture capital firm offered two million, two hundred thousand pounds. Unfortunately for them, the US exercised their final-bid option, buying it for one pound more.

"Our penultimate item: number forty is a film magazine from Apollo 12 astronaut Alan Bean's camera. He only took a couple of photos before the magazine jammed, so he ejected it then mistakenly left it on the lunar surface. There's a chance there could be never-before-seen shots in there, although who knows what seventeen years of exposure on the lunar surface has done? Bidding starts at fifty thousand pounds."

The bidding ramped up. The British venture capital firm who'd lost out on the last camera won this round for an amazing two million, three hundred thousand pounds.

Radcliffe consulted his notes. "And now for our last item! As I'm sure you're aware, Apollo 14 astronaut Alan Shepard smuggled the head of a golf club—a six iron to be precise—and two golf balls onto his flight. When he got to the moon, he attached the club head to the handle of a lunar excavation tool, creating the first lunar golf club. He shanked the first ball into a crater only a few yards away; the second one flew much farther. AdAstra was, after what we're told was a considerable search, able to recover the former one. We end today's auction with item forty-one: the first golf ball hit on the moon. Bidding starts at one hundred thousand pounds."

Somerville's had left this item for last, guessing it would be the most popular. The winning bid came from a representative for a PGA Championship multiple winner, for an astounding four and a half million pounds.

Radcliffe relinquished the lectern to Smythe-Jones.

"Well, that's it for today's auction. Thank you for coming. If you're a winning bidder, please see one of our assistants on your way out."

With the room now empty, Matt and Stuart huddled together.

"Jeez," Stuart said. "Tell me you did the math."

Matt nodded. "Forty-one million, four hundred thousand and three pounds," he said. "Somerville's take is thirty percent—that leaves us with... twenty-eight million, nine hundred and eighty thousand and two pounds."

"Not bad for a couple of week's work, eh?" Stuart replied. "Remind me how that gets divvied up?"

"Sixty-five percent of that—just over eighteen million—goes into AdAstra's coffers."

"That'll make Nigella happy."

"Along with the Columbus Prize winnings, we should have more than enough to build the Mark III," Matt added. "I get ten percent, or two point eight million pounds. The guys each get five percent—one-point-four million. You get seven hundred thousand—not bad for an ambulance chaser, huh?"

Stuart grinned. "And the foundation?"

"Two point two million. That'll make a big difference."

◎

Charles William Winston the Third muttered an expletive and flung the TV remote control at the screen. It shattered on impact, its pieces scattering across the carpeted floor. The television set, having just finished showing a recap of the first ever lunar auction five time zones away, blinked off in sympathy.

"The US government just gave Matt Barnes and his merry band of thieves almost four million dollars and all we got was a camera and bags of urine and feces?" he ranted at his executive assistant.

"And video of their recovery," the assistant added. "Hopefully that'll offer some insight into their technology."

"I doubt it," Winston said, glaring at his assistant. "Barnes is too smart for that." He shook his head, fuming. "If it's the last thing I do, I'm going to get my hands on his technology."

The assistant nodded. "Many people are digging into Barnes' latest papers—the ones he published last year in that British physics journal. I read them—I got the gist of the one about the high-strength superconducting electromagnets, but the other one, about multiple dimensions and an expanding universe, was Greek to me."

Winston nodded. "Yes, yes, I read them, too. He did his electromagnetism work while at Caltech. They never should have let that paper go." Winston was too egotistical to accept the fact that *he* was the reason Caltech lost out on that work. "As for the other paper, it's just a lot of nonsense," he said, waving off the matter.

◎

University of Arizona
1986 Convocation Ceremony

When the master of ceremonies announced Renny's name, he strode across the stage to the lectern, feeling awkward in his convocation robes.

Like an ape in a suit.

He shook hands with the Dean of the College of Science and accepted his diploma.

"Renwick Norman Harris, Graduate Minor in Planetary Science. The title of Mr. Harris's thesis is, 'Confirmation of a Paleocene-Era Meteor Strike in Southwestern British Columbia.' Mr. Harris showed conclusively that Crater Lake, British Columbia, Canada, previously assumed to be created by glacier scour, is actually an impact crater lake."

Renny turned to the audience as they applauded. His mother, along with Matt, Stuart, Josh, Gary, and Matt's parents, clapped the loudest.

Following an afternoon cocktail party for graduates, Renny took his friends and family on a tour of the Lunar & Planetary Laboratory building. He ended the tour at the lab where he'd spent several months toiling away, analyzing the drill samples he'd taken beneath Crater Lake.

"Matt, there's someone here I want you to meet," Renny said, winking. He steered Matt away from the others and towards a man with shocking red hair who sat at a bench in the lab's corner, peering into a microscope.

"Hey, Red!"

The red-haired man looked up, blinking several times to re-focus his eyes. "Hey, Renny. Congrats on your degree."

Renny nodded and motioned towards Matt. "Scott, this Matt Barnes, my best friend. Matt, Scott Hansen. Scott's a NASA astronaut—he's been on three space shuttle flights and lived on the US space station twice. He's here doing, what was it again, analysis of materials structures?"

Hansen nodded. He'd arrived at the LPL two months ago, ostensibly to conduct research into long-term exposure of the space station's outer thermal blanket to the harsh environment of space. His master's degree in materials engineering made the story seem plausible, but scuttlebutt said something different. Based on what Renny had gleaned from other lab colleagues, NASA administrators decided Hansen had, to use the military idiom, "screwed the pooch" on his last mission and forced him to take a leave of absence until they decided his fate. Coincidentally, the lab Renny was using to analyze his Crater Lake samples had the equipment Hansen needed for his research. But Hansen couldn't know that Renny knew more about the space station rescue than Hansen did; it hadn't been easy for Renny to keep his mouth shut these past months.

Hansen sized up Matt before speaking.

"Ah, Mr. Barnes! Saw you on the news," he said, referring to the recent lunar auction.

Matt nodded. "Nice to meet you."

"Poking through the Apollo landing sites has made you quite a few admirers, and some enemies, on this side of the Atlantic."

Getting no response, Hansen held up his hands. "Don't worry, I'm in the former category. I'd just as soon you'd brought *everything* back so we can study the effects of long-term exposure. Everyone here at the lab is dying to know how you pulled off the scientific coup of the decade. Didn't realize until just last week that Renny is part of your merry band of salvagers. He's normally a chatty guy, but somehow kept quiet."

Renny gave a sort-of-embarrassed shrug.

"Well," Matt said, "the World Court's on our side, and our operations are proprietary."

Hansen nodded. "Understood." A sly grin appeared on his face. "Say... during your salvage ops, you didn't happen to grab a chunk of the thermal blanket off any of the lunar module descent stages, did you? We use a similar material on Liberty's exterior and I'd love to see how it's fared after all these years."

"No, we haven't touched any of the landers. At least not yet." Matt glanced at Renny and raised his eyebrows. *Should I tell him?*

Renny nodded. *Do it!*

"Tell you what, Scott," Matt said. "We might be able to snag a piece for you, but I was hoping you could do us a favour in return."

Hansen's eyes lit up. "What?"

"Well, last year, just before Christmas—I think you were on the space station then—we misplaced a couple of items at AdAstra. I was hoping you might know where they are."

"I... I don't understand. How could I help?"

"I believe you have one of our fire extinguishers?" Matt said, deadpan. "I'd like it back. And my baseball cap."

Hansen's face turned pale; he dropped into his chair and looked up.

"How... how could you know about that?" he whispered. "There's only five people in NASA who know what happened."

Renny watched as Hansen connected the dots: the mysterious sphere appearing in space; the fire extinguisher; the Columbus Prizes; the lunar auction. Then the light bulb came on.

"That was you," he whispered. "Somehow, that was you."

It took Matt a few minutes to explain how the fire extinguisher appeared right in front of Hansen, literally out of nowhere. Hansen had many questions, most of which Matt couldn't or wouldn't answer. Then he went silent for a full minute, staring at Matt. He reached up and grabbed Matt's hand with both of his. His eyes were wet.

"You... you saved my life. You saved my kids from growing up without a father. How can I *ever* repay you?"

"Not necessary," Matt said. "I'm glad we could help. All I ask is that you keep this between us."

Hansen nodded, then leaned forward, resting his forearms on his knees.

"You look like you need some alone time," Renny said. "I gotta drop Matt off at the airport."

"Scott, nice to meet you," Matt said. "I have a feeling we'll be in touch."

An hour later, Renny pulled up to the curb at the departures terminal at Tucson International Airport.

"Well, Professor," he said as he pulled Matt's luggage out of the trunk of the rental car, "thanks for coming to my grad. I guess I'll see you in Cambridge in a couple of weeks. Can't wait to get started."

"No problem, Batman. Oh, I almost forgot. Got you a graduation present."

Renny stared suspiciously at his empty-handed best friend, then raised his eyebrows.

Matt reached into his back pocket and pulled out a folded-over envelope. "Here."

Renny tore it open and pulled out a single piece of paper.

"What's this?"

It was a British bank draft in Renny's name, drawn on a London HSBC account. His eyes bugged out when he saw the amount.

One million, four hundred and forty-nine thousand pounds.

"That's your cut from the auction," Matt said, smiling. "Best wait until you get to the UK before depositing it, or you'll get hit with some serious exchange rate conversion charges. Oh, and you'll have to pay British taxes on it, so don't spend it all. See you in a couple of weeks, Batman." He turned and headed into the terminal.

Renny just stood there, clutching the bank draft in his massive fist, his mouth agape.

◎

Two weeks later, Renny had wrapped up his affairs at the university. He said his goodbyes at the lab, packed his few belongings, and caught a short-haul flight from Tucson to Dallas Fort Worth International. There he boarded a British Airways 747 non-stop flight to London—he splurged and bought a first-class seat. Matt met him at Heathrow Airport; they took a cab into London, then the train from King's Cross to Cambridge. Matt had arranged for an apartment in the same building that he, Josh, and Gary and Nadia lived.

Renny was relieved to be done with school and thrilled to be back at AdAstra permanently. He was astounded at how much money the lunar auction pulled in—he, Josh, and Gary each received almost *one and a half million pounds*. For someone who'd grown up in near-poverty, Renny never thought he'd accomplish much in life.

Now I have an amazing group of friends, a master's degree, and I'm a millionaire. A multi-millionaire, if you convert to Canadian dollars.

As soon as his bank draft cleared, Renny had Matt drive him to Cambridge's sole luxury car dealership, where he ordered a cherry red BMW Z1 Roadster convertible, paying a premium to expedite delivery. Then he contacted a car dealership back home and arranged for a new car to be delivered to his mom's house.

She worked so hard to raise me on her own. The next time I go home I'm going to set her up so she never has to work again.

Renny felt guilty about receiving so much money from the auction, considering how little he'd contributed to the winning of the Columbus Prizes. He compensated by diving into his work, taking over one of the small, unused buildings nearby and building a modest lab so he could catalogue and analyze the moon rocks and dust they'd recently collected.

His friends also came to terms with their newfound wealth. Gary bought new cars for himself and Nadia: a silver Jaguar sedan for her and a black Land Rover 4x4 for him. The two started house hunting, looking for something local that befitted a junior university professor. Josh's needs, courtesy of his conservative upbringing, were almost as modest as Matt's. He did spring for a brand-new model of the old Vauxhall that Matt drove, then bought all the latest video game consoles and personal computers, including a Compaq Deskpro 386 and the latest Apple Macintosh. He also sunk a significant percentage of his windfall into Apple stocks, urging his friends to do the same.

"That stock's got real long-term potential," he predicted.

Josh contemplated making a large donation to the local Baptist church he attended almost every Sunday since arriving in Cambridge. But his ongoing crisis of faith caused him to re-consider.

Renny continued hounding Matt about his old car, only giving up once he realized Matt was keeping the "old girl" running just to bug him. Matt had left most of his newly earned money in the bank, sending a sizeable chunk to his parents.

◎

With AdAstra's coffers now overflowing, it was time to get serious about building the HYDRA Mark III. Even though Matt had more-or-less figured out *how* it would work, it took him and his friends several weeks to formalize the system-level requirements.

"We don't want to miss any important features, and we don't want to build anything we don't need," Matt declared.

Josh needed a state-of-the-art, networked computer system to run and monitor the Mark III and its complex support equipment. Gary wanted to replace the labour-intensive MoonClaw umbilical system with a robotic manipulator arm. Renny had no particular input to the Mark III design, but wanted his own, fully equipped, on-site geology lab: "the Harris Planetary Receiving Laboratory." And, since the Mark III would create a wormhole almost two metres across, they had to figure out how to move a human through it. Safely.

"We're gonna need spacesuits," Gary noted during one of their many planning sessions. "And someone to train us in how to use them. I'm a certified scuba diver, but working in spacesuits is a whole other ballgame."

Matt nodded. "I've got someone in mind."

"Before we get too far into the details," Nigella said, "we're going to need help launching this project. We have the money. Our top priority is hiring the right people—those experienced in constructing such a massive machine." There were murmurs of agreement from around the table.

"I know just where to look," Matt said. Later that day, he called AdAstra's travel agent and booked a trans-Atlantic flight.

TWENTY-ONE

Professor Bill Oldman was working his way through marking a tall stack of first-year physics assignments when a knock at his office door vied for his attention.

"Come in!"

A tousled head appeared in the doorway. "Hi, Uncle Bill!"

Matt Barnes!

It was two years ago that Matt, the brightest engineering physics student Oldman had ever met, actually *failed* his doctoral defence at Caltech. Oldman had heard rumours through the academic grapevine about what transpired and tried contacting Matt right away, but he'd gone home for the summer and was off-the-grid. Then a copy of his failed doctoral thesis arrived in the mail, courtesy of Dr. Feinberg; Oldman immediately called him to learn the details.

The physics community has always been rife with politics, especially in the States, but what Matt endured was some next-level machinations.

Then Matt had, surprisingly, taken a short-term teaching gig at Caltech, then gone off-grid again, surfacing six months later working at Cambridge as a part-time lecturer. That appeared to be the sad end to Matt's promising academic career, until his doctoral thesis was published in The Physics Journal B, sponsored by the Cavendish Laboratory. That same journal then published another paper of Matt's, one so radical it was either the rantings of a crazy man or the most genius of work to come along in decades. Or both.

"Matt! How the heck are you?"

"Great! Yourself?"

Oldman waved at the stack of papers in front of him. "Living the dream. What brings you to these hallowed halls?"

Matt smirked. "Just stopped by for a visit."

"Good timing on your part. I'm supposed to be going on sabbatical in January, but, well... I saw Columbus's press conference on the news, and the results from your auction. I always knew you'd succeed, but, wow!"

Matt nodded. "Thanks. We're having a lot of fun."

"The entire department's talking about it," Oldman said. "There's a pool going, betting on how you did it."

"What's your guess?" Matt said with an impish grin.

Oldman removed his glasses and rubbed the bridge of his nose. "Well, after seeing the video from the press conference, I went back and re-read your PhD dissertation—Feinberg sent it to me—looking for clues. Brilliant work, by the way—thirty-five Tesla, continuously! Then I read your 11-Space paper. Or tried to, at least."

"And?"

"To be honest, I only understood a fraction of what you wrote, but... some of its implications are, well... staggering." Oldman stared at Matt for a few seconds. "I think you've found a way to create an Einstein-Rosen bridge."

Matt tilted his head side-to-side. *Sort-of.* "Topologically speaking, yes," he said. "But in the classical sense of general relativity equations having solutions that include wormholes... no."

Oldman leaned back in his chair, feeling the blood drain from his face. "Topologically speaking? You mean you *can* create a mass-traversable wormhole?"

Matt nodded. "I could tell you more, but then I'd have to—as the saying goes—shoot you."

Oldman grinned. "And I'm guessing it has something to do with magnetism?"

"It's got *everything* to do with magnetism," Matt said.

"Jun Kim at MIT is doing some interesting theoretical work on E-R bridges using general relativity."

"I've read her preliminary work," Matt said. "It's based on using exotic matter with negative energy densities—you know, stuff that only exists theoretically. What I've done is completely different, actually works, and doesn't need a black hole or other form of matter that's not even known to exist. The key is the magnetostatic wormholes."

Oldman nodded enthusiastically. "I understood *that* part of your paper. Professor Bernhard here has a post-doc trying to create the magnetostatic wormhole you predicted in your paper. I hope you don't mind."

"Not at all—the key is the field modulation. I'll swing by and see him on my way out."

He speaks so casually about something so complex, so ground-breaking!

"Uncle Bill, I want to thank you for your encouragement during my four years here. Honing my experimental techniques helped make it possible to turn my theoretical work into reality."

Oldman welled up with pride. "My pleasure, son. Nothing makes me happier than seeing former students succeed. Damn... I'd love to see your wormhole machine in action."

He paused, staring at Matt. "So, why are you *really* here?"

"With our Columbus prize winnings and what we've raked in from the lunar auction, we're going to build a bigger version of our current... machine. It will give us a much larger wormhole."

"How much larger?"

"Right now, we can create a wormhole with a twenty-five-centimetre diameter throat. The new one will give us at least one point five metres. Theoretically, up to two metres."

Oldman's eyes bulged. "A two metre-wide, stable, mass-traversable wormhole? That'll require an almost infinite amount of energy!"

"If you think in terms of general relativity, then yes. Let's just say... I found a shortcut."

"How big will this new machine be?"

"Not as big as TRIUMF, but close," Matt said, referring to Oldman's pride and joy, the cyclotron facility at the south end of UBC's campus.

"Holy cow." Oldman felt an attack of information overload coming.

"So," Matt said, "getting back to why I'm here. We need people to help with our detailed design and construction. You're connected with all the major labs and accelerators around the world—I figured you'd know if there's anyone available who fits the bill."

"That is true," Oldman said, steepling his hands. "What skill sets are you looking for?"

Matt counted with his fingers. "One: a mechanical engineer familiar with large vacuum chambers and high-stress structures in the presence of intense magnetic fields. Two: an electrical engineer experienced in high-voltage DC power conversion and superconducting electromagnets. Three: an engineer-physicist who can help me design the permanent and electromagnets needed to create the wormhole. I *could* do that myself, but we're having so much fun right now with our orbital and lunar activities I don't want to spend *all* my time on the new machine. And, last but not least, we need a project manager-slash-engineer who can oversee construction of the entire facility. Someone experienced in building large-scale facilities like particle accelerators, nuclear reactors, that kind of thing."

"That's quite the shopping list."

Matt shrugged. "Building something like TRIUMF won't be easy, as you well know."

"What's your timeline? It took us three years from breaking ground to producing our first proton beam."

"Money's not a problem, so if we can get the right people... a year, maybe eighteen months at the outside. We have full support from the British government, and I want to get started right away."

Oldman chuckled. "Well, my boy, your timing couldn't be better. Thanks to our science-averse, conservative federal government, TRIUMF's operating budget for the next two years has been slashed; we'll be lucky if we can keep the lights on, let alone fling protons around. I've been in budget meetings for the past two weeks trying to figure out where to cut, and we've already started laying people off. Colleagues I've worked with for years are being let go. Even *my* time has been cut back. So there are good people here looking for work."

"Well, TRIUMF's loss may be my gain," Matt said soberly.

A thought came to Oldman. "You know, Matt, I'm scheduled to take a one-year sabbatical, starting in January. Wifey wants us to travel, but I want to do research."

Matt's eyes lit up. "Are you thinking what I'm thinking?"

Oldman grinned. "Wifey *has* always wanted to study *English* castles..."

"Could you come to Cambridge next week? We're doing a drill in support of a project some local students are doing—I could show you what we've done and what we're planning next."

"Deal!"

"Great! I'll have my travel agent contact you with the details. See you in Cambridge, Uncle Bill!" he said, disappearing out the door.

It's amazing how far Matt's come in only a couple of years! Failing a doctoral defence has ruined many an academic. And his recent paper... if half of what's in there is right, Matt may have found the Holy Grail of physics. I really should bone up on my advanced geometry and read that paper again.

◎

Bill Oldman's jaw dropped when the wormhole winked out of existence, the roar of vanishing air suddenly stopping. The immense room was silent but for the creaking of the HYDRA's support structure. He stared at the complex arrangement of permanent magnets and superconducting electromagnets mounted around the rim of the HYDRA Mark II's rings, trying to visualize the complex magnetic fields it generated to create a pair of magnetostatic wormholes, let alone an honest-to-God mass-traversable one.

"Well, what do you think?" Matt asked, smiling.

"If I hadn't seen it with my own eyes, I wouldn't have believed it," he muttered. He'd just watched them deploy a miniature, low-cost, optical telescope in high-earth orbit for a group of Cambridge astronomy undergrads.

"It never gets dull," Matt said, "and that was our 112th drill."

"Where do I sign up?" Oldman said.

Matt grinned. "I was hoping you'd say that. Let's talk about the plans for the Mark III," he said, ushering his former mentor into the conference room. It took Matt the rest of the day to walk through the system-level requirements and explain what he and his friends envisioned. By dinner time, they'd significantly refined Matt's high-level design; Oldman had suggested a few changes Matt hadn't even considered.

"Darn..." Oldman said, staring at the sketches on the blackboard. "I want to start *now*."

Matt nodded. "It is rather intoxicating. Should we talk salary?"

Oldman shook his head. "I'll be on sabbatical, so UBC's paying my salary. You're getting my services for free."

"Well, can we pay for your housing?" Matt offered.

Oldman mulled it over for a few moments. "Deal. Wifey's gonna be thrilled to spend a year in England. She's got a thing for castles."

Matt grinned. "How about we fly back to Vancouver tomorrow, then you can introduce me to those soon-to-be-out-of-work TRIUMF engineers?"

◎

A week later, Matt was back at AdAstra.

"How'd your shopping trip go?" Nigella asked at the Monday morning management meeting.

"Better than expected." Matt described the problem with TRIUMF's funding.

"Wow," she said. "I don't fully understand what TRIUMF does, but it sounds like it worked out well for us."

Matt nodded. "I've hired three ex-TRIUMF people. Ben Stellutti was their engineering manager. Dr. Deepa Chandra is an electrical engineer who specializes in DC control systems for superconducting electromagnets. Elaine Turner has a master's degree in mechanical engineering and twelve years' experience working with large vacuum structures. They're arriving within the next three months. Doctor Oldman and his wife come in January."

"Excellent," Nigella said. "Forward me their details and I'll get my assistant started on their work visa applications—our friends at the BNSC will expedite the process."

"So do we have time to grab more stuff off the moon now?" Gary said.

Matt nodded. "And there's two more VIPs I want to show our operations to."

"Who might that be?" Renny asked.

Matt smiled.

◎

A multitude of thoughts ran through Dr. Feinberg's head as the wormhole appeared in the centre of the spiderweb-like structure—which Matt Barnes had wittingly christened HYDRA—accompanied by a roar of departing air.

Feinberg shook his head in amazement. He was a brilliant man—a Nobel Laureate, no less—but the mathematics that lay behind this engineering marvel were beyond him. His protégé had taken a conceptual leap far beyond anything Feinberg thought possible—clearly, Matt's failed doctoral defence hadn't slowed him down.

In fact, it may have done the opposite.

Matt had spent two hours that morning trying to explain his "hyper-math," but Feinberg could only catch glimpses of what it meant. It was, to paraphrase noted sci-fi author Arthur C. Clarke, sufficiently advanced technology to be considered "magic."

The student becomes the teacher.

Josh Allen's voice boomed over the loudspeakers, startling Feinberg out of his reverie. "Drill complete. Deploy the packages."

Feinberg peered over the concrete wall as Gary Stocks used a wooden pole to push the first of three, half-metre-long cylindrical objects—lying in a fibreglass trough—into the roaring wormhole.

"Bomb's away!" Gary shouted as the cylinder disappeared with a loud sucking sound.

"Copy that," Josh said, holding a stopwatch. "Stand by for second deployment in ten seconds. Five, four, three, two, one, go!"

They repeated the procedure with the second cylinder, then again with the third, another ten seconds later.

"Executing normal shutdown," Josh said.

Feinberg heard and felt, in his bones, the HYDRA's odd, multi-harmonic tones shift in frequency an instant before the wormhole winked out of existence, accompanied by near silence.

"Now we wait for confirmation from the university," Josh said to Feinberg and the other guest present for today's deployment. Feinberg had been so enthralled with the HYDRA he'd forgotten he wasn't the most important person in the room.

Prince Edward, the Duke of Cambridge, sat at the control station beside Josh, exuding the confidence and grace expected of royalty. He was in his third year of studies at Cambridge, an avid astronomy buff and patron for this endeavour: a trio of very low-cost optical telescopes thrown together by students from the Cambridge astronomy department.

This wasn't Feinberg's first time around royalty; as a Nobel Laureate, he'd rubbed elbows with the King and Queen of Sweden, not to mention several US Presidents and European heads of state. But meeting the Prince was a real treat.

"Anything yet?" Josh said.

Matt was leaning against the wall, holding a telephone to his ear. He spoke a few words into the phone; ten seconds later, he gave a thumbs-up then hung up.

"They're receiving telemetry from all satellites," Matt said. "It'll take them an hour to calibrate, but everything appears nominal. We'll call this a success, at least from our end."

The Prince smiled. "Thank you, Mr. Barnes, for that amazing demonstration. Dr. Feinberg, sir, it was an honour to meet you." He stood up and turned to his security detail. "If we head over to the university now, we should be able to see the first images arrive."

His detail led him out of the room; Matt intercepted them at the door and engaged in a brief but animated discussion with the lead agent.

"What was that about?" Feinberg said after the Prince's entourage departed.

"Just trying to ascertain the whereabouts of one of his former security detail. We crossed paths a while back, and I want to get in touch with him."

◎

The following evening...

"Well, that makes eight," Renny said, as they exited a dodgy pub in the small town of Hereford, two hundred kilometres west of Cambridge. "Never would've guessed there'd be so many bars in such a small place."

"Well, Batman, at least we're on his trail now," Matt said. They'd almost caught up with their elusive quarry at the last pub, only to be told by the barman, "You just missed him, mate."

Matt was glad Renny had insisted on accompanying him on this quest. Patrons of these pubs didn't take kindly to strangers showing up and asking about one of the locals; that led to more than one tense standoff. Renny's bulk and demeanour prevented things from getting out of hand.

They were now wandering the narrow streets and alleys in what was clearly the roughest part of town; Matt felt safe, knowing nothing could go wrong when accompanied by someone who'd literally taken on armed terrorists with his bare hands. And at least one grizzly bear, if the story, which Renny still refused to confirm or deny, was true.

They found another nameless pub on a deserted street with mostly broken streetlights. Renny pushed open the old, creaky wooden door and cautiously led them inside; cigarette and cheap cigar smoke wafted out. Every head turned in their direction—more locals wary of outsiders. In a dark corner, Matt spied a dusty old claw arcade machine.

I must tell Gary about this place! But he should probably come during the day. And with Renny.

They found their quarry at the end of the bar. Seamus O'Donnell was perched on a stool, leaning against the wall, half-asleep. He looked up as Matt and Renny approached, bleary-eyed and squinting through the unkempt red hair that hung down over his eyes.

"Hi, Seamus, remember us?" Renny said.

Seamus looked back and forth at them several times before a look of recognition appeared on his ruddy face.

"'ow could I forget you two?" he slurred. "The Eagle pub! Was one of the proudest days of my career, saving the Duke himself!"

The current head of the Duke's security detail had given Matt the low-down on Seamus's personal situation, but Matt wanted to see it and hear it first-hand.

"So, Seamus, what are you up to these days?"

Seamus filled them in the best he could in his inebriated state, his speech slurred from his hours-long pub crawl. The gunshot wound to his right hand had fully healed, but the jacketed 9mm round fired by one of the Prince's would-be abductors nicked a nerve the surgeons weren't able to repair. That left him with just enough numbness in his trigger finger to lower his marksmanship and hand-to-hand combat scores to where he was no longer eligible to remain on active duty, let alone on the Royal's security detail. And to add insult to injury, he had just reached his twenty-second year in Her Majesty's British Armed Forces—his "golden year"—and faced mandatory retirement.

"So now all I got is a measly pension," he slurred, "an' the George Cross, presented by Her Majesty!" he announced to everyone within earshot, his chest puffed out. The lapel of his faded khaki army jacket sported a small gold pin—a replica of the George Cross bestowed on him by Queen Elizabeth. Matt and Renny had been at the public award ceremony when Seamus and his partner were decorated, then at a private one immediately after where they both received the George Medal "for gallantry in service of the Crown." Matt's medal sat in its velvet-lined presentation box in the top drawer of his dresser, under a pile of socks.

Matt looked to Renny, who nodded back. *Go ahead!*

"Um, Seamus, would you be interested in a job? I think we have something right up your alley."

Seamus had consumed too many pints to comprehend the question. "Wha?" he said, leaning against the wall, then falling sound asleep.

Matt tucked his business card in Seamus' front pocket. "Call me."

Two days later...

Seamus O'Donnell waited outside AdAstra's main gate while the security guard made a phone call.

What am I doing here? Seamus wondered.

The past couple of months had been rough—he wasn't coping well with the sudden lack of purpose after being retired-out of her Majesty's Armed Forces. Two nights ago, he'd gotten seriously bog-faced, not even remembering how he made it back to his tiny Hereford flat. It wasn't until the next morning that he found Matt Barnes' business card lying just inside his front door. Then some memory fragments returned; Barnes and his dangerous sidekick had showed up at the pub.

I think he said something about a job?

Seamus called the number on the card—the discussion with Matt was brief.

"I'd like to talk about some work. Can you come up to Cambridge? We'll make all the arrangements."

The next morning, there was a first-class ticket waiting for Seamus at the Hereford train station. It was a five-hour milk run from Hereford to Cambridge, circling clockwise around to the north via Birmingham, Leicester, and Peterborough. A pre-paid taxi was waiting at the Cambridge train station, which whisked him to AdAstra's compound northeast of town.

"Mr. Barnes will be out shortly," the security guard said.

Seamus nodded. While he waited, his professional training kicked in— he identified four ways to breach the fenced compound, subdue the guards, and storm the complex.

Old habits die hard.

A minute later, Matt came out of a nearby building, striding towards the gate.

"Welcome, Seamus. Glad you could make it."

Seamus just nodded, unsure why this brilliant man might want to hire him.

Matt ushered him into the main building and gave him a tour, ending in the hall where the HYDRA Mark II resided.

"So, laddie, why am I here? You mentioned something about work? You need a bodyguard? Got a rival you want me to get rid of?" Since retiring, several less-than-reputable individuals had approached him, offering well-paying work of a legally grey and morally questionable nature.

Matt chuckled. "No, no, nothing like that. We're embarking on a major expansion and construction effort here, and AdAstra could use someone with your skill set."

Seamus stared up at the HYDRA and shrugged. "Not sure what a washed-up SAS grunt could do for you—my skills are more on the... kinetic side."

Matt smiled. "We need someone to manage our security. First, there's the physical security of these facilities. We've already had several attempted break-ins. Then there's the human element—we're going to hire lots of people and I need someone who can keep a lookout for industrial spies and, possibly, agents from other governments. There's also cyber-security, making sure our computer systems are secure and our intellectual property safe."

"I don't know much about computers..." he mumbled. *Other than how to blow them to smithereens.*

"Not to worry. Josh Allen can handle the technical side, but he easily gets bogged down in details. We need someone who can maintain the ten-thousand-foot view. And there are probably other security holes we haven't even thought of."

I don't know what to say!

Matt continued. "We can offer you a salary of twenty thousand pounds per year, reviewed annually, with a commitment for a minimum of three years. Once we get our human resources staff going, we'll sort out details on life insurance, dental plan, etcetera. And we can help you find a flat in town."

Twenty thousand quid? That's more than double what I made as a career sergeant!

Seamus looked around the cavernous room, taking in the enormous machine and its high-tech control console.

I'm out of my league here. "Can I think on it for a spell?" he ventured, hoping he wasn't blowing a good thing.

"Absolutely," Matt replied. "Take all the time you need. We got you an open return train ticket, so you're welcome to head home anytime. Or we can book you into a hotel if you want to stay overnight."

Seamus thanked Matt and opted to take the train back—he enjoyed riding the night trains.

By the time his train pulled into the Hereford station just after two in the morning, he'd made his decision. He waited until morning before calling AdAstra.

"Mr. Barnes, I'm in."

◎

Matt looked at the crowd that formed a semi-circle in front of the HYDRA Mark II.

"Welcome, everyone, to AdAstra's first official staff meeting. Until we get the facilities in Building 2 ready, this will have to make do as our meeting room."

"First, I'd like to introduce the newest members of the AdAstra team." Matt motioned for Seamus to step forward.

"Seamus O'Donnell is our new Chief of Security. He's a just-retired sergeant from the British Army, spent ten years with the SAS and was seconded to the Royalty Protection Division. As you may have heard, Renny and I have seen Seamus in action. Up close. But that's just a rumour!"

There was a smattering of laughter and warm applause.

"Next up is Scott Hansen. Scott's a former NASA astronaut, has been on three space shuttle missions and has lived on the American space station Liberty. We convinced him to take a break from his research in materials science at the University of Arizona and join us."

"Fight, Wildcats, fight!" Renny hooted, proud of his newly adopted alma mater.

Hansen rolled his eyes.

"About time we got another fookin' ginger onboard," Seamus said, smiling.

Hansen nodded back.

The real story behind Hansen coming onboard wasn't well known. NASA was having ongoing problems with their space shuttle fleet—both technical and managerial—and were quietly scaling back flight operations, focussing on military missions and just keeping their space station Liberty running. Hansen, as "damaged goods" following his recent near-death experience, was no longer needed. The timing of Matt's offer of employment had been serendipitous for both.

Matt continued. "The HYDRA Mark III will create a wormhole close to two metres in diameter. To move payload and people through it into orbit and onto the lunar surface, we'll have to work in pressure suits—spacesuits, presumably—and it'll be Scott's job to train us on how to work in them. Once he finds us some, that is!"

More applause.

"And last but not least, Ben Stellutti," Matt said, motioning towards a burly, hairy ape of a man—a two-thirds scale version of Renny. "Ben was the engineering manager at UBC's TRIUMF cyclotron for ten years and part of its original construction team. He'll be managing the Mark III construction in Building 2, just east of here."

More applause.

"Two other former TRIUMF people will be coming to help with the Mark III, but they won't arrive for another month or two. I'll introduce them when they arrive."

Matt paused. "Next announcement. Nigella, our interim Financial Director, has agreed to come onboard permanently."

Lots of applause.

"Nigella has been working hard the past couple of months to organize AdAstra, business-wise. I'll let her explain what we've come up with."

Matt stepped back to give her the floor.

"Here's an overview of our corporate structure," she said. "AdAstra Enterprises LLC is a privately owned, UK-registered company governed by a board of directors consisting of Matt, Renny, Gary, Josh, and Stuart. The board sets the company's overall direction and strategic goals. Matt is on record as the owner and President, and Josh is Vice President.

"The company will have eight divisions, each with a division head who reports to the board. Right now, some—okay, most—of the divisions consist of only one person, but we expect that'll change as we ramp up operations with the Mark III. And yes, some of the division heads are directors.

"Matt is in charge of Research & Development, which includes the Mark III construction. He will also, for now, lead the Operations division, which decides what we do with the HYDRA. Renny will handle Planetary Sciences. Josh runs Computing Services, and Gary is in charge of Robotics. As Matt mentioned, Mr. Hansen will be responsible for Manned Space

Operations. Mr. O'Donnell will head up Security, which covers all AdAstra's security matters, including physical security, employee security, and cyber-security. I will run the Administration division, which includes finance, accounting, legal, marketing, and human resources.

"Any questions?"

Seamus was first. "How does the British government fit in? I can't imagine they're letting us do all this on our own."

Matt nodded. "Ah, thanks for reminding me. Great Britain is a signatory to the Outer Space Treaty, so there are conventions we have to follow to play nice with other countries. There's a small government agency called the British National Space Centre that has the mandate to coordinate all civilian space operations. They've assigned us a representative whose job it will be to smooth over any bureaucratic issues and deal with foreign relations. Basically, they'll run interference and help keep us out of trouble. The BNSC rep is a Mr. Byrd—he will attend our operations planning sessions and be present for most of our missions."

"What's the deal with our pay?" one technician said. "I heard there's going to be a change?"

Nigella smiled. "Yes, I should clear that up. The board of directors decided to do something unconventional. All AdAstra employees—everyone—will receive the same salary, currently set at twenty thousand pounds per year. That's well above the national median, which is roughly ten thousand pounds right now. We'll review that number every year, taking into account inflation, cost of living, and so on. Rest assured, it'll never go down."

There were appreciative murmurs from the crowd, most of whom typically made half that. There were few questions—the company was small enough that everyone knew what was going on.

"Thanks, Nigella," Matt said. "Well, that's all I've got to say. Next week we break ground on Building 2 and the Mark III!"

TWENTY-TWO

Under Ben Stellutti's guidance, construction of the HYDRA Mark III began in earnest. To create a wormhole nearly two metres wide, the support rings for the HYDRA's superconducting electromagnets had to be *five metres* in diameter. Matt calculated that the mechanical stresses on those rings would be an order of magnitude larger than on the Mark II, requiring an immense support structure. His original plan was a scaled-up version of the spiderweb-like structure in Building 1 that kept the Mark II from tearing itself apart.

"Why don't we put the whole fucking thing underground?" Renny suggested during one of their design review meetings. "Most of the ground in this part of the country is unconsolidated alluvium and peat sediments on top of deep sedimentary rocks. Might as well be quicksand. But we're smack in the middle of a big-ass pluton—an intrusion of hard, igneous rock. Let's bore a tunnel or blast a trench, then anchor the rings to the surrounding rock."

Everyone liked the idea. A cost-benefit analysis confirmed that trenching offered many advantages over boring a tunnel. With Renny providing his geological expertise, Ben hired a local excavation company to surface-blast a trench thirty metres long, four metres wide, and ten metres deep. Once they'd removed all the blast rock, they lowered a pair of excavators outfitted with hydraulic rock hammers into the trench. It took the excavator operators ten weeks to dig down and hollow out a cylindrical tunnel, five metres in diameter and thirty metres long. The owner of the excavation company was thrilled to have the work, and got to haul away several thousand cubic metres of rock for free; he planned on using it for fill at a construction project on the other side of town. It was Renny who nicknamed this expensive trench, "The Money Pit," which was soon shortened to just "the Pit."

Next to go up was Building 2's exterior, which surrounded and covered the Pit. Its design proved challenging, as ferrous materials, such as the rebar typically used to reinforce concrete, would affect the Mark III's powerful yet finely tuned magnetic fields. The building's two-storey-high walls were constructed from pre-fabricated concrete panels strengthened with polyethylene fibre and braced with titanium brackets. A barrel-arched roof, consisting of plexiglass panels supported by laminated wooden beams, covered the entire building. Tall sliding doors on each side of the building facilitated the movement of heavy equipment and materials in and out. Once the roof was up, the envelope of Building 2, eighty metres long by fifty metres wide by ten metres high, provided an acre of room to begin construction of the HYDRA.

The Mark III construction was a boon to the local economy. At any given time, AdAstra employed over a hundred people in various capacities: construction companies, local machine shops, and electrical supply outlets. Couriers and trucking companies made daily deliveries; restaurants and pubs provided take-away lunches for workers in the morning and served them meals and drinks at the end of each work day. Seamus O'Donnell and his small security team kept busy vetting every tradesperson who came on-site, and inspected every vehicle entering and leaving the compound.

Construction continued at an almost frenzied pace. Workers erected a two-storey office block inside the north end of the building; the south end was left empty but intended for support equipment and future laboratories. Ben was a tireless project manager, always watching, always thinking two or three or ten steps ahead, and never missing a detail. When the HYDRA's two machined aluminium support rings—five metres across—were lowered into the Pit by a travelling overhead gantry, Ben followed them down on a temporary staircase, barking orders at the gantry operator over a walkie-talkie. He watched over the shoulder of the worker assigned to torque each of the hundreds of stainless-steel bolts that anchored the rings to the surrounding bedrock.

Once the rings were precisely aligned, Matt and Dr. Oldman supervised the installation of the permanent trim magnets at strategic positions around each ring's perimeter. Matt was thrilled to have such an experienced engineer-physicist onboard, marvelling at Oldman's understanding of how surrounding structures affected magnetic fields. Once that task was complete, Oldman took a well-earned, month-long vacation with his wife to tour Scottish castles. Electrical engineer Dr. Deepa Chandra, the second of three former TRIUMF employees Matt hired, took over and supervised the installation of the twenty-two superconducting electromagnets, eleven spaced equally around each ring.

Each electromagnet was a coil of wire made from tiny filaments of niobium-tin—an intermetallic compound—embedded in a copper matrix. When cooled below 18° Kelvin (18° above absolute zero), the wires became superconducting, offering essentially zero electrical resistance and capable of generating powerful magnetic fields. Deepa was a world-renowned expert in the art and science of keep those delicate components operating at peak efficiency inside their cryostats—thermally insulated containers that liquid helium circulated through. The super-cooled helium was generated on-demand by two-stage mechanical refrigeration units fed by a pair of large helium storage tanks on the main floor of the complex.

While the mechanical construction was underway, Josh Allen was in "geek heaven," supervising the installation of the Mark III's computer control system. Mission Control was a large room on the second floor of the north end of the building, with floor-to-ceiling, wall-to-wall windows overlooking the main floor of the complex. Directly below Mission Control was the computer room, shielded by a Faraday cage to prevent damage from the HYDRA's intense magnetic fields. Four brand-new Data General Eclipse MV/8000 32-bit minicomputers, the most advanced computer available, sat on the room's raised floor (for cooling and routing cable bundles). Their 32-bit processors performed 1.2 million instructions per second, and each came with 2-megabytes of memory, a 9-track tape drive for data archiving, and an 80-megabyte, washing machine-sized disk drive that held the Advanced Operating System, or AOS/VS. A halon-gas fire suppression system kept the room safe from electrical fires.

Josh had named each of the minicomputers and assigned them specific tasks: Alpha handled the HYDRA control; Beta was for data recording; Gamma for the mission control operator interfaces; and Delta, for system and safety monitoring. He networked them together with high-speed serial communications links, creating an X.25-based packet-switched local-area network. Alpha communicated with the electromagnet control system hardware—designed and built by Deepa and in cabinets on the main floor—using a FieldBus high-speed industrial network. Cable bundles ran from those cabinets into the Pit, branching out to the individual electromagnets and the many sensors populating the HYDRA's two support rings.

Josh also oversaw the porting of the Mark II's software—which he and Matt had written in assembly language and PL-11—to the new computer hardware. Data General offered several programming languages for the MV/8000-series minicomputers; Josh converted the low-level software that executed Matt's complex hyperspatial math to Fortran, a computer programming language made for scientists by scientists. The rest of the software was being converted to PL/1—a procedural language developed by IBM—by a pair of top-notch Cambridge computer science students who were eager for extra income. At Seamus's insistence, those students worked on computers in a locked room in Building 1, had to sign an iron-clad non-disclosure agreement, and agreed to random searches when entering or leaving.

Thanks to Ben's tireless efforts, assembly of the Mark III proceeded at a brisk pace for eight months. Soon it was time to start testing.

"Okay, here's our plan," Matt said to the small crowd of engineers and technicians gathered around him on the main floor of Building 2. "Josh has completed basic testing of the mission control software. First, we'll check out the monitoring and logging systems—we want to make sure we can read the hundreds of sensors, calibrate them, and record their readings in real-time. Then we'll do the power-up testing of HYDRA's twenty-two superconducting electromagnets. Once all are working, we'll begin testing the drilling software."

◎

Deepa Chandra stared at the remains of superconducting electromagnet A-3, hanging forlornly from its support ring by a single, melted cable. A portion of the magnet's cryostat was embedded in the bedrock a metre away.

"Good thing we decided to evacuate the Pit during these tests," she said wryly to Ben Stellutti, who was standing beside her and poking at the cryostat's housing with a pencil. A layer of ice that had formed on the super-cooled electromagnet coil was rapidly subliming away.

"Looks like a mechanical failure of the housing," Ben said. "But why?"

"I saw a spike in the helium feed pressure three seconds before this happened," Deepa said. She'd been sitting in Mission Control beside Josh when he enabled the super-cooled helium flow to the electromagnet under test. "Josh's printing out the data log file so I can check the raw numbers, just to be sure."

"Any thoughts at this point?" Ben asked.

Deepa pursed her lips. "I suspect it was the second-stage pressure regulator in the refrigeration unit," she said. "We are using the best ones on the market, but their mean-time-to-failure isn't as high as I'd like. My design calls for triple redundancy, but we only got a partial shipment of regulators—the rest won't be here until the end of the week. This is the first magnet control subsystem we've tested that didn't have the redundant regulators, so I'm not too concerned. It doesn't appear to be a design flaw or a defect in the cryostat."

Ben shrugged. "These things happen in engineering test."

Deepa nodded sagely. They'd debated whether to wait until all the parts arrived, but decided there were enough other components in that subsystem that the benefit of learning something outweighed the risk of learning nothing.

By the end of the following week, Deepa had tested all twenty-two superconducting electromagnets, first cooling each one down to $4.2°K$ then increasing the coil current. Thanks to the breakthrough Matt had made during his PhD work, every electromagnet maintained a magnetic field intensity of 29 Tesla and held it for an hour.

During the short end-of-day progress meeting, Deepa gave an update.

"I'm very pleased with our progress. We'll start magnet training tomorrow morning."

"Could you explain this 'training' thing to me again?" Gary asked.

Deepa nodded. "We train the magnets to prevent quenching—an abnormal termination of a magnet's superconducting state, when part or all of its coil transitions to its normal, resistive state. This can happen if there are crystallographic defects in the coil's wires, if the rate-of-change of the magnetic field is too high, or if the magnetic field is too large. Or any combination thereof. It depends on the size of the coil, but it typically happens in a few seconds or less; the magnetic field energy gets converted into heat, which results in a boil-off of the cryogenic fluid."

"And there's usually a really loud bang," Bill Oldman added, echoing his decades of experience.

"As the magnetic field collapses, the coil current drops off quickly, producing kilovolt-level spikes and arcing. We have to get rid of that energy by shunting it into load dumps made of metal or fluid with a high heat capacity. To reduce the likelihood of quenching, we 'train the magnets,' what we magneticians call, 'bedding them in.' We run a magnet at low current, increase the current until it just starts to quench, then back off. If we repeat this process, increasing the current each time, the magnet retains its ability to run at higher currents without quenching."

◎

Test review status meeting (2 months later)

"Okay," Matt said, "let's go around the table and see where we stand. Josh, how's Mission Control looking?"

"We're in good shape. Beta—the logging computer—is debugged. We can log the full telemetry stream in real-time for up to four hours, which is how much a magnetic tape will hold. Gamma—the operator consoles—is ready, as are the initial graphical displays. I do expect, though, we'll create more displays as our operations evolve. We've done extensive testing on the monitoring subsystem—Delta—and as of yesterday evening, all sensors are working and calibrated. We have a relatively short bug list, and no critical or major bugs. I expect that once we start drilling, we'll uncover more bugs in Alpha."

Josh paused. "Oh, and the good chairs finally arrived." They'd been sitting in uncomfortable metal folding chairs for the past several months.

"Excellent," Matt said. "Uncle Bill?"

"All trim magnets are within expected limits," Oldman replied. "The static mag field is constant around the circumference of both rings to within zero-point-five percent."

"Good," Matt said. "Deepa?"

"We've bedded in all the electromagnets, and have no indications of quenching when running at full field strength. The helium refrigeration units are running within spec and we've installed the redundant pressure regulators."

"Great," Matt said. "Elaine?"

Elaine Tanner, designer of the large cylindrical pressure vessel that would sit inside the HYDRA rings—nicknamed "the Pipe"—nodded. "Construction of the Pipe is complete, and the manufacturer is starting their quality checks tomorrow. I'll be going on-site to monitor their testing until they're done. Assuming we don't find any problems, delivery is two weeks from today. My team has installed the vacuum system, and it has passed initial testing."

"Good," Matt said. "Gary?"

"Design of the robotic manipulator is complete, and I've ordered the parts. I expect to have everything ready by the time we install the Pipe."

Matt nodded. "Seamus?"

"The new security system will be complete by the end of this week. Internal and external cameras, motion sensors, the works. The security room is half done—it'll be ready on schedule. We've had four attempted security breaches in the past two weeks. Three were just nosey reporters. The fourth was a more elaborate attempt—my guys are still following the trail to see where it originated."

Matt looked worried.

"*Dinna fash yerself*, Matt. Everything is under control."

"Good," Matt said, having recently learned another of Seamus's Scottish phrases that roughly translated to, "Don't worry."

Matt turned to Ben. "Overall, how are we doing?"

"Just two weeks behind schedule," he said. "But remember, shit happens."

Matt paused. "Well done, everyone. It appears we have no show stoppers. Monday, we'll try our first drill."

◎

The walls of Mission Control shook and its windows rattled from the random vibrations coming from the HYDRA Mark III, deep in the Pit.

"No! No! No!" Matt shouted. "It's not working! Shut it down!"

Josh entered the command to abort the drilling sequence, and the HYDRA went through its orderly shutdown, leaving a grim silence in the control room. This, the twelfth attempt in the past two weeks to drill through hyperspace, was the same as the first eleven—a complete failure.

"Geez, my teeth hurt," Gary said, holding his jaw.

Renny was madly scratching his arms. "I feel like I've got bugs crawling all over me. That was some weird-ass, multi-dimensional fucking vibrations." He shuddered.

"We're not getting anywhere," Josh said, exasperated.

Matt sighed. "I don't know what I'm missing. The magnets are at saturation. The field strengths are nominal. Field modulation is *exactly* what it's supposed to be."

"Matt, we're seriously behind schedule—the Pipe is arriving tomorrow," Renny said, referring to the massive pressure vessel to be inserted in the middle of the HYDRA assembly.

"I know! I know!" Matt yelled, stomping out of the room, slamming the door behind him.

Josh stared at the door. "I'll go through the code again, just in case I missed something."

Matt locked himself in his Math Room for the next three days, only coming out to use the bathroom and grab the occasional snack. He found no answers staring at the blackboards, so he shuffled morosely down to the Pit. He sat on a stool and stared at the HYDRA assembly, looking for inspiration.

Something.

Anything.

The entire weight of the company felt heavy on his shoulders.

If I don't figure this out, we're screwed. Everyone's counting on me!

Towards the end of his second day staring at the HYDRA, AdAstra's machinist, Angus MacDougall, wandered in.

"Ach, sorry, Matt! I dinna mean ta interrupt yer thoughts," he said in his thick Scottish brogue. "I wanted ta get some measurements on the mounts for the Pipe so I can update the as-built drawin's."

Matt sighed. "No problem, Angus. Do what ya gotta do. I'm just trying to figure out why the drill won't work."

"I heard yar havin' some wee troubles. Ya looked gubbed, laddie."

Matt wasn't sure what "gubbed" meant, but he caught the gist of it. He stared up at the Mark III, reciting out loud a list of the things that did work, not realizing that Angus had pulled up a wooden crate and sat beside him, listening intently.

Matt went silent for several minutes, then Angus spoke.

"I dunna ken most a what yer sayin', but, if I unnerstan' ya correctly, yer sayin' ya can drill a wee hole threw what ya call 'hyperspace' with yer other drill, but ya canna with this bigger 'un?"

Matt nodded. "I've been over *everything*. It *should* be working."

Angus paused, deciding whether to speak up. "I dunna if this helps, but what ya described soun's like yer drill is skippin' oot."

"Skipping out? What do you mean?"

"Well, when I got ta drill a big hole in somethin' hard, I dunna start off with a large bit—it just skips across the surface, makes a mess o' the material an' breaks the bit. So, firs', I make me a dimple wit' a punch, drill a pilot hole with a wee bit, then work me way up te the size hole I need."

"Dimple. Punch. Pilot hole," Matt repeated while staring at the HYDRA. His eyes glazed over.

Angus shrugged and stood up. "Ach, sorry ta bother ya, laddie. I'll leave ya te yer thoughts."

Matt jumped up. "A pilot hole! THAT'S IT!" He grabbed Angus by the shoulders. "Angus, you're a freaking genius!"

Matt flew up the stairs to the Math Room, slamming the door behind him.

Three hours later, he burst into the lunchroom where Renny, Josh, and

Gary had congregated for a late afternoon coffee break; his eyes were red and puffy but he was grinning and clutching several pages of equations.

"I've got it! When I developed the equations to define the Mark II's magnetic drill pattern, I accounted for the secondary boundary conditions in 5-space but ignored the third-order ones because they weren't relevant at that scale. Well, the Mark III has a larger drill pattern, and those tertiary effects now *are* relevant—they *prevent* the drill from getting into hyperspace. Angus suggested dimpling, then drilling a pilot hole. You know—if you try to drill a hole in a piece of metal using a large drill bit, it just skips on the surface. You start with a small bit and work your way up."

His friends all nodded.

"I figured out how to form the 10-space mag field force vector into a tapered shape: narrow in the middle, then slowly widening."

He handed his clutch of paper to Josh. "Here's the updated equations and sequencing. How long would it take you to code this?"

Josh scrutinized the papers for several minutes.

"Seems pretty straightforward—some changes in the magnet PLCs and a few dozen lines of code in the main drill sequence state machine. What's this thing here labelled AMDF?" he said, pointing at an equation Matt had circled in red. "It looks like an impulse function, but in ten dimensions."

Matt nodded. "That's exactly what it is: the Angus MacDougall Dimple Function. Just before drilling starts, we have to create a small depression in 10-space—a dimple—so the tapered magnetic force vector can bite. Timing is critical—we have to create the dimple, then start drilling just *before* hyperspace rebounds. I have a good guess what the delta-t is, but we'll have to experiment to get it right."

Josh looked over the papers again. "This looks pretty easy. It should take me... four hours to code, and another day or so to test."

"Okay, let's get started on that tomorrow!"

Two days later...

"All magnets at full strength," Deepa reported from her console.
"Punch it," Matt said.

Josh rolled his eyes, and Matt added, "Yes, that pun was intentional."

"Okay, activating the dimple function," Josh said, typing away.

An odd-sounding thump reverberated throughout the building and the bodies of those inside it. Oddly, the event didn't register on any of the seismic sensors Renny had installed during construction.

"That's hyperspatial rebound in 10-space," Matt said, staring at columns of numbers scrolling past on the monitor, too fast for his friends to read. "Now we have to get the timing right."

It took half an hour to determine that drilling had to start precisely forty-two milliseconds after dimpling—close to what Matt had predicted.

"Forty-two!" Gary shouted. "Ha ha! Douglas Adams was right!"

Josh updated a configuration file with the "magic" 42 value, then reset the HYDRA's control system.

"Shall we do it?" he said.

Matt nodded. Josh typed in a single command.

Drilling proceeded without incident, identical to the Mark II except for the "thump" when the Angus MacDougall Dimple Function kicked in. Nine minutes later, the HYDRA Mark III let out a hair-raising shriek as its first wormhole opened two hundred kilometres into space, accompanied by a massive roar of departing air. Matt's full attention was on the video monitor showing a feed from a camera in the Pit.

"Diameter looks to be roughly sixteen hundred millimetres," he said.

"Weren't you hoping for two metres?" Gary said.

Matt nodded. "It'll get bigger once we drill in vacuum." He turned to Josh. "We're dumping a lot of air into space. Let's shut her down."

Josh complied, and the building fell silent.

Matt stood up with both arms over his head, fists clenched. *Victory!*

"Let's get the Pipe installed!" he exclaimed.

TWENTY-THREE

The Pipe, which had arrived a week earlier, lay alongside the Pit on the ground floor of Building 2. It came in two sections—Perspex (plexiglass) cylinders four metres in diameter and ten metres long. Its walls were ten centimetres (4 inches) thick, and each section weighed in at just over 7,000 kilograms. A cylinder that large would buckle under its own weight, so Elaine had designed Perspex stiffener rings spaced at equal distances that were ultrasonically welded to the inside of the cylinder walls.

Ben supervised as the overhead crane operator lifted the first pipe section off its wooden transport cradle with a sling harness, then slid it sideways until it hung over the Pit. Everyone watched nervously as it slowly descended the ten metres through the slot cut into the bedrock—kept centred by workers holding tag lines—to rest on waiting support brackets in front of the HYDRA's rings. Elaine and Ben climbed down the temporary staircase to inspect it.

"Looks good," she yelled up at Matt and his friends, who were watching from the safety railing installed around the edge of the Pit.

They repeated the process for the second section, laying it on the other side of the HYDRA. Under Ben's watchful eye, workers slowly winched the sections horizontally until they met between the HYDRA's rings. After an hour of minor adjustments, they had the two pipes level and perfectly aligned. Elaine came back up to join them.

"Um, why didn't we just order a single pipe twice as long?" Renny asked.

"Couple of reasons," Elaine said. "Too big to transport, and the manufacturer has never made one that long. I didn't want to risk it."

"So, how do we stick them together? Crazy glue?" Renny snickered.

Gary shook his head. "This is what happens when you miss design meetings, Bigfoot."

Renny opened his mouth to launch an appropriate retort, but Elaine cut him off.

"Ultrasonic welding," she said. "We *could* use an industrial version of cyanoacrylate—superglue—but welding gives a bond that is stronger than the material itself and acts as another stiffener ring. The Pipe's manufacturer has a team that does nothing but welding—they'll be here tomorrow."

Nonplussed, Renny continued. "And what's with the odd colour? It's got a bluish tinge."

Elaine sighed. "Normal Perspex—PPME, or polymethyl-2-methylpropanoate—ignites at 460°C, and our design requirement is at least 500°C. I had the manufacturer add a small amount of cobalt during manufacturing to raise the ignition point to just over 600°C, but that produces a colour shift."

"We need that temperature margin for one of our destinations, remember?" Matt said.

"Ah yes," Renny replied, realizing that he *had* missed at least one design review meeting.

"I'm going to head back down and double-check everything before the welders arrive," Elaine said.

The "welders" spent two full days setting up a custom fixture that surrounded the joint both inside and out. The actual welding took only three hours; Matt and his colleagues watched from above as the "welding head" inched around the joint, magically bonding the two pipe sections as an ultrasonic generator heated the joint with a pencil-shaped transducer. Elaine and her assistant—a physics grad student from Cambridge—spent another two days inspecting the joint, first visually, then with portable X-ray and ultrasonic imaging equipment.

Elaine meticulously reviewed the manufacturer's inspection reports before signing off. The next step was a test drill to see if the Pipe's presence affected wormhole creation (Matt was sure it wouldn't). All the readings during this drill were the same as before, the only difference being a significant change in the sound of the out-rushing air.

"Check out the acoustics," Matt said to everyone in Mission Control as a low-frequency rumble came through the floor. "The primary resonance for a twenty-metre-long open-ended air column is 17 Hz. We're feeling the first and second harmonics at 34 and 51 Hz."

"That's a fucking expensive flute," Renny noted.

With that milestone reached, Elaine supervised the installation of airlocks at each end of the Pipe, five-metre-long Perspex cylinders with doors at both ends. The outer doors were circular disks, hinged on one side with a face seal. The inner doors were pivoting disks, also with face seals but on opposite sides. Then the workers connected the vacuum system, a quartet of industrial-grade vacuum pumps situated up on the main floor next to Deepa's helium refrigeration system.

"My pumps will be able to bring the air pressure inside the Pipe from sea level down to a hard vacuum in thirty minutes," Elaine said confidently.

Once the airlocks were installed, she ran a series of tests to confirm not only that her pumps worked as designed, but that the Pipe could handle the pressure differential. She and her assistant had mounted strain gauges at strategic locations around the Pipe; as they lowered the Pipe's internal pressure, they watched the strain gauge readings up at Mission Control.

"We're at ten to the minus five atmospheres," Elaine reported. She scanned all the stress readings. "Looks good. Let's go down another step." The vacuum pumps chugged away for another ten minutes.

"We're at minus six," she said. "We'll leave it there for sixty minutes."

An hour later, the pressure inside the Pipe remained steady and the strain gauge readings were as expected.

"We'll call that a conditional pass," Elaine said, nodding to Josh and Matt. "But I want to repeat that test another nine times. Then high-pressure tests at one hundred atmospheres."

Matt nodded. "Ben has those scheduled to start on Monday. Next, we need to see what effect vacuum has on the drilling—we'll do that first thing tomorrow."

The next morning, nine minutes after drilling started, the wormhole appeared in the middle of the Pipe. Owing to the vacuum, its characteristic shriek was gone—at least the audible part. However, everyone still "felt" the shriek. Matt tried to explain.

"It's a hyper-dimensional version of sound, coming from 8-space. The human ear can't hear it, but the human body can feel it at the cellular level."

And there was no longer a safety concern of having air rushing into a bigger wormhole open to the vacuum of space. Matt stared at one of the video monitors for several minutes, gauging the size of the wormhole.

"It *is* bigger, isn't it?" Josh said.

Matt nodded. "Yup. I'd estimate about one point nine metres. We'll have to wait until Scott gets us trained in our spacesuits so we can go inside and make better measurements. But we're gonna be able to move *a lot* of stuff through that. Let's shut her down—it's Friday afternoon. Time to let everyone go home."

◎

Running a small but rapidly growing company was a new thing for Matt. Even though he'd delegated administrative duties to Nigella and day-to-day operations to Ben, Matt did his best to ensure every employee felt appreciated. Every Friday, freshly baked goods arrived in time for the morning coffee break, delivered by a local family-run bakery that had been in Cambridge for over one hundred years.

Matt designated the last Friday of every month as Employee Appreciation Day, when everyone gathered in Building 2's main conference room for lunch. Matt first gave an update on how business was going and what projects were coming up. Then he held a Q&A session where any employee could pose any question to any of the directors. Following a catered lunch, AdAstra's HR manager Annabelle announced employee birthdays, work anniversaries, and other employee-centric events of note. Then she brought out a large cake decorated with the names of everyone who had a birthday that month. And everyone got to go home early.

"Before we dive into lunch, I've got one more announcement," Matt said during his spiel at the October celebration. "Last month we encountered a major hiccup in getting the Mark III up and running, which put us three weeks behind schedule. It turned out to be a complicated engineering-slash-physics problem that Josh and I fixed, but the *reason* we *could* fix it was because a member of our team volunteered a seemingly unrelated observation. So we decided to start up a bonus program. Here's how it works: if you think of something, anything, that improves things around here, be it technical, logistical, security, human resources, workplace safety or whatever, we want to hear about it. Just tell someone on the management team. If your suggestion produces a tangible improvement, you'll get a commemorative trophy and a reward. That reward might be monetary, it might be something... else."

The staff murmured their approval.

"So," Matt said, "I'd like to announce our first winner. Angus MacDougall, get on up here!"

Angus was reluctantly shoved to the front of the room by his co-workers.

"Angus was instrumental in helping get the Mark III to drill into hyperspace. His observation, from a machinist's perspective, came at just the right time and helped me realize we needed to dimple hyperspace before drilling."

Matt turned to the table behind him and picked up a fist-sized object. "Angus, congratulations on being the first HydrAward winner!" He handed the Scot a horrendous clay statue somewhat resembling the mythical Hydra monster from Greek mythology. "Students at a local primary school made these; we have dozens of them, just waiting to be awarded."

Everyone applauded. Matt held up his hands for quiet.

"Earlier, I said each HydrAward comes with a bonus gift. Not only is Angus immortalized in the HYDRA control system software with the 'Angus MacDougall Dimple Function' or AMDF, he'll receive something more tangible. Apparently he has a passion for a famous Scottish poet?"

Angus nodded.

"Well," Matt said, "that poet's birthday is in January, so we've arranged a fully catered, authentic 'Robbie Burns supper,' complete with a piper, for Angus and his family."

Everyone clapped and cheered. Angus hooted his approval.

◎

By the end of November, the Mark III had endured a full month of rigorous testing. Many problems cropped up, but all were minor. One of the vacuum pumps worked intermittently, forcing its manufacturer to overnight-ship a replacement. There was a leak in one of the airlock seals that eluded Elaine for the better part of two days. Deepa had to tear down and rebuild an electromagnet that randomly quenched—she found a microscopic break in one of its wire bundles. Josh and Matt spent three days hunting a software bug that turned out to be rounding error in an open-source math library.

"All things considered, this is typical for such a complex system," Bill Oldman noted during the weekly progress meeting. "When we first powered up TRIUMF back in '73, it took us three months to iron out the bugs and get a proton stream going."

Renny's suggestion to put the HYDRA underground and secure it to the bedrock turned out to be a brilliant one. The added strength provided by this arrangement allowed the HYDRA to operate at 115% of its design specs, meaning they could open wormholes for minutes longer than originally planned.

◎

Stuart looked up from his copy of the Financial Times as his train coasted into the Cambridge station, the eighty-minute trip just long enough to get through the thick Saturday edition. He folded the newspaper and stuffed it into his briefcase, exited the train, and hurried through the railway and outside to the taxi rank. He caught the attention of the first driver, then climbed in the back seat.

"Where to, sir?"

"AdAstra headquarters, please."

"'Fraid I don't know that place, Guv'na. Got an address?"

"The old industrial area northeast of town."

The driver's eyes widened. "You mean Area 52? That's where they keep the aliens."

Stuart chuckled at the name the locals had given AdAstra's facility, known for both its high security and mysterious goings-on. "Yup, that's the place."

"Happy to oblige, sir." He flipped up the taxi's meter lever, switching the sign on the taxi's roof to show it was not available. Twenty minutes later they arrived at AdAstra's main entrance, blocked by an imposing security gate and dour guard.

"This is as far as I can take you, Guv'na. That'll be twelve quid."

Stuart paid the driver, tipping an extra three pounds, then walked up to the security gate and showed his AdAstra id badge.

The security guard recognized him but still scrutinized his pass, following Seamus's training. "Welcome back, sir."

"Thanks," Stuart nodded, then headed for Building 2, where he figured Matt and his friends would be.

He arrived at the building's side entrance to find it locked; a red light beside the door was lit up and rotating.

Ah, they're in the middle of a drill! He pressed a button below an intercom mounted beside the door.

Josh's annoyed voice came from the speaker. "Who is it?"

"Pizza Hut, here with your delivery," Stuart said, waving at the video camera mounted above the door.

"There's no Pizza Hut in Cambri—oh, hi Stuart." There was a loud "clunk" of a magnetic door lock being released. He pulled the heavy door open, walked inside, waited for the door to close, then climbed the wood staircase and walked the ten steps to Mission Control. Josh and Gary were focussed on their controls and the video monitors. Elaine and Deepa were at their consoles, monitoring their subsystems.

"Hey guys, what's happening at Chaos Control? Where are the others?"

"They're in the Pipe," Gary said. "Matt's taking near-field measurements of the wormhole."

Stuart looked out the floor-to-ceiling windows that gave him a panoramic view of the inside of Building 2. Looking down into the Pit, he could just make out the top portion of the HYDRA Mark III, its large, circular magnet assembly emitting wisps of white mist—the superconducting electromagnets chilled to nearly absolute zero. He felt the low-frequency hum reverberating through the floor and walls that signalled the HYDRA was doing its almost-unbelievable job of keeping the wormhole open.

He sat next to Josh, who acknowledged his presence with a brief nod while keeping his attention on the controls in front of him. One monitor, coming from a video camera inside the Pipe, showed two spacesuited figures. The larger one (obviously Renny) was holding a wooden pole, its end decorated with sensors; cables snaked back to several pieces of electronic equipment at the back of the chamber where Matt was monitoring. Another camera view showed Scott Hansen waiting in the airlock, monitoring Renny and Matt's life support equipment. Every few minutes, Matt instructed Renny to move the sensors to a particular location; Matt would then recite a string of numbers, which Gary jotted down, even though they were recording the audio and video feeds.

"I guess the spacesuits Scott got us are working out?" Stuart said.

Gary shrugged. "Mostly. Mine had a small leak during testing this morning, so Bigfoot took my place."

Scott Hansen's first assignment upon joining AdAstra had been to acquire spacesuits, a necessity for working in the harsh vacuum of space. His NASA credentials and two decades of networking in the aerospace industry got him a meeting with the president of the US company that made the spacesuits for the Apollo and space shuttle astronauts. Initial discussions had gone well and soon resulted in a signed contract. But just hours before Nigella was to authorize a wire transfer of the down payment, the US government slapped an export restriction on the suits, claiming they were "intellectual property of the US Department of Defence." That maneuver nullified the deal, setting Scott back to square one.

"I smell Charles William Winston the Third's stink on this," Matt had declared.

Scott didn't give up, eventually acquiring surplus spacesuits and their support equipment from the rapidly dissolving Soviet Union. The Soviets had designed their suits in a modular fashion, so he bought as many parts as he could so they'd have enough to tide them over until they could find a more reliable source. He was even able to build a suit large enough for Renny, although the gloves were tight around his massive fists. Then he put Matt, Gary, and Renny through a rigorous training program before he even let them try out the suits, covering everything from SCUBA diving to the high-altitude training required of military pilots.

"Where's this wormhole go?" Stuart inquired, noticing that on the back of Renny's spacesuit were faded red letters "CCCP."

"Low-earth orbit," Josh replied, his eyes swivelling between the video monitors and the HYDRA readouts. "Five hundred kilometres out."

Stuart glanced at the large electronic timer on the wall. "Hey, has this wormhole really been open for sixteen minutes? I thought ten or eleven minutes was the limit."

Josh nodded. "We've got the motion compensation disabled—it's what Matt calls an 'uncoupled' wormhole. We can keep it open much longer, but its tail is moving with the earth's rotation, more or less."

Five minutes later, Matt spoke. "Okay, guys, I'm done here. You got everything written down, Gary?"

"Aye-firmative, Matt. Can't say I understand what most of it means, though."

"Okay. There's one more thing to do before we bring out Wilbur," Matt said.

Josh consulted a printout tacked to his console. "Uh, Matt, according to our task list, Wilbur is *the* next *and* last item."

Matt chuckled. "I know. I want to make some close-up observations first."

"Uh, how close?" The worry in Josh's voice was obvious.

Stuart watched as the two spacesuit-clad figures swapped positions; Matt moving towards the wormhole while Renny stepped back to tend to Matt's safety tether.

"Just close enough, Mother," Matt said. "My tether's secure and Batman's got my back." They'd taken to referring to Josh by that nickname whenever he was being what they considered overly protective.

Matt shuffled to within a metre of the wormhole, then raised an arm until it was inches from the wormhole's mouth.

"Matt, that's close enough!" Josh cautioned.

"It's okay, Mother. This has to be done. Batman, one-half metre of slack." Renny obliged. Matt took a small step closer, stuck his hand in, then quickly pulled it back.

"Didn't feel a thing!" He moved his arm slower into the wormhole and held it there.

"Wow, I can feel the gravity gradient! It's a light tug back along my arm; very linear across the wormhole threshold..." He continued voicing his observations so they'd be recorded.

He held his hand there for several more seconds before moving his head until it was right next to the edge of the wormhole's mouth. He gently prodded its edge with a gloved finger.

"Wow, I can see the geometric folding of the manifold's potential surface!" He started rambling off a series of observations, "tensor-this" and "matrix-that," words and phrases only he could understand. He continued for several minutes, then paused and gave Renny a hand signal.

"Hey, Mother," Renny said, "How are our mains looking?"

Josh turned to check a set of readouts on the wall behind him. "Uh, mains are nominal. Backups are nominal. Why do you ask?" He turned back to the monitors. "MATT! WHAT ARE YOU DOING?"

Renny's question had been a deliberate, planned distraction; he'd given Matt just enough slack so he could stick his head right into the wormhole's mouth. Josh looked in horror at his friend, who was now a headless, spacesuit-clad figure.

"Wow!" Matt said, his voice static-y on the intercom. "Other than a slight lightheaded-ness from the gravity differential, I don't feel anything else. What a view! I can see stars, and part of the earth's curvature!"

"MATT! GET BACK IN HERE!"

Matt ignored Josh, rambling off observations for a tense thirty seconds. "Okay, Mother. I'm backing away now." Renny took the cue and pulled Matt's tether back a metre. "Damn, that was cool," Matt added.

"My turn," Renny said. The two traded places. Josh leaned back in his chair, throwing up his arms in exasperation as Renny stuck his head in the wormhole.

"Wow, look at the stars!" he exclaimed. "Hey runt, guess what? I can see Uranus!"

Gary looked at Stuart, rolled his eyes and shook his head in disgust. "What an idiot."

"If you two are finished playing around, it's time for Wilbur," Josh said.

"Copy that, Mother. We're getting him ready now." They moved their equipment out of the way and dragged a large object, wrapped in plastic, from the corner of the Pipe.

"Is Wilbur an acronym?" Stuart asked, trying to guess what the letters W-I-L-B-U-R might stand for.

Gary chuckled. "Nope. Wilbur is, or was, a hog we picked up yesterday from a local butcher. Pigs have very similar physiology to humans—we want to see what happens if the wormhole closes on someone."

"That's ghastly," Stuart muttered.

"We designed the HYDRA Mark III with safety in mind," Josh said, not taking his eyes off the monitors. "It's got three independent back-up power systems, each of which provides two hundred percent of the power needed to keep the wormhole open long enough to pull someone back then execute a normal shutdown."

"Eventually we're going to put people and payloads through," Gary said. "We want to know what happens to anything in transit if the wormhole suddenly closes."

"We're ready here," Renny reported. They'd positioned Wilbur on a wooden table along with several other test items, including wood dowels and aluminum bars. They slid the table close to the mouth of the wormhole.

"Roger that," Josh said. "Push them through."

Renny and Matt pushed the bench until it, Wilbur, and the test articles had half-disappeared.

"Okay, they're in position," Matt reported. The pair backed to the airlock door. "We're ready here for shutdown."

Josh entered a single command; the HYDRA's characteristic hum stopped, and the wormhole winked out of existence. He checked his readouts. "Good shutdown, Matt. No alarms."

"No issues here, Mother," Matt said. "We're still in one piece. Can't say the same for Wilbur, though."

The wooden table—technically half a table now—tipped over on its remaining two legs. The rear half of Wilbur, along with the remains of the other test articles, slid onto the floor of the Pipe.

"Looks like clean cuts here," Matt said, examining the items and half-pig. "Surgical, one might say."

Renny couldn't resist. "So I guess we know what'll happen to anyone caught transiting. Instant weight loss. Ha ha!"

He paused. "Pigs. In. Space," he droned in a low voice, an homage to a sketch from the Muppets TV show. "Bacon, anyone?"

"What. An. Idiot," Gary said again.

"Another successful drill," Matt said. "Okay, Josh, get us out of here."

"Roger that, Matt," Josh replied. "Red, Elaine, you're clear to start the re-compression sequence."

"Re-compression?" Stuart said.

"The suits run at an internal pressure of 5.8 psi with a higher oxygen content than normal air," Josh said. "We have to bring the pressure in the Pipe back to sea level gradually while adjusting their suit pressure and air mixture. Takes twenty minutes. If we go any faster, they'll get the bends."

Once the guys were out of their suits, they stowed Wilbur's remains in the "treasure room" freezer, then joined Stuart and the others in the conference room for a post-mission review. Everyone present got to comment on what worked, what didn't, and suggest improvements.

"No more unplanned tasks like that stunt you pulled today," Josh said.

"Consider us properly chastised, Mother."

"Hey guys, guess what?" Renny said. "For a few seconds there, I was the tallest man in the world—over five hundred kilometres tall. Ha ha ha!"

Gary shook his head. "You're an idiot."

Renny grinned.

It was the last Saturday in December before Christmas, and AdAstra employees began arriving at the Cambridge Regent Hotel just after five pm. The hotel's concierge directed them through the hotel's festively decorated lobby towards the largest meeting room, the notice board beside the room's double doors announcing "AdAstra Christmas Party." Most gravitated towards the open bar and appetizer table before breaking into small groups, the main topic of conversation being Matt's recent announcement that all AdAstra employees would get the next two weeks off, with full pay.

At six o'clock, Matt walked onto the small stage and tapped on the microphone. The room went silent.

"Hello, everyone! Welcome to the first annual AdAstra Christmas party. We plan to make this an annual event, assuming you enjoy yourselves tonight!"

There was a smattering of laughter throughout the room.

"Thanks to every one of you for your hard work and dedication these past twelve months. It was a good year. We got the Mark III up and running just a little behind schedule, and it's working as expected. Next year, we have big plans. Our first task in the New Year will be to get Gary's robotics working so we can grab more stuff off the moon and auction it off at outrageous prices!"

There were plenty of cheers.

"We've lined up our first unofficial commercial job—deploying some prototype satellites in Earth orbit. That's going to generate a lot of income!"

More cheers.

"After that, we have a couple of ambitious projects that will take us through to the end of the summer—we're keeping the details secret for now, but they *will* involve sending people through the wormhole."

More applause.

"I'd like to offer special thanks to our Canadian 'imports' for their hard work this year."

More applause.

"I'm happy to announce that Deepa and Elaine have both agreed to stay on permanently—they'll be keeping HYDRA's electromagnets and vacuum system up and running. Technically Deepa's not an import, though, as she originally hails from London. We also convinced Ben to stay—he'll be taking over as Director of the Operations division and will coordinate our day-to-day drilling activities."

The crowd cheered.

"What about Uncle Bill?" someone yelled. The staff had taken to referring to Dr. Oldman by his nickname.

"Unfortunately, Uncle Bill's sabbatical is over and he has to go back to UBC, where he'll continue to train the next generation of UBC engineers. You know, nerds like me."

"Speech, Uncle Bill! Speech!" someone in the crowd yelled.

People standing near Bill Oldman pushed him forward, and Matt waved him up onto the stage and handed him the microphone.

Oldman looked around the room at the friendly faces, people he'd worked closely with over the past eleven months, and smiled.

"Thanks to everyone for making Wifey and me part of the AdAstra family. I've enjoyed my time here helping get the HYDRA up and running, and thrilled to be part of your ground-breaking work. And Wifey got to see every castle on her list. We appreciate your hospitality—we'll miss you all."

He handed the microphone to Matt, then pulled it back.

"Oh yes, I almost forgot. I'm happy to be the bearer of exciting news from the world of physics! A colleague at CERN—the particle accelerator lab over in Europe—told me they've just submitted a paper to the Journal of High Energy Physics confirming they've detected the H-meson particle predicted by Matt's Expanding Universe theory. This might not seem like much, but in the physics community, it's a really big deal. It's another step in the validation of Matt's work, placing him amongst the greatest scientific minds, the likes of Feinberg, Bohr, Dirac, Schrödinger, and Einstein."

The audience hooted and applauded. Oldman handed the microphone back to Matt, who had turned a dark shade of red.

"Thanks, Uncle Bill. Wow, that is good news! We're going to miss you and Wifey, and you know that you're welcome back any time!"

Matt paused—the head of the hotel's catering team waved to him from the back of the room.

"Well, that's all I've got to say. I just got the signal that the buffet is ready, so please help yourselves!"

Matt and his friends waited until everyone else had a first pass at the buffet before they dug in, each of them sitting at a different table so they could socialize with the employees and their spouses. Once everyone was working through the dessert course, Matt stood up and tapped his glass. The room soon went silent.

"I promise this will be my last speech tonight! I hope you enjoyed the wonderful food put on by the hotel. We have this room booked until midnight and the bar remains open, so stay as long as you want. If you need a taxi ride home, just ask at the hotel front desk. Have—"

Matt was interrupted by a round of cheering.

"—have a great Christmas holiday and we'll see you in the New Year!"

TWENTY-FOUR

January 1988

Stuart sat in Mission Control's guest chair, between the consoles manned by Matt and Josh, and looked up at the large overhead monitors.

"What's going on?"

One monitor showed Scott Hansen and Gary inside the Pipe's airlock with spacesuits on but helmets off, fussing with a rack of equipment. The airlock's outer door was open; the inner one closed.

"We're testing Gary's latest creation," Matt said. "He calls it 'The Probe.'"

"That's a thoroughly unoriginal name," Stuart said.

"Agreed," Matt said. "It's a robotic manipulator arm, mounted inside the Pipe near where the wormhole mouth forms. It's got a suite of environmental sensors that measure temperature, air pressure, ionizing radiation levels, and solar flux density. There's also six video cameras—each pointed in a different direction—giving us a 360-by-360-degree view. We have a laser rangefinder good to one thousand metres that will also measure range-rate. And there's the star tracker, a gizmo the Cambridge astronomy department built for us: it triangulates its position by locating certain stars in the sky. We also added an omnidirectional, time-synchronized radio transmitter we can receive with a dish up on the roof—

that'll give us range and Doppler velocity. From now on, every time we open a wormhole, the first thing we'll do is stick the Probe through to confirm that the wormhole's tail is where it is supposed to be and the conditions are what we expect."

Stuart nodded. "Makes sense."

"Once Gary's got the bugs worked out, we plan to operate it remotely from here in Mission Control. But you're right, it does need a better name."

Gary's voice came over the intercom. "We're ready here, Control. How does it look?"

Matt consulted a computer monitor. "All sensors are reporting. Elaine, how's the vacuum?"

Elaine sat at a console next to Josh. "We're holding at ten to the minus five atmospheres."

"Give us somewhere to go!" Gary said.

"Okay," Josh replied. "Starting the drill."

Stuart had watched many drills, but this was the first with people already in the airlock. It turned out to be no different from the others. When the wormhole popped into existence, Josh keyed his mike.

"Okay, Gary, you're clear to deploy."

"Copy that, Control." Gary toggled a switch, and the Probe unfolded from its mount on the right side of the Pipe and positioned itself only centimetres from the wormhole. He toggled another switch and its sensor head telescoped outwards, the cluster of instruments disappearing into the wormhole's mouth.

"Okay, we're in," he said.

"Copy that," Josh replied. "Stand by."

Matt consulted a separate computer monitor dedicated to the Probe's sensor readings. "Okay, the star tracker is powered up and is imaging. Radio transmitter is powered up. We're getting telemetry from the sensor package. Pressure: ten to the minus five atmospheres. Temperature: six Kelvin. Solar irradiance: 1.36 kilowatts per square metre. Gamma ray flux: 4.3 photons per centimetre-squared per second. X-ray flux: ten-to-the-minus-eight watts per metre-squared. Electron flux density: five hundred electrons per centimetre-squared-per second. Proton flux: hmm... not getting anything from that sensor."

Matt stood up and consulted a panel on a rack of equipment on the wall. "Radio ranging is reporting five hundred and six kilometres. Doppler is plus twelve metres per second." He returned to his seat. "The star tracker has finished imaging and is in computation mode."

Matt turned to Josh and nodded. "Not bad so far, just a few glitches. Let's look at the camera feeds," he said, flicking a switch. Six monitors lit up. Four showed orthogonal views in orbit, two were black.

"Gary, there's no feed on cameras five and six."

"Hang on a sec," Gary said. He jiggled some connectors; the two black monitors lit up.

"Okay, all cameras are working now," Matt said. "Still nothing from the proton flux sensor."

A moment later, Matt's console let out a pleasant chime, and some text appeared on one of his monitors.

"Star tracker has computed a position. Coordinates look... completely wrong. It thinks it's in the Alpha Centauri star system."

"Pretty sure it ain't," Gary said, "given that we can see the Earth on cameras three, four and five."

"Agreed," Matt said. "I'll dump the tracker's raw data when we're done and forward it to the guys at Cambridge."

"Okay, but before we shut down, I'd like to cycle the Probe's joints."

"Copy that," Josh said.

Gary fiddled with his controls and the Probe telescoped back in from the wormhole, then stowed itself against the Pipe's wall.

Josh turned to Stuart. "It's taken him quite a while to get it to operate in a vacuum. Not the most forgiving environment."

After cycling the Probe in-and-out a dozen times, Gary declared his testing over. "Let's shut her down so we can start fixing our problems."

"Agreed," Matt said, nodding to Josh, who started the shutdown procedure.

I think I'll blow off my meetings back in London for the rest of the week, Stuart decided. *This looks like it's going to be fun.*

He ended up staying two weeks.

◎

"What the heck is that?" Stuart said, pointing at a contraption on the floor in the Pipe.

"I call it SpaceBot," Gary said proudly. "It's an ROV—a remotely operated vehicle—like the ones I worked on in the subsea industry. Its tether is a Kevlar-reinforced electrical umbilical with DC power, a communications cable, and several video coaxes. The vehicle itself is just a wooden frame with a couple of video cameras, some nitrogen gas thrusters, and a three-fingered grabber claw." He pointed to a small drum. "That reel is one hundred metres of umbilical that we can pay in or out. For now, we'll operate SpaceBot from inside the Pipe, mainly because we have to be in there anyways to deploy and recover it."

Stuart sat patiently in Mission Control day after day as Gary and Scott practiced deploying SpaceBot through a wormhole in low-earth orbit. After a week of ironing out procedures, it was time to try it for real. Destination: Mare Tranquillitatis, more commonly known as the Sea of Tranquility.

◎

"Good aiming, Josh," Gary said over the intercom, looking at the video feed from the Probe at a console in the Pipe's airlock. The wormhole they'd just opened was, according to the laser rangefinder, fifty-three metres above the descent stage of Apollo 11's lunar lander.

"Okay, retracting the Probe," he said, toggling a switch; it slowly withdrew from the wormhole and folded itself off to the side.

"Okay, you two," Matt said. "Deploy SpaceBot."

Renny and Scott, who were standing inside the Pipe's airlock in their spacesuits, shuffled through the inner door, pivoting it closed. They approached the wormhole, picked up SpaceBot, and pushed it through.

"Bomb's away," Renny said over the intercom. They backed away, leaving just a tether that disappeared into the wormhole.

"Getting good video," Gary reported. "I've got the targets on my monitor—they're close together, five metres from the descent stage, at my 3-o'clock." He checked a readout on his control panel. "Looks like... ten pounds of tension on the cable, so I guess that means lunar gravity is doing its job."

"Try not to disturb any of the footprints," Matt said. "We don't want to give the Americans more reasons to bitch about us violating their historical sites."

"Not to worry," Gary replied as he made a slow circle above the lunar lander. "The surface looks scrubbed clean for a good ten metre radius—I guess that was from the ascent stage's rocket exhaust."

"That would explain why the targets are so far away," Matt added. "The astronauts just tossed them out the airlock door when they went inside for the last time."

Matt looked to Josh, who nodded.

"Okay Gary, you're clear to move in," Matt said.

Gary activated a control and the umbilical reel payed out cable, lunar gravity gently pulling the SpaceBot downwards. The image of the lunar surface on the monitor slaved to the 'bot's video camera got larger, the image jerking each time Gary activated a thruster.

"Over the targets, moving in on number one."

As SpaceBot descended, the image of the white object on the monitor got bigger; it was a dust-covered white backpack with a faded NASA logo and "ALDRIN" stenciled on it. The camera was almost touching the backpack when three foam-covered claws appeared from the periphery of the monitor, 120° apart. The claws converged on the backpack's hose.

"Contact," Gary reported. "Reeling in the fish." The SpaceBot's umbilical winch started turning, and astronaut Buzz Aldrin's Personal Life Support System rose off the lunar surface, dangling from the claw.

A minute later, with help from Renny and Scott, SpaceBot was lying on the floor of the Pipe, the backpack next to it.

"WHO'S THE CLAW MASTER?" Gary shouted over the intercom. "I AM!"

Everyone cheered.

"Nice catch, Gary," Matt said.

"How much time do we have left?" Gary asked.

Josh glanced at an LED clock sitting on top of the console, its red numerals counting down. "Six minutes. Tops."

"Okay, I'd like to re-deploy and go for target #2."

"Your call," Josh replied. "I'll let you know when we're down to two minutes."

Renny and Scott pushed their just-acquired treasure off to one side, then stuffed SpaceBot back through the wormhole. It took Gary longer than planned to get it over the second target; Josh called for an abort when the countdown timer reached the two-minute mark.

"We'll get it next time," Matt said as Gary reluctantly winched SpaceBot back in. "Let's get our booty secured so the guys can begin their decompression cycle."

The next day, they retrieved Neil Armstrong's backpack, with Gary deftly grabbing it in record time. That gave him time to move SpaceBot to another target twenty metres away from the descent module. But, rather than grabbing the small, cube-shaped object SpaceBot hovered above, Gary activated its vertical thruster in short bursts.

"Looks like he's dusting off that box," Stuart said.

Josh nodded. "That's Apollo 11's laser reflectometer, for making precise Earth-Moon range measurements. It worked while the astronauts were there back in '69, but when they took off, the thrust from the ascent module's rocket covered it with dust. They took bigger ones up on Apollo 14 and 15 and deployed them further away from the lander, and they still work."

"You're doing a cleaning job from almost four hundred thousand kilometres away," Stuart said, shaking his head at the absurdity of the situation. "Does NASA know we're doing this?"

Matt smiled. "Nope. At least not yet. I'm gonna send them a bill."

They spent the rest of the week retrieving more lunar artifacts: a sizeable chunk of the Soviet Luna 2 probe that had crashed in 1959; two Apollo 17 life support backpacks and the lunar lander's ladder, which the astronauts had jettisoned once they'd climbed aboard for the last time; and from Apollo 16's 1972 landing site on the Descartes Highlands, the Far Ultraviolet Spectrograph/Camera. Astronaut John Young had set up the gold foil-covered telescope on a tripod only a few metres from the lunar module, taken photos and recovered its film canister, then left the camera where it was.

Once they'd sealed the artifacts in vacuum containers and locked them in their "treasure room," it was time to celebrate at their favourite local pub, The Eagle.

Stuart raised his glass in salute. "And I used to think those hundreds of hours playing the claw arcade games in pubs and bars back home were a waste of time. Here's to the best claw operator in the world!"

Gary stood up and took a bow, spilling his pint of beer. "Best in the solar system!" he bellowed.

"So, Matt, what's next?" Stuart asked.

"We'll get our video and photo documentation in order and issue a press release. We've got Somerville's standing by to run another auction. Then we're going to launch some satellites at an outrageous profit margin!"

"Show me the fucking money!" Renny roared.

The nondescript man sat in the guest chair of the office of the deputy to the Science Advisor to the President of the United States, waiting patiently while the well-dressed, well-coiffed man behind the desk ranted.

Dr. Charles William Winston the Third, PhD, mashed the power button on the remote control he'd been clenching in his hand, and the TV on his office wall winked off. He'd been watching the BBC live broadcast of AdAstra's latest lunar auction in London.

"Matt Barnes! Again! He just made forty million pounds selling off Apollo hardware. That stuff belongs to us!" he shouted. He flung the remote at the wall where it exploded into several pieces, surprising his normally implacable guest.

The guest waited until Winston ran out of breath. "I thought we were supposed to get the last bid on American artifacts."

Winston stared back. "We were. The State Department dropped the ball and my office didn't get the notification in time to send anyone to the auction."

"Barnes did donate some of the smaller items to the Smithsonian," the guest offered. "And I understand he dusted off an old science experiment left by the Apollo 11 astronauts?"

Winston grabbed a sheet of paper off his desk and angrily waved it. "Yes, I got a fax from NASA's chief administrator. He says their Lunar

Sciences department is thrilled now that Apollo 11's laser reflectometer is working. Would you believe that Barnes even sent NASA a bill 'for cleaning services'? One. Fucking. Dollar. The nerve!"

The guest shrugged, hiding his amusement. "That's quite the bargain." He guessed correctly that the rant wasn't over. Winston picked up another sheet of paper.

"Then this just came out. Researchers at CERN confirmed they discovered a new sub-atomic particle—the low-energy H-meson Barnes predicted in his paper. That guy just won't go away!"

The guest waited a few seconds. "I'm guessing you didn't call me here to talk about auctions or sub-atomic particles."

Winston shook his head. "I *know* Barnes developed his technology while he was at Caltech, so as far as I'm concerned, it belongs to us. I want the US to have wormhole capability, and I need you to get me their secrets!"

Winston's guest was a former intelligence operative now working freelance. He was "the" man important people like Winston hired to acquire items or snippets of information. He received a sizeable sum for his work, and never concerned himself with the character of the people who hired him, nor the legality or morality of his assignments.

"I'm already on it. I have several operations in play right now. At least one of them should bear fruit soon."

"I'm counting on you," Winston warned.

TWENTY-FIVE

Sir Jeffrey Russell leaned back in his chair beside Matt in AdAstra's Mission Control and looked up at the large video monitor suspended from the ceiling. He felt more than heard the unworldly shriek that heralded the creation of an artificial wormhole. A shiver ran up his spine.

To say that the past six months had been "busy times" for Russell and his team at British Aerospace would have been an understatement. His fledgling company, which had spent two years developing a fleet of low-cost imaging satellites, had been within days of signing an exclusive, long-term contract with a large American defence contractor when the British National Space Centre contacted him. That phone call led to a meeting with BNSC officials, then to another with Matt Barnes of AdAstra fame. It was in that last meeting that Barnes proposed using his revolutionary wormhole technology to put Russell's satellites into orbit. The offer was tantalizing: the satellites wouldn't be exposed to the intense shock and vibration during a rocket launch, so they could be structurally simpler. Russell was skeptical, even after watching the press conferences held by AdAstra and Alastair Columbus. But after signing a non-disclosure agreement that gave his legal counsel fits, he watched AdAstra deploy a short-lifespan radio telescope—built by a small team of Cambridge astronomy undergrads in under a month—into lunar orbit. He was hooked.

He backed out of negotiations with the Americans and tasked his engineers to redesign the satellites. They still had to be hardened to survive the harsh environment of space, but the mass saved by making them structurally less robust allowed for a higher-resolution optical system *and* an increase in fuel for their attitude thrusters. His launch costs—make that "transportation costs"—dropped by an order of magnitude, and his engineers predicted the re-designed satellites would remain in orbit a full year longer than his original business model assumed. His bean counters did a detailed cost-benefit analysis and realized this combination would make him a lot more money.

Russell turned his attention back to the activity in Mission Control, as Josh Allen's voice came over his headset.

"Okay, Gary, deploy the Probe."

"Copy that, deploying the Probe," came the reply in a perfect Irish accent. In Russell's short time working with AdAstra, he'd been impressed with Gary Stocks' amazing vocal talent. Russell also appreciated the increased professionalism in Mission Control. During his first visit, the "drill" operations had been, well... casual.

Too casual.

Now, Josh Allen was officially the Mission Director and ran the operation like an orchestra conductor, following a prepared checklist with every task sequenced. Contingency plans had been rehearsed, updated, then rehearsed again. Voice communications were crisp and business-like. It was like watching NASA run a space mission.

Russell looked back up at the monitor. The robotic arm unfolded, then telescoped its sensor array into the wormhole.

"Probe is in," Gary reported.

"Report sensor data," Josh said.

"Stand by," Matt replied. Thirty seconds later, he rattled off a series of readings.

"Latitude zero degrees. Longitude five degrees east. Altitude three thousand seven hundred and twenty kilometres. Speed is six point two kilometres per second due east." Matt looked at Russell and nodded. "We're where we're supposed to be, and going the correct speed and direction." He tilted his head towards an overhead monitor. "Check out number seven."

Russell saw the feed from one of the Probe's six video cameras, looking down over equatorial Africa.

"Longitude looks about right," Russell said. "Wow."

"Retract the Probe," Josh said.

The robotic arm withdrew from the wormhole and stowed itself off to the side.

"Probe is clear."

"Move the packages into position," Josh said.

Russell edged forward in his seat as activity picked up inside the large plexiglass cylinder that held the cold vacuum at bay. British Aerospace's precious space vehicles EarthCam1A and -1B lay horizontally in a fibreglass trough on a wooden platform; a trio wearing Soviet-era spacesuits carefully slid the platform towards the mouth of the wormhole. The satellites were to be deployed in pairs, separated in orbit by only hundreds of metres, providing a unique stereo-optic imaging capability.

"Packages are in position," Gary reported.

"Confirm vehicle data downlinks," Josh said. "Sir Russell, that's you."

Russell picked up the telephone handset in front of him, an open line to British Aerospace's satellite operations centre on the island of Malta in the middle of the Mediterranean Sea.

"Ops, this is Russell. Initiate communications uplinks."

Staff in Malta already had one of their many radio dishes pointed up at the wormhole's carefully calculated position.

"Transmitting now," came the reply.

A few seconds later, Gary reported in. "We've got a green light here on both packages," he said, referring to a small status panel on the side of each satellite.

"Comms link established on -1A and -1B," came a voice on Russell's phone. "All indicators are green."

Russell turned to Matt. "We're good to go."

Matt nodded.

Josh picked up a stopwatch. "Deploy package one," he commanded.

The trio inside the Pipe eased the trough forward until it was almost touching the wormhole. One figure remained on each side of the trough, while the third moved in behind.

"Ready?" came Renny Harris's deep voice.

"10-4, big guy," Gary said.

"Ready here," Scott Hansen said.

"Okay, here we go!" Renny gently pushed the first of the two-metre-long satellites through the wormhole.

"Bomb's away!" came Gary's signature call.

Josh started his stopwatch. When it reached fifty-five seconds, he keyed his mike. "Deploy package two in five-four-three-two-one, go!"

"Bomb's away!"

"Deploy the Probe," Josh said.

The spacesuited figures stepped aside as the robotic arm unfolded and its sensor package telescoped back into the wormhole. The monitor slaved to the Probe's forward-facing camera showed the satellites, one mere metres away, the other about a hundred metres beyond.

Russell spoke into his phone. "Both vehicles have been deployed. Report."

"Telemetry on -1A is nominal. Telemetry on -1B is nominal," came the reply. "All indicators are green. Inter-vehicle ranging reports one hundred point three metres. Now deploying solar panels."

Russell kept his eyes on the monitor and his ear glued to the phone as each satellite began the painfully slow process of extending its solar panels. Five minutes later, with the panels only half-extended, he felt a tap on his shoulder.

"We can't keep the wormhole open any longer," Matt said, pointing at the mission clock.

Russell nodded, so focussed on the goings-on at the other end of the telephone he didn't notice the Probe retracting and the HYDRA shutting down.

Russell breathed a sigh of relief. *Two down, eight to go!*

By the end of that week, they'd deployed the remaining eight satellites, each pair in a different orbit and already transmitting test images. Russell pulled a cheque out of his shirt pocket and handed it to Matt.

"No cure, no pay was our deal," Russell said.

"Happy to oblige, Sir Russell," Matt replied, accepting the cheque.

Twenty million pounds is a bargain! Russell expected to recoup these "launch costs" within three months by selling imagery to government and commercial interests.

◎

Following Russell's press release heralding the successful launch of his satellite fleet, word spread throughout the space industry. The media, now having accepted that AdAstra's no-longer-secret wormhole technology was not an elaborate scam, coined various names for this paradigm shift, each vying to "out-headline" its rivals:

"Space Race 2.0"

"Stampede to Space"

"The Era of Low-Cost Space Travel"

The scramble was on, and everyone—commercial companies, government agencies, academic institutions—clamoured for access to AdAstra's low-cost, low-risk, "space transportation" capabilities. They hadn't predicted this level of interest—Nigella stepped up, offering to take point on fielding the dozens of business proposals rolling in each week.

"We've got to hire a full-time Business Manager," she said at the first meeting of AdAstra's management team following Russell's news conference. She received nods of approval.

"Someone who can also be our point-person for media inquiries," Matt added. "I'm getting non-stop requests for TV and newspaper interviews," he grumped. "They just won't leave me alone!"

Several reporters had also taken to following Matt around town, ambushing him in public places and hoping for that exclusive interview, quote, or sound bite. Those tactics didn't last long—direct intervention by one of Seamus O'Donnell's larger security team members stopped most of them. The last holdout, a persistent tabloid photographer, threw in the towel after making the mistake of bothering Renny just once. He watched in horror as Renny slowly broke his prized Nikon camera into several pieces with his massive hands, then threatened to insert a piece into every one of the photographer's body cavities if Renny ever saw him again.

For every bona fide business proposal and media inquiry AdAstra received, there were several attempts to "acquire" their technology; that kept Seamus and his security team busy around the clock. The first time a delivery truck driver tried to smuggle in a camera and take pictures, the response was swift. Not only was the delivery company banned until it fired the driver, its subsequent deliveries were redirected to a separate quarantine warehouse where they remained until thoroughly inspected, the delays charged to the supplier.

Several times a month, someone tried the more direct approach, attempting to go over, under, or through the now two-layered security fence surrounding the AdAstra compound. Some attempts were creative, others more brute force in nature. Seamus's team rebuffed them all; sometimes they sent the intruders on their way with a "light" roughing up, other times the local constabulary was called. Word soon spread: *don't mess with AdAstra*.

Computer hacking wasn't a real thing yet, but Josh predicted it would become a global problem as the Internet grew. He regularly strategized with Seamus on ways to ensure HYDRA's control system and its complex software weren't compromised. When a magnetic tape—the quarterly operating system patch sent out by Data General to all its customers—arrived by courier two days early, Seamus noted the date discrepancy. Josh loaded the patch onto a MV/8000 minicomputer isolated from the HYDRA computer network; as soon as it rebooted, it erased its hard drive.

"I guess *someone* has given up on trying to steal our secrets and will settle for shutting us down," Seamus said.

His team spent weeks trying to determine the tape's origin, eventually tracing it through several numbered companies to one in the Philippines that bore the marks of being a shell corporation run by the US Central Intelligence Agency.

In addition to the attempts at outright theft and denial of service, there were more overt, yet "civilized" attempts to stop AdAstra. Caltech filed a civil lawsuit against Matt in California Superior Court, alleging theft of intellectual property—the physics department claimed Matt wrote his "Expanding Universe Theory" paper while employed by Caltech, thus they owned the copyright on his multi-dimensional theories. They asked for a restraining order to stop AdAstra's operations until the courts could resolve the matter. Caltech also filed a copyright violation lawsuit against the Cambridge University's Cavendish Lab and the UK-based physics journal that published the paper and Matt's "failed" doctoral thesis.

The US government also got involved. Their state department sent a diplomatic "letter of dispute" to the British government, claiming this was a matter that needed to be negotiated. They also tracked down everyone who'd successfully bid on American lunar artifacts during the recent auctions and served them with notice of lawsuit for theft of US historical artifacts. And, presumably to cover all their legal bases, they sued Somerville's New York branch, claiming they were an "accessory after the fact" to those thefts.

The American media's reporting of this "important international intellectual property dispute" was heavily biased, fully supportive of their government's efforts. Meanwhile, the media in the UK, Canada, Asia, Europe and, well, just about everywhere else in the world, reported on these legal maneuvers with slants ranging from amusement to derision.

"I'll bet Charles William Winston the Third is behind all this," Matt fumed during one legal strategy session with Stuart and the British government's legal counsel. "He's pissed at me personally for showing him up at Caltech, but also embarrassed because he was responsible for forcing me out. If I'd stayed at Caltech, they'd be taking credit for my work. Now that Winston's in a position of power, he's trying every trick in the book to get our secrets."

"Not to worry, cuz," Stuart replied. "They're running the legal equivalent of a full-court press, but my team has everything covered."

"And you have full support from the British government," the BNSC's Mr. Byrd added.

Matt sighed. "That's good to hear—we've got some high-stakes missions coming up and we need to focus on those."

◎

Josh waited the required thirty seconds for the Probe's sensor readings to appear on his monitor after it disappeared into the just-opened wormhole. He glanced at a video monitor showing the inside of the Pipe; it was crowded with four spacesuited figures: Matt, Gary, Renny, and Scott. Elaine and Deepa were manning their consoles in Mission Control, but Josh felt... alone.

I don't like having all three of my best friends together next to an open wormhole!

If something goes wrong, I could lose them all.

What if God decides to reach through and take retribution for our trespassing in His domain?

Or does God care?

Does He even exist?

The Probe's console chimed, and Josh shook his head to push down those worrisome crisis-of-faith thoughts. He stared at the numbers for a few seconds, checked the six video feeds from the Probe, then keyed his microphone.

"Everything looks good, guys. We're exactly where we're supposed to be. Four hundred kilometres altitude, Doppler shows a velocity-delta of twenty thousand kilometres per hour. Camera six is looking straight down at the UK. Unless I can convince you otherwise, let's get this over with." Josh glanced at Stuart in the seat beside him, raised his eyebrows and grimaced.

I'm not thrilled about this!

"Retracting the Probe," Gary said. The robotic arm withdrew and stowed itself out of the way.

"Ready, Matt?" Josh said.

Matt was in his spacesuit, lying in the elongated fibreglass trough used to launch satellites, his feet towards the wormhole. A communications umbilical and safety tether ran from a harness on Matt's suit to an anchor point at the rear of the Pipe.

"Let's do this before I change my mind!" Matt replied, trying unsuccessfully to sound brave.

"Audentes fortuna iuvat," Josh said. *May fortune favour the bold.*

"More like, Audentes fortuna stultum," Matt replied. *May fortune favour the foolish.*

Renny and Gary had come up with a simple yet ingenious method for moving a spacesuited person into the wormhole: a pair of wooden "pusher" arms, each with a concave end that pressed against the spacesuit shoulders, were connected by a wooden cross-beam just above the spacesuit helmet. A two-metre-long wood pole, attached to the cross-beam, was the "pusher rod."

"I'll go nice and slow, Professor," Renny said. He pushed on the pole, and Matt slowly slid towards the wormhole, stopping just before his feet reached the mouth.

"I feel a slight tingling in my legs," Matt reported. "That must be the gravity gradient. Let's keep going."

"Qapla', Professor," Renny barked, invoking the Klingon battle cry: *Victory!*

"Qapla' indeed, Batman."

Renny continued pushing, and Matt's feet, then legs, then torso, disappeared into the wormhole's mouth. Matt kept a running commentary as his head vanished, a monitor showing a video feed from his helmet-mounted camera. Renny pulled the pusher-pole back, leaving just the umbilical and safety line.

"I'm through," Matt said over the intercom. "Just a slight wave of vertigo when my head passed through. Probably the change in gravity messing with my inner ears."

He paused. "Wow! What a view!"

Josh could barely keep his fear in check. He glanced over at the red emergency shutdown button mounted on the console—it had a note taped over it: "DISCONNECTED." After seeing what a closing wormhole did to Wilbur the pig, Josh had insisted the button be disabled during their initial manned trials.

"Okay, Matt. That's long enough. Guys, bring him back."

Renny cautiously pulled on the safety line, and Matt reappeared, headfirst.

"Woo-hoo! That's was pretty cool!" he exclaimed.

They repeated the procedure four more times, Matt spending slightly longer in space each time.

"Fantastic!" he declared when the decompression sequence was complete and they'd taken off their helmets. Once Matt was out of his spacesuit, an emergency room attending physician they'd hired from the local hospital gave him a thorough medical exam, looking for side effects from wormhole travel. With AdAstra's blessing, he planned on writing a paper on the medical effects of wormhole travel.

In the following days the other guys got their turn. Gary had recently decided his Irish accent was "perfect" and had switched to Scandinavian—Swedish, he claimed. His running commentary as he passed back and forth through the wormhole sounded like an advertisement for a famous Swedish furniture company—it left everyone in Mission Control in stitches.

Renny was uncharacteristically quiet when his turn came, other than muttering "Holy shit, this is fucking awesome," once he was floating in space.

Scott Hansen was ecstatic during his turn, thrilled to be back in space, if only for a few minutes.

During the post-mission review meeting, they pored over the mission logs and medical reports.

"Well," Matt said in summary, "I don't see any anomalies. It appears to be safe for human transportation." He turned to Mr. Byrd, the BNSC representative, who usually remained quiet during these meetings. "Any questions, comments, or concerns?"

Byrd shook his head. "You've met all the safety criteria we've jointly developed. I have no objections."

Matt nodded. "That's great. I'll give Alastair Columbus a call so he can get the ball rolling."

◎

The main conference room at the Columbus Group's flagship hotel was, again, standing room only. Columbus had given only two days' notice that he was holding a joint press conference with AdAstra.

The hub-bub in the room died down as a side door opened and Columbus strode in, followed by Matt and his AdAstra colleagues. Columbus moved to the lectern.

"Welcome, everyone. I'm sure you're dying to know why you're here today, so I'll get right to it. Mr. Barnes will make an announcement first, which segues into mine. Matt?"

Columbus relinquished the microphone.

Matt cleared his throat. "Ladies and gentlemen of the press. I've got a brief announcement, will show some video, then will answer your questions."

He paused, waiting for the room to go quiet.

"The few past months have seen remarkable progress in AdAstra's space operations. As you know, last month we deployed ten imaging satellites for British Aerospace. We also deployed research-grade optical and radio telescopes into lunar orbit. And, as you may have heard, we recently took on a couple of advertising contracts."

That remark caused many in the room to chuckle. The world's largest beverage company had paid AdAstra a small fortune to deploy a ten-kilometre-long flashing banner with the company logo in a decaying orbit over the continental US. They'd deployed it just after sunset so it was visible in both America and Europe before it burned up in a fiery light show over eastern Europe. To top that, AdAstra deployed a radio transmitter onto the lunar surface that broadcast the well-known jingle from an American pizza restaurant chain's TV commercial on an unlicensed AM radio frequency for two days. Those advertising stunts earned AdAstra both kudos and derision from the public, along with almost thirty million dollars.

"But on to more important things," Matt said. "Last week, for the first time in earth's history, a human passed completely through an artificial wormhole. On May 4th at 0925 hours Greenwich Mean Time, we opened a wormhole at an altitude of four hundred kilometres above the UK. Wearing a spacesuit and safely tethered, I made five out-and-back transits, each lasting approximately one minute. Gary Stocks, AdAstra's robotics expert, then repeated my excursions."

Gary stepped forward and bowed.

"Next through was Renny Harris, our planetary geologist, then Scott Hansen, our director of manned space operations."

Renny and Scott each gave a simple nod.

The noise in the room increased. Matt held up his hands for quiet.

"I'll show video of our operations now."

The room lights dimmed then hotel staff started the projector, displaying the grainy video image on the pair of enormous TV screens set up on each side of the lectern. The room was silent during the ten-minute video as Matt provided a running commentary. When the room lights came back on, Matt turned to the audience.

"We have a copy of the video for everyone here. Any questions?"

"Mr. Barnes! You said 'for the first time in earth's history, *a human* passed through an artificial wormhole.' Does that mean you sent animals through first, like what NASA and the Soviets did in the early days of the space race? And, if so, what animals? Dogs? Monkeys? And was the RSPCA consulted?"

Matt shook his head. "We did not experiment on any animals." *No need to mention Wilbur.*

"Still," the reporter said, "it seems like an odd choice of words. 'Humans,' I mean."

Matt pondered the question. "Well, I guess it would be arrogant to assume that humans were the first intelligent life in the universe to create artificial wormholes. I guess I was being... cosmically humble? Next question."

"Mr. Barnes! You also said, 'completely through an artificial wormhole.' Does this mean that prior to May 4th, some person or persons had already been *partially* been through?"

"Yes, during our initial testing, I wanted to see what it felt like, so I put my arm through. Nothing weird happened, so I stuck my head through. We'd opened that wormhole to low-earth orbit, so it was quite the view. Renny here did the same."

Renny nodded several times, grinning.

"Mr. Harris! You're AdAstra's planetary geologist. Now that manned operations are possible, are you planning on expeditions to the moon?"

"You bet your sweet ass we are," Renny said, earning him stares of rebuke from Stuart and Matt.

"A follow-up," the reporter said. "Earlier this week NASA issued a pre-emptive statement regarding AdAstra's activities. They claimed that the title 'astronaut' is reserved for, and I quote, 'Americans trained by NASA's space flight program who have flown to an altitude of at least fifty miles.' Since your wormhole technology doesn't involve space *flight*, according to NASA, you can't call yourselves astronauts. How do you respond?"

Renny leaned towards the microphone. "I don't give a flying fu—"

Matt grabbed the microphone from Renny to stave off a media gaffe.

"First off," Matt said, "the *internationally recognized* boundary for space is called the Kármán Line, one hundred kilometres above sea level. The Hungarian-American engineer and physicist Theodore von Kármán proposed this as it is the theoretical altitude limit for airplanes. The US uses fifty miles—approximately eighty kilometres—which is roughly the boundary between the mesosphere and thermosphere. You'd have to ask them why they chose something different from most other countries.

"Second, the term 'astronaut' is a misnomer since it means 'star sailor' or 'star traveler,' and none of NASA's astronauts have been to another solar system. The Soviets use the more correct term 'cosmonaut,' which means 'space sailor' or 'space traveller.'

"Third, I wasn't aware that the US holds the trademark for the word 'astronaut.' I'm pretty sure that word first appeared in British author Percy Greg's science fiction novel 'Across the Zodiac,' which was published in 1880. But I didn't come here today to debate etymology."

Matt paused. "Just because we developed a short-cut to rocket-based spaceflight, that doesn't diminish our accomplishments. The four of us *have* been in space. But NASA need not worry—we don't refer to ourselves as astronauts. Or cosmonauts."

"Another follow-up then," the reporter said. "What *do* you call those of you who've gone through a wormhole to space?"

Matt glanced at his friends and smiled. "We came up with a better term. Since creating an artificial wormhole involves drilling through higher dimensions of space-time—what is colloquially referred to as 'hyperspace'—we decided that anyone who passes through a wormhole has earned the title *Hypernaut.*"

The room was abuzz as they all repeated the word and wrote it down.

"Mr. Barnes!" another reporter yelled. "What's next for AdAstra? More lunar exploration?"

Matt smiled. "Glad you asked. Officials from the British National Space Centre, who've been observing our operations, have qualified the HYDRA for manned space travel. So now I'll hand the mic over to Alastair Columbus, who, believe it or not, has an even bigger announcement." Matt stepped aside and joined his friends as Columbus moved to the lectern.

"Thanks, Matt. Now that AdAstra's wormhole technology has been demonstrated safe for humans, I'm going to collect on a promise Matt made me two years ago when he and his merry band of adventurers here won most of my Columbus Prizes and I handed them a small fortune. The team at AdAstra likes to assign interesting names to their noteworthy operations; this next one's going to be called 'Operation Flaming Arrow,' and yours truly will play a key role. Allow me to explain."

It took him several minutes to describe the details of Flaming Arrow, but, ten seconds in, the audience was rapt. Answering questions took the better part of an hour.

◎

AdAstra Monthly Planning Meeting
May 1988

Stuart scanned the familiar faces around the large table in Building 2's main meeting room. He'd missed the last planning meeting, as he'd been busy dealing with the many US-instigated legal attacks.

"April was a lucrative month," Nigella said. "Ten satellites deployed into earth orbit, and a one hundred percent success rate. Then there's those two advertising contracts."

"And we're fifty million pounds richer," Renny added. "Ka-ching!" He gave Gary, who was sitting beside him, a celebratory high-five.

"And we've put four people through the wormhole," Gary said.

"And brought four back," Josh added.

"May is going to be a busy month," Matt said. "Is everything ready for Operation Flaming Arrow?" He looked at each person sitting at the conference room table, receiving a nod back.

"Stu, you still good?"

Stuart squirmed uncomfortably in his seat. "We're navigating uncharted legal territory here. Columbus and his lawyers are happy with the liability waiver I drew up—they've signed and notarized it."

Matt nodded. "Good. After last week's press conference, Columbus has the media wound up. His team's ready to go—they just need a week's notice." Matt turned to Ben. "What do you think?"

Ben mulled over Matt's query. "There's several routine maintenance tasks that Elaine and Deepa have identified, and we should do a couple of dry runs, so... let's aim for... Thursday next week?"

Matt nodded. "I'll call Alastair after this meeting and tell him to pull the trigger."

"Just to be clear," Renny said, "once Flaming Arrow is out of the way, *then* we do Operation Gotham?"

Matt nodded. "You betcha, Batman. Unless something goes horribly wrong on Flaming Arrow."

"Gotham?" Stuart said. "I must have missed a meeting. I hope it doesn't have as many legal minefields as Flaming Arrow does."

Matt chuckled. "Nope." He looked across at Renny. "We're gonna put Batman on the moon."

Renny nodded, grinning. "Professor, it's about fucking time. I've been waiting my whole life for this."

TWENTY-SIX

Stuart glanced to his right to confirm that Angus, AdAstra's head machinist and self-appointed company videographer, had the video camera rolling. Angus nodded and Stuart turned to Alastair Columbus, who was donning a one-piece bodysuit with cooling tubes woven through almost every surface.

"For the record," Stuart said, his voice echoing inside the cylindrical airlock, "please confirm that you want AdAstra to provide one-way transport to the coordinates specified in our contract."

Columbus, more interested in his upcoming adventure, nodded brusquely. "Yes, yes, yes. We've gone over this several times with my legal team. I've signed off on it. I'm doing this of my own free will. I'm not crazy, blah blah blah."

Stuart nodded. "Okay, then." He turned to the video camera. "This is Stuart Barnes, legal counsel for AdAstra Enterprises LLC. It is zero-nine-thirty hours local on the 12th of May, 1988. We are in Building 2 at AdAstra's Cambridge facilities, and our client, Alastair Columbus, has verbally confirmed his understanding of the transportation contract he signed."

Stuart turned to the security camera mounted in the holding area outside the airlock. "Okay, Josh, we're good here."

Josh's voice boomed from a nearby loudspeaker. "Okay, Stu. Moving onto the next step in the checklist: complete suit checks."

Alastair's technicians helped him into his carbon-reinforced suit—not unlike a high-tech set of medieval armour—while another pair of assistants recorded the event with their still and video cameras. Stuart climbed the six flights of stairs to Mission Control, where Matt and Josh were in their customary seats at the control consoles. Elaine and Deepa manned their consoles, while another technician monitored the power systems. Mr. Byrd, the BNSC representative, sat quietly in the corner, grinning ear to ear, thrilled to be witness to this historic event.

Ten minutes later, Columbus's technicians were done.

"Knight One reporting suit checks are complete," Alastair said over his radio link.

"Clear and seal the airlock," Josh said.

A technician swung the circular plexiglass door until it mated with the face seal on the end of the Pipe, then locked the six latches around its circumference.

Josh ticked another item off the checklist before keying his mic. "Lock helmet visor."

Gary, Renny, and Scott were already in the airlock, having suited up in their second-hand Soviet spacesuits hours before to start their long oxygen pre-breathing and decompression cycle. Alastair didn't need to endure this procedure as his high-tech suit had a hard shell and its interior remained at sea-level pressure.

Scott reached up and locked Alastair's helmet, as the high-tech suit of armour did not allow its occupant to move his arms that high.

"Knight One's visor is closed and locked," he said.

"Starting pump-down sequence to one-quarter atmosphere," Josh said.

Elaine activated her controls. Through the glass window that looked down onto the main floor of Building 2, Stuart heard the faint but distinctive "chug-chug" sounds of the large vacuum pumps drawing air from the Pipe.

Five minutes later, Elaine reported, "We're at one-quarter atmosphere and holding."

"All's well in here," Gary replied. "All suit pressures are reading normal." The three figures on one of the video monitors all gave a thumbs-up.

"Roger that, Gary. Now completing the pump-down sequence."

The chugging sound grew louder as Elaine activated additional pumps. Twenty minutes later, the air pressure in the Pipe was at a hard vacuum and the four inside the airlock reported all was well.

"Complete magnet cool-down," Josh said.

"Increasing helium flow rate," Deepa replied. When Elaine had begun evacuating air from the Pipe, Deepa started pre-cooling the HYDRA's electromagnets. Now she was bringing them down to their desired temperature, only a few degrees above absolute zero.

"All magnets at three-point-eight Kelvin and holding," Deepa reported five minutes later. "No anomalies."

Josh nodded. "Initiating drill sequence."

Throughout the building, revolving red lights activated, reminding the workers present that the HYDRA's magnetic field was ramping up. Its unique low-frequency hum resonated throughout the building.

"All electromagnets at saturation," Deepa reported. "Field strength is nominal."

"Initiating drill sequence." Josh provided a running account as the drill progressed, with Elaine regularly confirming that the Pipe was still at a hard vacuum and Deepa reporting on the status of the superconducting electromagnets.

Nine minutes later, the HYDRA emitted its now muted shriek as it completed its drill through hyperspace.

Josh scanned his readouts. "All readings nominal. Next step: deploy the Probe. Let's see where we are."

Matt checked the video monitor to make sure all the spacesuited figures were out of the way, then thumbed a control; the robotic arm unfolded, stopping just short of the wormhole. Six video monitors mounted from Mission Control's ceiling lit up, displaying images from the cameras mounted on the end of the boom. The forward-looking camera tried in vain to auto-focus on the swirling mass of the wormhole mouth mere inches away.

"Extending the Probe," Matt said, flipping another switch.

The boom telescoped out. The video images briefly turned to static as the cameras traversed the infinitely small distance, then three showed various views of the Earth from a high altitude.

"Looks like we're right on target," Josh said. "That's the northern coast of Germany."

Matt nodded, consulting a raft of numbers on his monitor. "Ranging is good—altitude is one hundred and five kilometres. Doppler shows... geosynchronous speed for this altitude." Stuart had picked up enough orbital mechanics in the past two years to know Matt meant the wormhole's tail was moving at the same speed as the Earth's rotation.

Matt stared at a video monitor for a moment. "I confirm minimal ground motion."

Josh nodded, then consulted his checklist. "Okay guys, you're clear to enter the main chamber."

Gary opened the airlock's inner door, allowing Renny and Scott to usher Alastair, who could barely walk in his high-tech suit of armour, inside.

"Wow," was all Alastair had to say, even though this wasn't his first time near the wormhole—they'd done several dry-runs to wring out the procedures.

"Move Knight One into position," Josh said.

They lowered the armour-clad Alastair into a face-down position on the fibreglass trough, his armoured helmet a metre from the wormhole.

"Knight One, status check," Josh said.

"All systems A-okay."

"Knight One, perform chase comms check," Josh said.

"Knight One to Chase team, comms check," Alastair said, broadcasting from his suit through the wormhole to a small fleet of support helicopters north of Cambridge.

"Chase One to Knight One, in position at northern corner of recovery area. I read you four-by-four."

"Chase Two to Knight One, in position."

"Chase Three to Knight One, in position."

"Chase Four is on the ground at Mission Control."

"Launch team, take your positions," Josh said.

Renny and Scott eased the trough forward until Columbus's helmet was inches from the wormhole; Gary stood back, waiting, ready to assist if needed.

Matt keyed his microphone. "Alastair, last chance to bail."

A chuckle came over the radio. "No way I'm backing out now, Matt. Let's do this."

Matt glanced at Stuart. *Talk about liability!*

"Launch team, you ready?" Josh said. He got affirmatives from Renny, Gary, and Scott.

Josh consulted a monitor that displayed the position of the wormhole's tail relative to the desired coordinates, those having been calculated by Matt then triple-checked by Alastair's team.

"Standby for launch in nine seconds... five, four, three, two, one, LAUNCH!"

In unison, Scott and Renny slid Alastair forward in the trough and he disappeared, headfirst, into the wormhole.

"Bomb's away!" Gary said.

They stepped back and Matt redeployed the Probe. Its forward camera showed Knight One drifting three metres away.

"Knight One to Mission Control—good launch. Almost no rotation. Wow—what a view!"

"Copy that," Matt said. "Congrats, Alastair, you're officially a hypernaut! And the first untethered one!"

The mission plan allotted sixty seconds for Alastair to mentally re-orient himself, and he took all of that, babbling about his panoramic view.

"Okay, Knight One. Sightseeing time is over," Josh said. "Initiate pre-braking orientation."

"Knight One copies."

Columbus reached across and tapped a control on his left forearm. A small computer embedded in his high-tech life support backpack sampled the readings of a miniature inertial navigation unit for a few thousand milliseconds before deciding how fast he was travelling and "which way was down" before activating small nitrogen gas thrusters. Knight One slowly rotated in three dimensions until he faced due west, tilted forty-five degrees down with his feet pointing up towards the heavens.

"Orientation complete," Alastair reported, reading off numbers from his heads-up display. "Beacon lock confirmed. Retro-thrust is on auto.

Deceleration burn in... twenty-nine seconds."

Exactly on schedule, Alastair's backpack discharged a stream of white gas. He shot past and below the Probe; one of its cameras showed him dropping away to the west, rapidly leaving the wormhole behind.

"Okay, Josh," Matt said. "I leave this your capable hands. Stu, let's go!"

As Stuart followed Matt out into the hallway, Josh's voice boomed from a loudspeaker on the wall.

"Beginning shutdown sequence."

Columbus is really on his own now, Stuart realized.

They rushed down the stairs and through a fire door that exited onto Building 2's compound. A Bell 212 helicopter sporting the Columbus corporate logo—radio call-sign "Chase Four"—waited, its engine idling. They hustled onboard; the other rear seat was occupied by a Columbus employee with several film cameras hanging from his neck. Another Columbus employee occupied the co-pilot seat, cradling a state-of-the-art video camera in her lap. As soon as they'd buckled in and donned headsets, the pilot applied power; they lifted off and headed north.

◎

Two minutes earlier...

Alastair Columbus felt a momentary wave of vertigo when Renny and Scott unceremoniously slid him headfirst through the wormhole.

Matt said it was because of the sudden change in gravity.

"Okay, Knight One. Sightseeing time is over," Josh said. "Initiate pre-braking orientation."

Columbus sighed. *We should have budgeted more time for me to enjoy the view.* "Knight One copies."

He felt more than heard muted tapping from his thruster pack as he rotated in three dimensions. He caught a glimpse of the wormhole, the Probe sticking out and recording his maneuver. The suit settled onto an orientation forty-five degrees down towards the Earth, his feet pointing up at the dark sky. He could just make out the coastline of northern Germany, with Denmark coming into view as the Earth rotated eastward. His visor's heads-up display reported an altitude of one hundred and five kilometres, a horizontal speed of only two hundred and eighty-five kilometres per hour, and a negligible vertical speed.

Matt and his team nailed it! I hope the rocket scientists who built my thruster pack were as brilliant...

"Orientation complete," he reported. More numbers appeared on his HUD as his suit began receiving a signal from the radio beacon marking his landing site, displaying the horizontal and vertical distances to touchdown.

"Beacon lock confirmed. Retro-thrust is on auto; deceleration burn in... twenty-nine seconds."

The thruster pack activated on schedule, pushing him down into his suit. *That's a higher thrust than I expected, but it's manageable.* He glimpsed the Probe as he shot past and below it; he wanted to wave but the suit's limited dexterity prevented that.

His HUD showed his horizontal speed decreasing rapidly and his vertical speed increasing. His altitude, now one hundred and three kilometres, marched downwards.

The thrust continued for a minute, stopping at the instant his horizontal speed reached zero.

"Chase Team, Knight One. Burn complete," he reported. "Altitude is now eighty-seven kilometres, vertical velocity is five eight zero, and the earth is getting noticeably larger."

I've fallen twenty kilometres in under a minute! I hope my helmet cams are working!

"Knight One, Chase One. We confirm you're right on track."

Columbus rattled off his readings as he plummeted another fifty kilometres, his downward speed increasing to over *four thousand* kilometres per hour. His inner ears confirmed he was falling, but, since he was still in a vacuum, he couldn't sense his absurdly high speed as he rocketed past thirty-one kilometres, the altitude at which US Air Force officer Joseph Kittinger made his record-breaking freefall from a balloon back in 1960. Every few seconds, one of his thrusters pulsed to prevent him from entering a flat-spin, a dreaded aerodynamic condition that was almost always fatal.

"Knight One, we show you at thirty kilometres. Activate auto-entry mode."

"Copy that. Switching to auto-entry," Columbus reported, tapping a control on his forearm. His thrusters activated, rotating him into a heads-down orientation. A cone-shaped heat shield extended from the top of his armoured helmet, angling down to his shoulders. The joints in his arms and legs locked tight; the last thing he needed during a hypersonic re-entry was an arm or leg flopping around.

At twenty-five thousand metres, the surrounding air pressure was less than one percent of that at sea level, but those few molecules combined with Columbus's incredible speed to produce friction.

"Picking up some vibration and noise," Columbus reported. "Hitting the atmo."

Things happened quickly. The air friction produced drag, which slowed him and produced increasing g-forces. The friction also generated heat, which his high-tech space armour was designed to handle. As he rocketed into the thicker air, the temperature increased and the g-forces ramped up. The vibration made his HUD difficult to read, but the numbers appeared to show he was deviating slightly from his planned trajectory. He maintained a running dialogue, through chattering teeth, that his backpack's onboard flight recorder was dutifully copying to a small tape drive.

◎

Patrick Hanlon was on his daily morning toodle with his faithful golden retriever Maxine, walking the countryside of Chettisham, a small village in East Cambridgeshire, England. It was the same route he'd taken every day for over ten years.

The unmistakable "whop-whop" sound of a distant helicopter broke the morning quiet. Patrick had excellent vision for a seventy-eight-year-old and spotted a black speck, high up and ten kilometres to the north. Then he heard the sounds of two others off to the east and west.

Must be some military exercise, Patrick surmised.

Maxine sat down, looked up at the sky, and whined. A few seconds later, a sharp thunderclap shook them. Patrick had spent twenty years in the Royal Air Force and recognized the distinctive sound of a sonic boom. He looked up and saw an almost vertical contrail, just to the north. He sat down on a comfortable boulder, hoping he might see something interesting.

A minute later, Patrick spotted a red and white parachute drifting towards him. He eased himself up off the rock.

"C'mon Max. Let's go see if he needs a hand."

Maxine wagged her tail enthusiastically. He picked up his walking stick, gauged the wind direction, and briskly headed towards where he estimated the parachutist would land.

He'd guessed right—a minute later, he was directly underneath the parachutist and noticed something odd: the figure under the chute was much larger than a normal human. Two of the three helicopters he'd heard earlier circled overhead at low altitude.

Maxine growled as the parachutist touched down twenty metres away, then stayed upright for only a few seconds before toppling onto its back. Patrick approached cautiously—it looked like a high-tech suit of medieval armour that had come out of a blast furnace. Heat radiated from the suit with a ticking sound, curling the grass in a two-metre radius. There was a stylized but scorched "CG" symbol on the suit's chest, a logo familiar to everyone in the UK: the Columbus Group.

Patrick had been so focussed on this high-tech knight from the sky he didn't notice the helicopter that had landed not fifty metres away. Several figures emerged, including one holding a video camera and the other several still cameras. The youngest of them ran up and leaned over the parachutist. He released latches on each side of the figure's neck, then cautiously removed the helmet.

The face of the man inside the suit was a mess: his hair plastered to his sweating forehead, his face bright red, two bloodshot eyes, and a mass of blood congealing under his nose.

"Alastair!" shouted the young man. "Talk to me."

The spacesuited man looked around wildly, then his eyes came into focus. His mouth split into a wide grin.

"Woo-hoo! Now *that* was a ride!" He gagged and spat out a tooth.

Two more helicopters landed, disgorging what was clearly this high-tech parachutist's support team. One was a medic who fussed over him while the others helped him out of his suit.

◎

Ann Barnes had just returned from her morning grocery shopping when she noticed the light blinking on their answering machine. She punched the play button.

"Hi Mom. Hi Dad. Had an exciting day today. Watch the news. Bye."

What did those boys get up to now?

Ann turned on the television just in time for her and Nathan to catch the CBC's noon news.

"Our top story from the UK: noted British explorer, adventurer, philanthropist, and entrepreneur Alastair Columbus just successfully completed the world's highest sky dive. Wearing a high-tech spacesuit that looks remarkably like a suit of armour from the knights of old, Columbus plummeted to earth from an altitude of just over *one hundred kilometres*, smashing his previous record of twenty-one kilometres. According to his support team's radar tracking data, Columbus reached a maximum speed of just over five *thousand* kilometres per hour while falling through the vacuum of space before slowing rapidly as he entered the atmosphere, which starts at roughly thirty kilometres above sea level.

"Once Columbus slowed to several hundred kilometres per hour, he deployed a drogue chute to stabilize himself. He descended the final three kilometres under a main chute, landing in a field outside of Chettisham in East Cambridgeshire. Columbus, slightly injured during this incredible feat, said he'll make a preliminary video ready to the news outlets in time for tomorrow's evening broadcast.

"Our viewers are probably wondering how Columbus made his record-breaking skydive from such a high altitude. Well, he was transported into space using the secret wormhole technology developed by Canadian engineer-slash-physicist Matt Barnes and his team from AdAstra Enterprises. It was only two years ago that Barnes and his team stunned the world by winning several of the Columbus Prizes, so, in a sense, Columbus himself bankrolled today's record-breaking sky dive."

The reporter paused, switching to another sheet of paper.

"When Barnes published his scientific paper on multi-dimensional physics in 1985, the scientific community received it with a mix of skepticism and indifference. In the three years since, scientists have been working through his incredibly complex equations and theories and finding merit across the scientific spectrum. Physicists at CERN recently announced the discovery of the H-meson predicted by Barnes. Similarly, his theory is reportedly now being used to solve other perplexing problems in everything from fluid dynamics to cosmology to nuclear and quantum physics.

"Who knows what other amazing things may come out of AdAstra in the coming months and years..."

"Who indeed," Ann mused.

TWENTY-SEVEN

Ann Barnes stared out the window of the executive jet; the mountains of northern British Columbia passed below. She returned her gaze to the cabin and its luxurious surroundings, smiling at her husband across the narrow aisle as he leaned back in his large and comfortable reclining seat and sipped a glass of champagne and orange juice.

Talk about being in the lap of luxury!

Nathan read her mind. "Yup, not bad at all," he said. "And quiet, too, considering we're at 45,000 feet and travelling at Mach 0.8." He tilted his head towards the pair of video monitors on the front wall of the cabin. One displayed flight information: air and ground speed, altitude, and distance travelled. The other showed a map with the plane's flight path overlaid—a curved route northeast from western Canada, over Greenland, then south to Great Britain.

Two weeks after Columbus's orbital skydive made the news, Matt had called to invite them to AdAstra's Cambridge headquarters for "a special event."

"We're taking care of the travel arrangements for all our parents," Matt said. "Be at the Penticton airport at five pm on the twelfth."

Their taxi dropped them off at the entrance to the Penticton Regional Airport on the appointed date and time; the other AdAstra parents had also just arrived and were milling around outside.

"There must be a mistake," Gary's dad said. "I just checked inside—

there's no more flights scheduled today."

They stood there for a minute, deciding what to do, when a well-dressed flight attendant came out of the building, followed closely by a pair of airport workers pulling a large luggage trolley.

"The AdAstra party?" she said. "Please come with me—we'll take care of your luggage."

They followed her inside the terminal, then through a locked security door that led onto the tarmac where a gleaming Gulfstream 4 executive jet was waiting, its captain and co-pilot standing at the bottom of its gangway to greet them. Ann had been expecting an exhausting two-day journey to Cambridge via Vancouver and London—two flights, a train ride, and several taxis.

Instead, a single, luxurious flight of just under nine hours!

Ann glanced out the window again, pondering what the "special event" was that Matt and his friends had planned.

That orbital skydiving stunt—I hope the boys aren't going to try something equally silly.

But I wouldn't put it past them.

She looked aft; Josh Allen's father was explaining to Gary's parents and Renny's mother how they were "chasing the sun" around the North Pole as they flew the great circle route over Greenland to southern England. Ann unlocked and rotated her seat so she was facing the others. The smell of gourmet food wafted back from the galley just aft of the cockpit.

Soon the male steward approached. "Mr. and Mrs. Barnes, would you care for wine with your beef bourguignon?" Ann nodded.

Following a sumptuous gourmet meal, Ann tilted her seat back and fell asleep.

◎

Ann awoke seven hours later as the hum of the jet's engines changed pitch and its nose tilted down. The overhead speakers crackled.

"Ladies and gentlemen, this is your captain. We've begun our descent over central Scotland and expect to be on the ground at Cambridge City Airport in approximately thirty minutes. If you need to use the lavatory, please note I'll be turning on the Fasten Seatbelts sign in twenty minutes."

Exactly on schedule, the jet landed smoothly, taxied, and within a minute had stopped outside the airport's Business Aviation terminal. A bored customs officer came onboard, checked and stamped their passports then took a cursory look inside the plane.

"Welcome to Cambridge," he said.

Ann and Nathan were the first off the plane. A white stretch limousine pulled up beside the plane's left wing; Matt and Stuart got out.

Matt came over and hugged his parents. "Well, did you enjoy the flight?" he asked with a mischievous smile. "Enough legroom?"

"Honey, I can't believe that jet!" Ann gushed. "It must have cost a fortune to charter!"

Matt shrugged. "We just started chartering it, but our bean counter thinks it might be more cost-effective to buy it."

Nathan's jaw dropped. "Buy it? That jet must cost millions of dollars!"

"About two million pounds, actually."

Ann turned to Nathan, her eyebrows raised. *He's rather cavalier about that much money!*

"Mom, Dad, two million pounds is a drop in the bucket to AdAstra. And we have a very large bucket."

"Several buckets, actually," Stuart added with a grin, first hugging his parents, then his aunt and uncle.

The limo driver already had their luggage stowed; once they got comfortable in the leather seats, they headed west towards Cambridge. Ten minutes later they pulled up at the front entrance of the Hilton Cambridge City Centre Hotel, the staff waiting and treating them like visiting royalty. Matt and Stuart helped them get checked in, then took them downstairs to the main restaurant for their second dinner in twelve hours.

"Boys, we're just amazed at this VIP treatment," Gary's mother said. "Are things really going that well?"

Matt smiled. "Yup. It was slow while we were building the Mark III, but now, business is a boomin'." Stuart nodded vigorously.

"But son, all this?" Nathan asked, waving an arm. "The hotel, the limo, the executive jet? It seems a bit... much."

Matt shrugged "I know, Dad. Sometimes I find it overwhelming. But we're doing really, really well. We hired good people to help us grow smart.

And Stu here continues performing his legal magic, keeping us honest and our rivals outfoxed."

"We heard on the news about all the lawsuits against you boys," Nathan said. "How's that going?"

Matt smiled, looking to Stuart to answer.

"Pretty good, Uncle Nate. I've been working with lawyers in the British government. We've already quashed most of the lawsuits. The only one outstanding is the 'theft of intellectual property' suit in California. I've hired an excellent lawyer in LA—she's sure she'll get that one thrown out because Caltech doesn't have a record of anything being stolen. Everything's under control."

"How is the Mark III going?" Josh's dad asked. "And where are your partners in crime?"

"It's running great," Matt said. "You're going to see it in operation tomorrow morning. The guys would have been here to meet you, but they're busy getting ready for tomorrow."

Matt looked at his watch, grimaced, and stood. "I've got to get back to headquarters—lots to do before tomorrow's big event. Stu will pick you up tomorrow morning at nine. Enjoy your day, get some sleep if you can, and charge anything you need to your room." And with that, Matt and Stuart were off, leaving nine curious parents.

Ann and Nathan were waiting in the hotel lobby with the other parents when the stretch limo arrived precisely at nine o'clock. The chauffeur opened the door and Stuart climbed out.

"How were the accommodations?" he asked.

"Incredible," Ann replied, yawning. They'd all been up for hours due to jet lag and excitement.

"I'll be your chaperone-slash-tour guide today," Stuart said. "I don't get involved in operations, so when the guys are drilling, I just watch."

"Stu, what's going on today?" his father asked.

"It's a surprise, Dad." With that pronouncement, the guests enjoyed the scenery as the limo headed northeast. Twenty minutes later, they arrived at AdAstra's headquarters; a heavy-duty security gate blocked their path. A guard came over to the limo and Stuart rolled his window down. The guard leaned over and stuck his head in, then took a good look at the occupants, comparing each to photos on his clipboard.

"Hi, Eric," Stuart said. "How are the wife and kids?"

"Very well, Sir. Thank you for asking. So, where are you folks headed?"

Stuart paused before replying. "Uh, to have tea with the Queen at Buckingham Palace."

What's going on? Ann wondered.

The guard nodded. "My watch is broken. Do you have the time?"

"It's quarter past noon," Stuart replied without looking at his watch.

"Very well, then. Welcome to AdAstra," he said, tipping the brim of his hat with his hand. He stood up and nodded at his colleague in the guardhouse; the security gate rose.

"Stu, what was *that* about?" Ann asked.

"Yah," Nathan added, checking his watch. "I know I'm jet-lagged but I'm pretty sure it's only nine thirty!"

Stuart smiled. "Security. Even though the guards know us, they have to ask us security questions, which get changed every couple of weeks. If I got any of the answers wrong, he'd have sounded a silent alarm."

"Then what happens?" Ann asked.

He chuckled. "You don't want to know. Seamus, our Chief of Security, is ex-SAS and takes his job seriously. *Very* seriously. Companies *and* governments have been trying to steal our secrets, so every time one of them tries something, we respond then improve our defences. Seamus refers to it as 'a never-ending game of corporate whack-a-mole.'"

The limo wound its way through the compound, several acres of derelict buildings surrounded by a tall, double-rowed. chain-link fence topped with barbed wire and security cameras.

"What's with all the dishes?" Josh's dad said, referring to the small farm of radio telescopes they passed by.

"You'll have to ask Matt or Josh. Park over there, please," Stuart said to the limo driver, pointing to a parking area in front of a massive white building that had a huge number "2" painted on each side. Two shiny black Rolls Royce sedans were already parked there; a pair of burly men wearing business suits and dark sunglasses stood next to the cars, watching the new arrivals.

"What's with those guys? Is the Queen here?" Ann quipped as they exited the limo.

Stuart deflected. "Welcome to Building 2, where we keep the HYDRA Mark III."

Must be some other VIPs, Ann thought. *Another surprise?*

Stuart led them into the building's foyer, where Matt was waiting. He handed each of them a plastic visitor's pass on a lanyard. "Welcome to AdAstra. Please keep these with you at all times."

"Where's the rest of the Explorers Society?" Josh's dad said.

"They're getting ready for today's drill, so we'll see them shortly. Shall we start our tour?"

They began in a changing room on the ground floor, passing a few of AdAstra's employees who were just starting their shifts. Matt introduced them and traded a few jokes.

I'm glad to see that Matt has a good rapport with the employees.

"For your own safety," Matt said, "I'll ask you to remove any metallic objects before we go inside. Watches, rings, necklaces, etc. We're entering a high magnetism area and have to limit how much metal gets inside. Just put them in this tray—they'll be safe here."

Matt led them down a hallway, then through a tall set of double doors that opened inside Building 2.

"This is the main floor, what we call Level Six," his voice echoing in the cavernous room. "It's eighty metres long, fifty metres wide, and two stories high. This is where we keep the support equipment needed to operate the HYDRA."

"Where is the HYDRA?" Renny's mother asked.

"The Mark III is underneath us, five stories underground."

"Which is why this is level six," Josh's dad noted.

Matt nodded, then pointed up to a large windowed room one floor up. "That's Mission Control, up on Level 7. We'll head down into the Pit first."

Matt led them to a staircase and down four flights, along an access tunnel, then through a pair of security doors.

"Son, what are these doors made of?" Nathan, the engineer, asked, rapping one with his knuckles. It made an odd sound. "This isn't metal."

"Kevlar reinforced fibreglass," Matt said. "We limit the amount of metal in here, as it makes calibrating the HYDRA difficult. That was one of the biggest challenges in constructing this building." Matt led them onto a landing. "And here we are," Matt said with a flourish. "This is the Pit."

Wow!

They were two floors above a wide tunnel cut into the bedrock and extending thirty metres left and right. The pair of enormous rings that made up the HYDRA Mark III stood upright in the middle of the tunnel—a scaled-up version of the Mark II she'd seen before. The rings, covered with coils, magnets, pipes, and cables, were anchored to the surrounding bedrock. A massive transparent cylinder ran through the centre of the rings, extending down the tunnel in both directions.

"This is the HYDRA Mark III," Matt said proudly. "It uses super-conducting electromagnets to generate the intense magnetic fields needed to create a wormhole almost two metres in diameter. The cylinder is a pressure vessel built from high-strength Plexiglas, with airlocks at each end. The cylinder runs through the middle of the HYDRA, so the wormhole forms *inside* the chamber. We pump the chamber down to a vacuum so we can open a wormhole into space with no pressure differential. No out-rushing of air like with the Mark II."

"What's the range? I mean, how far away can you drill?" Josh's father asked.

"Well, theoretically, the topology of 10-space *should* allow us to go at least one AU. It depends on a lot of factors, mostly engineering ones..."

Mr. Allen's eyes bugged out. "An astronomical unit? You mean you can reach the inner planets and out past Mars?"

Matt shrugged. "Theoretically, yes. Like I said, the range depends on many factors. Drilling through hyperspace is an incredibly complex process, and we're still learning how to do longer-distance drills."

"What's in those pipes?" Gary's father asked, pointing at bundles of insulated pipes coming from above and plumbed into the HYDRA rings.

"Liquid helium. We cool the electromagnets to just under four degrees Kelvin—that's four degrees above absolute zero—and they become superconductors. I designed them during my doctoral work at Caltech." Matt looked at his watch. "Let's continue the tour—we have a schedule to keep."

Matt led the group back into the stairwell, down another flight, and along an access tunnel that led to one end of the cylinder.

"And here's more of the Explorers Society," Matt said.

Gary and Renny were on the other side of the transparent hatch, sitting on a wooden bench wearing long underwear and sporting oxygen masks. A third man with shocking red hair sat next to them.

"That's Scott Hansen," Matt said. "He's a former NASA astronaut and is in charge of our manned space operations."

"What are they doing in there?" Renny's mom asked.

"For today's drill, they're going to be... er... testing some of Gary's robotics in full vacuum. They're pre-breathing pure oxygen because the internal pressure of their spacesuits is below ambient pressure—the oxygen removes the nitrogen from their blood so they don't risk getting the bends. It's a standard technique astronauts use when doing a spacewalk."

Matt pressed a button on the wall intercom. "Hey, ladies, how's it going in there? Your parents are here, so watch your language!"

Gary responded with a wave and a 'thumbs up.' Renny bellowed, "Hi Mom!" which they heard through the thick plexiglass wall. Scott waved.

Matt looked at his watch. "Okay, let's head up to Mission Control."

Ann and the others followed Matt up the stairs to Level 7, then through a locked security door.

"Welcome to Mission Control," he said.

The room spanned the entire width of the building, its front wall a series of floor-to-ceiling windows that looked down onto the ground floor of Building 2. There were two rows of complex-looking consoles with computer monitors, keyboards, dials, and gauges.

It looks like NASA's Apollo mission control, Ann thought. She smiled at Nathan. He grinned back, thinking the same thing: *Our son (and his friends) built this!*

Josh looked up from his console and came over to greet his parents. Matt gave them a quick tour of the consoles.

"This is where Josh and I sit. We take turns acting at Mission Director." He motioned at the others manning consoles. "Everyone, this is Deepa Chandra and Elaine Tanner, our magnetics and vacuum experts. And

Arthur Cleese here—no relation to the John Cleese of Monty Python fame—is our power systems technician."

Matt glanced at a clock on the wall. "Okay, we're just about ready to begin. Stu will take you to the visitor's gallery. We'll talk again when we've completed today's mission."

"Which is?" Renny's mom said.

Matt grinned. "You'll see shortly."

What are these boys up to?

Stuart led them out a door and into the visitor's gallery, directly behind and slightly above the control room. A floor-to-ceiling window, running the width of the gallery, provided a full view of the control room; a row of dark large television monitors hung from the ceiling.

There were others in the gallery, an older, rumpled-looking man and a well-dressed, twenty-something young man. The latter was flanked by two "suits"—clones of the pair they'd encountered outside—who also eyed the new arrivals.

"Oh, introductions are in order," Stuart said. "Your Roy—"

The older man scurried forward. "Ah, Mr. and Mrs. Barnes! Dick Feinberg—we've never met, but I was Matt's supervisor at Caltech. I imagine you're as excited as I am to be here for this historic event!" He vigorously shook their hands, then introduced himself to the other parents.

What historic event?

Ann glanced over at the other young man present. Her jaw dropped as Stuart introduced His Royal Highness, Prince Edward, Duke of Cambridge.

How did Matt get British royalty to come?

What are these boys really up to?

Movement behind the glass caught Ann's eye. Matt had joined Josh at their space-age control consoles; a red-haired man arrived and moved to another console. Matt thumbed a button on his console; a pleasant "gong" sounded three times through the overhead speakers.

"Looks like they're ready," Stuart said.

Ann sat with Nathan in the first of three rows of comfortable chairs facing the window.

"Stu, what exactly is going on today?" Nathan Barnes asked for the umpteenth time.

Stuart shrugged. "Uncle Nate, the guys wanted this to be a surprise."

The gallery's overhead monitors came to life, offering different views of the HYDRA, including one that showed three spacesuited-figures in the Pipe.

Matt donned a headset; his voice came through the speaker. "Testing, 1, 2, 3. Welcome everyone! Today is drill number three hundred and seventeen. I'll be the Mission Director, but it's Josh who really runs the show."

Josh nodded.

"Okay," Matt said, "starting our checklist. Lock down the site."

The sound of alarm klaxons rang throughout the complex.

A minute later, the red-haired man at the adjacent console spoke up in a thick Scottish brogue. "Security reports all clear, laddies."

"Logging?"

Josh flicked a switch; a pair of magnetic tape drives on the side wall started slow, jerky motion; on an adjacent bank of video tape recorders, all the "record" indicators lit up.

"Recorders are running." He typed in a command, then waited until an indicator on one of his monitors turned from yellow to green. "Data logging to disk drive is active."

"Main power?"

"Cambridge Gas and Electric reports they're ready to handle the load," replied Arthur, the power technician.

"Backup power?"

"Generators are online," Arthur said as indicators crept upward and stabilized. "We're showing 300% capacity—backup power is ready!"

"Power distribution?"

"Status board is green."

"Cooling system?"

"Helium flow is good," Deepa reported. "Magnets at twenty Kelvin and holding."

"Guests?"

Stuart keyed the intercom on the wall. "All present, Matt. And more than just a bit curious."

Matt turned and waved at them.

"Comms check."

"Batman is ready to rock and roll," came Renny's deep voice.

"Ditto here," Gary said. "We're in the airlock."

"Backup is suited and ready," Scott reported. "Helmets are on and locked."

Matt nodded. "Begin pump-down."

"Starting up the pumps," Elaine said.

"Drill control?"

"HYDRA is powered up and in standby mode," Josh said. "All systems are in the green."

Josh and Matt leaned back in their chairs.

Stuart turned to the guests. "Right now, they're pumping the Pipe down to a hard vacuum. It takes twenty minutes."

Exactly on schedule, Elaine reported, "Pressure reading ten-to-the-minus-five atmo and holding."

"Okay, everyone," Matt said. "Just like in the dry runs. Commence drilling sequence."

Dry runs—they've done this before?

"Increasing coolant flow to all magnets," Deepa said. "Field strength coming up nicely." A minute passed.

"Magnetic saturation reached," she reported. "We're steady at three-zero tesla on both rings. No anomalies."

"Okay," Matt said. "Begin drilling."

Josh typed in a command. Everyone in the visitor's gallery both heard and felt the strange, low-frequency sounds generated by the HYDRA.

Stuart turned to his guests. "The HYDRA is now drilling through hyperspace towards today's, er... target. Matt says this one will take about nine minutes."

The odd-yet-melodious tones coming from the HYDRA rose and fell, with Josh regularly calling out the drill's progress.

"Ten percent, eight minutes remaining."

"Twenty percent, seven minutes."

...

"Ninety-five percent, thirty seconds."

Half a minute later, Ann felt more than heard the muted and unnatural shriek as the wormhole opened. A blurry blob appeared on one of the overhead monitors.

"Okay guys," Matt said after he scanned his readouts and got a thumbs-up from Josh. "You're clear to enter the inner chamber."

Scott swung open the inner airlock door and entered, followed by Renny and Gary.

"Deploying the Probe," Matt said.

A robotic arm unfolded and telescoped into the mouth of the wormhole. Video appeared on another monitor, showing a stark brown and grey rocky valley.

Matt consulted a readout. "Rangefinder says fifty-five metres altitude. Negligible range-rate."

"Copy fifty-five metres," Josh said. "Descending now." He tilted a joystick forward, and the image changed.

"Range now forty metres," Matt said. "Thirty, twenty, ten, five, three. That's perfect right there!"

Josh released the joystick and an indicator on his monitor changed from yellow to green. "Auto tracking engaged. We have ten minutes."

"Stu, does that wormhole go where I think it does?" Nathan said.

Stuart nodded. "That's the surface of the moon, Uncle Nate."

"Commence phase two," Matt said.

"Saddling up," Renny replied. With Scott and Gary's help, Renny carefully lowered himself into a half-cylindrical cage, not unlike the type used to transport commercial divers to the depths.

"Bigfoot is ready to go!" Gary said, after making several adjustments to Renny's suit.

"Copy that," Matt said. "Confirm backup power."

Arthur consulted his readouts. "Generators are running at full power. We have three hundred percent backup power."

"Okay, guys. You're clear to deploy the shuttle," Matt said, trying unsuccessfully to hide the nervousness in his voice.

"Hey, Batman?" Matt said.

"Yes, Professor?"

"Qapla'!" Matt barked, invoking the Klingon battle cry: *Victory!*

Those boys! Ann thought. *Doing this amazing work and still quoting from Star Trek.*

"Heghlu'meH at jajvam!" Renny rumbled in response.

"Not on my watch, Batman," Matt replied, glancing over his shoulder at Ann and grimacing. Ann had, by raising Matt, picked up enough Klingon to understand Renny's reply: *Today is a good day to die!*

Gary's voice came over the intercom. "If you two trekkies are done, I'm going to beam him down now."

He activated a control; the cage Renny was laying in advanced towards the wormhole, pushed by a thick, telescoping aluminum pole.

Renny's mother jumped out of her seat. "Wait a minute! He's going through the wormhole?"

Stuart put his hand on her arm. "Don't worry, Shirley. The guys have rehearsed this many times." She sat down, only slightly placated.

One monitor showed Renny disappearing feet-first into the wormhole. On another monitor, video from a camera mounted on Renny's helmet showed the lunar surface as the cage slowly descended.

"Three metres, two metres, one metre, half a metre, and… stopped," Renny said. Ann, and everyone else in the gallery, unconsciously leaned forward in anticipation.

"You're clear to proceed, Batman," Matt said.

"Okay," Renny replied, "I'm stepping off the shuttle." The view from his helmet camera tilted as he looked down at his feet. One spaceboot-clad foot came into view, cautiously stepping forward onto the lunar surface.

"Hi Mom! I'm on the Moon! Oh fuck. I mean, oh shit. I mean damn. Oh crap, I mean, that's one big step for me, one giant leap for the Explorers Society of Canada!" Renny announced. His helmet camera view tilted back up to the horizon, then slowly panned left and right. "Wow, this is fucking awesome!"

Renny's mom shook her head. "I've been trying to get him to tone down his language since he was a kid. Haven't had much luck." She shrugged.

"Congratulations, Batman," Matt announced. "You're the first Canadian to walk on the moon!" He turned around and grinned at the spectators in the visitor's gallery.

Ann, along with everyone in the gallery, applauded.

"Gravity feels pretty good," Renny reported, hopping a few times. He turned towards the shuttle, plucked a long pole loose and walked a few steps before jamming it into the lunar surface. Once it was secure, he reached up and unfurled a flag held open with wires. It sported the Explorers Society of Canada logo, with its distinctive red Maple Leaf and the mythical Ogopogo sea monster cavorting in the waves.

"I claim the moon on behalf of the Explorers Society of Canada. I can do that, right?"

Matt chuckled. "Sorry, Batman, that's a big negative. Treaties and all that."

"Bummer."

"You have one minute. Time to pick up some rocks."

"Roger that." Renny pulled another shorter pole from the shuttle—a set of metre-long trash tongs. He grabbed random rocks and scoops of dust and dumped them into a bag hanging from the shuttle.

"Every rock tells a story," he said, eliciting the standard groans from his friends.

"Okay, Batman, time's up. At least for this go-around."

"I know, I know... stick to the plan," Renny said, sighing. His helmet camera panned left and right as he took one last look at the stark vista. "Damn, there's so much to explore."

"I know, my friend. We'll be back soon enough."

"Alright, I'm stepping back onto the shuttle." It took him a few seconds to wriggle into the framework. "I'm in. Beam me up, Scotty!"

"Energizing," Gary said, activating a control. The video feed from Renny's camera showed him slowly rising from the lunar surface, then cut out as he passed through the wormhole. The airlock camera showed him appearing head-first, the shuttle stopping when it was above the wooden support table.

"Shuttle is clear!" Gary reported.

"Begin shutdown sequence," Matt said. Josh entered a command, and the wormhole winked out of existence.

"Welcome home, Moon Man!" came Gary's excited voice. Everyone in the gallery cheered.

Renny lay there patiently while Gary detached the sample bag and placed it in a sealed container. Then he and Scott helped Renny stand up, and they made their way to the airlock.

"Okay, we're in the air lock, and both doors are secure," Scott announced.

"Begin re-pressurization sequence," Josh said. Elaine toggled several controls.

As the air pressure in the chamber rose, their spacesuits became more flexible. Scott adjusted a control on the back of Renny's and Gary's backpacks. Gary did the same for Scott.

"Why aren't they taking off their helmets?" Renny's mom said.

"That question I *can* answer," Stuart said. "The air inside their suits is almost pure oxygen and half the pressure at sea level. We have to bring them gradually back to regular air mixture and pressure or they risk getting the bends, like scuba divers. Takes thirty minutes."

Shirley nodded, relieved to see her son back safe and sound.

Matt came into the visitor's gallery. "Well, was that exciting? We have to do our mission debrief—that'll take a couple of hours. Stuart will take you back to the hotel now, and we'll meet you there later for a little party we're throwing."

Later that day...

Arm in arm, Ann and Nathan walked into one of the hotel's conference rooms that had been set up for a medium-sized dinner party. Everyone from AdAstra was present. Renny's mom was standing beside her son, repeatedly hugging him and praising his accomplishment.

Matt stepped to the front of the room, and let out a loud, "Oi!"

The room went silent.

"Family, friends, and members of the AdAstra team. Thanks for joining us to celebrate today's historic event, one with many 'firsts.' Renny, get your butt up here!"

Renny, who already had a good buzz on already, stumbled up, beer bottle in hand.

"Ladies and gentlemen, may I present Hypernaut Renny Harris, the first Canadian to walk on the moon, and the first human on the moon since

1972."

Renny gave an inebriated bow, and the room erupted in applause. He grabbed the microphone from Matt. "I'd like to thank my mom, and I'd like to thank Josh and Matt for not shutting down the wormhole while I was in transit and cutting me in half, like that pig."

A sprinkling of uncomfortable laughter went through the crowd.

There must be a story behind that, Ann realized. *I probably don't want to know...*

Matt surveyed the room. "Today's mission was truly a group effort," he said. "Thanks to every one of you."

He paused, getting a signal from the hotel staff. "Okay, the food's ready, so let's eat!"

After dinner, Ann and Nathan mingled, chatting with many of AdAstra's employees. Everyone thought highly of Matt and his friends.

During a lull in the party, Ann caught her husband's eye and shook her head. "This really is a lot," she said, referring to the opulence of the room, the gourmet food, the general air of excess.

Nathan nodded. "But look at what they just accomplished. Let them have their fun tonight. We'll chat with him in the morning."

Ann nodded. *Tonight is for Matt and his friends.*

TWENTY-EIGHT

Ann and Nathan had just sat down for breakfast in the hotel restaurant when Matt walked in. Their flight home wasn't until mid-afternoon, so they had plenty of time to relax and chat. As they worked through their proper English breakfasts—artery-clogging plates of fried eggs, fried bacon, fried toast, fried tomatoes, etc.—Matt rambled on about their adventures at AdAstra. After the waitress took away their plates, Ann gave Nathan an uncomfortable glance. Matt noticed.

"What's up?" he said.

"Son, we need to talk," Nathan said.

Matt's face took on that expression a kid gets when they realize their parents aren't happy.

"Son, we're impressed with everything that you and your merry band of explorers have accomplished," he said. "Impressed doesn't cover it. Amazed. Astonished. Proud beyond belief. But—"

Ann jumped in. "But the *excess*, Matt. The executive jet, the limos, this luxurious hotel." She glanced at Nathan. "We're worried all the money you're making is going to your head."

Matt was silent for a few moments as he pondered their concerns.

He nodded. "It may seem like we've gone a bit overboard." Matt paused again. "Yes, we are making *lots* of money. We deserve to be rewarded for our hard, and at times dangerous, work. And I see nothing wrong with spreading it around to family and friends." He went silent, mulling over something important.

"Your flight doesn't leave until three pm," he said. "I've got a few things to take care of at HQ this morning, but how about I meet you out front at, say, 1130? There's something I'd like you to see."

Intrigued, they both nodded.

◎

Ann and Nathan walked out the front door of the hotel and rebuffed the doorman's offer of a taxi when Matt pulled up in his old Vauxhall.

Ann smiled. *At least he hasn't succumbed to fame and fortune and bought an expensive car.*

He drove them to an older part of town, navigating several narrow streets before parking in a side lane. Ann scanned up and down the street, sensing something amiss. A general air of... not decay, but... poverty.

"This way," Matt said, leading them around the corner and up the front steps of a dilapidated old stone building. He motioned towards the structure.

"This is Bell Meadows, one of five state-funded primary schools in Cambridge. In this part of town, most of the children come from homes where, at most, one parent works." Matt held the door for them.

Why is Matt taking us into an elementary school?

An older woman, sitting at an old desk behind the dingy office counter, looked up. "Mr. Barnes! I mean Matt! Glad to see you again!"

"Hi, Felicity. I brought my parents by for a visit—I hope that's okay?"

She nodded. "Of course it is. You're always welcome here." She turned to Ann and Nathan. "So, you're Matt's parents. Welcome! Welcome! You must be so proud of him."

Ann acknowledged the compliment with a nod. *Why would a receptionist at a public school say that?*

Felicity motioned to the clock on the wall; both hands were almost pointing at twelve. "Mind yourselves... chaos begins in two minutes!"

"Thanks for the warning," Matt said cheerily.

He led them down the main corridor past several classrooms, the familiar sounds of teachers teaching and students learning coming from behind the closed doors. Ann detected the unmistakable aroma of food as

Matt ushered them through a pair of swinging wooden doors into a large room full of tables and chairs. At the back of the room was a modest kitchen staffed by two busy young women. One of them looked up, smiled, and waved. Matt steered them in her direction.

"Matt! It's so nice to see you again!" she said, still smiling. She was in her mid-to-late-twenties, five feet six inches tall, had medium-length auburn hair, a pert nose, and twinkling hazel eyes. A white cooking apron, stained with various food groups, covered her slender figure.

"You... er, you too," Matt stammered.

"Son, aren't you going to introduce us?" Ann said.

"Oh, yah, I, uh, Kate, these are my parents, Ann and Nathan. Mom, Dad, this is Kate."

Ann shook her hand. "Nice to meet you, Kate."

"I, uh, brought them by for a visit—I hope that's okay?" Matt said.

"Of course!" Kate said. "You'll be staying for lunch, then?"

Ann and Nathan turned to Matt, who nodded.

Kate looked up at the clock; the second hand was almost at the twelve-o'clock position. "Well, it's about to get busy in here, in three, two, one..."

The noon bell rang and the hall corridor came alive with the sounds of students happy to be out of class. Seconds later, the doors burst open and children poured in, the few with bag lunches heading for tables while most headed in their direction.

"I suggest you stand back," Kate said with a smile. "They're a hungry bunch—like piranha fish—get in the way and you might lose an arm or a leg. Excuse me for a moment, would you?"

They moved out of the way as the children queued up in a somewhat orderly manner, grabbing trays and loading them with sandwiches, salads, bowls of soup, bread rolls, fresh fruit, and glasses of milk or juice. Once the line dwindled to nothing, Matt motioned for his parents to get their lunches, then they moved to an empty table.

Ann looked around the room. "Uh, Matt... why are we having lunch in an elementary school?"

"Well..."

Kate arrived with a tray of her own and sat down across from Matt; her gaze lingered on him. "So you're Matt's parents—you must be so proud of him!"

"We've been hearing that a lot lately," Ann said.

"What's he's doing at AdAstra *is* amazing," Nathan added.

Kate shrugged. "I suppose." She gestured to the room. "*This* is what's impressive."

Then she noticed the look of confusion on Ann's face.

"Let me guess, he didn't tell you?" Kate said. "Funding this meals program? It's making *such* a difference to these kids. Many teachers are already seeing improvements—better concentration, more energy, higher grades."

Matt blushed. Their conversation was interrupted by the sound of a lunch tray crashing to the floor, followed by laughter. Then crying.

"Excuse me," Kate said. "Duty calls."

Ann and Nathan looked at Matt. "You funded this?" Ann said.

Matt nodded. "I didn't want you going home thinking all the money we're making is going to our heads. I remember all those Christmases and Thanksgivings we served lunch and dinner at the retirement centre. And the Christmas Hamper program when we delivered gift bags to families in need. You taught me the importance of helping those less fortunate. Just after I started teaching at Cambridge, one of my colleagues mentioned that many of the kids going to these state-run schools arrive without a proper breakfast and almost nothing for lunch. I had to do *something*. Kids need proper nutrition or they'll never be able to reach their full potential. I tried funding an unofficial breakfast program here, but the school's headmaster was leery of a stranger showing up and offering money. Go figure.

"So Stu helped me create a non-profit organization to fund a breakfast and lunch program. Seven and a half percent of AdAstra's gross income goes directly to that organization—it's called the ANB Foundation, a registered charity in England and Wales, and Stu and I are its directors. AdAstra is doing really well, so the foundation is now funding identical meal programs in the other four state-funded schools in town. We're also expanding to include nearby cities, and I want to create a college and university tuition fund for kids from low-income families."

Ann and Nathan silently absorbed this revelation. They had many questions, but when Kate returned to their table, they opted for small talk.

They learned she volunteered here on her days off and was a Nurse Practitioner at the local hospital.

"I'm afraid I must get back to work," Kate said, standing up. "We always make extra sandwiches in case any child wants to take some home. Ann, Nathan, it was a pleasure meeting you both. Matt, do drop by again, soon?" she said with a smile, then returned to the kitchen.

Matt looked wistfully at Kate as she returned to the kitchen, then let out a long and rather pathetic sigh. "She's gorgeous, isn't she? And her accent..."

"Son, what does 'ANB' stand for?" Nathan asked.

"Huh...?" Matt said, his attention miles away.

Ann snapped her fingers inches from his nose. "Earth to Matthew!"

Matt shook his head. "Oh, ANB. Right. Well, on the public-facing stuff, 'ANB' stands for 'A New Beginning.' But its legal name is the Ann and Nathan Barnes Foundation." He paused. "I hope you don't mind."

A tear came to Ann's eye. "Matt, we're... we're speechless."

"Son, I don't know what to say," Nathan said. "We're so proud of you."

Matt shrugged. "These kids have you two to thank as much as me."

Ann couldn't help but notice that Matt kept glancing over at Kate, busy working behind the counter.

"Kate seems nice," Ann said. Matt's face lit up at the mention of her name. "She likes you too, you know."

Matt rolled his eyes. "Right."

"No, really."

"Really?" Matt said, confusion on his face. "How can you tell?"

Ann chuckled and shook her head.

Matt grabbed her arm. "No, seriously, Mom. *How can you tell?*" His voice took on a tone of exasperation. "I understand the physical universe better than probably anyone on the planet, but I don't understand women. I can't tell what they're thinking. Argh!"

"It's alright, son," Nathan said. "You'll figure them out, eventually. I haven't quite yet, but I'm working on it," he said, only half-seriously.

"I don't know," Matt said, watching the object of his interest, metres away yet light-years distant. He sighed, then glanced at his watch. "Well, we should head back to the hotel so you can check out."

When they reached the school's front door, Ann paused, then winked at Nathan. "Hang on, I didn't thank Kate for lunch. I'll be right back."

Ann returned a few minutes later; Nathan and Matt were waiting outside, commenting on the state of the local architecture.

"That Kate's a lovely girl," Ann said as they walked towards the car. Matt sighed and nodded, his shoulders sagging.

"Here," she said, handing Matt a scrap of paper.

"What's this?"

"Kate's phone number. Call her. She'd love to go out with you sometime."

"*Mom!*"

Matt dropped them off at their hotel so they could pack. Two hours later, a limousine was waiting in front of the hotel.

"It feels weird to check out and not pay the bill," Renny's mother said. Ann nodded in agreement.

The limo ride was brief, and all the members of the Explorers Society of Canada were waiting at the airport to bid them farewell.

"Make sure you watch the news when you get home," Matt said. "Stuart arranged a press conference to announce our recent lunar excursions."

◎

Matt stepped up to the microphone, his friends beside him. The meeting room at Alastair Columbus's flagship hotel was full of journalists— mostly science and business reporters—who quickly went silent.

"Good afternoon, everyone. I'm Matt Barnes, president of AdAstra Enterprises, here today with my colleagues to give you an update on our space operations. I'd appreciate it if you'd let me finish my presentation, after which we'll entertain questions.

"With our larger and more powerful HYDRA now online, we've made a leap forward in lunar exploration activities. Last week, on the morning of June 5th, we opened a wormhole just above the lunar surface at the Sea of Tranquility. At 1133 hours, Greenwich Mean Time, Renny Harris, AdAstra's planetary geologist, transited the wormhole in a spacesuit and stepped onto the lunar surface. He spent four minutes and twelve seconds there, during which he planted a flag, left a commemorative plaque, and collected moon rocks and dust. There were several witnesses to this historic event, including a representative from the British National Space Centre, our family members, Nobel laureate Dr. Richard Feinberg, and His Royal Highness, the Duke of Cambridge."

Matt paused as a murmur ran through the audience.

"On subsequent missions, AdAstra personnel deployed several scientific packages and retrieved more artifacts abandoned by previous lunar expeditions. In the coming months, we have many more lunar missions planned, both for scientific and commercial applications."

The room erupted in a clamour; Matt held up his hands.

"Please! Please! I have more to say. Then we'll show some video and I'll open the floor to questions."

The clamor died down.

"I'd now like to introduce hypernaut Renny Harris, AdAstra's planetary geologist, who set foot on the moon on June 5th. Renny is the second human to pass through an artificial wormhole and the first Canadian to set foot on the moon. He's also the thirteenth person in history to walk on the surface of the moon, the last being—"

Renny leaned in to the microphone. "I'm also the first native person to go into space and to walk on the moon."

Matt turned and stared at Renny for several seconds. "As... as I was saying, the last person to walk on the moon being American astronaut Eugene Cernan back in 1972."

Renny nodded to a loud round of applause.

"Next," Matt said, still staring at Renny, "hypernaut Gary Stocks, our robotics expert, who designed the equipment we use to move people and equipment through the wormhole. Gary is the third human to pass through a wormhole, and the second Canadian to walk on the moon."

Gary made a formal bow as the audience applauded.

"And third, hypernaut Scott Hansen. Scott is a former NASA astronaut, one of the newest members of the AdAstra team, and is in charge of our manned space operations. He's the fourth human to go through a wormhole, the thirteenth American and fifteenth person to walk on the moon."

Reporters started clamouring with questions. Matt held up his hands for silence.

"Now, if you don't mind, we'll show some video of these recent expeditions. Can we turn the room lights down?"

Hotel staff played a series of video highlights of his friends' brief trips to the moon. There was lots of chuckling over the many "bleeps" in the audio during Renny's running commentary, not to mention his first words being, "Hi, Mom!"

"Okay, *now* we'll answer your questions."

"Mr. Harris! What was it like to travel through the wormhole and step onto the moon?"

Renny grinned. "Pretty fuc—, I mean, pretty cool. Going through the wormhole is rather uneventful. It's only a fraction of a millimetre long, so there's no sense of passing *through* anything. I felt a brief wave of vertigo transitioning from earth to lunar gravity, but that's it. Standing on the moon was incredible, even if I was there only for a couple of minutes. I can't wait to go back."

The next question came from a writer from Popular Science magazine. "Mr. Harris! Mr. Barnes said you left behind a flag and a plaque. What was on the plaque and which flag did you plant? The Union Jack? The Maple Leaf?"

Renny smiled. "We thought someone might ask that." He nodded at Gary, who pulled a small bundle of fabric from his coat and unfurled it.

"The flag isn't from a country," Matt said. "It sports the emblem of a little-known organization called the Explorers Society of Canada, or ESOC. The four of us started the ESOC when we were in elementary school, and its motto is *Audentes fortuna iuvat*, Latin for 'May fortune favour the bold.' As for the plaque, well..."

His friends beside him all chuckled.

"... we're not going to divulge what's on it."

"Mr. Hansen! NASA invested a lot of time and money in your astronaut training. Do you feel you've betrayed your country by using that training to further the interests of an organization in another country?"

Scott bristled. "Not at all," he said tersely. "NASA and I parted ways a while back. There's lots of former NASA personnel now working at companies, universities, and research institutes all over the world."

"Mr. Barnes! You mentioned you left scientific packages on the moon. Can you give us more details?

Matt shook his head. "No. We've signed contracts with several academic institutions and commercial businesses to deploy their equipment on the moon. The details are... proprietary. You'll have to wait until they publish their research and/or issue their own press releases."

A well-dressed man raised his hand and stood up.

"Mr. Barnes. You mentioned earlier that during your second and third lunar missions, you recovered more artifacts from the moon. Care to elaborate?"

Matt noticed the man wasn't wearing a nametag listing his affiliation. He glanced over at Stuart, whose expression was one that screamed, *Caution!*

"I'd be happy to," Matt said. "What organization do you represent?"

"I'm the assistant director of the Smithsonian Air and Space Museum."

"Fair enough," Matt said. "We recovered the two backpacks—technically called the PLSS, or Portable Life Support System—left behind by the Apollo 16 astronauts. We would have picked them up last year, but they wouldn't fit through the wormhole created by our smaller HYDRA."

"Those backpacks are property of the US government."

Stuart jumped in. "That, sir, is incorrect, and you know it. The World Court has ruled that any non-functional items left on the moon are fair game. We plan to auction them off a few weeks, and, as during our last auction, will give the US government the option of last bid."

A London-based business reported jumped in. "Mr. Barnes! What about the lawsuits filed against you and AdAstra?"

Stuart waved his hand dismissively. "We've already dealt with most of them. They're just pathetic attempts by the US government to steal our technology and stop our operations. We're not concerned."

"Mr. Barnes! I just read that a group of South African scientists have experimental data confirming one of your Expansion Theory's claims about gravity. What do you say about that?"

Matt shrugged. "I haven't seen their results, but that's good to hear."

The questions continued for another half hour, mostly attempts to get technical information on the HYDRA.

◎

Charles William Winston the Third glared at the television screen on his office wall as the re-broadcast of AdAstra's press conference ended. *Matt Barnes! Again!*

"Wow," said the nondescript man invited to Winston's inner sanctum through a side door. "That's some amazing shit he's doing over there."

Winston glared at the man. "I pay you good money and so far, you haven't produced anything I couldn't get through public sources. And now he's grabbing more of our Apollo hardware!"

"What about Hansen?" the man said. "He's American. We could appeal to his sense of national pride."

Winston shook his head. "I already put out feelers, and he rebuffed us. NASA grounded him after that fiasco at the space station, and he's got no interest in cooperating. He and his family have moved to the UK; his loyalties lie with Barnes now."

"My guys have tried several times to gain access to their facilities, but their security is too good. We're going to have to work a different angle," the man said. "The human angle."

Winston hit the 'pause' button on his VCR, freezing the image of a smiling Matt Barnes surrounded by his AdAstra team. "There, the fat one," Winston said, pointing at the overweight young man standing beside Matt. "Joshua Allen. Looks like a deer caught in a car's headlights. He's their computer genius—he'll have what we need."

Winston slid a thin file folder across his desk. "Here's everything I have on him."

"You're sure about this?" the man said, thumbing through the pages.

"Make it happen," Winston commanded. "The last page is a list of the information I want. And make sure the operation can't be traced back to this office."

"Understood."

◎

"Well, that went fairly well," Stuart said as they gathered for a post-press conference de-brief at a pub near Columbus's hotel. "You—what's wrong, Matt?" Matt was staring at Renny, an odd look on his face.

"Batman, what was that about you being a native?" Matt said.

Renny's eyebrows went up. "Uh, because I am?"

Matt was silent for several seconds, staring intently at his friend with a dark brown complexion, thick black hair, and bushy eyebrows. Then the lightbulb came on. He looked around the table at his other friends. "Shit, am I the only one who never noticed?"

Gary shook his head and chuckled. "Apparently so."

Josh and Stuart both nodded.

Renny chuckled. "Professor, you may be the smartest person on the planet, but apparently you're colour blind. I'm a member of the Gitxsan First Nation, Fireweed Clan. So was my dad."

Matt was silent for several more seconds, processing this revelation. "Well," Matt said, "fuck me."

"Anyways," Stuart said, "as I was saying, you guys did a good job of fielding questions. Mostly," he added, glancing at Renny, who shrugged.

"Dropping an f-bomb on TV would not have been a good thing," Josh said.

"Whatever," Renny said, nonplussed. "I caught myself in time."

"I still think it'd be worthwhile to polish your presentation skills," Stuart added.

Renny snorted. "You mean charm school?"

"Call it what you want," Stuart said. "It would be wise to keep the media on your side. Otherwise, they might start digging for dirt."

"We've got no dirt, but it's a good point," Matt said after a moment's reflection. "Can you set it up?"

Stuart nodded. "Our firm uses a company that would be good. So, what's the plan for the next couple of weeks?"

"Maintenance," Matt said. "We've worked some of the subsystems pretty hard. Deepa wants to replace two of the electromagnet coils—her failure model predicts they might quench in another cycle or two, and we don't want that happening when we're putting humans through. Scott wants to upgrade a couple of components in the spacesuits. Josh and I are going to take a deep dive into the recent mission logs, in case there's anomalies we didn't notice during the missions."

"And don't forget, *you* have a phone call to make," Stuart said, smiling.

"Phone call? To whom? You found us a new customer?"

"Your parents made me promise to remind you to call Kate."

Matt's face cycled through several shades of red.

"Matt's got a girlfriend... Matt's got a girlfriend," his friends chanted.

"I'm outta here for three weeks," Gary said. "Nadia and I are off to Egypt on a dig."

"I'm going on a trip, too," Renny said. "I'll be back in a week." The tone of his voice made it clear he wasn't interested in explaining.

◎

A rental pickup truck turned into the gravel parking lot at a poorly maintained cemetery on the outskirts of Tumbler Ridge, a small town in the northeastern corner of British Columbia, Canada. A tall, heavyset figure emerged from the truck and strode with purpose past many neglected burial plots, stopping at a gravestone that bore the inscription: "Norman Renwick Harris—loving husband, father, and geologist. 1932-1959."

The lone figure stood in silence for several minutes, then brushed the snow off the top of the gravestone and carefully placed a grey-black, fist-sized, pockmarked rock on it.

"This is for you, Dad," Renny said. "I'll be back soon with more." He took a long look at the foothills of the Rocky Mountains before heading back to his truck.

In the following days, the few visitors to the cemetery noticed the rock—it was common to leave gifts, flowers, and other personal mementos—but gave it no further thought. None would have guessed it had recently been hand-picked off the surface of the moon.

◎

Kate McDonough had just returned to her flat following a dayshift at the hospital when the phone rang. It had been a long, tiring day in the emergency ward, with several taxing trauma cases, including one involving a child, a bicycle, and a plate-glass window. All she wanted to do now was have a long, hot shower and unwind with a salad and a glass of wine. She considered letting the call go to her answering machine, then decided otherwise.

"Hello?"

"Uh, hi Matt, this is Kate." A pause. "I mean, hi Kate, this is Matt. Matt Barnes?"

She smiled. "Hello, Matt. It's good to hear from you. How are you today?"

"Uh, good. How are you?"

Their small talk lasted several minutes before being interrupted by the shrill beeping of her work pager. She glanced at the code on the small liquid crystal display.

"I'm sorry, Matt, but I just got paged to work—it's an emergency."

"Oh, uh, okay. No problem."

"But I'd like to continue this conversation in person." She took a deep breath. *Here goes...* "Would you like to get together sometime?"

"Uh, yah, that would be great," Matt replied. "I could call you tomorrow night—maybe we can arrange something for the weekend?"

"Perfect. Gotta go, Matt. Thanks for calling!" Tired as she was, Kate had a spring in her step as she headed out the door.

TWENTY-NINE

Kate was thrilled when Matt called the following evening. They made awkward small talk for a few minutes before he sprung the question she was hoping for.

"Er, would you like to go for a walk one of these days?"

"A brilliant idea," she said. "I don't start work on Saturday until six pm if that works for you." She'd been hoping he'd suggest something casual, something low-key. *Just in case it turns out to be a bust. Hope it doesn't, though. I hardly know him, but I have a good feeling about this man...*

"Uh, yes it does. I, uh, don't know the town that well," he said, "so if you have any suggestions...?"

"I've got a perfect route in mind," Kate said. "Can you meet me tomorrow morning in front of the Castle Inn pub at, say, eleven?"

"Great!" Matt said. "See you then!"

◎

The weather forecast called for a warm day—typical for early June in Cambridge—so Kate dressed casually: jeans, a light blouse, and a pair of faded trainers. She parked her blue Austin Mini a block from the pub, arriving five minutes early to find Matt already waiting out front. She was relieved to see he was also dressed casually: khaki shorts, a polo shirt, and trainers.

"Ah, I love a man who's prompt!" she said, beaming. *I really do!*

Matt smiled nervously. "Better an hour early than a minute late."

I like this guy already.

"So, where are we going today?" Matt said.

"I thought we'd start with the toodle along the Cam, then bimble around town. Sound good?"

Matt looked confused, then smiled and shrugged in agreement. "I literally don't know what you just said, but I'm game."

She giggled. "Splendid!" *This brilliant young man has trouble with basic British slang.*

They strolled north, following the meandering River Cam. Kate, acting as tour guide, rambled on about the historic buildings, bridges, and parks. They stopped to watch locals "punting"—paddling on the river in small boats, or "prams." She considered herself gregarious, but found conversation with this young man a tad awkward. The simplest of natural things distracted him: ripples on the surface of the river, the spacing of a flock of birds flying overhead, the way sunlight filtered through the trees.

He sees the world differently than most people do. Almost child-like.

Eventually they both relaxed, Kate talking about her work as a nurse practitioner and Matt about his lecturing at the university. She'd seen snippets of Matt's press conferences on the news and was impressed by his modesty—he only mentioned his amazing work at AdAstra when she posed specific questions, and gave only vague answers.

They must keep everything rather secret there...

Over the course of the next three hours, they covered five kilometres, circling the town clockwise and ending up at the picturesque King's College bridge—almost back at their starting point.

"Would you like to get something to drink?" Matt said. "Maybe a bite to eat?"

Kate nodded. "I'd love to. Any place strikes your fancy?"

Matt looked around to get his bearings. "On days I'm teaching, I grab a sandwich at the café in the Mathematical Sciences building. But it's closed on weekends. Um, my friends and I often go to The Eagle pub. It's over there somewhere," he said, pointing vaguely east. "They have pretty good food."

"Sounds lovely. I've never been there, but I hear it's nice."

They crossed the huge grass courtyard of King's College, then wound their way through a labyrinth of backstreets until they found the pub. The lunch rush was over, the place almost deserted; they grabbed a quiet corner booth.

"What can I get you?" Matt said.

"I'll have a bitter—IPA if they have it, thanks."

He headed to the bar to order drinks, returning with two pints of India Pale Ale, a bowl of salted peanuts, and a menu. She'd watched him at the bar and noticed that he hadn't paid the barman.

When he sat down, she leaned towards him. "I know you're relatively new to this country, but did you know you're supposed to pay when you order?" she whispered, trying not to embarrass him.

Matt looked momentarily confused. "Oh, yah, it's okay. We hold many of our informal planning sessions here, so I have a running tab."

"A running what?"

"A running tab." Matt paused. "Oh, I uh, guess that's a Canadian expression. I think here you call it, er, 'on the slate'?"

"Ah," Kate said. She stared at him as he sat down.

"So. Matt Barnes. World-renowned physicist. Lecturer at Cambridge. Man who's been through a wormhole—'hypernaut' I think is the term you used when I saw your press conference on the telly. What prompted you to become a philanthropist as well?"

Matt relayed anecdotes from his childhood: his parents dragging him to the town's homeless shelter and retirement centre every Christmas and Thanksgiving.

"So, I guess I can thank my parents for instilling a sense of... not so much charity, but... social responsibility?"

He rambled on, sharing his story of learning about Cambridge's hungry school-kid problem from a colleague at the university. "I contacted the principal—I mean headmaster—at Bell Meadows. He liked my idea, but wasn't thrilled about accepting money from a stranger who walked in off the street. My cousin Stuart—he's a lawyer, I mean solicitor—helped me start up the ANB Foundation. Things moved quickly after that; the school was happy to receive money from a registered charity." He took a sip of his ale. "How did you come to volunteer there?"

"A nurse I work with—Margie—her husband teaches there. She mentioned the breakfast program was starting up and they needed help preparing and serving food. I work a four-on, four-off shift pattern and don't do much on my days off."

Kate could see Matt was getting uncomfortable with so much sharing. *It's a lot for a first date.* She smiled, glanced around the pub conspiratorially, leaned towards Matt, and lowered her voice to a whisper. "You know, a couple of years ago, I heard a rumour about this place."

"What was that?" He leaned in.

Damn, he smells nice. "Well, I'd just come back after my four days off. During my start-of-shift handoff, I was told there were three patients under guard in the ICU. Heavy guard. Not just the local constabulary, mind you, but no-nonsense military types. Possibly SAS. One patient had two gunshot wounds and was in critical condition. Another looked like he'd walked in front of a bus—broken arms, broken ribs, internal injuries. The third had been on the receiving end of a beating or a wild animal attack—his face was bashed in and one of his hands badly mangled."

"Wow. What's that got to do with this pub?" Matt whispered back.

Kate glanced around, making sure no one was listening.

"Rumour was they were IRA terrorists that tried to kidnap the Duke of Cambridge. At this very pub. He's known to pop in here occasionally with his security detail. But there was nothing, absolutely nothing, in the news. Just rumours floating around town."

"Wow," Matt said. "No other witnesses?"

Kate shook her head. "Everything was kept on the hush-hush, and we were instructed not to discuss it. Apparently three other men came in by ambulance at the same time but with minor injuries. Rumour was they were pub patrons, injured in whatever it was that never happened. The police had the entire wing they were in sealed off for two whole days. Another rumour was that royalty paid a visit. Possibly Her Majesty!"

"Wow, royal intrigue," Matt said.

Kate stared at Matt. "The Duke attends classes at the university, doesn't he?"

Matt nodded. "I've taught him the past two years."

"You've *met* Prince Edward?" she said.

Matt nodded. "Nice guy. Outstanding student. He was at AdAstra last month when we put Renny on the moon."

Wow! Every British citizen dreams of meeting royalty sometime in their life.

They chatted for another half hour, then ordered an early dinner—a Thai salad bowl for her and a steak-and-ale pie for him. The pub was still nearly empty, with only a few patrons coming and going.

Kate was staring into Matt's baby blue eyes when, from her peripheral vision, she noticed someone standing beside their table.

"Ah, Mr. Barnes, returning to the scene of the crime, I see?"

Kate looked up. It was a young man, well-dressed but with a faded University of Cambridge baseball cap pulled down to his eyes. A pair of hard-looking men flanked him.

Oh my God! It's Prince Edward!

Matt smiled. "Uh, hello Edward, I mean, uh, your Highness." He grimaced at his breach of protocol, then glanced around the pub to see if anyone was nearby. "I could say the same about you—crime scene, I mean," he blurted out.

Kate was embarrassed on Matt's behalf. *You don't talk to royalty that way!*

The Prince smiled, amused at Matt's impetuousness.

"It's okay, Mr. Barnes. I'm incognito," he said, winking. He turned to Kate. "And who might this lovely lady be?"

"Uh, your Royal Highness, may I introduce Kate—"

"Kaitlin McDonough, your Highness," she blurted as she tried to get up from the booth, not sure whether to do a proper curtsey. The Prince motioned for her to stay seated.

Matt finished his introduction. "—McDonough. Kate, His Royal Highness, Prince Edward, Duke of Cambridge."

"Pleased to meet you, Miss McDonough." He held out his hand. She shakily accepted.

Oh my God! The Prince shook my hand!

"The... the honour is mine, your Highness."

Oh. My. God.

Matt broke the uncomfortable silence. "Your Highness, would you care to join us?"

Kate turned to Matt, her eyes wide and jaw dropped. *Commoners don't ask royalty to 'join us'!*

The Prince smiled. "Much as I'd like to, Mr. Barnes, I doubt my minders here would permit that." He glanced at his security detail. Both shook their heads slightly, one tilting his head towards the door.

"As I thought. Turns out we must be leaving. Mr. Barnes, thanks again for inviting me to your demonstration last month. I was honoured to be witness such a historic event, and to meet your charming parents. Miss McDonough, it was a pleasure meeting you."

Kate could only nod. The Prince and his detail left the pub, leaving her momentarily speechless.

"Well, what a coincidence," Matt quipped. "We were just talking about him."

"That... I just met Prince Edward! He shook my hand!"

Matt smiled. "He's human, just like the rest of us."

No, he's not. He's... he's royalty!

Hang on...

"Matt, what did the Prince mean when he said, 'returning to the scene of the crime'?"

Matt blushed. "I'm, uh, not allowed to talk about it. Sorry." He awkwardly rubbed a faded scar on his forehead.

She stared at him.

There's more to this man than meets the eye.

They finished their now-lukewarm meals. Kate glanced at her watch. "Oh dear, I must be off soon. My shift starts at six."

Matt walked her back to her car. Then came that awkward moment, the 'end-of-first-date goodbye.'

Kate took a deep breath. "I had a wonderful time today, Matt."

"I... I did, too," he said. "A wonderful time."

Another awkward pause.

Kate took a deep breath. *Here goes...*

"Matt, I find you to be an utterly fascinating person. I hope we can do this again sometime soon?"

Matt's goofy grin was adorable, and all he could do was nod. She leaned over and gave him a peck on the cheek. *He smells really nice!* She got into her car and drove away, watching Matt in the rear-view mirror, still standing there, grinning and waving.

◎

Later that evening...

Like many software geeks, Josh Allen liked to sleep in, arrive at work around ten am, then work well into the evening. So, it was not surprising he did his grocery shopping when most people were home, getting ready for bed.

He'd stopped at the local Tesco on his way home from work and bought his usual week's-worth selection of less-than-nourishing food. He wheeled his grocery cart—*they call it a "trolley" here*—out to his car and put his groceries into the car's "boot." He was about to return the trolley to the store when two men blocked his path, having appeared out of nowhere. They were both dressed in black and had features best described as "nondescript."

"Hello, *Mister* Allen," the first one said. The other man just stared.

"Uh... hello," Josh replied nervously.

"Nice night, isn't it?"

"Uh... I guess. Can... can I help you?"

The man smiled. "Actually, you can. You're AdAstra's computer whiz, aren't you?"

Josh looked around the parking lot—there was no one else around. He nodded nervously.

"How are your parents, Jack and Louise? Jack is still working at the observatory? And Louise volunteers at your church."

"My... my parents? How... how do you know about my parents? Who are you guys?"

"I'll ask the questions here. And your sister—she's still living in Vancouver with her husband and three wonderful kids, right?"

Josh's jaw dropped. "Huh.... what do you guys want?"

"We need you to get us some information."

"Li... like what?" he stammered. He flinched as the man reached into his pocket and pulled out a slip of paper.

"This."

Josh looked at the piece of paper. *Root password. Gate security codes. HYDRA drawings. Source code. Jeez!*

"I... I can't get these," he stammered.

The man's smile was pure evil. "Oh yes you can, unless you want something bad to happen to your parents."

Josh locked his knees so he wouldn't collapse.

Must stall for time. "This... it'll take me a while to gather all this."

"I know," the man said. "Meet us here next Thursday, same time. If you don't show up, something bad might happen to your parents. Or your sister. Or her kids. Understand?"

Josh could only nod.

"And don't even think about going to the authorities. We'll be watching you. We get one whiff of you not following our instructions, it'll be your family who suffers."

"Yah, suffer...," said the other man, speaking for the first time.

Josh stared at the piece of paper; when he looked up, the two men had vanished. He got into his car, shaking violently for five minutes before he was calm enough to drive back to his flat.

He didn't sleep a wink that night, tossing and turning, getting up and peeking through his closed curtains every time a car passed by his block of flats. All he could think about was his parents. And his sister. *Should I tell the guys, or not?*

◎

Josh arrived at work the next morning later than normal, exhausted. He shuffled up to Mission Control and sat down at his console, staring at the blank monitor.

"Extra late today, huh?" came a voice from behind. Josh nearly jumped out of his skin.

"Jeez, Josh. You okay?" Matt said. "You look like hell."

"Didn't sleep well."

His friends sensed something was troubling him and gave him space; he used that time to mull over his predicament. Finally, he'd had enough, and approached Matt on Friday afternoon.

"You got a minute? There's something I want to run by you."

"Can it wait until Monday?" Matt replied. "I've got a *date* tonight A second date with Kate!" Matt beamed.

"Oh yah, I forgot," Josh said, deflated. "No worries. It'll keep." Matt's friends had taken a keen interest in his bumbling attempts at dating.

◎

Josh spent days pondering his dilemma: protect his family and betray his friends, or be true to his friends and risk his family.

Why would God allow my parents to be harmed—is He testing me? Or... maybe there isn't a God?

These conflicting thoughts robbed him of sleep every night. By Thursday morning he'd made a decision. But he also knew he was too weak to make the right decision.

"I'll be right with you," Josh said to his friends, who were heading into town for lunch. "Just gotta take care of something. I'll meet you outside in ten."

Josh went downstairs to the computer room and mounted a blank tape on one of the tape drives. He sat at the operator console and began typing, the tape reels started jerking as files were copied from the hard drive. He almost lost bladder control when a deep voice came from behind. "I thought you were coming for lunch," Renny said.

"I... I... was just... starting an... an incremental backup before I do a system upgrade this afternoon," he stammered.

"A little jumpy, are we?"

"Sorry, I... I... not sleeping much lately."

"No problem."

He stared at the spinning tape drive. *Is this the right choice?*

That evening, Josh pulled into the parking lot of the Tesco supermarket at his usual time. He'd just gotten out of the car when the two men who'd accosted him last week reappeared.

"You have what we talked about?" the leader of the two said.

Josh nodded nervously. He reached under his front seat and pulled out a paper bag containing an 8-inch magnetic tape. "Mmm... mostly," he replied. "I couldn't get the drawings because they haven't been digitized yet. Bu... but the source code is on here," he said, thrusting the bag at them.

The man smiled. "Good for you. And the other information?"

Josh nodded, fumbling in his pocket for a couple of Post-It notes. "Here... here's the admin password and the security gate passwords. But we change them every two weeks."

The man stared at Josh, who started shaking.

"Good work," he said. "I guess your family will be safe. For now."

"But we might want more from you another time," the other man added. "You can go now."

Josh obediently got into his car. When he looked up, the two men were gone. He began shaking violently, and barely had time to get the door open before retching onto the pavement.

The next morning...

Josh felt a certain comfort having his three closest friends sitting next to him in AdAstra's meeting room. Seamus stood at the head of the table, giving what he referred to as his "after-action report," or AAR.

"They were amateurs. Rank amateurs," Seamus declared. "After Josh handed over the blank tape, we followed them. They didn't check for tails or employ *any* counter-surveillance techniques, and drove straight to a motor inn on the outskirts of town. We gave them an hour to get settled then popped in for a chat."

"Josh," Matt said, interrupting Seamus, "on behalf of all of us, thank you for trusting us. That couldn't have been an easy choice."

"Are my parents going to be okay?" Josh blurted.

Seamus held up his hands in placation. "Laddie, your family was *never* in danger. These guys had a thin file on you and your family, nothing more. They were bluffing. Anyhow, we 'persuaded' them to call their contact and set up a meet. We scooped him on an old farm road a few clicks out of town. He was a tough nut to crack, but eventually he coughed up a name. It was easy to connect that name to the person behind this entire scheme."

"Who was it?" Matt demanded.

Seamus told them.

"I knew it!" Matt shouted. "That motherfucker!"

"What's the plan for the two who threatened Josh and his family?" Renny said, with a gleam in his eyes. "Do you still have them on ice, or whatever you call it? I'd like to be alone in a room with them for a few minutes." He cracked his massive knuckles menacingly.

Seamus chuckled. "Not to worry, lads. Those two won't be bothering Josh, or anyone else, ever again. You have my word on that." The finality in his tone made the message clear: *You don't need to know, you don't want to know.*

"As for their contact," Seamus said, "we still have him. Any thoughts on what we should do?"

Matt nodded. "Seamus, I'd like you to release him. There's a message he should deliver to his employer."

◎

"What do you mean, you got nothing?" Dr. Charles William Winston the Third roared at the man sitting across from his desk. Holding this meeting in the evening meant a lesser chance of his staff seeing his guest. Or hearing the yelling.

"Allow me to explain," the man said calmly. "The guy I hired I've used many times as a cut-out for jobs in the UK and on the continent—he's been very reliable. At least until now. He hired a pair of ex-military types he's worked with before. Those two confronted the target and used the information you provided to pressure him, and he appeared suitably frightened for his family. He showed up as expected with a magnetic tape and security codes, so they thought they'd been successful. Turns out he'd chosen loyalty to his friends over family—or he figured our guys were bluffing—and went to Seamus O'Donnell, AdAstra's security chief. O'Donnell bagged our two guys and worked them over until they gave up my cut-out's name. Then he faked a meet and bagged the cut-out."

"Shit!" Winston said. "What's my exposure here?"

"In theory, zero. There were three layers between me and the target.

Four layers for you."

"You said, 'in theory.' What about in reality?"

The man was clearly uncomfortable. "Well, O'Donnell gave my cut-out a message to pass on."

"Message?" Winston fumed. "What do you mean, a message?"

"A message from Matt Barnes."

"Well, what's the message?"

The man paused. "The message is, 'Nice try, Chuck. Better luck next time.'"

I think I'm going to have a stroke, Winston thought.

◎

Kate waved as Matt drove away from the front entrance of Addenbrooke's Hospital, then hurried inside to find out why she'd been paged "999" on her day off.

Well, so much for our third date!

Their second date had been a near perfect repeat of the first: a long walk around town followed by refreshments at a local pub. There'd been a lot less awkwardness the second time around; they both opened up more, talking about their respective careers, current events, and so on. Making plans for a third date proved difficult, owing to Matt's hectic workload and Kate's four-on, four-off hospital schedule. It took them several weeks to find a date that worked.

Their third date began with Matt picking her up at her apartment in his beat-up old Vauxhall. He took her to a quaint Italian restaurant smack in the middle of downtown Cambridge. As the evening progressed, Kate found herself more and more charmed by this young man across the table. He was polite to the waiter, and attractive in a nerdy sort of way. Matt wasn't a hunk, but then raw machismo did nothing for her.

Besides, I'm not exactly an English Rose. Well, maybe a rose with a few crooked teeth.

Kate was a self-admitted *sapiophile*—attracted to intelligence—something Matt had plenty of. But intellectual arrogance turned her off, which explained why she'd never dated any of the hospital's young and attractive doctors (although she'd been asked out frequently).

There was something unique about Matt—his incredible intellect was tempered by a sincere modesty she found utterly charming. His conversational skills were sorely lacking, but he tried hard and seemed genuinely interested in her, her work, and her interests. Even when he talked about the amazing things AdAstra was doing—opening wormholes, exploring the moon—he didn't come across as boasting. And he seemed to derive just as much satisfaction from the work the ANB Foundation was doing. Kate realized she was also a philanthrophile—*is that even a word?*—attracted to someone who used their money to help others.

"So, what are your plans for the ANB Foundation?" she asked over a scrumptious tiramisu dessert for two.

Matt smiled. "We're expanding the school meals program to several of the surrounding towns. We just hired a full-time business manager to solicit corporate and private donations, and they're trickling in. Since I'm on the board of directors—actually Stuart and I *are* the directors—I've instructed the foundation to start a scholarship fund so kids from low income or otherwise disadvantaged homes can go to university, college, or trade school."

"Trade school?" Kate asked.

"Oh, sorry, that's a North American term. I think here you call them vocational, or technical schools?"

"Ah, yes. That's brilliant, Matt." Kate stared at him. "And I heard on the news that AdAstra is doing really well. Looking at the car you drive, one couldn't tell. I've seen your friends driving their fancy new cars around town. Do you not pay you well there?"

Matt looked momentarily embarrassed, then smiled when he realized she was just taking the piss. "A car is just transportation, and now I keep it just to bug Renny. You know, when he and I were at university, we shared a 1974 Datsun for three years. He grew up poor—just him and his mom, renting a house and living paycheque to paycheque. Yes, he did just buy himself a pretty fancy sports car, but I don't begrudge him, or any of my friends, for wanting to live it up a bit."

Kate smirked. "And, according to the rumour mill at work, he's become quite popular with the single ladies in town."

Matt shrugged. "Renny keeps his personal life to himself. Say, speaking of Renny, did you notice that he's native?"

Kate nodded. "Of course. Why do you ask?"

"I've known Renny for almost twenty years, and I never realized it until he mentioned it during our last press conference." He shrugged. "Makes me wonder what else I'm missing about my friends."

Wow, this man is so humble he's adorable!

"Well, everyone in town thinks you are an amazing bunch of crazy Canucks."

Matt grinned. "Thanks. We've all worked hard and taken personal risks to get where we are today. Especially Renny—it took a lot of guts to go through the wormhole and step onto the surface of the moon."

Kate nodded. "I saw that video on the news, and the one of you floating through the wormhole into space. That took a lot of courage, too."

Matt shrugged. "I guess. But that's different."

"How so?"

"Well, I know *everything* about how the HYDRA works—the math, the physics, the engineering—so I can objectively evaluate all the risks. Renny only partially understands the technology, but he *trusts* me and Gary and Josh. That takes a special courage."

Kate nodded, impressed (again) with Matt's modesty. "Speaking of risk, what's it like to go through a wormhole? Must be kind of creepy moving from your facility right into space...?"

Matt nodded. "When we were doing our initial testing, I stuck my hand through, then my head, with no ill effects. The first time I went completely through, I didn't know what to expect. Then I realized there wasn't much to it. The wormhole is infinitesimally short—a fraction of a millimetre—so you're not going *through* anything. I found it scarier being locked inside a used Soviet spacesuit. Thought I was going to throw up. I don't think I'll ever get used to being stuck inside one of those."

Kate was silent, digesting Matt's comments. *Brave and modest.* They chatted for another hour before agreeing to go for a walk to digest their delightful yet calorie-rich meal. After Matt paid the bill, they strolled hand-in-hand through Cambridge's market square, looking in the shop windows.

Matt stopped and turned to her.

"Kate, I'm having a great time tonight. I... I can't read people well, so I can't tell if you're feeling the same." He gave a sort-of shrug that screamed frustration, maybe even panic.

Kate stared into his blue eyes. She smiled and nodded, then leaned towards him for their first kiss. It was awkward and thrilling at the same time. She was about to ask Matt to come back to her apartment when a shrill beeping came from her purse.

Oh no, not again!

She pulled out the offending black box and pressed a button to silence it. She glanced at the LCD readout.

"Something important?" Matt said, hoping it wasn't.

Kate sighed. "It's the 'all-hands-on-deck' code—must be a multiple trauma. We've been short-handed all week. I... I really should go."

"My car's only a block away. I can have you at the hospital in five minutes."

Kate nodded numbly. *Damn...*

"I'll make it up to you," she promised.

THIRTY

Matt looked around the long mahogany table in Building 2's main conference room. Gary, Josh, Renny, Stuart, and Nigella were in their usual places; one chair was empty.

"I see our BNSC rep is running late," Matt said. "Let's do our business update now—we can move on to operations when Mr. Byrd arrives."

"Screw business," Renny said. "How'd your date on Saturday go?"

Matt blushed.

"That good, eh?" Renny said.

"Yaw, ve vant da deeetails," Gary added, nailing the sing-song Swedish accent he'd perfected this year.

Matt shrugged, uncomfortable discussing personal affairs with Nigella—a relative stranger—present.

"It... it was great. Great dinner, we went for a walk. Then she got paged into work."

"Oh!" Renny bellowed. "The Professor got cock-blocked by a pager!"

Matt's face shifted from red to maroon.

"Jesus, Renny!" Gary said, shaking his head. He only called Renny by name when he did something way off-base.

"Oh, too far?" Renny said.

"Uh, yah."

Renny turned to Matt. "Sorry, Professor."

Matt nodded, accepting his best friend's apology.

"You did get her flowers, didn't you?" Gary said. As the only one of the group with a steady girlfriend, he was their "expert" on the female of the species.

"Flowers? No."

Gary rolled his eyes. "As soon as this meeting is over, call a florist and order her flowers. Roses. A dozen. Have them delivered to the hospital. Nigella, help me out here. All women like to get flowers, right?"

She raised her hands, palms out. "I'm not getting involved in your personal affairs." Then she caught Matt's eye and gave him a subtle nod. *Of course we like flowers!*

Matt gave a tiny nod back. *Thanks!*

"How'd we do at the auction last week?" Matt said, changing the subject to something less embarrassing. Renny's recent lunar field trips were primarily rock-hounding, but he had recovered more man-made artifacts.

"Good," Nigella said. "The Apollo 16 backpacks fetched a cool five million pounds each. Actually, John Young's sold for five million and one pounds because NASA exercised their final-bid option. Assorted moon rocks sold for another two point three million. So, minus Somerville's cut, we netted just over eight million pounds."

Everyone at the table applauded. Matt's friends would each receive almost half a million pounds; Stuart, a quarter-million, and Matt, close to a million.

I really should check my bank account one of these days! Gonna have a big tax bill this year.

"That's six hundred grand for the ANB Foundation," Matt said.

"I think it's time Matt bought a new car," Gary declared.

"He might get a fourth date if he gets a car that was built in this decade!" Renny added.

Everyone laughed.

"Moving on," Matt said. "Unless we want to piss off the Americans by stripping their lunar modules, we're into diminishing returns on our lunar salvage-and-auction business model."

"Agreed," Nigella said. "We need to move to a more structured revenue model."

"I still want to bring back one of the American flags," Renny said, referring to the ones planted at each Apollo landing site. "It would lock cool mounted on the wall in Mission Control."

"I strongly discourage that," Mr. Byrd said, who'd just walked in. "That would likely provoke an international incident."

Renny shrugged. "Whatever. Fuck 'em if they can't take a joke."

"Renny, while I appreciate your enthusiasm," Nigella said, "that's not a sound business strategy."

"Okay, how about this: when we were at the Apollo 16 site last month, I took a good look at the lunar rover they left behind. I want to bring it back, piece by piece, and rebuild it here."

The room was silent while everyone digested Renny's audacious plan.

"Bigfoot, that's brilliant!" Gary exclaimed.

"If the rovers are non-functional, I don't see any political issues," Mr. Byrd said.

"Won't it take a lot of work to disassemble?" Josh cautioned.

Renny smiled. "Not really." He reached into his backpack and brought out a thick binder, dropping it on the table with a loud 'thunk.' "This is Boeing's original technical manual for their lunar rovers—I came across it in the U of A archives. Thought it might come in handy someday, so I made a copy. They built the rovers in a modular fashion; Red and I have poured over this manual and we figure it would take about six trips to break it down into pieces small enough to fit through the wormhole."

"I like it," Matt said. "We'll need a codename."

"Operation Chop-Shop," Renny said.

"Okay," Matt said, "You and Scott come up with a detailed plan. On to new business. Nigella and I have reviewed all the proposals received to date and identified the ones we think are worth considering. Nigella?"

She nodded. "I'll start with the Earth-orbit ones first. The European Space Agency wants to deploy three prototype navigation satellites, like the GPS ones the US is sending up. They're testbed platforms and they have them almost ready to go. India wants us to deploy a communications satellite. British Aerospace—Sir Russell's company—has another two dozen imaging satellites to go up. On the non-technical side, the UK's largest manufacturer of chocolate bars wants to deploy a kilometre-long lighted sign to advertise their newest candy bar—something visible from the ground at night. The largest funeral home chain in the US wants to put the ashes of cremated people into space, where they'll burn up."

Nigella looked around the table. "Did I miss anything?"

Mr. Byrd cleared his throat, then slid a single sheet of paper across the table. "Our Foreign and Commonwealth Office received a formal request from the US State Department. On behalf of NASA, they are requesting we begin negotiations to provide regular supply drops to their space station Freedom."

The room went silent and everyone looked at Matt—they were all aware of the animosity between Matt and one of the US President's deputy science advisors.

Matt broke the silence. "Well, given the considerable effort they've expended to acquire our technology and/or shut us down, I sure didn't see that coming. Let's table this one for the moment, shall we?" He turned to Nigella. "And on the lunar side?"

"That garnered more interest," she said. "We've had proposals from no less than a dozen universities around the world to transport various sensor packages and robotic rovers to different places on the moon. The UK wants to build the first permanent moon base—they're going to partner with the fledgling Canadian Space Agency. That same funeral company I mentioned earlier also wants to create a lunar cemetery for ashes of its premium customers. The Italians and the Chinese both want to transport materials and personnel to the far side of the moon so they can set up radio observatories. Oh, and here's an odd one. A law firm in Malta has a wealthy client with terminal cancer who wants to die on the moon."

"Wow," Matt said. "Okay, let's go around the table on each proposal, so everyone can give their input, then we'll vote. Mr. Byrd, please speak up if there are any political and/or international relations issues we should be aware of. Let's start with the orbital ones."

Everyone agreed on almost all the orbital proposals—the only issue was scheduling. Josh insisted on one change to the candy bar advertisement proposal: it was his favourite snack since moving to the UK, and he wanted a guaranteed lifetime supply.

"You've got several million pounds in the bank, and you want free chocolate bars?" Renny said incredulously.

Josh shrugged. "It's the principle. I may not always have money, but I will always have those chocolate bars."

"Whatever," Renny said, shrugging.

The only proposal that gave everyone pause was the supply drops for the US space station. The table was evenly split—Nigella, Stuart, and Gary were in favour, primarily because it provided a guaranteed revenue stream.

"Besides," Nigella said, "NASA is still having problems with their space shuttle program and is desperate to keep the station running, so we could set whatever price we want. And Matt, wouldn't it feel good if the president's deputy science advisor had to come cap in hand?"

"Yah," Matt said with a gleam in his eye, envisioning *that* meeting.

Gary explained why he was in favour: one of his childhood dreams had been to "go camping" in orbit someday. He figured that if AdAstra was running regular supply missions to the space station, he'd be able to arrange an overnighter there.

Mr. Byrd voiced his support. "Money aside, it would be good for international relations."

Matt, Renny, and Josh were strongly opposed, primarily because of the lawsuits and other legal roadblocks the US government had recently thrown up.

Renny, as usual, was the most blunt. "I think we should tell them to go fuck themselves. I smell a ruse backed by your old Caltech pal to get access to our facilities. We shouldn't trust them."

The lively discussion continued for another ten minutes, then Matt spoke up.

"Scott and I have been kicking around an idea involving the US space station. We think it's workable, at least in the short term." It took him a few minutes to explain.

"Audacious," Stuart said.

"Wow, that's fucking brilliant, Professor," Renny declared.

"Okay, I'm convinced," Gary said. "I'm changing my vote to 'no' on one condition."

"What's that?"

"That we call your plan 'Operation Chicken Little.'"

"Nigella, what do you think?" Matt said.

She shook her head. "You guys never cease to amaze. I can't see how this 'Chicken Little' will bring in more revenue than regular supply drops would, but it would definitely turn the media spotlight back on us. It would also make us some serious enemies in the US government."

"Mr. Byrd, what do you think?" Stuart said.

Byrd looked uncomfortable. "Well, as Nigella said, this will probably antagonize the Americans. But, since the World Court has already ruled that non-functional equipment is fair game for salvage, I don't see any legal issues. Possibly diplomatic ones, though. I imagine the timing would be critical."

Matt nodded, looking at Nigella and Byrd. "Good points, both of you. But *this* is personal. I ran the idea past Alastair Columbus a few months ago—just the broad strokes—and he's fully onboard."

Nigella shrugged. "It's your company. Let's take a coffee break, then discuss the lunar proposals."

◎

Everyone agreed to support the proposals for robotic vehicles and remote sensor packages from companies and universities in the UK, Canada, Europe, and Asia. From basically anywhere except the US.

"Any they've all offered to pay quite reasonable fees for our services," Matt said.

"I think we should set a fixed rate for academic institutions," Matt said.

"An interesting idea," Nigella replied. "How much were you thinking?"

"One dollar per deployment," Matt proposed. "We want to encourage academic research."

"That would be a brilliant public relations move," she said. "But, to keep things simple, we should make it one British pound."

Everyone agreed. There was also full agreement to support the UK-Canada moon base plan.

"We have to reject the far-side radio observatory proposals," Matt said. "The moon is tidally locked to the Earth—one side always faces the Earth so it's not possible to open a wormhole to its far-side."

The "cemetery on the moon" and the "I want to die on the moon" proposals provoked much discussion. The eventual consensus was that leaving human remains behind likely violated the "don't litter" clauses in the Outer Space Treaty and the Lunar Agreement.

"I'll take this one," Stuart offered. "I'll work with the BNSC to get further direction from the World Court." He looked at Mr. Byrd, who nodded.

"Hang on," Gary said. "Some perspective here? The Americans and Soviets left a lot of crap on the moon under the guise of 'exploration.' And, in the Americans' case, literally bags of crap. That's gotta be, what do you call it, legal precedent, for littering? No one's been bitching about the US cleaning up their landing sites."

"That's an excellent point," Stuart said, making a note on his legal pad. "The US will look pretty silly if they make noise about this."

"You know," Renny said, "I don't see how leaving a bunch of ashes—which are already sterilized—on the lunar surface could be considered littering. When it's my time, I think it would be cool to have my ashes in a lunar crematorium, looking down on the Earth."

"Actually, it would be a columbarium," Matt said. "A crematorium is where the dead are cremated. A columbarium is where funerary urns are kept."

Renny rolled his eyes. "Whateverrrrrr."

"Okay," Matt said. "We've covered all the lunar missions. Does anyone have a pet project they want to bring up? I have a sneaking suspicion Renny does. I mean, beyond that expensive lab we just built."

Renny had spent close to half a million pounds of AdAstra's money building a fully functional and hermetically sealed geological research laboratory at the far end of Building 2. It was a planetary geologist's dream lab, equipped with everything from rock hammers and diamond saws to microscopes to soil analyzers and mass spectrometers. It even had a state-of-the-art X-ray crystallography machine. In short, everything he'd need to examine and analyze soil, rock, and atmosphere samples from wherever the HYDRA might take them.

"You bet yer ass, Professor," Renny said. "The Harris Planetary Receiving Lab is just wasted space unless we can feed it. I want to check out the moon's South Pole."

"Why there?" Nigella asked.

"Water," Renny said. "It's the holy grail for lunar exploration. Any self-sustaining, manned moon base will need water to make both air and fuel. You see, the moon's spin axis is at a right angle to the ecliptic plane, unlike the Earth's, which is tilted twenty-three degrees. There's craters and basins around the South Pole that haven't seen sunlight for millions, maybe billions, of years. If there's frozen water anywhere on the moon, the South Pole is the first place to look. And, if there's any exotic geological compounds left over from when the solar system formed, that's likely where they'll be."

He sounds like an academic, Matt realized. *My friend has come a long way...*

Gary must have been reading Matt's mind. "I think we should start calling *you* 'Professor,' big guy."

Renny opened his mouth, then closed it, for once unable to come up with an appropriate response to Gary's extremely rare compliment.

"Speaking of ashes on the moon," Nigella said. "I have a troublesome ex-husband I'd like to send there. Last I heard, though, he's still breathing. Is that a problem?"

"Not if we can get him into the Pipe," Renny quipped.

There was a smattering of nervous laughter—no one was sure just how serious Nigella was. No one wanted to ask.

Josh changed the subject. "I think we should do some freebie missions for school kids around the world."

"What did you have in mind?" Matt said.

Josh shrugged. "I dunno. Science experiments. Heck, why don't we let them decide? Let's hold contests and see what the kids come up with."

"That would be great PR," Nigella said.

"My turn," Gary said. "I want to build survey robots. Solar-powered ones that can run around on their own for days or weeks. Hell, maybe they can help Bigfoot hunt for water."

Everyone in the room agreed.

"Okay, then," Nigella said. "Our next step is to get signed contracts. We'll need our customers to commit to payload delivery dates."

"I'll start drafting the contracts," Stuart said.

"Great," Matt said. "We know what we want to do. Now we have to figure out the *how* and the *when*."

◎

A week later...

Matt stared at the wall of the main conference room, looking at the master project schedule that Ben Stellutti was constantly updating. The critical path on most of the commercial jobs they'd accepted was payload delivery. Nearly all the customers wanted more time—months, not weeks—as they hadn't expected to get the "green light" so soon. That was pushing many of the "sexy" missions into next year.

Oh well, looks like our missions will keep us just busy enough, but nothing too risky.

Elaine and Deepa were both pushing for more time to keep ahead on the maintenance of their critical subsystems. Security Chief Seamus was fretting over how much "foreign" equipment—the customer payloads— would be coming into the facility. He also wanted to limit the number of customer representatives allowed in the building.

Ok, Matt thought. *We've got a realistic and conservative schedule with time allotted for contingencies. Ben assures me we should be able to get most of this done by Christmas, the rest, early in the New Year. Plenty of time for HYDRA maintenance. I'll still be able to teach a course or two at the university. And I'll have more time to spend with Kate! I hope nothing unexpected pops up.*

◎

By early September, Matt was on top of the world. The AdAstra compound was buzzing with purposeful activity; everyone was focussed on their tasks, preparing the HYDRA Mark III for its first "official" commercial jobs. Ben was doing an outstanding job, maintaining the master operations plan and scheduling customer payload deliveries. Ben recommended limiting operations to two drills per week to allow time for routine maintenance of HYDRA's many complex subsystems—his schedule reflected that conservative approach.

The physics community was abuzz over several recent discoveries tied to Matt's Expansion Theory. A team of Italian radio astronomers detected a neutron star that exhibited an atypical surface temperature, leading them to conclude it was a quark star, matter composed exclusively of free quarks—something predicted by Matt's theory. Also, a group of South African scientists, intrigued by one of the gravity-related implications in Matt's paper, had published their results on an experiment that was elegant in its simplicity. They'd dropped aerodynamic-shaped lead weights, instrumented with high-accuracy accelerometers and radio transmitters, down a ten-kilometre-deep mineshaft. Once they analyzed the data from hundreds of drops and accounted for a multitude of factors such as air temperature and drag, they discovered a miniscule, but statistically significant drop in gravitational acceleration the deeper the weight fell. This was contrary to the accepted theory of gravity (not to mention Einstein's general theory of relativity), but exactly what Matt's theory predicted.

Then Dr. Feinberg called late one night, letting him know that the debacle surrounding his failed dissertation defence had, after years, come to a head. After a long investigation, Professor Clarke had been placed on indefinite leave pending the outcome of a disciplinary hearing. Feinberg also said there were rumblings that Caltech's board of directors was considering overriding the "fail" mark Clarke had given Matt.

It's been five years—why now?

Maybe I will get my PhD after all!

But do I want it?

And Matt's personal life was going great. He and Kate had just celebrated their three-month anniversary and were spending as much time together as their often-conflicting work schedules allowed. Neither had a lot of prior dating experience—Kate a bit more than Matt—and by mutual agreement were "taking it slow." But human nature being what it was, their attraction was becoming increasingly physical; Matt was anticipating them soon taking the next "big step."

Matt was also looking forward to resuming his lecturing role at

Cambridge, but his start-of-term teaching package was weeks overdue. After the fiasco at Caltech, he was justifiably paranoid about getting caught in office politics, something he knew he had a blind spot for.

Have I been overlooked?

When Matt phoned the Cavendish Lab to find out why he hadn't received his lecture assignments, Professor Samuelson's assistant gave him a cryptic response: *Be at the faculty lounge dining room at noon on the 12th.*

◎

Cambridge University Faculty Lounge

Matt took in the ambience of the oak-panelled dining room. *I'd call this room's aesthetic, "early-modern drab."*

Sitting at the table were Professor Samuelson and three senior department faculty: Professor Emeritus Adams, who'd done ground-breaking work in condensed-matter physics and had once been in the running for a Nobel Prize; Professor Walker, who specialized in string theory; and Associate Professor Singh, a magnetician.

The waiter served a round of drinks, then, following a subtle nod from Adams, disappeared without taking their lunch order.

Why am I here? Matt wondered.

"This get-together has been long overdue," Samuelson said. "Since your 'failed' doctoral thesis was published in Physics Journal B two years ago, several researchers around the world, including Professor Singh here, have been successful in constructing high-strength superconducting electromagnets based on your design."

Matt nodded. "I know Professor Bernhard at UBC is looking to use them at TRIUMF."

"Can't say I comprehend your underlying math," Singh said, "but you can't argue with thirty-five Tesla."

Matt chuckled. "That's exactly what Dr. Feinberg said."

"And your '11-space, expanding universe' paper has been getting a lot of traction lately," Samuelson said. "CERN found the H-meson, a Caltech doctoral candidate thinks he's detected the H-neutrino, and the news about that quark star is amazing. Then there's those South Africans and their gravity experiment. Imagine, gravity not being a point source—who'd have thought? Not to mention your secret wormhole technology we keep hearing about on the news. No one has teased that little gem out of your equations yet, but there seems to be no end to the discoveries lurking therein."

"Well, I do refer to it as my 'Theory of *Almost* Everything,'" Matt replied, hedging his bets.

"I've got a post-doc looking into your predictions about magnetostatic wormholes," Singh added.

Matt nodded. *It's not a prediction—we create two every time we use the HYDRA.*

"If you don't mind," Samuelson said, "we have a few questions about your doctoral thesis."

Matt shrugged. "Not at all. Fire away."

The questions came slowly, mostly from Singh. How did the multiphasic modulation work? How did he ensure laminar flow of the liquid helium? How did he overcome the dielectric heating problem?

This feels like a thesis defence, Matt thought. *Or a job interview.*

The questions continued for a half hour, and the waiter still hadn't come to take their lunch order.

Then there was a long, uncomfortable silence. Samuelson looked in turn at Singh, Adams, and Walker, getting a brief nod from each.

What's going on here? Matt thought. *I wish I could read body language better...*

"Mr. Barnes, thank you for indulging us," Samuelson said. "I'm sure you're wondering why we're giving you the third degree."

Matt nodded and swallowed hard. *I knew it. Here it comes...*

"We've decided that your role as an unaffiliated lecturer has come to an end."

A multitude of thoughts tore through Matt's head. *What did I do wrong this time? Who did I cross? What departmental politics did I run afoul of? Fuck!!!*

"You're... you're firing me," Matt said, his shoulders sagging and the colour draining from his face.

"No, no, Mr. Barnes, you completely misunderstand me! Given your impeccable academic record and recent publications, we feel a more *senior* position is appropriate. Put simply, we just can't have someone of your caliber working as a part-time, unaffiliated lecturer. This little get-together today was, technically, your doctoral thesis defence."

"And you passed with flying colours," Professor Adams said.

"Sorry for the subterfuge," Singh added.

"I don't know what to say," Matt replied, "other than, thanks?"

"I took the liberty of starting the degree approval process last week," Samuelson said. "It'll take another week for the paperwork to work its way through the bureaucracy, but I'm confident you'll be able to take part in the Degree Congregation at the end of September. Congratulations, *Doctor* Barnes."

Well, this turned into some lunch!
I gotta let the guys know.
And Kate!

Tuesday, October 3rd

Matt joined Josh, Deepa, and Renny in Building 2's lunch room for a late-morning coffee break after completing the last in a series of test drills to validate Deepa's new electromagnet control algorithm. They'd just brought the facility out of lock-down and called for a break; Deepa and three technicians were watching a cricket match on the television mounted from the ceiling in the corner of the room.

"Who's winning?" Matt said. The technicians laughed.

It was a running joke at AdAstra that the brilliant Matt Barnes could not fathom the "simple" rules of cricket. That he'd recently been "hooded" by Cambridge and was now *Doctor* Matt Barnes, PhD, somehow made it even funnier. Matt took the good-natured ribbing in stride.

The wall phone rang with a distinctive double-tone that signified an outside call being transferred from reception.

"Ah, right on time," Renny said, glancing at the clock on the wall. "I see British Telecom still hasn't fixed our phone system." Seamus O'Donnell had decided that, for security reasons, all external phone lines should be disabled during a drill. That was easy to implement—Josh had one of AdAstra's electrical technicians wire a switch at the HYDRA console that controlled power to the phone system's main control box. Unfortunately, there was a glitch in the phone system hardware: after power-up, the phones remained dead for twenty minutes, then random phones throughout the complex would start ringing without actual incoming calls. Renny ignored the phone.

A minute later, the phone rang again. Renny growled, heaved his enormous frame out of his seat, and shuffled to the phone.

"Lunch room." He listened for a few seconds. "Yah, he's here, you can put the call through," Renny turned to Matt. "Reception has a call for you, *Doctor* Barnes." Since Cambridge granted Matt a PhD, Renny had taken every opportunity to use the long-overdue honourific.

Matt took the phone from Renny's massive hand. "This is Matt Barnes."

He listened for several seconds before turning to his friends and rolling his eyes.

"Oh, I did, did I?" Matt said, chuckling. "Hilarious, Gary." He hung up.

"What was that about?" Renny said.

Matt shook his head. "Our resident comedian, playing another one of his practical jokes. Gary's Scandinavian accent is superb—he sounds just like the guy from the Ikea commercial."

Renny snorted. "More like the Swedish Chef."

Even the three techs chuckled, then turned their attention back to the cricket match. Deepa rolled her eyes.

Gary's predilection for crank phone calls using his repertoire of accents had become legendary throughout AdAstra. He'd convinced Deepa that India's most-famous cricket player was in town and wanted to take her to dinner. Elaine had likewise been one hundred percent sure that the Dublin, Ireland-based lead singer of the world's best-selling rock band had phoned to offer her VIP seating at their next London concert. And to this day, AdAstra's receptionist swore that the Scottish actor voted "the sexist man alive" had called to wish her a happy birthday. Gary recently announced he was "just about done" with Swedish and was moving on to a more challenging accent: Newfoundlander.

A minute later, the phone rang again. This time, Josh answered it, then handed the phone to Matt, who listened for only a few seconds before interrupting.

"Again, Gary, nice try," he said, hanging up.

Just as the phone hit the cradle, Gary walked in.

"Hello, ladies," he said, heading for the coffee machine. His friends stared at him.

"Whaaat?" Gary said.

"That wasn't you on the phone?" Matt said.

"What are you talking about?" Gary replied.

"Nothing," Matt said. "Never mind."

Gary shrugged. "Whatever."

A few minutes later, Stuart burst into the room.

"Where's Matt? Oh, there you are! Why aren't you answering the phone?"

"Are you in on this, too?" Matt asked.

"In on what? You guys gotta see this." He grabbed the television's remote control off the table and switched to BBC One, eliciting howls from the cricket-watchers. They had to wait for the commercials to end.

"And returning to our top news: the Royal Swedish Academy of Sciences just announced this year's winner of the Nobel Prize in Physics. The award is going to Canadian scientist Matthew Barnes, who's been working in the UK for the past four years, teaching at Cambridge and—"

All eyes in the room turned to Matt; he was staring at the TV, pale as a ghost. The phone started ringing again.

"Oh, shit...," he said.

THE END

(of The HYDRA Chronicles – Vol. 1)

THANKS!

Thank you for purchasing "n-Space: The HYDRA Chronicles – Vol. 1," the first in a series of the adventures of Matt Barnes and his friends as they explore the solar system using the HYDRA. I know you could have picked other books to read, and I am extremely grateful you chose mine.

If you enjoyed this book, I'd like to hear from you and hope you could take the time to post a review on Amazon. Your feedback and support will help me improve my writing and make the next books in the series even better!

If you follow this link to my Amazon author page, you'll be able to create a review:

www.amazon.com/stores/Bruce-Butler/author/B018N5OQUS

Again, thanks!

www.brucebutler.ca

ABOUT THE AUTHOR

Bruce Butler is a semi-retired professional engineer with a lifelong passion for science fiction. He grew up in Penticton, BC, Canada, then attended the University of British Columbia where he received a Bachelor of Science degree in Computer Science and Physics. He worked in the Vancouver-area high-tech industry for thirty-five years, in telecommunications, subsea robotics, autonomous marine vehicles and mining equipment, industrial remote controls, vessel surveillance, and marine navigation. Bruce still does some GPS-related consulting work in the Middle East.

Bruce's first book was a persuasive non-fiction book titled, "Letters to a Driving Nation: Exploring the Conflict between Drivers and Cyclists." His second book, "Into the Labyrinth: The Making of a Modern-Day Theseus," is a true account of his work on a classified Canadian defence research project at the end of the Cold War.

Bruce is now branching out into science fiction with "n-Space: The HYDRA Chronicles – Vol. 1," the first in a series of hard sci-fi stories chronicling the adventures of engineer/physicist Matt Barnes and his friends as they explore the solar system using their fantastic HYDRA. Bruce is also working on a techno-legal novel with his partner Lorna.

In his spare time, Bruce likes to cycle, open-water swim, and take part in the occasional Ironman triathlon or long-distance open-water swim event.

You can find Bruce these days in the south Okanagan Valley of British Columbia, Canada, where he's building his dream house on ten acres of undeveloped land.

Bruce is active on social media:

Twitter: @ButlerAuthor
Facebook: facebook.com/profile.php?id=100013563048281

Contact info:

Email: bruce@brucebutler.ca
Web: www.brucebutler.ca

AUTHOR'S NOTES

Even though this is a work of (science) fiction, its timeline is loosely based on the world I grew up in (starting in the 1960s). That said, I have taken a few factual deviations from that timeline:

- The UK *was* a signatory to the 1967 Outer Space Treaty and ratified it.
- The Poincaré Conjecture was solved by Russian mathematician Grigori Perelman in 2002 or 2003.
- Apollo 11's laser reflectometer did not get covered in a layer of moon dust when the astronauts ignited their ascent stage engine. It continues to bounce back photons to this very day.
- The real Crater Lake (Chapter 4) is in Crater Lake Provincial Park west of Keremeos, BC. For literary purposes, I moved it to the summit of Okanagan Mountain where Baker Lake is—a remote lake my friends and I camped at as teenagers.

For the record, I independently came up with Matt's "fire extinguisher solution" (Chapter 1) years before I saw the 2013 movie "Gravity."

I have purposely omitted details about The Ritual of the Calling of an Engineer (Chapter 7). It is a private, but not secret, ceremony open only to Canadian engineering candidates or those who have already undergone the ritual. As I took part in this ceremony in 1993, I am bound by its rules so have only included information already in the public domain.

There is no spillway in the Penticton Reservoir (Chapter 9); it was inspired by the real-life "glory hole" spillway in Lake Berryessa, Napa County, California.

Details on the math behind solving the Rubik's cube came from Wikipedia. Information on the TRIUMF cyclotron at UBC came from: https://cycops.triumf.ca/cycfac.htm.

Matt's Latin insults came from *www.latinlanguagephrases.com/witty* and the book, *"How to Insult, Abuse & Insinuate in Classical Latin"*, Michelle Lovric & Nikiforos Doxiadis Mardas, Ebury Press, Random House, London, England, 1998. ISBN 0-09-186445-3

The Klingon phrases came from:

www.wired.com/2016/09/klingon-phrase-guide/

www.omniglot.com/language/phrases/klingon.php

Matt's "Theory of Almost Everything," was inspired by author Mark McCutcheon's "expansion theory" in his book, *"The Final Theory: Rethinking our Scientific Legacy,"* Universal Publishers, ISBN 978-1627341592.

I based Matt's theory about "electromagnetic wormholes" on this paper:

Greenleaf, A., Kurylev, Y., Lassas, M., Uhlmann, G. Electromagnetic Wormholes and Virtual Magnetic Monopoles from Metamaterials. Phys. Rev. Lett. 99, 183901 (2007).